Sean Patrick

O'Mordha

Book 2
A Pirate's Legacy:

The Urchin Pirate

Celtic Publications
Sparks, Nevada

Celtic Publications
2515 – 4th st.
Sparks, NV. 89431

ISBN: 978-0982984291
ISBN-10: 0982984294

Artwork by Angela Dahle

Cover by Bill H. Moore

Printed in the United States of America

To

Ephraim Douglass Moore

Photographer / Writer / Graphic Designer / Traveler
And his sidekick, Murphy

Where I was at that age, but maybe a step or two ahead.

CONTENTS

(Continued)

CONTENTS
(Continued)

ACKNOWLEDGMENTS

Working with talented people is always a pleasure, and when one of those people is multi-talented it can leave you feeling a bit in awe. **Angela Dahle** is awesome. She writes, she draws, and lots more, while continuing the important role of wife and mother – and she's family, but I am not being predjudice. Thanks girl.

See what I mean:

http://angelapenadahle.wordpress.com/

Author's Notes

I have tried to depict the beliefs and practices as they were historically. In 1600 the French had their own measurement system and would not have used terms we are familiar with today. The system is explained in context, but to help, here is a quick reference guide. Except for the Toise, it should appear familiar. It should be noted that until adoption of the metric system, measurements in France had so many variation to be insane.

The French System of Measures in 1600

1 Puce   = 1 thumb width or about 1 inch*
1 Pied   = 12 Puce or about 1 foot
1 Toise   = 6 Pied or about 6 feet (2 yards)
1 Lieue = 14,400 Pied (aka: a league or 3 miles)

Therefore:

50	Toise	= 100 yards
100	Toise	= 200 yards
500	Toise	= 1000 yards
750	Toise	= 1500 yards
1000	Toise	= 2000 yards
1500	Toise	= 3000 yards

*Refers to current American measurements

The Ship's Bell System

Before mechanical time pieces, time at sea was measured by sand using a half - hour glass. One of the ship's boys watched the glass and turned it when the sand ran out from the top half. Immediately after turning the glass, he struck a bell as the signal he completed this vital function. From this evolved the tradition of striking the bell once at the end of the first half hour of a four hour watch, twice after the first hour, etc., until eight bells marked the end of the four hour watch. The process is repeated for the succeeding watches. The exception to this is during the Dog Watches. At the end of the First Dog Watch, only four bells are struck, and at the end of the Second Dog Watch bells are struck in this manner: 6:30 PM - one bell; 7 PM - two bells; 7:30 PM - three bells, 8 PM - eight bells. The time from 4 PM to 8 PM, First and Second Dog Watches were for only 2-hours each so that the crew could eat their evening meal, usually served at 7 PM.

Bells During a Watch

(For the Mid Watch as example)
(0000 = 12 o'clock midnight)

0000 Watch begins
0030 1 bell
0100 2 bells
0130 2 bells, pause, 1 bell
0200 2 bells, pause, 2 bells
0230 2 bells, pause, 2 bells, pause, 1 bell
0300 2 bells, pause, 2 bells, pause, 2 bells
0330 2 bells, pause, 2 bells, pause, 2 bells, pause, 1 bell
0400 2 bells, pause, 2 bells, pause, 2 bells, pause, 2 bells
        (8 bells - End of Watch & Start of Next)

The Watch Schedule

Mid Watch   –   Midnight to 4 AM (0000 – 0400 hrs.)
Morning Watch   –   4 AM to 8 AM (0400 – 0800 hrs.)
Forenoon Watch – 8 AM to 12 Noon (0800 – 1200 hrs.)
Afternoon Watch – 12 Noon to 4 PM (1200 – 1600 hrs.)
First Dog Watch –   4 PM to 6 PM (1600 – 1800 hrs.)
Second Dog Watch – 6 PM to 8 PM (1800 – 2000 hrs.)
First Watch   –   8 PM to Midnight (2000 – 0000 hrs.)

Sean O'Mordha

Chapter 1

† Off the Lorient Coast †

Captain Malcolm Campbell stood at the rail atop the aft castle watching the flurry of activity on the main deck below. Minutes before, the *Lady Catherine*'s crew was about their duties when a lookout sounded the alert propelling them to receive company as a Caravel bore directly toward them. At a thousand yards, a flag bearing the black emblems of an hourglass and cutlass on a blood-red field unfurled from the approaching ship's stern. Capt. Campbell snorted disgust.

"Shall I give the order to haul in sails, Cap'n?" the Bosun asked.

Campbell stood mute, staring at the approaching ship, his round, weathered face darkening with anger.

"Cap'n?"

"No, you shall not, Mr. Page," he shouted, slamming

a fist on the rail. "I am not about to let some mangy, French miscreants have their way as if the *Lady Catherine* were some whore. Mr. Dorsett, make ready your cannon."

This was not the captain's first encounter with pirates in the thirty-six years at sea. General practice was to let them aboard and yield a bit of cargo to save the rest, but such course was risky when dealing with unpredictable scavengers. They could take the whole ship, selling both cargo and ship, or hold the lot for ransom. In that case, captain and crew would see no payment. Thirteen months weathering storms and insufferable heat, haggling with unscrupulous traders, finding worthy crew to replace those lost, keeping the crew from totally indulging themselves in Oriental pleasures, refitting the ship for the return, enduring the boredom of a long voyage, all for nothing. And considering what was aboard, the stakes were too high to play their games. Despite being disadvantaged, in Capt. Cambell's mind it came down to all or nothing.

The Caravel had been in wide use for hundreds of years throughout the Mediterranean and Atlantic. Columbus' favorite, the *Pina*, was such a ship. Originally employed for fishing, its use spread to carrying cargo and passengers because it was especially good in shallow waters. Being fast and agile made it a favorite of pirates, too. Campbell judged this one to be about seventy-five feet, in the sixty-ton range.

The *Lady Catherine* was a low-charged Carrack, built for transporting large amounts of cargo on the open seas. Laden with 400 tons of cargo, she was a lumbering cow in comparison. Campbell now regretted having concurred on leaving half her guns behind so to haul more cargo, but they had been sufficient to dissuade Chinese pirates near Calcutta. A few well-placed shots ended their career, permanently. The more

Campbell thought on it, the more determined he became. Plymouth lay four days ahead to end a successful expedition. A rich cargo filled the ship's hold, and he certainly wasn't interested in yielding the chests in his cabin.

Normally, a warning shot was the most needed to persuade a pirate's victim to haul in her sails. Boarding was then a cordial affair. The pirate captain reviewed the ship's manifest, selected what he desired, and shared a bottle of wine with the merchant captain while the crew off-loaded those items. It had been a long time since the last ship tried to resist, so this pirate was surprised when clouds of gray smoke erupted from the merchant followed by plumes of water spraying over his bow and amidships.

The battle raged for nearly two hours as the ships exchanged shots. Despite having seven guns per side to the pirate's four, the *Lady Catherine* took the brunt of the assault. Quick and nimble with a well-trained crew, the Caravel was too illusive to hit, reloading fast enough to fire two shots to the *Catherine*'s one. However, the pirate captain began tiring of this game of cat and mouse. His intention was not to sink their prey, but anger was beginning to get the best of his judgment.

Moving the rudder bar to bring his ship behind the *Catherine* allowed all four guns to fire two rounds of shot into her big stern. Coming around to lay down a broadside into the port side, the pirate held fire. The merchant's sails began to lose wind. The maneuver had damaged the rudder. Striking the white pennant with its blue St. George's cross, the *Catherine* signaled surrender as her crew scrambled aloft to haul in sails fluttering uselessly in the wind. If they filled without control, she could turn over.

Those who knew this pirate captain tended to chart wide of his course. Forced to flee his beloved Scottish highlands, he sought exile in France; unhappy with the situation, he grew increasingly restless as the years passed. A powder keg with a short fuse, he had a reputation to explode, which of late had been often. Climbing aboard the English ship he was at his worst. Standing on the main deck, he glared up at the merchant's captain standing on the high rear castle, hands behind his back, staring ahead past the bow.

"Your name," he demanded.

Fists clenched, jaw jutting forward, the captain looked down and raised one eyebrow. The pirate wore the Mac Arthur tartan.

"Campbell," he said with contempt.

"Campbell! I thought to smell something foul as I come aboard." Mac Arthur spat on the deck.

Sharing a common ancestor, the two clans had been at odds for years as the Campbell branch sought power and lands at the expense of their once powerful cousins spawning the saying that there were but three scourges in Argyll, the bracken, the rabbits, and the Campbells.

"Hand o'er the manifest," Mac Arthur demanded, trying to control a swelling rage. It was hard as knuckles turned white about cutlass in one hand and pistol in the other.

"Go to hell with rest of the Mac Arthurs," Campbell replied.

"I lost a father and brother to Campbell treachery at Loch Awe. To hell with you," Mac Arthur screamed, and raising a pistol, shot the man dead. Then with blade leveled at the throat of the nearest ship's officer he said, "Now, someone had better produce that manifest, or this young officer is next."

"It be in the captain's quarters," the quartermaster said.

"Farley, go with him and retrieve the document. And bring me something to drink. I've need to cool my thirst."

Seated next to an up-ended barrel, feet propped up on it, Mac Arthur sipped a glass of wine while perusing the manifest.

"Farley, listen to this," he said quietly to his first mate, and read from the manifest. "Pepper-two-hundred tons; cloves-twenty-five tons; cinnamon-fifteen tons; mace-two tons; nutmeg-two tons; balsamic resin-fifteen tons; cochineal dye-ten tons; ebony-ten tons; and saltpeter-seventy tons."

"Impressive, Cap'n," Farley said. "Very impressive. Their captain did well. Pity." The two laughed.

"Ah, but there is more, old friend. Amber, twenty tons; silk, fifty tons; high quality cloth and tapestry, thirty tons." Mac Arthur looked up and smiled broadly. He saved the best for last. "Pearls, emeralds, rubies, sapphires, eight chests; gold coin, ten chests; silver coin, fifteen chests."

The grin stretching across Farley's weather-beaten face bared dark and missing teeth. "No wonder he put up a fuss."

"How long to repair the rudder to get this ship underway?"

"Renaldo says by mornin'. Ye thinkin' of takin' the whole of it?"

"This ship alone is worth more than we have taken altogether these past three years, nay, seven. We have truly come across Aesop's golden goose."

At that moment a rope-thin boy on the short side of seventeen leaped from the low, forward castle to race headlong across the main deck, forcing through the men gathered on deck, and up to where the pirate was enthroned, all the while yelling at the top of his lungs. "Cap'n! Cap'n!" His bare feet skid to a squealing stop, almost upending the barrel Mac Arthur was using as a footstool. Gasping a moment for breath he finally managed to say, "Cap'n, sail off the port bow. Looks to be a English warship."

"How far, Mr. Granger?" Mac Arthur asked.

"Mr. Peddibone puts it at three leagues, Cap'n."

Mac Arthur looked at the flag flying from his ship's mast. "He bears against the wind. That gives us no more than three hours. Damn! Mr. Farley, gather up the chests from the departed captain's quarters and put them in my cabin, and load as much saltpeter as we can carry. I am sure the King of France will welcome that generously. He always has need for making more powder. Have the quartermaster show you where it is located. And Farley, be quick about it. You have two hours."

"Aye, aye, Cap'n."

"Mr. Granger, you and the other powder monkeys replenish our supply of powder and shot, and Mr. Granger . . .," he then whispered something in the boy's ear before sending him scampering off.

With the merchant's crew pressed into service they hoisted the cargo from the hold and swung it over to the pirate's ship. Meanwhile, Mac Arthur resumed his chair, propping boots on the barrel, and sipped wine while reading the ship's log, specifically the crew list. After a time he stood to check on the progress of the transfer before staring absently at the approaching war ship. Such moments allowed time to ponder the druid's words and to wonder. The woman had come the day after news arrived that his father and oldest brother were dead by Campbell hands, betrayed and drown in Loch Awe. He had barely reached seven.

"There is no more left for the Mac Arthurs here," she said to his mother and remaining older brother. A painful truth. "Go to France where the others have fled. There the boy will raise the name of Mac Arthur as a banner of fear in the hearts of the Campbells and the English, and begin the course that will return unto the

Celts their days of glory."

The pirate's Caravel carried a crew of seventy-two, mostly Scots and French with a couple renegade Dutch. Farley was the oldest, the teacher. One step ahead of debtor's prison, he was impressed into naval service when yet another round of bickering broke out between France and England. There was a mutiny, but he had been wise enough to jump ship and stay in France thus averting a date with the hangman. The others who sailed with Mac Arthur had similar stories of seeking escape from oppression, deprivation, forced servitude, prison, or the gallows.

An hourglass sitting on the barrel-table tracked time. At the end of the second turn, Mac Arthur looked over the top of the log at the approaching warship now a league off, then at his ship. She was setting low in the water, much of the saltpeter aboard.

Approaching the captive officers gathered on the main deck, he said, "I see by the crew's list there is an Alfred Maitland aboard. Which is he?" No one answered. "I don't intend to repeat myself," he growled, pulling a cutlass from its scabbard. The boy of fifteen he had threatened earlier stepped forward.

"And what relation would ye be to Lord Maitland of Thirlestane?" The boy hesitated. A backhanded slap to the face knocked him to the deck, drawing a trickle of blood from a split lip. Grabbing him roughly by the shirt, the pirate lifted the boy easily with one hand until his feet dangled nearly a foot off the deck and the pirate could thrust his unshaven face in the lad's face. "Answer the question."

"He's my uncle," the boy struggled to reply as the collar of his coat choked his windpipe.

"Very good." He lowered the boy gently. "Mr. Granger, accompany Mr. Maitland to collect his things. He shall be coming with us. I am sure the Lord of

Thirlestane will pay handsomely for the return of his nephew."

When the young man turned to look at another officer, the panicked gesture was not unnoticed.

"And who shall ye be?" Mac Arthur asked.

The young man of early twenties didn't answer.

"I really have had quite enough of English stubbornness," Mac Arthur said, and without warning drove his sword into the young man's chest. "When I ask a question, I expect an answer."

"Lt. Braithwaite. He's Midshipman Maitland's cousin, sir," another officer answered as they gently lowered wounded man to the deck.

"Another Maitland? Too bad. Toss him over with the captain."

"But he's not dead," the officer bending over the wounded man pleaded.

"Just a matter of time. I never leave an untidy ship, but in this case I am pressed for time, so unless you care to join him . . . *clear the deck.*"

Seated on the gunwale, rope in one hand, ready to swing back to his ship, Mac Arthur pointed his pistol at the captain's cabin in the aft castle and fired. Granger had set a partial keg of powder and a keg of lamp oil near the entry. The resulting explosion started a fire, controllable, but the English warship would stop to render aid, affording extra time for the heavily-laden pirate ship to escape and disappear into the fog hugging the Lorient coast.

Chapter 2

† The Urchin of St. Nazaire †

Heavy, dark clouds laid an oppressive gloom over the French port of St. Nazaire all morning, sporadically releasing their load to drench the town. The flood of water then carried accumulated filth into sewage troughs running down the middle of the streets and on to the ocean. In the harbor, nearly a hundred ships lay at anchor or moored alongside a pier like one Caravel in particular. Its cargo now off-loaded into a government warehouse, no amount of water cleansing the town could wash the filth from this ship's deck.

As the latest Noachian deluge dwindled to a fine drizzle, a sailor stepped from an apothecary shop near the wharf, halting momentarily at the eye of a dark, tunnel-like alley. Taking a pinch of newly purchased tobacco, he dropped some into the bowl of his pipe, packing it with the callused stub of his left index finger, all the while savoring the sweet, spicy smell soon to be enhanced when lit. He loved the sea, but not having the world move about underfoot was a blessed relief as he leaned against the building and inhaled.

He wasn't a large man, neither in height nor in breadth, therefore didn't appear a threat. That superficial observation belied the truth. Mellow, often jovial and pleasant even when drunk, he appeared to be nothing more than a sailor of some means, a calculated deception. The shoes he wore pinched his feet and would be delegated to the bottom of his trunk soon after returning aboard ship. Both trousers and shirt hung loose over his slender frame, the shirt made of broad-stripped muslin, the trousers of cotton. Aboard ship, he wore a bandanna to keep the sun from blistering a balding head, but while ashore, a three-sided hat offered an air of importance. It also collected the rain, diverting it from his face to roll off somewhere behind.

After so many years at sea, his face was burnt the color of old leather and just as wrinkled. A short beard covered most of it, salt and pepper colored, mostly salt, suggesting he was getting along in years, although the young ones dare not mention it. He was still quick and agile, and with time had learned the savvy of survival.

Making port to sell their goods and purchase supplies, his ship had come appearing as a coastal merchant. Locals and the commission house representatives knew better. The captain made his purchases aboard Spanish, Dutch, or English ships making the goods much less expensive and all the more desirable. The government agent who the captain dealt with this time was delighted. Paying less than half the going rate of hauling saltpeter from the East Indies, both parties were satisfied with the transaction.

This cruise had been very rewarding, putting a sizable share in the crew's pockets. Some headed for the taverns and brothels, some to their homes and families. It would be some time, if at all, before the family men returned to the sea, but finding replacements was not hard. For this sailor, there was no returning to England, therefore continuing an estranged life. The tobacco shop always became his first stop ashore. The tavern was second for a pint or two, but no more, then a couple of other shops, and a good meal before returning to home aboard ship.

Stepping from the shop, he felt comfortable that the quantity of tobacco purchased would last this time. Re-lighting the bowl of his well-used pipe, the man gently nursed a tiny spark until a small, grayish cloud wrapped about his head. A sigh of contentment flowed over and through him, but that was short-lived as a growing tumult up the street drew his attention.

Taking advantage of the rainy respite, people swarmed onto the street seeking quick passage to their next destination. With much noise, they suddenly parted like the Sea of Reeds before Moses as a heedless youth flung down the street. Their obvious concern was to avoid being splashed by the spray of muck-laced water each of the urchin's bare feet sent up as they struck the pools and rivulets of water. Skirting the edge, he barely avoided a miss-step into the sewage trench. Not far behind the child, the sailor spied three soldiers in pursuit. Women shrieked. Men laughed and shouted encouragement for the boy to run faster, and derisive execrations at the soldiers, knowing they were safe as long as they continued chasing the boy. The sailor slipped into the shadows of the alley.

Suddenly the gangly waif, a loaf of bread latched tightly in small, bony fingers, planted his feet and turned sideways in an attempt to stop, sending up an arcing wall of muddy water. Now facing the alley, he began in that direction, but scrawny legs flailed fruitlessly as feet acquired little traction on the wet cobblestones. Realizing the futility of continued flight, the lad unerringly made an experienced dive beneath a pile of ragged canvas thrown against the sidewall several feet inside the alley. The sailor smiled and with less hesitation plopped his backside onto the canvas, pinning the boy beneath.

"Git yer foot under," the sailor said, giving the exposed foot a pat with one hand while casually drawing on the long-stemmed pipe.

Just as the filthy appendage disappeared, the soldiers rounded the corner, also sliding to a mud-spraying stop. The sailor just cocked his head in the direction of the alley as the first solider glared at him with an insolent look. There had been a time, when young and wild, he killed a man for the same loathsome look, but age had tempered him somewhat, so only returned an ambivalent stare. With a snort, the sergeant led his soldiers down the alley to disappear around the far corner.

Standing, the old sailor addressed the canvas, "Better git yerself out, lad. They be back quick enough."

The rags heaved. A loaf of bread appeared with grimy fingers still tightly locked around its golden crust followed by scrawny arms, a wild, bushy head, and then an equally emaciated body.

"You nearly broke my ribs," the boy said.

The sailor smiled pleasantly and again cocked his head to indicate for the boy to move along down the main street. With a flip of his curly tangle of locks, the urchin turned as gangly legs once again flailed the drenched pavement, and disappeared into the crowd.

Resuming his seat on the canvas, the sailor quietly puffed his pipe until the soldiers returned a short time later—walking. As they passed, their sergeant again gave the sailor a dour look, stopped, took the butt of his rifle, and slammed it into the canvas very near the man's hip. The sailor didn't flinch, although he wanted to.

"This soldier could use a lesson in civility," he thought, but only smiled and drew on his pipe, blowing a smoky ring at the soldier.

The sergeant and another stomped out onto the street looking for more trouble, but the third, a young man with white hair tied into a ponytail, lingered. The sailor looked at him questioningly.

"What is your name, sir?" the young soldier asked. He was polite.

"Farley. Just Farley, young sir."

"Yes. I hoped it might be. The sergeant is hunting the boy, Mr. Farley. It would be well if he is not seen in St. Nazaire after this day," the young soldier said so that his voice would not carry. Using the point of a bayonet, he gently lifted a piece of canvas to cover a dollop of mud. "He sleeps under the wharf near your ship."

Farley returned a curious look before issuing a faint, understanding smile as the soldier turned away in response to the coarser sergeant's shout to stop lingering.

Chapter 3

† The Mysterious Friend †

ᗷent over the body lying face up on the deck, the doctor pressed an ear against the bare chest before looking up sadly.

"Sorry, Cap'n, I think he's dead."

A young man kneeling on the opposite side touched two fingers against the victim's neck, then taking hold of the doctor's hand placed his fingers there. The older man wasn't really a doctor. Such were in too short supply for the number of ships at sea. The best available were men with the bare knowledge of first aid, and for this well-meaning man, that stretched the description thinly.

"Well, I'll be! He's alive! Just barely, but there's somethin' there," the doctor's voice cracked with the strain felt under the assignment.

"Take 'im to your quarters," the captain ordered.

The patient was completely disorganized. Words sounded far off and echoed so badly in his ears to be almost unintelligible, much like when he and other boys played in the sewer tunnels back home. Upon hearing the word, "dead," he wanted to scream, "No!" but the words refused to form upon his lips. Then someone touched his neck to prove he was indeed alive. Following was the vague awareness of being cradled in someone's arms like a baby and carried into a dark chamber where hands played over his body—poking, prodding, feeling.

"Other than that nasty knot on his head, there doesn't appear to be any broken bones or internal damage," the doctor said.

The patient tried to move. A man's voice spoke forcefully. It was in English and mostly incomprehensible, but he understood the hand pushing his body to lay flat. That was good advice as movement made the world even more distorted. To calm the wild, nauseous-promoting spin in his head, the boy tried focusing on what had happened.

That he wasn't aboard the *Fleurette* or among his shipmates was obvious. What had happened? His mind settled on the African port of Casablanca. That seemed a good place to start.

The Brigantine *Fleurette*, his ship, set sail from Casablanca, broke as usual. Captain Jean-Paul bore a commission from the French government to prey upon English ships, but a loose interpretation of the document suggested anyone, so long as they weren't French or didn't display the protective French pennant. In short, they were privateers, and for nearly four months they plundered a few ships along the Spanish coast into the mouth of the Mediterranean and south along North Africa coast. The ships encountered carried little more than cheap trade goods, which brought a meager return on the market. The ships, themselves, were old and worth even less.

No sooner had the *Fleurette* dropped anchor at Casablanca than the King's commission representative arrived to claim his share. The remaining was portioned out among the crew. Four days in Casablanca and the purveyors of indulgences possessed it all. The next two weeks at sea were not prosperous either, until spotting an English Carrack low in the water making its way south.

Frankly, Captain Jean-Paul expressed surprise they were able to approach so close to the merchant as if they didn't care. The *Fleurette*'s crew had already run the starboard guns out, as many crowded the rigging in anxious preparation to board like demented scavenger birds.

"François take the forward falconet and put a shot alongside. I prefer to take her in one piece."

"But they have so few guns, Captain," François whined with youthful exuberance, the excitement coursing through his lean body with such power his skin itched. It was the same feeling as when swinging recklessly through the rigging like the hairy, African brutes in the trees.

Jean-Paul smiled patiently from under his tri-cornered hat with its ostrich feather wagging playfully in the wind and waived a hand for François to move forward. The boy felt better, though, when the merchant rolled out its guns, a gesture of putting up some resistance. It was the acrid smell of burnt sulfur and the fear that stimulated him.

Aiming the swivel gun was difficult because of the rolling swells, and knew he was to land the shot as close as possible. Of course, if it did hit, too bad, just an accident. When the ball struck the water a scant, few toise off the *Agnes*' starboard side he was reasonably pleased, and set himself to loading powder and shot when he heard the crew scream. Looking up he was mortified to see the merchant turning directly across their path. The *Fleurette* put hard over to avoid a collision with the bigger ship.

François turned to scream back to the helmsman to turn the other way, across their stern not with them, but it was too late. They came parallel, guns pointing high into the air as the merchant came level. The *Fleurette's* bowsprit drove into a large swell sending a torrent of water sweeping over the bow. Powerful, wet fingers seized the boy, ripped the jib line from his grasp, and carried him overboard. As his head surfaced, François heard the unmistakable thud of cannon fire. Watching his ship sail past, he looked up to see shrapnel rip everything in sight—wood, rope, sail, and crew. Friends plummeted into the ocean torn and bleeding. The *Fleurette's* stern had just left him behind when a second series of reports turned much of his ship's port side into kindling.

He could see the merchant clearly, now. She had more than just the usual seven deck guns per side! What were supposed to be holes for the sweeps had become harbingers of more cannon barrels. From the merchant's deck issued the measured rumble of more shots. The *Fleurette's* mainsail swayed violently. When the merchant's guns on the sweeps deck fired, his ship erupted into a horrific series of explosions. The once beautiful ship that had been his home split in twain. Minutes later all that remained were shards of planking, a few barrels and sundry burning debris bobbing on the surface. Struggling to stay afloat in the choppy seas, François tried making for one of the barrels, passing a tri-cornered hat with a broken ostrich feather.

A strong swimmer, he had nearly gained the nearest barrel when several pieces of timber crested a wave and bore down on a collision course. His only escape was to dive. That was the last thing François remembered until regaining consciousness, apparently aboard the victor. He understood very little of what his captors said, except that it was about him. One of them was an older man, the other not much older than he.

"He's in shock," the younger man said.

"Quite right," the older agreed, flipping a wool blanket over the boys soaked torso. "He needs something hot inside. Peter, fetch me some tea. Hold on. I think he said something. Sounds like French."

"He's asking where he is," the younger man said.

"You speak French?

"I can."

"Well, this will make things easier. Good. Here's the tea. See if he will take a bit of it."

The younger man shifted into François' native tongue, gently encouraging him to take the warm fluid. Head lifted, François sipped. "Tea! Damn English and their tea," he thought. "If it will just halt my teeth from chattering."

"The doctor wants to know where you hurt."

"All over."

"Anywhere specific?"

"No. What about my shipmates?"

"You are the only survivor."

"How could a mere merchant sink the *Fleurette*?"

"This is not exactly a merchant ship."

François groaned as his head fell back onto the wood table he lay upon. "Well, that has been the run of our luck! Poor or worthless merchant ships, and now this! A man-of-war in disguise," he thought.

~   ~   ~   ~

"How's your patient, doctor?" Capt. Doublass inquired as the evening group gathered in his stern

18

cabin.

At noon the Captain and his officers gathered for a meal and to conduct ship's business; however, most evenings, the *Agnes'* captain, David Douglass, and others gathered for socializing, stimulating discussion, and relaxation. This select group included his father and owner of a merchant fleet, Sir Archibald Douglass, the ship's doctor, Roland Dorsey, their young passenger, Emanuel Guzman, and officers not on duty.

"Quite well, considering," the doctor replied. "He's talking a little. I can't understand a word, of course, but Mr. Guzman here speaks French quite well. That he's alive is nothing short of amazing. In the bow, apparently. Lucky he was thrown over before their powder went up."

"And what 'ave ye learnt of 'im?" Sir Archibald said in his heavy, Scottish brogue.

"From the French port of St. Nazaire. Seems harmless enough."

"He was manin' the gun that first fired upon us." Captain Douglass' reply was brusque, his usual manner. "I dun no consider 'im that harmless. He'll be under guard 'til the doctor says he can be put in irons."

"Then what?" Mr. Guzman asked.

"I'm no sure." The captain was obviously wrestling with the dilemma. "We can no turn 'im over to the authorities on the islands comin' up. He'd mouth all over what happened and then our secret would be out."

"It sounds like the only options are to take him with us . . . or make him walk the plank," Guzman said.

"Good Heavens, man! Walk the plank? You've listened to too many stories, my boy," the doctor said. "The only option is to take him along, of course. He's bitter at the loss of his shipmates, of course, but to keep him in irons the whole way would be inhumane. I'm

19

sure he could be useful."

"That will depend upon 'im. There be other options. In the meantime, a guard will be on 'im at all times, less he be in irons," the captain instructed.

~ ~ ~ ~

Speaking little English, the lone survivor of the *Fleurette* felt isolated and depressed at the loss of his friends so it was good he slept through the night and next day. When he finally began moving and able to stand late the third day following the encounter, Captain Douglass llowed him on deck for fresh air.

He was sitting on the forward cargo hatch under the close watch of two sturdy seamen when a young man approached and sat next to him and in perfect French said, "My name is Emanuel Guzman. What is yours?"

"François." The boy was wary. "Guzman? I've heard of that family. Guzman is Spanish. Very rich. Very powerful. Some say even more than all the kings of Europe. Spain is an enemy of the English."

Ignoring the comment, the young man continued, "I prefer to be called Manny. How old are you?"

François faltered a moment before answering. "Sixteen."

Manny smiled inwardly.

"So, how is it you were on that privateer?

"I am . . . I was the cabin boy."

Manny challenged his veracity. "They let cabin boys shoot cannon at ships?"

François turned his face away to stare at the gently undulating swells.

The "cabin boy" was large for his true age, tall, about five-seven, taller than many adult men. Well-built and muscular, he could pass for sixteen, perhaps more to a less observant person. His wide shoulders and deep chest tapered hourglass-like to a narrow waist and long legs. Trousers that came to just below the knee were, like his shirt, badly torn, exposing smooth, hairless skin—dark, reddish brown from many months at sea. The light brown blanket of curly hair with large ringlets hanging into the eye was sun bleached. Strong features etched the canvas of his face, not overly dominant, giving him a very pleasant countenance.

"No matter," Manny passed off the challenge. "So how did you come to be aboard that ship?"

"I was living on the streets. One day the soldiers were chasing me for stealing a loaf of bread. They would have put me in prison or worse, but a sailor helped me to escape."

"You were pretty young then. Too young to be alone," Manny baited him casually.

"I was six. I could take care of myself."

"But that soldier wanted to kill you."

"He almost did. Learned where I slept. He was about to slit my throat when he was struck over the head. The sailor who helped me hide the day before said one of the soldiers had warned that I was in danger and told him where I could be found. He saved my life and took me to his captain. I sailed with them. I had no family after the great sickness."

"Was it the *Fleurette* you first sailed upon?"

"No. It was a Caravel, the *Lillian St. Ives*. I sailed on her two years until my friend did not wake up one morning. Jean-Paul was Quartermaster then. Soon after, we arrived in port and he was given command of the *Fleurette*. I served with him five years. They always treated me well. I worked hard. I never wanted for food or a place to sleep. They were my family," the boy said angrily in an accusing tone.

"I'm sorry."

"You were lucky. The *Fleurette* could have blown this ship apart," François snapped, "would have if that stupid helmsman had turned to port instead."

"In a normal battle, maybe, but this is not a normal ship."

Later, after taken and bound with chains below decks, François realized the truth about his age had been exposed. This Guzman was good at extracting the truth; however, a disconcerting feeling permeated their conversation. The man seemed to already know things about him, and the sensation in the back of his mind was that François had seen this Guzman before, but could not quite place where they might have met. It was like grasping ethereal fog.

Each afternoon two sailors brought François top side for fresh air, and each time Manny sat with him. There was something very haunting about the friendly Spaniard. Even stranger about his captor was the unusually white hair with a touch of silver on someone so young, and green eyes that seem to penetrate to one's soul. François had seen an albino during an early voyage with Jean-Paul on the *Lillian St. Ives*, but this could not apply as Manny's skin was like burnt amber. Another thing was his ability to speak different languages with perfection. Despite François' hatred of everyone on this ship, it was difficult not to look at this person and feel something akin to what he had felt for Farley and Jean-Paul.

Feeling strangely comfortable and secure in Manny's presence, they talked for hours. His new friend seemed ignorant of many things, obviously a bookish, city person on his first sea voyage. Yet, occasionally he mentioned things only a visionary would know, although he tried to cover these slips.

What François did learn was that the *Agnes* sat

so low in the water because of the bigger cannon se-creted below decks capable of hurling a nine-pound ball. A normal merchant ship used four-pound balls, therefore it was no surprise they bored so deeply into the *Fleurette's* heart. Their destination was a Spanish fortress in the New World where the ship's owner in-tended to retrieve one of his best merchant ships, and this young man who had befriended him was intent on freeing a relative from that prison. François slowly be-gan to resign himself to a prisoner's fate when at sun-set four days after the *Fleurette*'s demise a call came from high up the main mast.

"Land ho off the port bow."

Captain Douglass checked his charts and smiled. Twenty-eight days from Kirkcaldy, Scotland, they sighted Lanzarote, the eastern most of the volcanic Ca-nary Islands, exactly on course. Continuing southwest, they slipped along the eastern shore of that island and then its neighbor, Isla de la Fuerteventura before an-choring in Puerto de Rosario's harbor.

Despite being dominated by Spain, the mer-chants there were more than willing to provide the needed supplies—for a price—and it was sufficiently remote to conceal their true course. If asked, they were bound for the African cape, when in fact their destina-tion was the New World. Only the officers knew that.

A few days in port helped rejuvenate the crew, as well. The devastating destruction of the privateer adversely affected their morale. With the passage of time, a fair wind, and this stop, morale would begin to return, but this good medicine was not to last.

Once leaving port and clearing the island, they turned westerly toward the island of Gran Canaria, and then almost due west. As the island's coastline began to slip away on their right side, François found a weak-ness in his chains. With the guard gone, he gained freedom. From a gun portal, he saw that land was not that far off. Believing this might be his only chance, he cautiously made for the ship's hold.

Slipping the latch and opening a door, he peered in and smiled. Neatly stacked inside the heavily shielded compartment were a hundred powder kegs. Quietly slipping in, he popped several bungs and spread a sufficient trail of powder to allow time to escape. He was about to touch the fuse when a shower of water spilled over his shoulder, wetting the powder, extinguishing the fire in hand, and drenching him. Wheeling around, he came face to face with the young cabin boy, Peter, who threw the empty bucket at him and yelled for help at the top of his high-pitched voice. His only chance was to flee, but where?

Captain Douglass and Manny Guzman were engaged in conversation near the wheel when a ruckus spilled out onto the deck. The pirate boy sprang from the forward hatch with a screaming Peter in hot pursuit. Tackling him to the deck, the two rolled about in desperate combat. Peter might have been small, but tenacious as an octopus.

Capt. Douglass flew down the ladder, bounding toward the melee with long, agile strides where he encircled arms around Peter. Seaman Fitch pinned the French boy's arms. Manny nicknamed Fitch, Clytius, after the giant killed by Hecate during the war with the Olympians, because of the man's massive size and flaming red hair.

"What's goin' on?" Captain Douglass demanded with a deep, thundering voice commanding attention as he slowly turned Peter loose.

"He tried blowin' us up, Cap'n." Peter's voice squeaked between gulps of air.

The captain looked at his cabin boy then at François whose chest heaved beneath hair plastered to his face and still dripping water. There was no retort, only a blazing hatred in his brown eyes, a hatred that transcend anything he'd ever witnessed, prompting a shiver to ripple down his spine. It was as if looking into the eyes of an enraged devil. Quickly diverting his eyes for fear of being consumed, the captain's nod to the bosun conveyed the unsaid command to check below.

Upon return, his report was chilling. "There's a powder trail to barrels in the main magazine, sure 'nough, Cap'n. Somebody splashed water all or it."

"I threw a bucket o' water on it, Cap'n," Peter explained. "It's all I could think to do."

"Well, done, Master Peter. It be fortunate ye were there."

"I wouldn't 'ave if Mr. Gusman hadn't asked me to fetch somethin' fer him."

"All aboard the *Agnes* be in yer debt."

"We can no take 'im on this venture, David," his father announced while pushing his portly, barrel-chested frame through the throng of crewmen encircling the confrontation. "He's far too dangerous."

"Aye, I know. We've no choice. Mr. Gardiner, lay a rope over the yardarm. Peter, best ye go below."

"You're going to hang him?" Mr. Dorsett protested.

"He tried blowin' us up, Doctor. Only by the grace of God and Master Peter he would 'ave succeeded. We can no take 'im with us, now. He poses too great a danger to the *Agnes* and her crew, and to our mission. Besides, he's a pirate."

"What about dropping him off on a deserted island," Dorsett pleaded, trying to find a way to save the boy's life, but François took matters into his own hands. Driving a heel onto Clytius' instep, elicited a howl and loosening of the hairy grip enough for him to slam an elbow into the man's ribs. Wrenching free, he took two steps to fling himself overboard. Everyone sprang for the gunwale and watched as the boy float in the ship's wake, and rapidly left behind.

"Launch the skiff, Cap'n?" the bosun asked.

The captain remained silent as the boy's head bobbed in the gently rolling waves, falling further behind the ship.

"Cap'n?"

"No, Mr. Muir. He chose 'is course. Continue on." Captain Douglass' reply was nearly inaudible as he slowly returned to his spot next to the helmsman. Feet apart for balance, hands clasped behind his back, he stared stoically forward, a pained expression etched deeply on his weathered face.

Chapter 4

† The Plank †

François might not have known much English, but understood the word hang. At that moment a massive wave of panic swept over him like the one which ripped him from the bow of the *Fleurette*. As a child in St. Nazaire, he had seen such an atrocity. The victim kicked and gasped for what seemed an eternity until turning black-faced and silent. The whole, gruesome affair left a nightmarish scar etched deeply in his mind. Out of a deep-seeded promise never to succumb to such an indignity, he tore free and leapt overboard, but bobbing like a small cork on a very big ocean suddenly didn't seem like such a great alternative.

Watching the *Agnes* continue on, the last face he saw was that of Manny Guzman. While the others peered over the rail looking somber, his only friend aboard that ship smiled from the stern rail while giving an informal salute—not as if to say "good-bye," but "good luck."

The trailing rope for anyone who fell overboard to grasp slipped pass, he watched with some detachment as the knotted end came within grasp and away. The boy realized the thin thread attaching him to human life was slowly being stretched until the tall, main sail vanished, snapping that invisible thread completely. At that moment, encased in a tomb-like silence, he felt overwhelmed by a feeling of incomprehensible loneliness.

He had seen land not far off, but in growing depression could not remember in which direction it lay, and from this level, he could not see it. Faced with certain death, he contemplated how it would come.

"Most probably I'll just fall asleep from exhaustion and drown," he thought. Then his pragmatism returned a debilitating funk. Land had been off the *Agnes'* starboard stern. Remembering the direction of the swells in relation to the ship's travel, he determined the direction to go. He was sure it couldn't be more than two leagues, a distance he easily swam many times. With renewed hope, he stretched out an arm, preparing to swim when he happened to look off to his right as a fin broke the water's surface. He hadn't considered sharks.

The motion of kicking his legs to keep afloat would have drawn them. Knowing there was no avoiding this fate, a moment's pain—hopefully—followed by oblivion, but that was a wish. A crewman who fell overboard off Corsica screamed a long time before disappearing beneath a bloody sea. He slapped the water to draw the creature's attention. The fin moved closer.

"Come on, beast! Let's get this over with," he yelled.

The fin disappeared beneath the surface. Closing his eyes, François braced for the searing pain that would come with its deadly grasp to drag him down. Nothing happened when he thought it should. Becoming aware of something in front of him, François open his eyes to stare into the glassy, black eyes of a bluish-gray dolphin. The suddenness of the large creature's smiling presence startled him so that he reared back and cried out, splashing water with his hands. The creature chattered excitedly while bobbing its head up and down as if to say, "Yes, yes, yes."

Beyond, several more dolphins leapt from the water. François stopped kicking and began to sink until the creature arced into a dive, brushing against his legs as if trying to lift him up, and then rising to the surface to literally place a big dorsal fin into his hand. Moving off, the creature began towing him. Unsure what was happening, François lost his grip, but the dolphin spun around with amazing agility to repeat the motion. It obviously wanted to pull him somewhere.

Holding more tightly, François allowed his apparent rescuer to drag him through the waves until realizing that being on his belly and trying to hold his head up wasn't going to work for very long. He let go, positive the creature would return. With a quick pivot, it did, whereupon the boy turned onto his back to drape an arm over the dolphin's back and grasp the fin. Another moved along the opposite side to take his other arm. Feeling their bodies undulate against his, they began the journey, but it wasn't in the direction he had determined land to be. After a time, two other

dolphins slipped in to take over, thus the relay continued as darkness overtook them. François lost track of
time and finally consciousness.

Chapter 5

† Marooned †

Lying in a hammock beneath a tattered, wool blanket, Mariah stared up at the laced branch roof overhead. The morning sun was finally penetrating the forest surrounding her simple, one-room cabin, but she wasn't enthusiastic about rising to another boring, routine day—eating, tending the garden, spending the warmth of the day staring at an empty ocean. With a heavy sigh, she rolled out of the hammock to stand and neatly fold the blanket. Her daddy expected that when he was alive. Gazing out the window at the black beach and deep blue ocean beyond, her breath stopped. There was something on the beach.

"Oh, no, not another one!"

She loved the friendly dolphins inhabiting the waters. There were many which seemed to delight in joining her during swims, but sometimes one would come onto the beach. She didn't know why. At such times, she would push them back into the water, caress them gently, and talk them into returning to their world.

Scrambling down the rocks from the plateau where the cabin perched, her bare feet dug into the deep, soft sand, each step bringing her to the realization that the dark form was not one of her marine friends. The closer she came the faster her heart pounded—it was human.

Falling to her knees beside the figure curled on its side, she gently rolled the lifeless form onto its back and placed a hand over his heart. There was life. Lifting her head toward heaven, the girl swept aside the long hair cascading over her face as tears streamed down brown cheeks.

"Thank you, God. Thank you."

~   ~   ~   ~

François stirred as his mind begrudgingly returned to reality, realizing he was no longer in the water, but nestled beneath a scratchy, wool blanket. Eyes still closed, he came to believe that he was awaking from an incredible dream, except his hammock wasn't swaying, and the aroma of something cooking slipped into in his waterlogged nostrils, something far too good to be ship's fare. His stomach knotted from hunger.

"Hello," a soft, angelic voice called out.

Looking to one side he saw her, a brown figure with a touch of olive coloring, black hair hanging to the waist. The simple, loose, clothe dress draped over her shoulders and tied about the waist did little to hide a lithe figure.

"Hungry?"

François sat up slowly, keeping the blanket close to cover his nakedness.

"Where am I? Is this heaven?"

"No," She giggled softly, "just a very lonely island. The ancient mariners called it Isla del Meridian. Now they call it El Hierro. I found you on the beach. How did you come to be here?"

"I . . ., I." He couldn't tell her the truth, that he was a pirate who jumped overboard to avoid being hanged. "I fell overboard. The ship sailed away. I was about to drown when a dolphin, several of them, came and began pulling me."

"God has answered my prayers, and my dear friends were his angels."

"Huh?"

"I have been alone ever since Papa didn't come back. The sea took him two years ago. He was fishing. A storm came suddenly and . . ." She diverted her gaze and fidgeted with a cooking pot.

"I'm sorry."

"I have prayed every day that God grant me but one wish, a companion."

"If you are alone, then who . . ." He stuttered. "Where are my clothes?"

"If you mean those rags, I hung them outside to dry, but they are beyond repair."

"But . . ."

"You have slept a long time."

"When did you find me?"

"Two mornings ago."

"That long!"

"If not for hearing you breathe, one would have thought you to be dead. You have the look of a sailor. How long have you been to sea?"

"A long time," he hedged, wanting her to think he

was older, careful not to be tricked like on the *Agnes*.

"I have always lived here. I rarely see other people. Sometimes, when I need something, I walk to the old Bimbache settlement of Amoco north of here. The Spaniards call it Valverde. A native Guanches village is not far to the south, but even they go to the west side of the island, to Sabinosa, to trade for flour and other necessities. The name comes from a spring there that has many curative powers, or so they say. The natives are good people."

"How far are they? These towns you mention."

"Valverde is less than a half day to the north. The Guanches village is much closer to the south. Sabinosa is a day's travel west. It is harder to reach because of the rugged terrain. I go there as do most of the villagers on this end of the island because the soldiers there are not so mean."

"Perhaps I can get clothes there?"

"I still have Papa's clothes. You are about the same size except for around the waist, but I can make them fit."

"Thank you," he said, taking a steaming bowl of potage from her hands, being careful the blanket covered his lap.

"How old are you?" he asked while rapidly devouring the seafood and vegetable concoction.

"Fifteen."

After eagerly downing a second helping his stomach hurt less, but there was a nervousness rooting deep inside his gut causing him to shiver as his eyes followed every flowing move the girl made. Soon, darkness began to envelop the room until it became increasingly difficult to see anything except the tiny glow of embers in the small cooking fire just out from the open door.

"I have no candles or oil for the lantern, so when it becomes dark it is time to sleep," she said as the last of the crude eating utensils were stowed.

A second hammock hung near the opposite wall, barely an arm's distance away. Even that close he could only tell she was lying in it by the sound. He lay back. François had never been this close to a woman, not that he hadn't tried, but Jean-Paul asked him to wait, and his shipmates conspired to keep him a virgin. It didn't matter. He was still tired, and with a full stomach, he fell asleep almost immediately.

Slowly the dim, early morning light began filtering through the forest surrounding the cabin like a thick cloak. Lying on his side, blanket pulled over his head; François struggled to reconstruct everything that had happened since jumping overboard. Now it all seemed so distant and unreal. Relegating it all to just a very bad dream seemed the best course until hearing the soft rustling sound of someone stirring about, softly humming an enchanting melody. He remembered the girl's words, "I prayed to God to send me a companion."

"God? There is no God," he again told himself. After the death of his parents, life became a squalid, hand-to-mouth existence except for a brief time until finding refuge among the privateers. While life became better, it was still hard, death from a myriad of things a constant companion. Yet, he could not deny the miracle that brought him to this island and this beautiful girl. He didn't intend to remain long, but he wasn't in that big a hurry to leave, either.

"Good morning," she said cheerfully as he stirred.

Pulling the blanket from his head, François found himself gazing into the face of a huge reptile who greeted him by flicking its tongue, gently popping him on the end of his nose. With a scream, he lurched backward and flipped unceremoniously from the hammock, bumping his head on the compacted ground. Burying himself beneath the trailing blanket, he heard the girl burst into laughter as something heavy raked across his legs from feet to hip.

"Oh, don't go. He didn't mean to frighten you."

François peeked from beneath the blanket to see a great, black creature lumber out the door.

"What is that?"

"That is Diablo."

"I know it is a devil, but what kind?"

"There are giant lizards on the island. That is Diablo. I call him that because he is so black. He eats the bugs that would infest this place. He is quite friendly, but I'm afraid you frightened him."

"I frightened *him*?"

"I have not been to the garden since you arrived, so there is only some fruit to eat. It grows wild on the mountainside."

"That would be good," he said, sitting cross-legged with the blanket around his hips all the while keeping a wary eye on the door. Taking a bite of fruit, some juice ran down his chin. "This is good."

"I suppose you are anxious to find another ship."

"I . . ." He hesitated.

"Do you feel strong enough to walk? I would like to show you something."

"I can manage," he replied, tightened the blanket around his waist. "Ah, what about the clothes you spoke of?"

"Why?"

"What if someone comes along?"

"Who? No one comes here. Besides, the blanket covers you."

"Yes, but," he stammered, continuing to hold back.

Her laughter was light and celestial. "Oh, I am just teasing. Let's see what we can find in Papa's chest."

Relaxing a bit, he liked being teased, especially by this girl whose countenance glowed like the evening sun. The trousers were a bit short, but the waist worked fine, needing only a piece of rope to hold them in place. The shoes did not fit, much to his delight. Sandals were easily adapted to his larger foot. The cotton shirt hung to his knees as it should to form an undergarment once tucked into the trousers. Loose and baggy around the chest, it helped make it feel cool in the warm sun.

Clothed, she led him south along the back of the beach to a trail skirting upward across the face of the mountain. About half way across he stopped to gaze out at the sea.

The mountainside angled steeply, diving into the surf crashing upon its rocky base. From this position, the concave beach was a small oasis snuggled between two long projections of tortured basalt reaching into the sea like outstretched arms. The one directly beside them had a large hole through the seaward end.

The rectangular cabin of thatched walls and roof set perched on a small, level piece of ground well elevated well above the beach and inside a thick, protecting forest. Slightly below and to the side of the cabin, a fresh water stream pummeled rocky boulders trying to slow its excited charge to the sea before it leapt from the cliff to crash upon the beach where ocean waves washed up to meet it. To François, this was too idyllic—too story-like to be real. Such a place could only be heaven, yet . . .

With a gentle tug, Mariah coaxed him onward until reaching a point where the trail divided, one part going out along the top of the southern arm. The other headed inland through a V-shaped fissure splitting the mountain. Another stream tumbled through this defile to plunge into the sea far below on the opposite side of the arm from the beach.

Continuing upward through the gash, they entered the cool shade of pine trees, their needles moaning a soft serenade in the wind. After a time François heard the sonorous sound of water as if poured into a barrel. As the ground leveled, they stepped from the thick vegetation and onto the bank of a large pool fed by water diverted from the stream. To the back, a waterfall dropped a gentle shower into a smaller pool then ran into the larger pool before the whole began a dash to the ocean.

"Papa built this for us to bathe in," she said, removing her sandals before slipping the loose-fitting dress over her head and carefully stepping into the pool. There she sank slowly beneath the glass-like surface until her head seemed to float on the surface like a light brown, glass globe. François secretly gasped upon seeing her remove the dress exposing a thin, cotton undergarment.

"Come in. You will find it very relaxing. The water has a way of renewing the body."

François hesitated. His timidity was obvious and vexing. Mariah giggled softly.

"You haven't become shy of water, have you? It really isn't very deep," she again teased, standing to demonstrate it barely reached to her waist.

He chuckled nervously and fidgeted before slipping off the sandals and loosening the rope belt to pull the shirt over his head. As that was his undergarment, removing the trousers was out of the question. As his foot touched the water, he snapped it back.

"The water's hot!"

"That's what makes it so refreshing. We are able to take a hot bath every day, not as the English, who only bathe once a year."

Gingerly re-inserting a toe, and then a foot, François cautiously entered the pool. Never had he experienced such a thing, but once submerged to the neck, he found that it felt surprisingly good. Every inch of his skin tingled as if tiny fingers worked to wash away layers of hidden dirt even though he bathed regularly aboard ship—with buckets of ocean water.

"Papa once told me the whole island is a volcano. The stream by our house is rainwater from the surface. It is cold. I followed this stream to its beginnings in the hills near our garden. This water comes from inside the mountain."

"It tickles."

"Yes. Isn't it wonderful? Papa said there are minerals in the water that do that."

Submerged to their necks, knees danced on the sandy bottom as heads floated upon the surface like two large bubbles. The girl suddenly sprang from the pool to stand under the waterfall.

"Try this," she called out.

The pool had taken away all the fatigue felt since arriving. Eagerly stepping to stand with her, it was not what he expected as the water cascading from above hit him.

"Aaaaaah!" Leaping away, wrapping arms around himself, he practically stood on one leg in a half crouch. She laughed again, a rollicking, happy sound that echoed among the rocks. "It's freezing!"

"You sound like a girl not a big, brave sailor."

Uncoiling to stand tall, François steeled himself and moved to her side, but like a firefly, Mariah flit back into the pool. Joining in the game, he was amazed how his body seemed to fill with its old, high level of energy. The water did renew the body. So did her laughter.

After a third time, he came out from beneath the gentle spray of cold water to sit upon a huge, rounded boulder in the sun. The warm rays that fell upon his back had never felt so good as he watched the girl, seated on another boulder pull a broken comb through the long, fine stands of her hair. He was beginning to like this place very much.

"So how did you come to this lonely island?" he asked.

"Papa was a soldier in the Spanish army. He saw my mother while in Morocco. They fell in love at once. She was a sheik's concubine—a bit of a problem. Papa arranged for a small boat in which they could run away. He thought that once back in Spain it would be all right, but someone betrayed them. To save political relations they gave him to the sheik and was sentenced to beheading. Mama helped him to escape. They commandeered a small boat, crossed over to Spain, and landed in a small fishing village.

"They had a good head start, but the sheik sent ships after them. A kindly fisherman warned them in time, and they were able to escape once again, but just barely. This time they sailed out of the Mediterranean and made land along the Sahara coast where they hid for several months. When they felt the search had quit, they pointed their boat for these islands, but it would not be possible to stay at any settlement even though they were all Spanish. A war ship had made port ahead of them and left notice of a sizable reward, so they continued to search for a safe place to make their home. A storm came up and drove them upon this beach. It has been a wonderful place.

"You told me what happened to your papa, but what about your mama?"

"She died giving birth to me."

"I'm sorry."

"Do you have family?" she asked, shaking off the memory.

"No. My parents died from the plague when I was six."

"Then we are both orphans."

François shrugged agreement.

"It is not good, being alone." There was a pause before she blurted, "I would like you to stay." Her olive-tinted face darkened in a blush.

In that moment François' thoughts of returning to the sea seemed to evaporate. "I would like that, for a while," he said, feeling the heat rise to his own cheeks.

Chapter 6

† Companions †

Seated cross-legged on a rock in the warm sun next to the pool, François thought about the tumultuous years of his short life. His parents were becoming a vague, wispy remembrance, but there were certain things never to be forgotten. His father worked on the docks. He remembered hearing them say that they had little money, but his mother always seemed to have food on the table, and they had a place to live where the roof didn't leak as it did with his friends. The one thing he would never forget was their love. His mama and papa loved him, and they loved each other.

Never a day passed that François' father didn't pick him up, tousle his thick, unruly mop of hair, kiss him, and play with him after a long day's work. He kissed François' mama, too, often holding her hands as they talked softly. When it came time for bed both tucked him in as she sang a tender song. Sometimes both sang together, then papa would say a prayer before both kissed him goodnight.

The death of his parents was a wrenching experience difficult for a six-year-old to understand, an experience that literally tossed him onto the cold streets of St. Nazaire. He would have died had it not been for the old Jew and his wife who took him in, gave him shelter, and love until they too, were torn from him.

Back on the streets, a soldier wanted him dead, not that he was innocent of provoking such hatred. Meeting the old sailor, Farley, began life at sea with both good and bad times until the destruction of his ship and loss of another family. Then occurred the miraculous shepherding by dolphins to the one place a girl lived alone which was . . . well . . .. He abandoned the concept of a God when his parents died, despite what the old Jews said. The more he considered these events the more difficult denial became.

Once his mind began to accept the possibility of God, it seemed his eyes opened, perhaps answering another puzzle, the one about Manny Guzman. François felt having seen him before, but where? It came to him in picture-like fashion during a dream early one morning. Someone similar to Manny stood in the background when the old Jews suddenly appeared to shelter him until they were forced to leave the country in yet another wave of anti-Semitism.

The old sailor had told François a white-haired soldier knew François was hiding beneath the canvas in the alley and warned about the dangerous sergeant. Could it have been the same man aboard the *Agnes* who offered friendship? Certainly Manny Guzman seemed to know much about François, and what would happen to him in the future. If the impossible were true, Manny Guzman could not have been so instrumental in his life unless he was an angel, and if even one angel existed there must be a God. But why did his life merit such attention? Upon these thoughts he was deeply engrossed when Mariah curled up behind him and began running the broken comb through his hair.

"Ouch!"

"I'm sorry. Your hair is so tangled. Have you never combed it?"

"No. Combing hurts. I just cut it off when it gets too bad."

"Oh, no! It is so beautiful, but I don't want to hurt you. I'll stop."

"No. . .. Don't stop."

Dipping the comb into the pool, Mariah re-wet portions of his locks. Using nimble fingers to tease first one then another stubborn tangle free, the matted strands came free, but the process would extend over many days. Despite the discomfort, François endured it because she was close. He felt as when in the arms of his mama and papa, and the old Jewish woman—comforted and secure. During this time they talked, she about life on the island, he about life at sea.

After a time, and a few "ouch!"-es, they continued their journey upward through the forest on a relatively easy trail except for one part that traversed loose talus. After Mariah pointed out the direction they must take, François led out with the girl close behind. Half way across he heard the flat, plate-like rocks begin to move. Turning quickly, he leaned into the side of the hill, digging his feet into the loose debris. Balancing himself with one hand, he reached out with the other to grab Mariah's hand as she began a precarious slide toward a ravine. With a strong pull, he brought her flying to his side, where she encircled his torso with both arms. He instinctively put his arm around her waist, holding her securely.

"Thank you," she said, breathless. "It does that. One has to be careful."

Locked closely together each looked into the other's eyes. François' breath stopped, but not his heart as it pounded loudly. Nervous, embarrassed, they parted slowly to silently resumed the climb, but neither released the handhold.

Another ten minutes or so the two stepped from the trees into a broad meadow at the base of a rocky pinnacle, a large, green island nestled within a garland of thick pines and black volcanic rocks. The grassy vegetation undulated like lazy swells as a breeze skipped playfully over the surface. From around the edge of the rock formation a clear stream flowed silently from a thumb-like extension of the meadow some distance beyond. Between the outcrop and stream, a rectangular plot of exposed soil broke the waving grass.

"That is my garden. The stream is the same passing the cabin. I come here every day. I must. The soil is so rich everything grows very quickly, especially that which is not wanted."

"It's very beautiful here," he replied, reluctant to release the girl's hand as she picked up a bundle from beneath a tree. Removing the oil clothe wrap exposed a shovel and hoe.

François had done many things in his short life, but not farming. It was not easy, but he found satisfaction from the labor. Here, in the open, the warm sun, tempered by a cool breeze blowing in from the sea was a feeling he had not experienced before. Aboard ship, even in the best of weather, one had to be constantly alert to retain an upright stance as the deck shifted with each roll of a swell.

Not long after starting work, he tossed the shirt aside then removed the sandals. He enjoyed the feel of the warm, soft earth oozing between his toes. As the shovel began to unearth produce, he became filled with a sense of security. On the streets of St. Nazaire he was always hungry. There were times at sea he faced a shortage of food and water, uncertain if the captain could pilot them through fickle winds and currents to a port in time. Here, there didn't seem to be that challenge. As long as they faithfully tended the earth it would yield one's needs. On the edge of the forest, one of the giant lizards stood sentinel upon a flat, rocky outcrop.

"That is Alita, the noble one," Mariah said.

François grudgingly had to admit she was beautiful, for a lizard. A bit smaller than Diablo, two rows of pale orange patches along each side with a little orange coloration toward the middle of her belly marked an otherwise brownish-gray hide. When condescending to move from her throne, Alita strode with solid, meaningful steps, broad head held high.

"Do those creatures only eat insects?"

"Oh, no, they eat plants, too."

"I should think a creature that size would do great damage to this garden just passing through, let alone snacking along the way. It would seem a ready plate. Why do they not bother?

"Papa had lots of trouble at first, and then one of the old Guanches from the village showed him how to make a liquid to spread around the outside. They do not like the smell, so they keep away. They do patrol the outside, though, and eat many insects."

"Perhaps we could use some by the cabin door."

Mariah laughed, "You don't like Diablo's visits?"

"His is not the kind of face one likes waking to in the morning."

"And what kind of face do you like to awake to?"

"Yours," François blurted.

Her laughter slid to silence as they looked at each other with serious countenances for a moment before both giggled softly, a surge of heat coloring their cheeks. Changing the subject, they returned to gardening.

That evening, seated upon a large rock overlooking the cove from the cabin's perch, Mariah resumed the self-appointed task of untangling François' curls. As the shadows lengthened, the ocean turned progressively darker until disappearing into the blackness that swallows the world. Their idle talk continued a while longer until retiring to separate beds.

So, the two eased into a routine of rising early, climbing the mountain to tend the garden, and stopping on the return to lounge in the hot pool. Later they would frolic in the surf with the excited dolphins, and partake of their produce. What François found most pleasurable was simply being in Mariah's proximity, especially as she continued prying the tangles from his hair.

The next morning François awoke early. Sleep had been fitful. Since first brought aboard ship as a six year-old, he hadn't slept on land again. Even when disembarking in port he returned at night so he was accustomed to the rhythmic sway of a hammock. He woke several times during the night, startled, wondering why there was no motion until remembering where he was. Not only that, but he had gained a sense of comfort by the sonorous sounds of male companions snores. The soft purr of a woman barely an arm's length away stimulated an unusual nervousness.

Although the cabin was still in deep shadows, the sun shone brightly on the ocean beyond. Having the need to relieve himself, he slipped quietly outside to an area Mariah's father had chosen for a latrine, some distance from both the cabin and stream. Finished, he thought to explore a bit, taking a faint trail leading to a small clearing where he found a number of slender poles, carefully cleaned of bark, and held off the ground by tripods, except for a much thicker one buried upright in the ground with a flat stone at the base.

"Papa used that to measure how much I grew," Mariah said as she entered the clearing from behind. François jumped slightly. He hadn't heard her approach. "This first mark is when I could first stand by myself, and then each year he would make another mark," she continued, speaking of the vertical pole. "This is the last mark he made before being taken away."

François studied a series of notches into the wood. "The *Fleurette*'s carpenter taught me about measurements. Each long mark is a pied. The smaller ones between are a puce. That is a thumb's width." He laid his thumb between two of the smaller notches. It fit. "There are twelve puce to each pied. So you were five pied, three puce when he died."

"Yes," she replied quietly.

"Let's see how tall you are now."

She stepped onto the flat stone so that François could make another notch in the pole. "You are now five pied, seven puce. That's taller than most of the women I've seen."

"Papa was tall," she said, pointing to a notch at the five-eight level. "Let's see how tall you are." François stepped onto the rock. "Five-seven. We are the same."

"What are those other poles for?"

"It is a calendar. Papa built it based on the lunar calendar of the Hebrews. He often spoke of the many books he had read, but I only have a Bible here. He used the Bible to build this devise to keep track of time."

"The old Jews spoke of it, too, but I don't remember much."

"From when the sun sets to its next setting is a

day. There are seven days to the week corresponding to the seven days God created the world. The seventh day He rested. Papa was careful not to do any manual labor that day. He would teach me to read using the Bible, and sometimes went for long walks, and then sit looking at the ocean, and talk. This mark begins the yearly cycle. It is . . ."

"The month of Nissan," François suddenly remembered. "It is when the Jews celebrate Passover. I loved that time. There was so much food and singing. He had a terrible voice."

"Each of the small marks indicates the days, but Papa said that here it really wasn't that important to know what day it was except for the Sabbath. The other pole shows the number of years I have been here."

His fingers ran lightly over the history pole. They began when her parents arrived, showed when Mariah was born and her mother died . . . and when her father died. There was a fresh incision.

"This is when my friends brought you here."

Returning to the cabin, François donned a shirt, but didn't tuck it in. After eating fruit, they traveled along a trail parallel to the stream. The steep climb brought them to the garden far faster than the other way.

"This is the way we usually went then returned by the pool. It was always good to bathe after working. However, today I want to go on to the Guanches village to trade our produce. Perhaps they will have some lamp oil," she said.

At the garden site, François quickly divested himself of sandals and shirt, working the soil to clear it of sprouting weeds and harvest produce. With the addition of his strong back, Mariah realized they could carry more, improving their bartering position. Before leaving, François went to the stream to wash off the dirt and sweat.

The lava rock cliff was like a finger ending 300 pied from the stream with the meadow wrapping around it. Using six pied to make a Toise, the vertical cliff face ran nearly one-hundred Toise south before curving and heading toward the ocean. At this point, a wide crevice split the face creating a place they could easily climb to the top. Within 150 Toise this trail joined another which Mariah said ran the length of the island along the top from south to north. From this height the ocean spread out far below to their left like a dark blue silk cloth shimmering in the sunlight.

"If you stand on that hill you can see the other side of the island and Sabinosa," she said, pointing to a rise some distance west of them.

François found it difficult to follow the trail at times. There was always something new and fascinating to look at from weirdly shaped rock formations, to trees bent into tortured shapes by the wind, to strange and beautiful animals. So fascinated, he didn't notice when the trail started to descend until spotting houses and wisps of smoke, and then people.

The natives smiled and greeted Mariah warmly. He received the same warm welcome, especially when introduced as a French sailor. Such greetings were not necessarily true for Spanish soldiers or the missionary priests. However, he did notice a few sideways glances cast in his direction by some of the young men that didn't appear friendly.

The Guanches were some of the last remnants of visits by Phoenicians, Greeks, and Carthaginians. Many succumbed to Spanish-born violence, sickness, and assimilation. Slightly shorter than François, they tended to be slender with longer faces and narrow noses, reminding him of some eastern Mediterranean people he had seen over the years, light to dark brown in color with matching hair, although there were a couple who were more blond. They wore a garment to the knees, not unlike his shirt except it was sleeveless, made of goatskin, and fastened about the waist by a thick, cloth belt. Little girls flitted about in a smaller version of the blouse while their counterparts darted here and there wearing only a wrap about their loins.

Trading accomplished quickly, they were disappointed the villagers did not have sufficient flour, which meant a trip to Sabinosa, perhaps in a week. Business concluded, they sat talking and eating. Of course, the villagers' curiosity centered on François, plying him with many questions about his travels. He had to be careful not to mention the reason for his sailing. That aside, this was a thoroughly enjoyable time, and as children escorted them part way up the trail, he looked forward to returning to spend more time. They had much he wanted to learn.

Shadows lengthened considerably by the time they reached the hot pool. François was concerned lest it would get dark soon, making the decent along the steep trail to the beach dangerous, but Mariah seemed unconcerned. As before, she slipped off the outer dress and waded into the pool, except this time when she reached the far side, she removed the thin undergarment and placed it on a boulder. Her bare back remained to him as she submerged and began rubbing her skin, a way to loosen and remove the day's dirt and perspiration. Remaining on the bank, François stared and swallowed hard.

"Well, are you going to wash or not?" she called out over her shoulder.

Hesitating, he removed his sandals and shirt. Once submerged, he slid the trousers about his ankles, and began scrubbing. A few minutes later the girl stood, still keeping her back to him and replaced the garment.

Stepping out, she sat upon a rock to comb her hair. The place was in dark shade, but it was still light enough to see.

After a time she said, "When you finish come sit here and let me work on your tangles some more," and patted the rock next to her, continuing to be oblivious to the fading light.

"The Guanches are a very friendly people," he said after struggling to put the trousers back on underwater.

"So long as you are not a Spanish solider or priest," she said, resuming work on the curls.

"From what they said, a justifiable position. I did notice a couple of the young men look at me when they did not think I noticed. They did not look so friendly."

She laughed. "I am unmarried, and they are of age to seek a wife. I think some consider you competition."

François' laugh had a nervous edge.

Exiting the forest at the foot of the volcanic arm, François relaxed. Although cast in shadow, it was much brighter away from the trees, making him less nervous about the descent. When they reached the beach, Mariah headed for the old tree trunk embedded in the sand. To François' surprise there was a large fish lying next to it.

"If you bring that along, I can begin fixing a meal," she said. Then as a response to his quizzical looked she added, "My friends deliver something every day. They have done that ever since Papa left."

François slept better that night, perhaps growing accustomed to the lack of movement, but probably more from the work and travel. From beneath his blanket the next morning he could hear the girl's soft singing as she prepared something for the morning meal. He still felt full from last night. Slipping the blanket back, he found himself staring into Diablo's beady, black eyes. The lizard's long tongue was unerringly accurate as it snipped the boy's nose. In triumph, Diablo turned and waddled out the door.

Mariah burst into laughter. "He has been standing there ever so long waiting to greet you."

François swiped his nose with the back of his forearm. "Great. A morning kiss from a devil. A boy devil even. Can we do something to block him from coming and going at will?"

"I suppose, but I don't really want to hurt his feelings. I think it is very nice he likes you."

The next couple of days turned hot, hotter than usual according to Mariah. Because of his arrival, they decided to expand the garden. It was hard work ripping out the grass and matted roots then pulverize the soil into something workable. The added heat didn't help as sweat rolled off as if doused by a bucket of water. During a visit to the Guanches village a week later, an old woman inquired if he had hurt himself, noticing that his walk seemed troubled. Wearing a large number of necklaces and woven, palm leaf diadem, she was the village shaman.

François was too embarrassed to admit the heat and sweat had chaffed the insides of his thighs, but one look in his eyes, she knew instantly.

"Spread this where the skin is red," she said, handing him a small container of grayish cream, "then wear this. It is called *taparrabos* in the coarse language of the Spaniards." Her face screwed up, acting as if the word left a sour taste as she gave François a length of soft cloth similar to that seen used by the men at work.

Staring at the folded cloth then at a couple of young men nearby, he was at a loss how to put it on. Understanding, she smiled faintly and summoned one of her sons whose glare said he considered François competition.

"Cirano, show Mariah's friend how this is worn." After the two disappeared into her home she called out, "And use the medicine." She sounded almost exactly like the old Jewish woman, terse, yet loving.

Applying the cream to the inside of each thigh brought on a brief stinging sensation, quickly followed by cooling. Rash soothed and garment in place, he thought it best to alleviate another problem.

"I notice you look at me with anger," François said, following Jean-Paul's admonition to meet one's adversary head on.

"Do you plan to make Mariah your woman?" Cirano said.

"Mariah took me in and nursed me back to health when I was marooned upon this island."

"You have no desire to make her your wife?"

"I am still a bit young to marry."

"Oh," the young man replied, sounding relieved.

"But I am considering doing so." François surprised himself with that declaration.

"Would you fight for her?"

François looked at him. Despite being several years older, the two were much the same in size. His answer was resolute. "Yes, I would fight for her. How would you suggest we resolve this?"

"I would wrestle for her," Cirano said, sounding very confident. François had seen him engage another larger than he during their last visit. He won handily.

Replacing his trousers, François extended a hand in a sweeping motion as an invitation for him to step outside.

The other young men and boys instinctively knew what was about to transpire as the two headed for the traditional area suitable for wrestling on the beach. Cirano tossed off his tunic as the others encircled the area.

The same height as François, Cirano was heavier and well-muscled with a prowess that earned him a reputation as unbeatable, but imbued a cocky attitude. If he thought this newcomer could be defeated quickly, the Guanches was surprised. There had been several aboard the *Fleurette* who wrestled as a pastime. Naturally, François was one of them, and his speed and strength visited trouble upon the contender from the first. Encouraged by cheers and taunts of peers, Cirano fought back, but knew that ultimate victory would happen only if François made a mistake.

Toes digging into the sand, each vied for a hold to leverage their opponent to the ground, there to role and flail, repeatedly securing a hold and breaking loose, until nearing exhaustion. Finally, François managed to slip an arm under Cirano's and lock fingers on the back of his neck. Forcing his head down, François stepped behind to replicate the hold with the other arm. The young man was helpless as he tried to throw Mariah's man from his back, but ended falling onto his belly. With François' weight bearing down on his back, Cirano found his face pushed into the sand, unable to breathe. Realizing his predicament, François rolled onto his side, maintaining the incapacitating hold. Cirano struggled to break free until relaxing and admitting defeat.

The two stood, brushing sand from their bodies. Cirano felt humiliated as friends and relatives chided the loss. François knew that was not good. Capt. Jean-Paul said a man had enough enemies without going out of the way to make more.

Extending a hand he said, "You are the best wrestler I have ever encountered. If not for a stroke of luck, you would have defeated me. Friends?" The young man looked at François, smiled faintly, and accepted the offer.

Escorted by the onlookers, the two walked into the ocean to wash off the sand. François had worn his trousers during the match. Old and thin to begin with, they did not survive the match at all well. Hanging in rags, he was glad to have the undergarment as he removed the shredded trousers and tossed them aside. Cirano said something to one of the other boys who took off back to the village. When the two exited the water, the boy had returned with a tunic.

"A gift for my new friend," Cirano said, handing François the goatskin tunic and belt. "Perhaps we could wrestle when you come again?"

"I would love to. It was great fun," remembering something else his captain had mentored. "It is not always necessary to win to be a victor." He had little doubt Cirano would be more than ready to win the rematch.

Besides finding the Guanches to be a happy and kind people, they were also generous, beginning a lasting relationship. The trip home the next morning meant a steep climb to the top. Upon reaching the top, François sat on a large rock.

"We need not stop. I'm fine," Mariah said.

"Good, but my legs are tired. Wrestling Cirano took a lot out of me."

"What was that all about?"

"Oh, just a man thing. Having fun."

Upon reaching the hot pool, the two washed. Exiting, she sat upon a large boulder to comb her hair as he continued to float around, reluctant to leave the soothing water.

"Do your legs feel better?" she asked.

"Yes. The irritation is gone."

"They have a great knowledge of plants. Come sit so I can work on that hair of yours," she said, patting the rock next to hers. "You and Cirano were not wrestling

for fun." She did not sound accusing. It was just a state-
ment of fact."

"No."

"Because of me."

"Yes."

"And you won me?"

François faltered.

"I am glad."

François thought it wise to change the subject.

Upon returning to what was becoming home,
they stowed their traded goods. Being early, François
went to the beach to wait for the dolphins to bring their
daily catch. Stretching out on the sand by the buried
tree, the cool, sea breeze mediated the warm sun. Coupled with the gentle roll of waves upon the beach he
was lulled to sleep until rudely awakened by a spray of
water.

Sitting up and gazing seaward, he noticed several
of the creatures watching as one rose up. Still sleepy-
eyed, he became vaguely aware of something sailing
through the air. Realizing at the last second what the
object headed directly at him was, there was no time to
react. A sizable fish struck him full in the chest, knocking him backward on the ground. Startled, he thrashed
about until realizing what had happened then glared at
the dolphins who seemed to be laughing their short
snouts off at the human's strange antics. From then on,
he engaged in the game by trying to catch the slippery
delivery. It was difficult and the fish often flopped free.
At those times, the dolphins bounced their heads and
laughed. When the boy did manage to hang on, the tossing creature would rise up on its powerful tail to swim
backward in a show of great excitement. The extent to
which they seemed almost human was surprising even
to playing tricks. When his catching prowess improved,
they tossed a large lobster ashore. François barely man-

aged to duck the flying pinchers.

Several weeks later, while waiting for the daily delivery, a particularly large dolphin appeared. Coming as close to shore as possible, it barked a couple of times and tossed water at François, obviously wanting him to come into the water. For whatever reason, he hadn't been back in the ocean since arriving except at the Guanches village after wrestling.

Having the urge, he jumped up and darted into the surf as if trying to catch the wily creature, which spun about and leapt in an arc to momentarily disappear beneath the surface before poking its head above water, just out of reach. François continued swimming toward him with long, easy strokes. Once again it turned, jumped, and swam away to reappear just out of reach. This game they played until nearing the hole through the end of the southern arm at which time the creature came along side and presented a fin meaning it wanted to tow him.

With a wag of its powerful tail, the dolphin began to cross the cove until reaching the end of the north arm of rock, and stopped. When François turned loose, it disappeared. Wondering what game it was playing, he looked around. It was then he noticed how much the southern arm appeared to resemble Diablo, his snout pointing seaward, the hole like an eye, the body stretching back to the mountain from which it sprang, the tail extending to formed the uppermost peak.

The creature reappeared, presenting a fin once again to tow him back, but this time they rounded the end of Diablo's head to enter the boulder-strewn cove on the far side. With amazing dexterity, they slipped around the rocky projections. To François' surprise they came upon the entrance of a cave well hidden behind the rocks and a curtain of water pouring from the top— hot water. He wanted to explore the dark cave, but that would have to wait until traveling to Sabinosa where they could trade their produce for flour and oil.

He wouldn't have to wait that long, however. Cirano and his sister came to visit not long after discovery of the cave. At first, François thought the Guanches might have a trade in mind—Mariah for a very pretty sister, but that was not the case. The girl and Mariah had become close friends and wanted to visit. Cirano, under the guise that it might not be safe for a young, unattached woman to travel alone with Spaniards about, tagged along. He was actually itching for a rematch. The two stayed for nearly a week with a match almost daily accompanied by working the garden and swimming with the dolphins, something the young man had never experienced before.

When François mentioned the need of lamp oil, Cirano showed him how to extract resin from a pine tree and produce several products, one being a lamp oil substitute, the other for making torches. Although the torch quantity was not great, he sparingly used some to fashion two torches allowing travel some distance inside the cave. When the first died, the second was used for the return to daylight, although he later determined that such precaution was unnecessary. A swift stream flowing out of the cave provided safe exit without the need of a torch. In later months, he would venture deep inside the mountain.

Returning home, Cirano and his sister crested the basalt hill and disappeared, leaving François and Mariah standing in the meadow feeling empty. They thoroughly enjoyed the company.

"Perhaps we could visit them in a week or so," he said.

"But we could not stay so long or we'd lose everything in the garden."

With a deep sigh, he agreed. "But even a day or

so would be good."

After a stop at the pool, they returned to the beach where a fish lay by the old tree.

"Let's cook it here," Mariah said.

"Collect some firewood and I'll dig a hole," he said, dropping to both knees to begin scooping out a pit.

As the sea began turning dark, they sat side by side on the beach, the waves teasingly darting up to splash their feet.

There was always something to talk about, but Mariah was silent until asking, "Do you miss sailing upon the ocean?"

Now François was silent. It had been nearly two months since the dolphins brought him to these shores. Every day the sea, now stretching out at his feet, beckoned him to return with undulating fingers.

"It is strange, but no. Sailing is all I have really known. Ports were nice to visit, but I never felt comfortable until back aboard ship. Perhaps someday I shall return, but not now."

"Like all sailors, you must have experienced many women."

The remark caught him completely off-guard. He coughed softly, stammered, and hesitated before answering with a hint of a nervous squeak, "No."

"You are a virgin?"

"Well . . ." He spluttered. "I, well, when I was younger it was not a problem, but when I became older Captain Jean-Paul asked me to stay away from women whenever we came to port. I honored his request, but it became increasingly difficult. Then, the last time, in Casablanca, he said that we would be there several days while putting aboard fresh stores. We had a little prize money and the men were excited. We had not been in a port for a long time. All they talked about was finding a woman. This time the Captain said nothing to me. I believed he thought it was time. As I left the ship, he was standing by his cabin door, smiled, and gave a slight nod. It was his way of saying I could do something.

"My shipmates laughed and teased me as we neared port, and they whispered among themselves as we left the ship, but I did not care. I should have known they planned to keep me from finding a woman. No matter what I tried, someone was there to stop me."

"You must have been very frustrated."

"I felt like a cannon with too much powder, ready to explode into a hundred pieces. I was so angry that when we sailed I went below and . . ." He halted, unable to admit that he had cried.

"I am sorry. Such feelings can be very painful. It has been very difficult for me as well, not knowing if I should ever have a husband."

"But all you would have to do is go to Val-verde or Sabinosa. The men there would fall over each other with the thought they could have the hand of such a beautiful woman." He stopped short, astonished at what he just said. A sudden rush of heat flamed his cheeks.

"Yes, I could have. I went there once with that thought. Something seemed to stand between me and them. I remember Papa told me that one day a man would come into my life, and I would know he was the one God intended for me. He believed such arrangements were made in heaven before we lived on earth."

"I have never heard such a notion," François said. "Have we no choice? Is all our life planned out that we are just puppets to play out a scene for the gods?"

"No. Papa said men and women are born free— free to make choices. The things that happen to us in life are the consequences of those choices. If we make the right ones we eventually find our true mate. If we live an honest life and ask for special things, they will be granted to us."

François wondered if Mariah could be right. Serving on the *Fleurette*, thrown overboard moments before its destruction, being brought to this place, somehow, it felt right as if all that had happened was meant to be. He never gave it much thought until now. Could a pirate achieve such a thing, living an honest life? Reaching out, he took her hand. She squeezed his fingers gently, more like a caress. His body shivered as if suddenly chilled.

"Will you become my husband?" she said so softly François wasn't certain he had heard correctly, then felt as if someone had just dropped a cannon ball on his body.

"I, I, I . . ." He stammered.

"I'm sorry," she said quickly, pulling her hand away, lowering her head so that the long hair covered her face.

He knew she was blushing and then heard a soft sniff. "Is she crying?" he wondered. "Mariah?"

There was no reply.

"To become a husband is a great commitment. The old Jews who took me in after my parents died talked of that often. My parents lived as if it were so. I have never committed myself to anything except surviving. I would like very much to have you as my wife, but I cannot let it be on a lie." He took a deep breath before spitting out the truth. "I am large, but the truth is that I am barely fourteen years."

Lifting her head, the girl turned her face toward his. There were faint glistening trails along her cheeks. She had been crying. Leaning forward, arms encircled one another as they embraced. Suddenly he felt her body tremble as she began to sob, hot tears dropping upon his shoulder to trickle down his back. Then her head lifted so that they once again stared into one another's eyes.

"I'm sorry," she said, her voice cracking. "I, too, must be truthful. I have been afraid you would leave, and thought marriage might keep you here."

"Well, so much for marriages made in heaven," he teased.

"But they are."

"Perhaps, but fourteen is too young, although I have known of such things happening in France."

"Perhaps we should wait."

"Yes. The old ones who took me in were good people. I remember he said that a man should never make a promise, especially before God, unless he intends to keep it. To do otherwise would be a great sin." François cleared his voice and began resolutely, "Mariah, I swear before God that I betroth my soul to yours, and if this indeed is a union arranged in the heavens, then I promise to become your husband upon my sixteenth birthday."

"And I swear before God that I betroth my soul to you, and we shall wait, but Papa said that the sea is a man's mistress. Will you be able to resist her temptations?"

"In all honesty I do not think so," he said honestly, "but you shall be the only woman I know."

Mariah smiled, and leaning forward, kissed his cheek, the first time a woman had done that other than his mother.

As the days passed, François explored the cave and the bottom of the cove, especially below Diablo's snout. The rocky appendage drove straight to the bottom which was quite deep, requiring all the air his lungs could hold to reach it. That got him to pondering some possibilities.

Not long after this discovery he sat alone on the furthest point out on what he called the Dragon's Head contemplating the future while staring idly out across the open water. Overhead, thick, white cotton ball-like clouds seemed suspended in the light blue sky, casting spots of shadow upon the ocean while sunlight slipped through open areas creating a sparkling effect to dance upon the waves. A person didn't see such variety from the low level of a ship's deck, but high up on the mains'l . . . He spent a lot of time perched near the top spar. Lashing himself to the mast, François would close his eyes, feel the movement of the ship, and become one with it.

Standing, François ventured near the edge of the point to look down at the water. The dark shapes of the dolphins moved continuously far below setting him to wondered how they would react if he suddenly dropped in on them. Closing his eyes and spreading arms, the boy let the wind play with him as it did on the mast until he felt himself swaying with each breath of wind. Just then, a gust lifted him onto his toes. Fighting to regain balance, it was as if some great hand nudged him over the edge.

The first instant he was surprised, but realized he would not die. Many times he and others had leaped from the top yardarm on the mainmast. Straightening his body as an arrow, he pierced the surface and shot downward, turning to reverse the descent. Moments later his head popped above the gentle waves amid the excited chatter of the dolphins. Filled with the daring and adventurousness of youth that had inspired him to swing through the *Fleurette*'s rigging like an African ape, he made for shore and back to top.

Mariah just exited the cabin when she saw François thrown from the basaltic arm. Her heart stopped as she cried out in despair. Relieved when he surfaced and swam back to shore, she was astonished to see him race back up the steep trail and deliberately fling from the cliff. He loved the exhilaration of freedom with arms spread like a soaring frigate bird, letting the cool wind blast his face. It was quite different for Mariah. She retreated from the cliff's edge many times before finally coaxing the courage to join in the diversion.

Swimming with the pod was a great adventure. That Mariah referred to them as her "guardian angels" was, well, silly. After all, they were just sea creatures, personable and playful, but still an animal, until one day after having just plunged from the cliff François was swimming lazily back to the beach when one of them came along side and began chattering excitedly.

He thought the creature wanted to play as they often did, but this time something about its excitement moved him to look seaward. Not three hundred pied away was the fin of a great shark headed directly toward him. There was no way to make land in time. Unexpectedly, the dolphin pushed its blunt snout into his stomach and lashed the water with its powerful tail, literally propelling him toward the shore with such force that he rolled up onto the beach like a ball. The creature then wiggled free of the sand and disappeared. Regaining his feet, François raced to the north side of the cove to climb upon a large boulder from which to see better into the clear water.

Once he was safe, the dolphin turned to nimbly dart around the lumbering behemoth until shooting up from beneath, driving its snout into the shark's belly. It tried to retaliate, but another dolphin shot out of nowhere, hammering the beast in the side. Then another and another of the pod appeared, each ramming the beast. Blood trailed away as it sought escape, but François knew it would never return from the depths of the ocean where it headed. Perhaps there was something to Mariah's claims. Perhaps they were guardian angels.

~   ~   ~   ~

Keeping track of days and months would have been impossible in a climate that is perpetually spring or summer if not for the ingenious system built by Mariah's father. However, asked when he had been born, François was ignorant.

"Some time before summer, I think. I remember it always rained a lot," he said.

"Then why not use the day you arrived here? When they left you behind in the sea, that world considered you dead. When you came ashore here, it was as if you were born."

They chose the day François appeared on the beach, a reasonable choice. Contentment easily hedged up around them. Still, sometimes while seated on the tip of Diablo's snout, staring upon the endless ocean, François remembered the days of his past, heard the song, and felt the sea tugging at him.

As the date of his birth neared, he remembered the promise made Mariah to become her husband. He grew increasingly nervous and excited about that prospect, and then François remembered the young man who befriended him aboard the English ship. Although he thought there would be little hope of a future at that time, during their conversations Manny Guzman had said things suggesting one.

"You need not despair. I you will have a long and interesting life," Guzman said during one of their conversations when François was feeling particularly depressed by his captivity. "I believe you will be comfortable and well cared for in your old age, and proud of your decedents, one in particular."

At the time, François' mental state was so negative to have let the remarks slip pass. Now, they made him wonder and wish to see Manny Guzman again, to ask him questions. Regrettably, that opportunity was probably lost forever. He then wondered if Manny's mission to rescue a relative had been real. If so, had it been successful? He prayed it to be so.

François had not come to entirely believe in Mariah's and Jean-Paul's God; however, he had to admit that a higher power must exist. Things that happened to him during the first years of life could not have been charted by chance. Perhaps someday he could believe. In the meantime, Mariah spent time each day teaching him to write and read using her father's Bible, continuing where Capt. Jean-Paul ended. Having a natural ability to pick up languages, he furthered his skills with Spanish and Arabic, what he learned from shipmates and Mariah from her father.

Chapter 7

† Pirates †

The rich, volcanic soil continued to yield a generous garden, but unwanted things seemed to grow faster. Tending the plot daily was necessary to survival. Also, there were a half dozen giant lizards of various ages in the vicinity patrolling the periphery, dining on native vegetation and insects. The younger ones in particular eyed the lush garden greedily. The Guanches' oily concoction kept them at bay, but required application at regular intervals, and especially after a rain.

"I'm thinking to try some of the repellent at the cabin," François jokingly suggested again.

"Did he kiss you again this morning?"

"No, he does not kiss me. He snips my nose with that tongue of his every morning."

"He really likes you."

"I wish he would find a girl lizard."

"Diablo is a girl."

Francois stared at her not knowing what to say. A girl lizard making advances was more than he could handle.

"I am just joking. He is a boy. You can tell by the coloring, but what if the oil keeps you from entering as well? Then the two of you would have to sleep together by the stream." Her teasing continued in good form.

François visibly shuddered at the thought causing her to laugh. Actually, he had grown fond of Diablo and his sometimes-unexpected visits, but not that fond. He certainly appreciated how well the inside of their cabin was clear of insects. One morning, just as consciousness re-entered his mind following a sound sleep, he felt the telltale tickle of a creature on his chest. Just as he opened one eye to see what it might be, a black line flashed into view and the colorful insect was gone.

"Thank you, Diablo," he mumbled and rolled to one side as the thick tail swept across the floor beneath the hammock following the remainder of the body out the door, one of the rare times François was not greeted affectionately.

Life might be primitive, but stable, a first in his life, with little thought of returning to the sea. Life changed greatly since arriving, so had he—physically. Clothes once belonging to Mariah's father no longer fit causing him to rely solely on native dress. Visiting the calendar eighteen months later to make an entry, they once again checked their respective heights. Mariah remained at 5-7, but François had added three pied to stand 5-10. He had filled out, adding more muscle. When he, Cirano, and others went to the beach to wrestle or sit talking, there was always a group of eligible young women close by. Then one evening, as he and Mariah sat on the old tree buried in the beach, she broached a subject he had given thought from time to time, but dismissed as yet far into the future.

"Tomorrow you will be sixteen."

"Already?" Mariah kept the calendar so he hadn't check it for a long time and honestly thought the date was still months away.

"It will have been two years since you arrived."

Banging heels against the petrified log, he remembered the promise. A great hollow feeling opened in his stomach as he shivered despite the pleasant warmth of the evening.

"Is there a holy man in Valverde?" he asked, his voice soft, hard to hear above the waves.

"Sometimes. Why?"

"To marry us," François said, hoping she didn't notice the slight quiver in his speech. "I heard the old Jew say several times a Rabbi or holy man was necessary for such things. A Rabbi, a priest, someone to seal the contract."

"Papa said priests are used very little for such things. Aristocracy sometimes will use them like that, but more often, they just request a letter of permission from Rome . . . with payment, of course. People such as us simply pledge themselves to one another. Papa said that when a man and woman exchange a pledge before God it is more meaningful. It's like what you said about taking an oath. That was how Papa and Mama married."

Standing, François stretched out a hand to help her off the log so that they stood facing one another other while the surf gently lapped at their feet. Una-

70

ware to either, the pod of dolphins silently gathered, floating in silent attendance just offshore.

"Mariah, I do love you and would have you as my wife. I promise to provide for you and protect you for as long as I live. And this I swear to you and before God."

"I love you François with all my soul and promise to be faithful to you for the duration of my natural life, to keep your home, and bear your children as God is my witness."

Then something came to mind he heard from the man who befriended him on the *Agnes*. It was as strange as anything he ever heard, but beautiful and something he wanted in this relationship with Mariah.

"Manny Guzman said that when we die as to the world, life continues in a heaven where we can be with those we love forever. That is something I would like very much for us. I would ask that God allow our love to extend beyond this life and through all time and eternity," he added.

Arms encircling one another, their lips drew together as they kissed—their first kiss—a seal to their pledges. Parting slightly, each stared into the other's eyes, smiling, then kissed a second, much longer time as the sea erupted into a froth as the dolphins leapt and sent forth a great, joyous chattering as if proclaiming to the world that a union proposed in heaven had now been sealed on earth.

~   ~   ~   ~

Each day François and Mariah climbed the steep grade to their garden until two months after exchanging marriage pledges she became ill, vomiting as if aboard a ship in heavy seas. He didn't want to leave her side.

"The garden needs tending and food brought down. Go. I will be all right," she insisted.

There was no fever, but the vomiting continued sporadically for the next week leaving her feeling weak. Curtailing non-gardening activities, he stayed close and worried. There was a barber in Valverde who doubled as a doctor capable of little more than verbose explanations and magical concoctions. They had been powerless to help his parents or friends aboard ship providing François little faith or trust in such people. If not for Manny Guzman, one of them would have had him buried at sea alive. However, being just as ignorant to the many ills that can inflict the body, he felt forced to turn to these men, like it or not, hoping they had some notion of what they were doing.

Fortunately, their Guanches neighbors came to the rescue. Though weak, Mariah insisted accompanying her husband when he took produce for trade to the village as usual. While sitting apart as the transactions took place, the old woman with the many necklaces and green, palm diadem stepped to her side. After looking Mariah in the eye, she affectionately stroked the girl's cheek and smiled.

"You look tired, daughter."

"I have not felt well."

"You are sick in the mornings?" Her raspy voice croaked somewhat like a frog.

"Yes. Most of the time."

"Take this before sleeping. It will help."

As usual, native herbs worked their magic. While the vomiting abated, Mariah continued to remain tired, making passage to the garden infrequently. However, one day several months later she felt well enough to make the trip. As he worked, Mariah spread a ragged blanket on a softer part of the ground next to a cave overlooking the garden where she waited patiently for her husband to finish. Occasionally looking up, he would smile while wiping the sweat rolling from his brow. It was a large garden now and she tried to help, but simply had no energy to work for very long.

Putting an arm around her waist, he took her back to the blanket. "You wait here, and let me finish," he said softly.

The sun seemed hotter this particular day due to a lack of air movement. It had rained a little during the night leaving the air feeling heavy. Stripping to taparrabos kept his clothes from becoming saturated with perspiration leaving him to contend with a sticky coating of sweat and dust. That was easily managed with cooling trips to the stream. While seated in the shallow water sponging off, he noticed the high, thin clouds were becoming denser. Well off shore other clouds began growing to great heights, both harbingers of an approaching storm.

Starting much earlier than usual and deliberately hurrying, the work was finished well before the sun reached its highest point. Sitting side by side beneath a large conifer, they quietly gazed into one another's eyes.

"Shall we go back down?" she asked after a time.

"I would like to explore to the north a bit, if that would be all right with you?"

"Please be back before dark. It looks to storm, and it is not safe to travel across the mountain at such times."

"The storm is four or five hours away. That should not be a problem." Standing, he helped Mariah to her feet. "I worry about you going back down alone, though. Why don't we stay here tonight?"

"All right."

François was always curious and loved to explore and this was not the first time they had stayed in the cave so he could do so. Although the opening was barely an adult's height, it quickly opened into a large area and no matter what the weather outside, a gentle, warm wind from deep inside the island always made it comfortable. She smiled weakly as her husband disappeared into the forest, following the trail skirting along the spine of the volcanic island like a piece of sinew binding the south lands to the north. Once out of sight he broke into a steady jog that would quickly devour miles.

The herbs seemed to control the vomiting, but he worried because the illness persisted so long. Now Mariah's tummy began to swell. He wanted to have a discussion with the barber in Valverde. The town was not so far he could not be back before the storm struck.

François traveled steadily for some time along the trail high above the rocky coast, mulling over his concerns, until an odor reached his nostrils. Coming to a sudden stop, he looked around and sniffed the air. Smoke! There had been no lightning with last night's rain. There had been no lightning for several weeks, which could only mean someone was in the area, except Mariah had said there were no villages in this part of the island. She had fished the coastline with her father and the island plummeted into the ocean with no beach, although there were a few places a single cabin might be built.

Carefully making his way forward, sniffing the air continually, he came to a small stream moving off the high plateau on its final plunge to the sea. Looking down the defile, he could just make out the faint, grayish-white wisps of smoke rising above the treetops into the calm air.

The ground was less rocky on the right and there seemed to be a trail of sorts paralleling the stream, but François was cautious as he silently worked his way down until spotting a small clearing. The smoke was rising from the remains of a hut. Some trees nearby had been burned, but with everything still wet from the rain, the flames had not spread far. What grabbed his immediate attention was the body lying face down in the clearing out from the smoldering remains. Slipping into heavier brush to be better concealed, François gradually worked up the courage to take a closer look. That's when he caught sight of another body near the burnt structure, lying face up, its bare chest impaled by a cutlass.

There obviously had been a battle, so where were the victors? Moving closer, he had a better view of the minuscule beach. There was a longboat pulled onto the sand, but no ship. As he got even with the smoldering hut, he spotted blackened remains in the ruins. That made three.

Hunkering down in the thick, steamy brush, he patiently watched before mustering the courage to venture out. Whoever had won appeared to have left—if there had been a victor. Walking through the carnage, his scavenging instincts took hold as he pulled the sword from the man's body, and then collected what interested him most—several pistols, a rifle, cutlasses, powder and shot, things he had been totally without since arriving. Whatever Mariah's father possessed in that regards had gone down with him. The longboat was providence-sent. Now he had an easier way to travel to the few, scattered seaside villages to the south and carry more produce to trade.

Finding no signs of life, François relaxed and began picking up more things, piling them neatly near the stream. In the process of removing a thick leather belt from one of the dead men, he detected the soft crunch of dirt beneath a foot. Wheeling around, he found himself staring at a thin, grizzled weasel of a man, who was stealthily sneaking up from behind, ready to run him through the back, but who now stood frozen in mid-stride.

"Come to steal what's mine, mate?" He snarled through scurvy teeth.

"You seem to have a sword, and there be plenty. I could use one, too," François replied, trying to sound calm while sizing up the attacker.

"Liar! You be wantin' Squirrel's treasure."

"Treasure? What treasure?"

The weasel raised his cutlass overhead and with a scream, charged at François, who threw a fist of dirt at the man and rolled aside. Grabbing a cutlass from the ground, he stood. Stymied for an instant, the attacker lunged again. François instinctively slashed back, deflecting the blow.

"Think ye know hows to cross swords with a pirate, do ye, boy?"

François could tell his attacker was drunk—something of an advantage to François as they battled around the dead man in the center of the clearing.

"Well, ye be good, boy," the assailant wheezed, his breathe coming in gulps as sweat poured down his face. Realizing he was in trouble, the weasel began looking around nervously for a way out. "Who taught you?" François denied him the benefit of an answer.

Capt. Jean-Paul had taught him. Mariah's father had taught her. Taking up sticks, the two frequently "dueled" until she become ill. The sparring helped one another to improve their technique. François' silence infuriated the man, who jumped into a desperate round of swordplay trying to get in close, but he was nearing exhaustion. François knew to keep his distance. Then from behind, the boy heard the crack of a pistol. In what seemed like slow motion, Squirrel froze as a hole appeared in his forehead, followed seconds later by a flow of blood as he fell backward.

The boy felt the shot whiz past his right ear. Leaping left, he sought the little cover behind a small rock before the pirate's body hit the ground. Making a quick estimate, the shot must have originated from somewhere in the undergrowth on the backside of the burnt cabin. He thought to detect the faint wisp of smoke in the thick brush. Still feeling exposed, he darted for a larger boulder. Expecting another shot, there was none, so he crept closer to the bushy area. Just upon reaching the undergrowth, he heard a soft gasp. Jumping through the foliage, he came face to face with a little girl crouching next to a man, who had a pistol pointed directly at François' heart.

"Hold it there, lad," the man gasped.

His shirt was soaked with blood and there was a rattle in his voice. François lowered his sword.

"What's going on?" he asked.

"Those terrible men wanted something my daddy has," the little girl replied.

The man's strength was ebbing. He had to lower the heavy pistol.

"Ye not be one of them." His voice was strained and rattled.

"I was on the *Fleurette* when a man-o'-war sent her to the bottom."

"Heard the *Fleurette* disappeared. Never knew what happened. What was the name of the man-o'-war?"

"The *Agnes*."

"Out of Glasgow?"

"Aye."

"That not be a warship. It be one of ol' Archibald Douglass' merchant boats. How could he be sinkin' ships? A lucky shot?"

"They were firing big guns secreted on the sweeps deck. Their shot cut through the *Fleurette*'s timbers like a hot knife. I got thrown overboard. Lucky not to be aboard when they hit the powder . . . I guess," he continued to explain. "They fished me out and put me in chains. I heard them talking something about going to a Spanish port in the New World to take back a ship that belonged to them. Had a Spaniard aboard named Guzman."

"Aye. I've heard of that family. Better than royalty. Heard tales of such an adventure, too. Fired a Spanish fort and sunk some of their fleet. Made it easier for a time to plunder their treasure ships, but how'd you git on this God-forsaken rock?"

"That's a strange tale. I hated them for killing my shipmates, so when I knew we were close to land I figured to touch off their powder and make it even, but the cabin boy caught me. They were making to hang me so I jumped overboard. They sailed on leaving me behind. I was about to give up when some dolphins appeared. One of them put his fin in my hand and started swimming off. I hung on for the want of life. Next thing I know I was here." François almost mentioned Mariah, but reconsidered and remained silent on that detail.

"Well, that be a tale indeed, boy," the man coughed, spitting up blood.

"Can I take a look at your wound

"No need," The man coughed again, a trail of blood issuing from the corner of his mouth. "Nothin' to be done. You live in the town north of here?"

"No. Near a village to the south."

"You seem a good lad so listen close. I ain't got

much time. There be a rock a ways back in the trees. Split in half it is. Buried in that split is a small chest. It be yours," he said with great difficulty while removing a key from around his neck and holding it out to François.

"Daddy?"

"I'd beholdin' if you'd take Lucy here and see she's properly cared for. She ain't got no body else."

"Daddy?"

"I can't mend this, little one," he said tenderly as she began to cry. He stroked her tear-stained face. "There be more . . ." he began, but went into a coughing spasm until his body went limp.

François let the little girl, perhaps seven or eight years old, cry next to her father while he retrieved the chest. The small, round top box, twelve puce long by eight wide, was heavy. Using the key, he opened the lock and looked inside. He was stunned. The chest nearly overflowed with gold coins, obviously the treasure the pirate was babbling about. Returning, he heard shouting down on the beach. Taking a quick look, he spied another longboat arriving from a sloop now anchored off shore.

"Come on," he said to the little girl, but she refused to leave.

"I said come on. The pirates are coming back," he insisted, taking her wrist and pulling her away. "We'll come back when it's safe."

Buckling a leather belt across his chest to hold a cutlass, François grabbed two pistols, quickly checked that they were loaded and primed, and shoved them into another leather belt lashed about his girth, then hung a bag of powder and shot over his shoulder. With the small chest clutched to his chest and the little girl in tow, he made for the high country before they would be seen. It was a desperate climb for he knew the flag flying from the ship, and its crew, some of the cruelest cutthroats to sail any ocean, feared by all, and loved only by the devil himself.

Gaining the top, François stopped long enough to see if anyone followed. Satisfied the pirates apparently hadn't seen them, he continued the desperate flight back to Mariah. Once the pirates didn't find the treasure, they would sail the coast.

The little girl faltered. It was obvious she couldn't continue at such a break-neck speed. After hiding the chest behind a dead log just off the trail, he slung her feather-like body onto his back, and continued moving forward until arriving at the garden after what seemed an eternity. To his great relief Mariah didn't have a fire going. Setting the girl next to his bewildered wife, he staggered up to a ridge overlooking their beach and sighed. The cook fire at the cabin had gone out which would have signaled the cabin's location; otherwise it was well hidden by the trees.

Leaning against a boulder, his lungs burned from the exertion, his heart pounded viciously, his whole body ached. Allowing himself time to recover, he finally stumbled back on rubbery legs to where Mariah cradled the girl in her arms listening to the story of her father's death through mutual sobs. François collapsed face down on the blanket.

"Are we safe?" Mariah asked.

"I think so. They didn't see us. I was afraid the cooking fire at the cabin might still be smoldering. It's not. They won't know we are here."

Mariah's complexion paled as she held the girl closer. Despite being in good condition, the events of the last hour had taken a toll. Following a short rest, they moved into the cave, after which François ventured through the ravine to the basalt arm as a warm rain began from a squall ahead of the main storm.

The pirate ship was just passing their cove at half sail, lingering long enough to scope the beach, but seeing nothing it continued on until out of sight. They were safe, but that didn't preclude the possibility some of the pirates might have remained behind at the other camp.

Returning to the cave, he moved everyone deeper into its bowels and made their stay as comfortable as possible, and kindled a fire, but not for warmth. Outside, thick, black clouds spread out to unleash the storm over the island.

Chapter 8

† Captain Aloysius Shaver †

Shortly after beginning his career in farming François made a discovery, the importance of which he would have no idea until years later. Not unlike himself, a young, spirited, and determined lizard somehow crossed the Guanches' repellent to invade the garden. During a comical chase that had Mariah virtually rolling on the ground with laughter, it ducked into a mass of bushes next to the rock cliff not far from where François and Mariah often sat to rest. Upon wading into the brush, sure that the creature was cornered, he found the opening to a cave.

Drawn by curiosity, François ventured in, but without a light he was only able to go a few feet. Clearing the dense brush still didn't allow enough light for deeper penetration. A simple torch only piqued his curiosity, as the cave was much larger than imagined.

During particularly warm days, it provided a comfortable respite. With this storm upon them, it would be a dry haven and hiding place from any pirates who may have stayed ashore. Obviously, he was feeling paranoid, but that often meant the difference between life and death.

With Mariah and Lucy safely inside, he built a comforting fire. Reassured neither flame nor smoke would be seen, they settled back to wait out the storm that howled, flashed, and thundered while crying great drops. By morning, the wind tempered and the rain faded to a light drizzle, although the sky remained darkened by thick clouds.

"I am going to the cabin to retrieve blankets and what other things we need that I can carry," he said, hanging a leather pouch over his shoulder containing powder and shot, and shoving a pistol under his belt.

"Please be careful," Mariah said with a nervous edge to her voice as she kissed him.

With cutlass in hand, he made his way along the now slippery trail, pass the pool, and down the mountainside to their cabin. The steeper trail along the stream would be impossibly slick and treacherous after all the rain. With the coastline shrouded in a thick, gray mist, he felt uneasy approaching his home for the past two years. Fear-sparked imagination tickled his mind to feel as if being spied upon, but there wasn't time to wait and watch. He hurriedly gathering up their needs, wrapped them in an old oilcloth, and slung the lot over his shoulder.

Turning to leave, he startled at a presence in the doorway. Dropping the armload of provisions he reflexively had cutlass and pistol in hand before the items hit the ground. It was Diablo. François felt a weakness in his legs as the adrenalin charge abated. In response he cursed the beast who flipped a tongue at him, turned, and lumbered away.

"I'm sorry," he shouted after the breast, then chided himself, "You are beginning to sound like Mariah. It's just a lizard. It has no feelings." Still, he felt badly.

Remaining paranoid, heart pounding, he started back up the side of the mountain, constantly looking over his shoulder, but there was no indication that anyone else was about. What did occur, though, was a sudden downpour that instantly turned parts of the trail through the gorge into a muddy river forcing three steps for every one forward. By the time he reached the pool, he crumpled beneath bushes that afforded some protection from the rain. His lungs burned and legs ached from the exertion. After a time he dragged himself out, and despite continued rain, resumed his journey until staggering into the cave, totally exhausted.

During his absence, Mariah and Lucy had time to gather pine boughs from the thickest parts of the forest where they would be driest making two piles near the fire. When he arrived, the girls quickly laid several blankets over the largest pile to complete a bed. He would have collapsed into it, wet clothes and all, except Mariah insisted he remove them, a nearly impossible task as his fingers were numb and hands shook. Curled beneath two blankets, François lie down, quickly falling asleep.

Awaking around what should have been noon, thick clouds continued to lay down a steady mist, masking any notion of time. He might have slept longer except for Mariah's retching outside the entrance. In the haste, he forgot the herbs in the cabin. Squatting next to a crackling fire, he smiled weakly at the little girl. She was tiny for her age.

"I wish I could help her," he said, nodding his head in Mariah's direction.

"You will need a midwife when the baby comes," Lucy said.

François' butt met the ground with a bounce as he dropped backward. In both their lives, neither François nor Mariah had occasion to learn about the details of pregnancy. His mouth locked open with the sudden realization he was to become a father.

When the old woman at the village gave them herbs to settle Mariah's stomach, she never said anything about Mariah being pregnant. Why should she? Everyone understood about such things, except François. He felt stupid. Even Lucy understood—little Lucy, who seemed far too wise for her few years. Hers had not been a sheltered life.

Going to Mariah's side as she re-entered the cave, he wrapped an arm around her shoulders and said, "Lucy says we are to have a child."

"Yes," Mariah answered. Tears began to trickle down her cheeks. "Lucy told me. Isn't it wonderful?"

"Yes."

"You do not sound very happy."

"I feel very . . . I don't know about such things. Your illness . . . it never occurred to me . . . I am very happy."

"I was beginning to wonder, but I was as ignorant about this as you."

They giggled, and then kissed.

"I should like to name him Jean-Paul."

"And what if it is a girl?"

François paused. "Yes, what if it is a girl?" he thought. "We will name her after your mother."

"Papa would have liked that," Mariah replied, and they kissed again.

After a meal of raw vegetables and fruit, François went out to tend the garden despite a continuing mist. It was a mass of mud, really unworkable, but what he needed was space and time to think. Later, perched on Alita's throne, legs drawn close to his chest, he released his mind to become engaged in deep thought as the fine, warm drizzle soothed tired muscles. A baby. He was to be a father. He worried silently. "What if something did not go well with the birth? Mariah's mother had died in childbirth. They would need someone to help when the time came. Lucy said a midwife. Perhaps someone from the village could help. He would ask the old woman."

By midafternoon, Mariah had mostly recovered from the weakness of her morning sickness, so François took some food, left a primed pistol with her, and headed out along the rim trail armed with a short sword and double-barreled pistol. He had said it was to give the little girl's father a decent, Christian burial, but beyond that he wanted to scavenge whatever remained that would be useful, especially the longboat. However, there was a nagging doubt the pirates would leave it.

Coming to the place where he had hidden the small chest of gold coins, he decided to leave it in place for now and continue on. There was one last, brief deluge before the clouds parted allowing the sun to break through and begin to bake the earth dry. When he reached where the stream began its run to the sea, steam rose from the ground, and sweat cascaded in rivulets down his body.

The trail hadn't been easy when the ground was dry. Now it was a mud-greased plunge, forcing him to divide the time trying to keep from sliding out of control, making no noise, and staying alert for any movement that would indicate pirates had stayed behind. His body still ached from yesterday's trek and the morning's ordeal. This only multiplied that fatigue. It was with some relief he discovered that the girl's father and the dead pirates were already buried, except for Squirrel. His body hung from a tree upside down. As for the cutlasses, pistols, and rifles François previously gathered, they were gone.

Kicking about, looking for anything salvageable, François wandered through the burned remains of the hut, a simple structure no larger than the one he and Mariah inhabited except this had a wood floor. That was all that remained after the fire. Standing in the middle, he surveyed the ashes, disheartened. Nothing was left to salvage. He was sorely disappointed.

Taking a step to leave, the plank beneath his foot bent down throwing him off balance. Trying to keep from falling, his next step fell heavily on the floor and the boards gave way. Dropped into a hollow space, the suddenness and jarring fall dazed him slightly. Seated on the damp ground, he shook his head and looked around. To his delight, he had fallen amidst a cache of clothes, rum, powder, several pistols, a rifle, and a cutlass with a beautiful engraved, ivory handle. There were also wood working tools and a keg of spikes. In a back corner was a pile of neatly folded canvas and coiled rope. While lifting these latter items out of the hole, he uncovered another small, round-top chest exactly like the one given him the preceding day bringing to mind the last words Lucy's father uttered, "There be more . . ."

Fingers quivering excitedly, François picked at the lock—a skill learned on the streets of St. Nazaire. Wetting dry lips in anticipation of finding more gold coins, he lift the lid. It did! A fortune in Spanish doubloons! On top of the coins was a small object rolled up in cotton fabric treated with oil to make it waterproof. Hands once again began shaking nervously as all the lore and legends of piracy stimulated his wildest imaginations.

Carefully peeling away the wrap revealed a parchment. There could be no doubt. It was a treasure map! Quickly re-wrapping it so as not to appear disturbed, he replaced it in the box and fastened the lock. After setting it beneath a pile of rope, he headed for the beach, issuing a sigh of relief upon spotting the boat thrown up onto the beach. A careful inspection showed it still seaworthy. The pirates apparently didn't want it, but he certainly did. Moving all the discovered booty would take a week of laborious trips to carry it back to camp. With the boat, he could do it in one trip.

Loading the boat still took nearly two hours after which he rigged a mast and fashioned a sail before being able to buck the waves and catch a breeze that would carry him away from the boulder-strewn shoreline. After so long, it felt good to be on the sea once again, and with this prize, François felt extremely pleased.

An outgoing tide aided François to tack at a safe distance along the dangerous coast, studying it closely, but as Mariah said, there was little of interest. The mountain-island dove steeply into the sea leaving no usable shoreline until coming to the basalt wall marking the northern limit of their small beach. Swinging around its blunt end, he suddenly came into view of the pirate ship. There was no turning back. By their gestures, he had been spotted.

The aging sloop lay to anchor in the middle of Dolphin cove, *Devil's Blade* painted across her stern in blood red. The words showed no weathering. It was Captain Aloysius Shaver's ship, yet no it wasn't. François was familiar with the *Devil's Blade* and this creaking, barnacled piece of sea junk wasn't the ship he knew. The pirate's flag flew from the stern, but he couldn't imagine Hogshead Shaver sailing something like this. Whatever the situation, it was not good. Unexpectedly,

François found himself praying aloud, "Please, God, keep Mariah and Lucy hidden and safe."

Nearly all his life François had denied the existence of a God, but after becoming aware of some of the things that had transpired in his life leading up to the time with Mariah, he suddenly found himself speaking to one. A crack in his encrusted soul was open. He worried not about himself, but for his wife, their child, and Lucy. All he could do now was pilot ashore to meet the pirates face to face.

Pointing the bow toward the center of the beach, he watched carefully as a small group of men came out to meet him. In the center was a tall, thickset man with a large, feathered hat and fancy, brocaded long coat. The captain had gotten the nickname Hogshead because of his large head and broad, flat nose. The thick, bushy tangle of facial hair gave the appearance of a wild man, but that was to hide a long scar on the man's left cheek. Yet anyone familiar with the pirate didn't need to be up close to recognize him. There was never mistaking the arrogant swagger used to conceal a limp.

Capt. Jean-Paul spoke of him differently from the stories that circulated. "Capt. Shaver is a thoughtful man. At least he listens to what others have to say, but once he charts a course, a hurricane couldn't change it. He hates liars and devious men. I think those at our meeting came to understand that, as well as his temper. Certainly the English have tasted of that temper."

Dropping sail, François let the bow drive onto the beach and threw a rope out for one of them to catch. Jumping into the water, he took two steps ashore to greet them.

"Ahoy."

"Ahoy," Shaver said with a voice that sounded like a wood beam being dragged over gravel. "And who might ye be?"

"François, Captain Shaver."

"Well, François, pleased ta be meetin' ye. And how be it ye know who I am?"

"I saw you at a meeting of pirates a few years back. You're a man who stands out in a crowd, sir," François replied, priming the pirate's ego.

"Do I now? And how be ye upon this desolate rock?"

"I was sailing with Captain Jean-Paul on the *Fleurette* when she went down. The captain spotted an English merchant and had intentions of boarding her. It was a new Carrack sitting low in the water and looked to be easy prey, but she had more guns than a wart hog has hairs. Big ones, too. I was on a swivel in the bow and got thrown overboard with the first salvo, then they must have hit the magazine; sent her to the bottom with all hands–except me."

"That be hard ta 'ear, lad. Word about she were sunk in a storm. Jean-Paul weren't much of a pirate, not ta be speakin' ill of the dead, he jist weren't very lucky. Always somethin' seem ta turn sour fer 'im, but mark me words . . ., he were a good man. Might too honest, but someone ye could count on . . . in a fight and otherwise. Now that I be thinkin' upon it, be ye that brat that was always tuggin' 'is coattails?"

"Yes, sir."

"Ye've grown a might. So, how'd ye end up 'ere?"

"Don't rightly know, sir. The merchant left me to drown. Thought that was my lot until some dolphins came along and started towing me. Don't rightly remember much after that. I'd taken a hit to the head by some timbers off the *Fleurette,* so don't remember much until I woke sprawled on this beach. That was almost three years ago."

Shaver looked over François' shoulder at a couple of his crew inspecting the contents of the longboat.

"Jist powder, musket, canvas, rope, and the likes, Cap'n."

"And where'd ye get all that?

"Found it up the coast a piece. Heard gun shots yesterday while hunting. Gunshots means people. That was curious. No one lived in that area I knew about. When the rains quit, I set out to find whoever it was. Found this place all burned down and some poor soul strung upside down in a tree. Not much I could do for him."

"Did ye cut 'im down?"

"No, sir. It was a warning and that would bring bad luck."

"So ye went gatherin' all this stuff?"

"Aye, sir. Couldn't see it go to rot when I could put it to good use here."

"And jist where'd ye find all these goodies?" a one-eyed sailor butted in.

"Under the floor of the burned out place." François had an instant dislike for this one.

"Well, Shelly, that be the one place ye didn't look," Shaver said.

"Wouldn't have found it myself if I hadn't fallen through while kicking through the rubble."

"So where's the chest? If'n you found all this you must have found the chest, too?" Shelly challenged.

"In the bow by the rope and canvas," François answered coolly.

Shelly leaped into the boat tearing through the pile of rope and canvas, finally holding the small chest over his head with a triumphant yell.

"Jist bring it 'ere, Mr. Shelly," Shaver said, rolling his eyes, obviously annoyed.

With the chest in his large, rough hands, the pirate looked it over carefully.

"Ye see what's inside?"

"No," François lied. "The lock looks sound. It was getting late and I wanted to get back here before dark. Figured there was time enough to look after getting all this stowed. By the sound there's coinage inside."

Shaver reached inside his cotton shirt and extracted a key on the end of a long, leather cord. Fitting it into the lock, it popped open easily. Handing the lock to François, he opened the lid carefully and stared for a long moment before breaking into a wide grin.

"It be 'ere, lads," he said, waving the map and handing the box to François who stared inside as if he hadn't seen the contents before.

As the boy began to finger the gold coins, ignoring Shaver' preoccupation with the map, Shelly tore the box from his hands and snapped the lid shut.

"Ye say ye ne'er set eyes on this?" Shaver asked sternly.

"On my honor," François said.

"'E's lyin', Cap'n," Shelly countered. "How'd he know there be gold coin inside?"

"By shaking the box you dumb lout," François' response was curt and defiant.

Shelly made a lung for François' throat only to find a pistol pointed directly at his long, hooked nose.

"Even the worst shot can't miss from here," François said with a cold firmness that even surprised him.

"Now, boys, settle down. Young François 'ere's been honest with us, Mr. Shelly. Could've lied and tried to keep the treasure fer 'imself."

"Is that a treasure map?"

"Aye. Cap'n Jeremiah Markel's treasure. Some of the best gold the Spaniards stole from the heathens in the New World." Markel had been one of the first of the pirates to successfully prey upon the Spanish treasure ships until killed during a raid on one of the smaller forts. "Since ye found this fer us, lad, you be entitled to shares."

That was an offer any pirate with a grain of adventure and lust for wealth wouldn't pass, and three years ago François would have leaped at the opportunity.

After a pause he said, "Well, I be passing on that, Cap'n Shaver."

"What say ye?! Ye want to stay marooned on this rock?"

"Well, I ain't exactly marooned any more. I got this boat to sail away anytime."

"So what be so important 'ere ta make ye wanna stay?" the captain's suspicions were raised.

"When I got thrown up on this beach I found a village south of here a piece and I met this girl. It's a bit sparse, but I like her comfort. Besides, she's fixing to have a baby and figure I need stay 'til that happens."

Shaver's right eyebrow shot up as a big grin split his mouth as he erupted into an equally big laugh.

"Well, that be good enough reason . . . I suppose . . . but I won't be leavin' ye empty handed. 'Ere," he said, taking the chest of coins from Shelly's greedy grasp and handing it to François. "Will ye be acceptin' this as yer share?"

"That's mighty generous of you, sir," he replied, returning the pistol to his belt and taking the box.

"As ye say it be mighty bare, 'ere 'bouts. Would there be anything else ye could be needin'?"

François recognized Shaver' question was a subversive way of verifying his tale.

"Well, I was hoping to find some flour."

Shaver's laugh sounded like distant thunder. "Mr. Shelly, fetch back what the lad needs and be quick about it."

"Thank you kindly, Cap'n Shaver. Such things are

hard to come by. I have to travel to the port up north. We don't have a cart or donkey, so it's hard carrying much back."

Shaver laughed. "Bring the lad some salt as well. We got plenty."

Irritated, Shelly ordered a couple crewmen to fetch the provisions then returned to hear Shaver inquiring more about the merchant that sank the *Fleurette*.

"Did ye happen ta see the name of the ship that sunk the *Fleurette*?"

"Aye. I won't forget that name any time soon. Some day when I take leave of this place, I'll find her and blow her bottom out. It was the *Agnes* out of Glasgow."

"The *Agnes*. The *Agnes*," Shaver rolled the name of the ship off his tongue while stroking his beard in thought. "Ain't that the ship owed by that pompous, fat Scot? Ne'er more than 16 guns." A good seaman knew the ships plying their waters.

"I saw more guns on his sweeps deck."

"Did ye 'ave any idear what 'e were up to?"

François shrugged and remained quiet. He knew, but didn't think it wise to let on he had been aboard.

"'Eard told a English ship shot up a Spanish fort in the Carib. Figured it were jist a tall tale. Might be why the brethren 'ave sailed a wide birth from 'is ships lately. That wily Scot be up ta somethin' fer sure, and my guess be 'e's carryin' important cargo. Well, we'll jist have ta take a peek . . ., after we make another stop," he said, waving the map as the sailors gathered around and laughed.

"I would prefer to sink her myself, but I might be here awhile. If you do, I'd appreciate word so I know things have been squared with my shipmates."

"Fair request, lad. Well, 'ere be yer provisions. I

hates leavin' ye behind, but know the warmth of a good wench can be mighty invitin'. We'll be leavin' a couple ores as well."

François watched as the pirates returned to their ship before hauling the caskets of flour and salt up to the cabin. He had purposely left the chest of gold coins on the beach knowing Shaver was watching through a spyglass and wanted to portray the notion that the provisions were more important.

They were setting sail as he returned to begin carrying the salvage up to the shelter. The *Devil's Blade* was an ink spot on the ocean as he hauled the longboat further onto shore, turning it over, and securing it to the salt-hardened tree. He was more than pleased at having pulled off the tale and actually come out ahead. As Capt. Jean-Paul always said, "Treasure maps have a way of coming up empty, but gold coin in the palm of your hand is for counting."

By the time the last of the salvage was stowed, it was too dark for travel so he waited several hours until the moon rose higher. Although only three-quarters, it provided enough light to negotiate the trail along the stream. Slipping quietly into the cave, he approached the small fire, trying not to disturb the girls, but the subtle crunch of dry soil beneath his feet echoed in the cavern.

Standing before the fire, he felt a tickle on the back of his neck so announced softly, "Mariah, it's me."

In the dark beyond, he heard the click of a pistol hammer returning to its safe, closed position. Squatting next to their dying, cooking fire, he added a bit of wood before opening the small chest. While hungrily devouring a mixture of fruits and raw vegetables he told Mariah and Lucy his fantastic story.

"There's another chest hidden on the trail to Valverde," he said.

"Lucy told me. God has smiled on us. Now come to bed."

Slipping out of the tunic, François crawled beneath the blanket. Mariah scooted close along his side, put one leg over his, and gently stroked his chest, a prelude to a frisky cuddle. However with all the exertion of the past two days, and the burden of poverty suddenly lifted from his shoulders, François fell fast asleep.

Chapter 9

† Another Map †

The next day dawned bright, but sultry, as the three made short order of the daily garden work, leaving François enough time to retrieve the other chest of gold before the sun raised an insufferable steam bath. Returning just in time for lunch, François handed the girl the box.

"Your father intended this gold for you," he said. "I will keep the other for us. You ladies stay here where it's comfortable. I'm going down for a hot bath. My nose says I need a soak and my head needs time to think."

Walking south along the base of the cliff, he came to where the trail climbed to the top and on to the

Guanches village. Trees flourished here thanks to protection from the wind and the abundance of water spewing from the earth. It was here the hot water bubbled up to begin its run to the ocean. There were intermittent breaks in the cliff allowing one to access the top if willing to sacrifice a bit of skin from hands and shins. There was no trail following the stream, which forced François to negotiate rubble and zigzag around huge boulders broken from the cliff. One spot required an almost hand-over-hand ascent and sliding descent.

He had hoped to find a way around the talus slope on the original trail so to make it easier and safer for Mariah to travel between the garden and beach. Following the stream was not at all promising. Deciding to cut through the brush back to the original trail, he discovered a spot that angled down through a natural swell hidden by heavy growth. It was obvious the lizards and other creatures had long used this passage. A little modification would accommodate human height.

Satisfied this was a much better route, he set blaze marks high up on a few trees as a reminder. Much satisfied, he headed to the pool, tossed his garments, a sweat-soaked taparrabos, and sandals aside, waded to the middle, stretched out his arms and fell backwards into the water. Gradually tight and sore muscles relaxed. Standing in the cold spray of the waterfall urged waning energy to return. After a few alternating plunges, he proceeded through the gap, tossing his clothes over some bushes before walking out onto the volcanic ridge. Without hesitation, he dove into the ocean, instantly joined by his watery friends as if expecting him.

Returning with Mariah's medicine, he was anxious to share his discovery; however, the girls seemed more excited, waving excitedly as he crossed the grassy meadow. Their shouting prompted him to break into a run.

"François, look what Lucy found," Mariah called out from a distance as the little girl waived something dark in her hand.

Taking the object, François stared transfixed before stuttering, "Where did you find this?"

"Lucy was counting the coins in the chest her father left for her and found it on the bottom," Mariah explained.

It's a treasure map, isn't it?" Lucy said.

"It's identical to the one I gave Captain Shaver. I recognize the shape of the island and some of the landmarks."

"But why two maps?" Mariah asked.

François studied the paper closely before making a disturbing discovery.

"No. This is different. It's the same island, but the location of the treasure is different. This shows it on the opposite side."

"Could it be another treasure?"

"I don't think so. One map is a fake."

"If the pirates have the fake, they will be back."

"Yes, but it will take them four or five months."

"What can we do?"

"We will have to move. Make it appear we left. I will bring everything up from your father's cabin. We can make a new home in the cave."

Mariah looked hurt.

"I will build a house. A very nice house."

"You can do that?"

"Jean-Paul apprenticed me to every job abroad ship, but the time spent with the ship's carpenter was the most enjoyable. I now have tools. Yes, I can do that."

For three days, François and Lucy undertook the laborious task of hauling all their possessions up the mountain. He refused to allow Mariah to help except to organize the cave. That completed, he and Lucy obliterated the trail through the mountain cleft with boulders, even transplanting vegetation. In a month or so, the whole area would appear undisturbed. By judicious use, he could still venture down to the ridge for diving, but there would be no telltale signs of a trail leading through the gorge to their new mountain home. They did the same for the steeper trail leading up along the cold stream.

Once that was finished, he set foundations stones and felled the first trees, shaping and fitting the ends tongue and groove. The arrival of Cirano, his new wife, and sister were a god-send. Mariah had company as the women tended the garden, leaving François and Cirano to sweat profusely log by log as the walls raised. Eventually they built a devise with block and tackle to lift each piece into position. Several days into the project more men from the village appeared and within two days, the roof poles were set. The old Guanches woman sent more herbs and Mariah felt stronger to help collect thatch, which were then handed up to a couple of older men skilled in lacing them together to make a water-tight cover. Completed far sooner than expected they could move in, but not until after a celebration brought everyone from the village including the old woman who pronounced a blessing on the home.

François was quite pleased with the work. He'd made some mistakes along the way, but learned how to work the wood better so that it fit snugly. The women chinked the cracks with a mixture of gray clay and tough saw grass from the seaward slopes, adding pine pitch to create a weatherproof seal. He designed the window openings with shutter closures. A rock fireplace would help dispel any chill.

The overall structure was a rectangular-shape covering the mouth of the cave using the rock face as the back wall. It had three doors. One exited out to the front where he planned to add a covered veranda. Another was located off the kitchen to the outside cooking area. He place a third entry at the back of the kitchen leading into the cavern that had been serving as a shelter and now would provid dry storage, and if necessary, escape.

The cavern had another entrance overlooking the western portion of the meadow. Over this he built a door and planted vegetation to hide it. The cave itself wove its way into the bowels of the island coming to a waterfall that drove the stream out to join the sea on the south side of volcanic arm protecting Dolphin Cove. This discovery, however, he kept secret.

A week after the dolphins deposited François on the beach a big storm overran the island shaking the original cabin so violently they feared it would collapse and bury them. When another such storm struck several weeks after moving into the new home the seaside house lay in ruins. The winds of that storm bent the surrounding treetops, but the meadow set in a protective bowl. Their new home was solid and safe. Moreover, it was comfortable and dry. Secretly, though, François missed Diablo's visits.

Cirano's mother, Rhea, came to live them during the last two months of Mariah's pregnancy. So did the youngest of her brood, three girls, and two boys ranging in age from three to twelve. That was especially good for Lucy, having someone close to her age to play with. François never had that opportunity after leaving St. Nazaire. This provided an opportunity to discover the joys of what becoming a father would be like.

He was very happy having found a safer way to the hot pool for Mariah, but she stopped using it at the midwife's suggestion. He continued daily visits with the children while she bathed in the stream. However, there were times he went alone to the cove to swim with the dolphins and sit on the beach, or on the headland, using the quiet time to think on their future.

Such times were also a struggle as he felt the siren's call to return to the sea. Acquisition of the longboat created a great temptation, but each night, cradled in Mariah's arms, those yearnings became less loud and slipped further away. He had found something stronger and more desirable, the permanency and contentment longed for. As for the treasure map, well, maybe someday he thought to follow it, but for now he had all a man could want—a good woman, a home, and money, for the chest contained considerable wealth. However, the gold was no good if not used, and on that, François began forming a plan.

Chapter 10

† The Pirate's Daughter †

The life of a seaman was hard and dangerous. If they returned home at all, it was not unusual to be less whole than when they left. A seaman turned pirate multiplied the risks a hundred fold. Returning, a single man fared better than one who was married, for the latter never knew what to expect upon entering the door of his home. The woman could be there waiting, or not. Years of being alone, maintaining a house and children, struggling on the edge of poverty took their toll. Such happened to Lucy's father.

Broke, James Bannister was easily enticed by a

lucrative offer and signed on as an officer aboard a privateer armed with a letter of marque. This official license permitted their ship to attack and capture enemies of the English government. In this case, they had permission to prey upon French, Spanish, and Portuguese shipping coming from the New World. The intent was to capture and bring the ship before an admiralty court, but that was impossible when patrolling at far distances. Taking the best of the captured ship's cargo they transported it to the nearest port with a government representative who took their share. It was dangerous work, not just because of the ensuing battles, but also because what happened to James' ship.

The attack on a French merchant did not go well. Cannon balls were not especially accurate and in the heat of battle, several struck below the waterline. Transferring the crew to their ship, James went aboard the listing vessel looking for its captain. Upon opening the door to his quarters, the man turned and fired a pistol as James entered. The ball narrowly missed him, striking a seaman following at his shoulder. James instinctively pulled the trigger on his pistol, killing the captain instantly. In the man's hand was a parchment. Stuffing it in his shirt, he scooped up a small chest of gold coins and the ship's log and returned to his ship where he turned the gold over to his captain. He forgot about the document until removing his clothes to lie down. The parchment was not more than six inches wide and ten inches long, soiled and crumpled, but still readable. The longitude and latitude fixed an island not far from the island of Jamaica. A detailed drawing showed a dotted line, landmarks, and paces. What made his heart pound was the signature of Jeremiah Markel and a date thirty days following the pirate's acquisition of the largest treasure ever relieved from the Spanish, and two months before being killed.

That event happened eleven years before, but the legend grew with each telling. Any thinking man knew that the stories were now far out of proportion, but still, the treasure would be sizable. The document had obviously changed hands many times until coming into his possession, but that it bore a curse never occurred to any of its owners until too late.

The ship's log did not mention the map. An entry eluded that the French captain came by a gift after sparing a Dutch captain's ship and life. The quartermaster told what he knew and James admitted seeing something in the dead man's hand, ignoring it to collect the gold. James' own captain lamented had he known about the map, he would have searched until the ship anchored in Davy Jones' locker. James never mentioned the map, not out of greed, but because of a persistent warning in his head that said to keep it hidden.

Upon arriving home after nearly fourteen months at sea, the authorities greeted the crew with less than open arms. England and France signed a truce three weeks before the French ship was engaged and sunk. That communications were next to nonexistent was beside the point. They committed an act of piracy and must suffer the consequences. It was all political, but deadly, nevertheless.

James was still aboard ship when he saw the soldiers arrest his captain and first officer. As they came aboard to take the rest of the crew into custody, he managed to secret himself below until darkness allowed escape.

The only place he could think was home. It would not be safe for long, but he had to see his wife and daughter. What he found was an empty house and devastating news. His wife died a few months before, and his daughter taken to his wife's older sister whom he thoroughly despised. Complicating matters, soldiers showed up as he stood at the door of a neighbor receiving the bad news. At the neighbor's insistence, he quickly slipped inside their home until the soldiers left allowing him to proceed to a village several miles away to find his daughter.

Determined not to leave the girl to the sister-in-law, he scooped Lucy up and fled, taking passage that eventually brought them to the Mediterranean. There he secured a small boat, again just ahead of the authorities, and searched for a place to hide. His problems only multiplied when he divulged to what he considered a friend that he possessed the map to Jeremiah Markel's Spanish treasure. He learned only minutes before an armed gang arrived that this friend sailed on the *Devil's Blade*.

For the next few weeks, he barely managed to stay ahead of Capt. Shaver, eventually landing on a small piece of shore on the Island of El Hierro. He thought them to be safe on this desolate rock and beached the boat, using its lumber to build a small, but hospitable cabin. But the curse followed. Shaver had spies in Valverde who alerted him that James was in the area. Not waiting for the pirate to arrive from neighboring Gomera, the spies struck out in a longboat to search the coastline themselves.

Lucy spotted the pirates first as they landed on the rocky beach. Cornered, James put up a desperate fight. That they were drunk gave him an advantage. The cabin caught fire during the battle, but just before putting the last to flight, he caught a ball in the chest.

Helping her father into the thick brush, they waited for the remaining pirate to return. James knew there was no help for himself, the panic for his daughter's safety greater than the pain of his mortal wound.

When the young native appeared, he knew there was hope for Lucy, but then the surviving pirate crept from his hiding place to attack the new arrival. James was about to fire a shot to at least alert him, but the young man turned and incredibly engaged the experienced pirate with the best swordsmanship he'd seen in many years. However, James wasn't in any condition to last much longer and when the opportunity presented itself, he shot the last pirate.

Until her mother died, Lucy's life had been one surrounded by love and comfort, if not wealth. That changed drastically. Life with her aunt was hard and often painful, physically and emotionally. The appearance of her father was as if seeing an angel. Despite having to endure the hardships of fleeing ahead of the authorities and pirates, she clung to every minute with her father as he clung to her. Now ripped from him forever, the little girl felt as if the heavens were pressing down to crush her. Cradled in Mariah's arms, she found comfort. Orphaned, she had come among orphans who understood her pain. Over the course of the next months, Lucy was able to begin putting the tragedies of life behind while helping Mariah and François build their home and become a family.

~   ~   ~   ~

François remained close as Mariah's time neared, continually plagued by the specter of what happened to her mother. Sleep was fitful. He leapt to her side at the slightest contraction despite having Rhea with them. All he could do was hold Mariah's hand, but while that was enough for now, it would not be sufficient when the time came.

Lying together one night, cradled in her husband's strong arms, she said softly, "François, I don't want to be alone when the baby comes."

"Rhea will be with you, and Celena," he said, referring to Rhea's twelve year-old daughter. "Lucy will be there, too."

"I want you to be there."

"During the birthing? It is not permitted."

"Who said?"

"Just the other night Rhea said that all was ready and when the baby arrived and it was proper, she would send for me. Remember?"

"Yes, I remember. I want you to be there holding my hand."

"Rhea will not permit such a thing."

"Are you not the master of this home?"

"Yes, but . . ."

"Are you afraid of Rhea? You who fought with pirates afraid of a woman?"

"This is different."

"Now I know how the Spanish should transport their precious treasures. Employ women. Why they would only need half the crew."

François felt his wife bouncing lightly. She was laughing."

"Oh, all right. I will speak with Rhea and seek her permission."

He truly tried to bring up Mariah's request several times, but the conversation never got beyond "Mariah has asked . . ." It was as if the Guanches mother knew what he wanted and deftly switched the conversation to something else.

Having finished the morning's garden work, he was coming back from the stream when he saw Rhea's silhouette in the door. Lucy and Celena were working in the outside kitchen. Leaving their chore, the girls ran for the house. He broke into a run, coming into the front room seconds behind the girls. In the back where their bedroom was located, he heard Mariah's cries. He stepped in.

"Men are not allowed," Rhea said as she bustled about getting linens ready.

"I will stay with my wife," François answered. She stopped and stared at him more astonished than angry. "I was present when this all started, I shall be at my wife's side for the finish." He was surprised at how firm he sounded.

Rhea didn't argue. There wasn't time. Seated next to his wife, François took her hand in one of his, and patted the perspiration from her brow with the other. Her smiled appreciation was a mere flash as the contractions lifted her head from the bed.

He felt so helpless, more than at any other time in life, seeing the pain etched on her delicate face, listening to the cries, oblivious to Rhea's directions for her to push. When Mariah's eyes closed and she relaxed, he began to panic. Then he heard a song more beautiful than any Siren, the first cry of their child.

"It's a boy," Lucy announced.

François turned to look at the squirming, crying, messy bundle after Rhea finished cleaning and swaddling. Taking the child in his arms, François turned back to Mariah who smiled weakly and cradled it in her arms. As Rhea and the girls tidied up, François gently brushed a finger along the chubby, soft, brown cheek, knowing it was time to put the chest of gold to use.

Chapter 11

† Maître de Beaucoup Trucs †

Valverde had always been the largest village on the island, but François seldom traveled there, preferring to trade for necessities at the seaside village of Sabinosa on the southern flank of El Golfo. Situated at the base of the long, western slope, it had a small Spanish garrison that didn't ask questions. The couple of times he and Mariah did journey to Valverde, he let her complete any trading and shopping while staying out of sight. At the time he wasn't sure why, but that decision proved wise. Known only to one person living on the outskirts of town, he was about to pull off a bold charade.

Having left Mariah home, he remained inconspicuous as possible as he approached the edge of town and headed to the most important first stop, a store run by a jolly, rotund widow, Señora Custadio. Making her acquaintance during previous trips to Valverde, Mariah became like a daughter, and as any observant mother, the Señora spotted the special glow in the girl's eyes on their last trip to town. Like a good mother, she finagled the reason from Mariah and insisted meeting the young man.

She was the only person in Valverde to actually meet François as they spent that night at her home on the southwest fringe of the settlement, and the only person other than Mariah to know his true identity. A prudent woman with a past, she kept the secret faithfully. For this trip, she was the only person who could fulfill François' first requirement.

"I need a suit of clothes befitting a land owner, but I desire them to be practical as well as fashionable," he said.

Eying his native garb she grinned widely and teased, "So, the young seaman is truly dropping anchor to make my Mariah happy?"

"We have become husband and wife, yes. And we have a child."

The woman placed pudgy hands on both her cheeks and squealed loudly before squashing his face with them, pulling him down to plant a kiss on his forehead. "I am so happy for you both."

He liked the short woman shaped like a large cask with dark blue eyes and perpetual winkles of joy and mischief at each corner. With black hair knotted in a bun, the Señora was a slightly larger and younger version of the old Jewish woman in St. Nazaire.

"Clothes? Oh, definitely." She looked him over carefully while wrinkling her nose as if smelling something bad. "Oh, definitely. Something less . . . rustic?

Well, let's see." She hummed a perky melody while sorting through an assortment of breeches and hose arranged neatly in cubicles behind a long counter. "Try these."

Casting about, he looked for a less public spot.

With a hearty laugh she said, "Oh, and I was hoping for a peak," before pointing to a small doorway covered by a beaded curtain. In the back, he had just tied the fly on the knee breeches when her large arm reached through the curtain dangling a white linen shirt. "And this," she said adding a waist-length, black jacket with silver thread.

Reappearing in the store, she looked him up and down before flitting behind and using the flat of her hands to smooth a wrinkle here and there.

"Not too bad. Perhaps a ruff. Do you need a ruff? No. That would be impractical. A cravat? Definitely, you need a cravat, but not with lace. Fine linen, and red. Let me show you how the Croat soldiers tie them. A gentleman I once knew showed me how to do the knot. Quite distinctive. No one on the island knows how to do this, not even the governor-general, though he tries. If they asked I would teach them, but who would ask a peasant woman? Now, a hat. There," she continued to critique after adding the items, "You look very much like a gentleman from the continent who would come to town . . . leading a donkey," she chortled merrily looking at his sandaled feet.

François winced at the thought. In St. Nazaire, he never wore shoes after his parents' death, even as a sailor, he seldom wore the simple seaman's shoe, and on the island he wore sandals only to traverse the rocky terrain. He didn't like the confinement, but both were quite pleased with the results as he stood before her in glistening brown, stovepipe boots.

François felt very different now clothed in a

white shirt whose sleeves ended in modest ruffs at the wrist. The cravat was a simple, long, narrow strip of cloth neatly knotted under his chin, the ends hanging to his breastbone. Over this he wore the jacket, leaving it unbuttoned. Black, knee-length breeches with a slight ballooning at the bottom, the ends tucked into the soft leather boots. Señora Custadio literally topped off the new man with a black, flat-brimmed hat.

"Here," he said handing her a gold coin from a leather pouch hung around his neck.

Her mouth opened as she stared at the irregular, round piece of metal.

"Anything wrong?" he asked.

"This is far too much. I don't have enough to give back the difference."

"That is quite all right. It is for all you have done for Mariah and now me."

"Where did you get this coin?" she asked, biting the coin and becoming very serious.

"Is it not good?"

"It is very good. Where did you get it?"

"Let's just say, in payment for my services."

"There will be questions when I attempt to use it."

"After today, that will not be a problem.

Adding a scabbard for his cutlass with the fancy, ivory handle, and holder for the pistol, he packaged his old clothes in a small, leather valise. Bowing slightly from the waist, François kissed her hand as he had seen Captain Jean-Paul do on several occasions when encountering a woman of culture. His next stop was at the desk of the minister of lands who looked up from a ledger with a puzzled expression.

"I wish to secure certain acreage," François said.

"Oh, really. And for whom do you entertain this request?"

"Myself."

"Ah, yes. And just what acreage are you considering?"

François went to a map of the island hanging on the wall and traced an outline of what he wanted.

"That is a great deal of land for someone so young." The fat man wheezed a laugh.

"How much?"

"I don't have time to play games with children. Go trouble someone else," the minister replied, waiving him off.

François jiggled the leather pouch containing coins. "How much?"

The minister was now fully attentive and an hour later François left holding papers to a huge plantation, paid in full. His next stop was at the house of a man who had cattle and goats for sale.

"And how many would you like?" the man asked, skeptical of the request.

"How many do you have?"

"Forty six cows and thirty seven goats."

"Very good."

"You wish to buy them all?"

François pulled out the leather bag and handed him several coins. "I would be interested in acquiring a few more as well, say fifty cows and an equal number of goats. One hundred sheep should be enough to begin. I will also need herdsmen. Your recommendations of capable men would be greatly appreciated."

The man faltered, staggered by the suddenness of receiving so much money all at once. Finally, he said, "I have a son and two nephews. They are only ten and eleven, but very good with the animals. If you desire someone older I have a brother who was crippled in a fishing accident, but he is most capable to handling such a task."

"I trust your judgment regarding their capabilities. I should require all four. Your brother can be the overseer. I shall pay him one silver real a month, and the boys a half silver real a month each, in addition to providing shelter and food, as soon as it can be built, of course."

"So much!"

François laid down five reals. "I would like them delivered to my plantation by the end of the week," François continued, handing the man a map with directions.

"Most assuredly. And whom shall they ask for?"

François had given that question considerable thought while formulating his plan and let the response roll off his tongue with a flair, "Don François Evreux de St. Nazaire."

François could not remember his real last name so used that of the man who had been his captain, mentor, and friend, Jean-Paul. Of course, to give it a dash of flair he added the city from which he came, a common practice among the wealthy.

This newly discovered power was very enjoyable. "What do you want, boy?" growled in contempt suddenly became, "Whatever you wish, Don François."

His last business stop was the home of a vintner where he not only placed an order for grape vines from Spain, but arranged for the necessary skilled workers and equipment as well. By this time, it was late afternoon. Wanting to continue building notoriety by following Señora Custadio's recommendation and going to the Land's End, an old, but well-kept hostel for a meal and room. That's when trouble appeared in the form of a man attired in a fancy military uniform, a soldier at either shoulder. His hard-soled, black boots made a loud thudding noise as he strut across the wood floor toward François' table where a simple, but nourishing stew had just been served. The room went deathly silent.

"I would like to have a word with you, Señor," the soldier said arrogantly.

"Fine," François answered, deliberately slurping his meal. He seemed to have a natural knack for irritating soldiers, the reason he tended to avoid them.

"My name is Manuel Ortega Hidalgo, Captain of his Excellency, Governor-general Francisco Alvaro Hernandez y Zárate's garrison."

"Nice to meet you. I am François Evreux de St. Nazaire, but you probably already know that by now. What can I do for you?"

"You could stop eating long enough to provide me with some information," he pushed.

"I have had a very long day arranging my business affairs, Captain Hidalgo, and this is the first I have eaten since morning. I believe that anything you want to know can be answered between mouthfuls of this delicious stew," François replied snootily, responding in like manner to the soldier's attitude.

"Where did a boy get so much money, especially Spanish crown gold coins?"

François looked at him with an air of contempt.

"I don't believe my personal financial affairs concern you, Captain."

"It does if those coins are stolen."

"Are you accusing me of being a thief?"

"Only you can answer that question."

"Oh. Very well. I'm not a thief," François said, and casually returned to the stew.

The blade of a sword came down on the table next to his hand and with a threatening voice the Captain said, "I want to know how you came by those coins?"

François' former captain schooled him well as how to remain in command of any situation so not to be intimidated. Pushing his chair back slowly, François tapped his lips with a napkin and stood. Despite a youthful face, his height and breadth by this time were equal to any full-grown man and somewhat better than the cocksure officer confronting him.

"If you must know, Captain, any monies that I possess were freely given my family by King Philip, himself," he replied with a measured tone.

"A Frenchman?" The comment dripped with animosity. "You are French, am I correct?" the Captain said, continuing to point his sword at François.

"Very astute, Captain. It must be my accent. Do you speak French?

"Not likely," he spat.

"Hm-m-m. Well, My father was Captain Jean-Paul Evreux, Master of the Fleurette.

"Just as I suspected! A pirate."

"A privateer, Captain, by writ of the King Louis of France and counter-signed by King Philip to prey upon our common enemy, the English and Dutch," François replied sounding irate. "As you should know, such appointment does not come to ordinary men. I am the heir to the Maître de Beaucoup Trucs."

"And does the King know that you have his gold?"

"Quite frankly, Captain, I have tired of this conversation and your boorish behavior."

"You filthy French pirates steal anyone's gold."

That was a clear challenge designed to humiliate and infuriate François, and goad him into rash reaction. Jean-Paul repeatedly warned and schooled him to control anger, "An angry man's mind becomes clouded and makes mistakes, the body becomes rigid and slow to respond." It took all the composure he could muster.

"Your behavior, Captain, is really inexcusable, but I will forgive that as it is obvious you were raised poorly."

The slap across François face was instantaneous and stung. His immediate reaction was to draw his pistol and shoot the man, but struggled even harder to maintain control by rolling his tongue around inside his mouth and taking a deep breath.

"I accept your challenge," François said coolly.

"You feel you are man enough to duel?" Capt. Hidalgo laughed.

"As much as I regret this, it seems my only recourse is, to phrase it in a vernacular suitable to your status, to carve your peasant gizzard into fish bait."

"Corporal, go to the barracks and retrieve my dueling pistols."

"I believe the choice of weapons is mine."

The Captain smiled and bowed, insolently spreading his arms.

"We have the necessary equipment," François replied touching the hilt of his sword. The accompanying soldiers laughed.

"Shall we step outside, then?"

"That would be a pleasure," François replied, then before turning to leave, said to his hostess, "Dear, madam, please keep this delicious stew warm. I should not be long."

The large open area behind the cantina was suitable for the fight, but François wanted this to be on his terms. He had to anger the man.

"Would you like a real sword?" the Captain asked with a smirk, offering him a rapier from one of his soldiers as François removed his jacket and handing it to hostel owner's young son.

"I have no need of a woman's toy," he replied drawing his cutlass deliberately, "Especially if from a philistine son of a female dog."

That achieved the desired response as Hidalgo

catapulted protocol and lunged forward.

The cock-sure officer had thought to make short order of a boy, but found himself in a true battle. If François had become proficient with any weapon it was the sword as he parried and countered everything presented. The Captain silently acknowledged having met a worthy opponent as the conflict spanned every inch of the dirt courtyard.

François presented the appearance of being completely relaxed as long hours of practice and drill flowed through his arms and feet. When he and Mariah hadn't practiced together, he kept in shape by practicing on the beach or by the garden with an imaginary foe. Cautious not to become overly confident, he played with this man as a cat might with a ship's rat.

"Really, Captain, is this the best you can offer?" François chided.

The officer offered no reply as sweat began to pepper his face.

Back and forth the battle raged, each kicking up clouds of dust, causing on-lookers to scatter out of the way until Jean-Paul's words again came to mind. "The longer a duel continues, the more chance something will go against you."

"Well, I really have better things to do. The smell of that stew is most inviting" François said, deciding to end the engagement, and with a flick of the wrist laid the man's shirtsleeve open, drawing blood from a scratch.

"Oh, I am so sorry," François apologized, and promptly laid the other sleeve open. "There, you have a matched set. That should allow more air to circulate and cool your obviously tiring body."

That second maneuver completely surprised Hidalgo as could be seen in his eyes.

"Perhaps you need more ventilation," François

continued and promptly laid the front of the man's shirt open with such ease that it now brought fear into Hidalgo's eyes.

As the Captain tried desperately to recover and counter, François creased his right biceps drawing more blood. Then he struck the man's left forearm especially hard with the flat of his blade nearly causing him to drop the weapon.

"It would seem, Captain, I have the ability to carve you up in many little pieces, so would you like to prolong this farce or shall we end it now?"

Hidalgo pulled back quickly to where one of his soldiers stood with musket in hand. Throwing his sword down he grabbed the rifle, pushing the soldier away, but before he could point the heavy weapon, a cutlass cartwheeled through the air impaling his right shoulder. Looking down at it with an expression of great surprise, Hidalgo slowly slumped to his knees, glazed eyes looking up at François then back at the hilt of the ivory handle.

Walking up to the Captain, he kicked the rifle away, put a foot on the man's chest, and pulled the blade out while shoving him backward onto the ground. Displaying an air of contempt, François took Hidalgo's jacket from one of the soldiers, using it to wipe the blood off his sword before tossing it back and deliberately replacing the blade in its scabbard.

"Your physician can hopefully mend him. Extend my condolences to the Governor-general for damaging one of his officers," he said to the stunned soldiers who quickly recovered and carried the wounded man away.

"Serves the misbegotten swine right," the hostel owner spoke angrily from the back door.

"That deserves a round of drinks," a merchant said coming up to hand François his jacket.

A well-dressed man had appeared at the door

moments after Capt. Hidalgo entered the cantina, and stood in the back as the duel ensued. Jean-Paul frequently played a memory game with François so that he could quickly scan his surroundings and place everyone and everything. This person was memorable because he stood alone in the shadows. "Be especially careful of such men," Jean-Paul warned. When the soldiers gathered up their captain, the man had gone.

A rollicking party ensued making it obvious the captain was not popular, but François did not partake of anything stronger than a single glass of wine. An hour later a very thin man in black attire, a white ruff about his scrawny neck, and greased down hair beneath a cloth skullcap strode into the cantina.

"Begging the gentleman's pardon," he said stiffly, "His Excellency, Francisco Alvaro Hernandez y Zárate's, Governor-general of the Island of El Hierro, sends his sincere apologies to Don Evreux for the behavior of one of his officers, and begs your forgiveness." It was a formal, courtly message. "His Excellency extends a personal invitation to Don Evreux to accompany me to the Governor's palace where he may express his apologies in person and offer a hand of friendship."

"His apologies are graciously received; however, I regret to decline the generous invitation until I can make myself more presentable. Perhaps an hour, if my hostess can prepare a hot bath in that time?"

"I'll have your bath ready out back momentarily," the robust woman said, having anticipated this need as she had done all night.

"I shall wait," the starchy messenger responded.

Securing a clean glass, he half filled it with wine. "Please, enjoy some refreshment while I bathe. Madeira. An excellent vintage." François then retired to the rear of the establishment once again, this time proceeding to the bath house off to one side. Not long after becoming comfortable in a froth of soap bubbles, he noticed the hostel owner's son suddenly divert his eyes to the door behind him. Instantly, François knew he had been careless not to position himself to watch the door. His only indication of what was happening was the reflection in the boy's eyes. They reflected being momentarily startled, and then dislike, but not of eminent danger.

"Good evening, sir," François said not turning around while his mind flashed through possible scenarios.

"Good evening, Don Evreux. I hope you will pardon the intrusion," a smooth, baritone voice said as footsteps moved softly over the wood floor around to François' left side until coming into view. It was the man in the shadows, of average height and stature, well suited for blending. He sat on a bench so to face François. He did not appear armed, at least with a sword, but his long coat could easily hide a small pistol or knife. "You handled yourself well against Capt. Hidalgo."

"Thank you. He is an accomplished swordsman."

"Quite so. Pistol or sword, he has never lost a duel. You have had considerable training."

"My father was a firm taskmaster about such things. You stood in the shadows during our disagreement, but did not remain to introduce yourself at the celebration."

His left eyebrow rose over dark eyes in surprise. "You noticed? Very observant, considering the circumstances." Turning to the boy who was watching him as a hawk would a mouse, he said, "Fetch Don Evreux and myself some wine," and tossed the boy a coin.

When the lad was out of earshot the man said, "Capt. Hidalgo is the presence of the governor. I am his eyes and ears. You have made some substantial purchases since arriving this morning."

"And you, too, would like to know where someone my age acquired such a large sum of money."

"Ah, here is our wine," the man said. "The lad does not waste time." The boy handed each a glass then ensconced himself near the stove to tend the heating water to both see and hear what was happening. The man's smile was very faint as he glanced at the youth. "As to your question, yes, I would be interested, if you would be so kind."

"To know if I am a thief?"

The man chuckled. "You guard yourself well, Don Evreux."

"As well a man should who carries a large sum of money. But I am not averse to discussing the matter with someone with manners."

The man lifted his glass slightly to acknowl-edge the compliment.

"The Evreux's are merchants; as such they conduct business with Spain as well as other countries. We have done so for many generations. That has placed us in a position of trust with the governments of both France and Spain."

"I am familiar with the Evreux family. And how is your father . . . Jean-Paul?"

"Dead."

That took the man off guard momentarily as indicated by a slight movement of his eyes.

"He engaged an English merchant that turned out to be a warship in disguise. His ship went to the bottom with all hands. I was aboard another vessel and was able to escape, and continue here."

"My sincerest condolences, Don Evreux. I only knew of your father by the things I have heard. He might have been a privateer, but was foremost a gentleman. I knew him to be under French writ, but not Spain as well."

"Such things are not always mouthed about

freely for obvious political reasons."

He nodded agreement. "Politics can be a very slippery slope to traverse. So what brings you to El Hierro?"

"Fulfillment of a promise made when I was barely weaned."

"Ah, a marriage contract."

"Yes."

"And the girl lives on El Hierro?"

"Yes."

"And you are not going to tell me the young woman's name?"

"Mariah, daughter of Señor Leocadio de Clare du Languedoc."

The man's left eyebrow shot up higher this time. "On El Hierro?"

François merely smiled.

"You obviously found the young woman and now plan to make El Hierro your home."

François tipped his hardly touched glass of wine toward the man to say, yes.

"Well, I have delayed your preparations long enough and kept the governor waiting, although I am sure he has no notion of the time. He keeps himself . . . busy."

"You haven't mentioned your name," François said as the man stood to depart.

"I am sometimes called Ojos Oídos," he said.

"Before you leave, Señor Eyes and Ears, I am curious. That bulge on the left side of your coat. Would you have used it if my answers were not suitable?"

The man chuckled. "Not here. The lad there has been playing dangerously close to your pistol and I know that he understands how to use it, and the knife you bathe with would only make an altercation at best a draw. Not good odds."

After the man left the hostel owner's son came to pour a bucket of clean water over him to rinse, then unexpectedly dumped a bottle of perfume over his shoulders that ran down both sides.

"So, you know how to use a pistol," François said as he toweled off.

"Si, but I did not know you bathed with a knife."

"Neither did the señor. Keeping one hand in the water was a ruse, my only defense against one such as that. He is a man who weighs his odds carefully. That is why he has lived so long in such a position. Your help has been greatly appreciated," he said, handing the boy a silver coin. "What is your name?"

"Onika."

An hour later François stood in the foyer of the governor's mansion fully aware he could be greeted either as a peer, or arrested and executed. However, if the governor planned treachery, he would find himself divested of more soldiers before it was over. That was François' arrogantly fatalistic, pirate attitude, but the short, portly man waddled out of a side room with a big smile.

"Don Evreux, I am Francisco Alvaro Hernandez y Zárate," he said, then paused before continuing hesitantly, "I was told you were young, but . . ."

"You were not expecting someone quite this young."

"I, well, ah," he stammered.

"No offense taken, Excellency."

"Please, come let us go into my study."

The room was large, but not nearly as intimidating as the reception area, with a pair of doors leading to a balcony overlooking the port some distance below and empty ocean beyond. A huge, mahogany desk, a bookshelf, and lots of souvenirs and trophies filled the room.

"I want to personally apologize for the behavior

of my commanding officer. He aspires, but is lacking."

"Apology accepted. I believe he has learned a valuable lesson."

"I dare say. Wantonly attacking persons such as you is inexcusable. He will, of course, be relieved of command."

"That will not prevent what must surely transpire in the future. He is not the sort to take humiliation lightly."

"You are quite correct. Perhaps it would be best if he returned to Spain."

"And have an opportunity to learn the truth? That would not be acceptable," François thought. "He is a fighting man, your Excellency. Such skills would be totally wasted in Spain. Perhaps it would be best for such a man to be sent where there is more action suited to his skills?"

"Yes, of course, the New World. Definitely. Yes. You are quite right," the governor agreed as he handed François a beautiful, silver goblet half filled with wine. "Málaga. From my family's vines."

The governor's guest swirled the reddish liquid around the inside of the goblet and sniffed. Its sweet fragrance had a definite smell of alcohol. A fortified wine. The governor took a healthy swallow. François sipped.

"I am curious as to how you got here, Don Evreux. There are not so many people that new arrivals are not immediately noticed."

François was under no delusions that Señor Ojos Oídos had made his report. "I arrived some time ago actually. You are probably aware that Señor Leocadio de Clare and his daughter were living quietly along the coast south of here."

"Vaguely," the governor lied, having no idea, although he seemed to remember hearing something about a hermit on the island in that area.

"Señor de Clare was the younger brother of the Fifth Duke du Languedoc." He used the name of a prominent Spanish family.

"I had no idea!"

"Despite the differences our governments have from time to time, our two families have for many years been associated through business ventures throughout Europe, and therefore have been close. There was some unpleasantness within his family and Marquis du Languedoc sought life elsewhere. However, before leaving, he entered into an agreement with my family for the marriage of his daughter to me.

"We were mere children at the time and surprised by his departure, but knew him to be an honorable man that would respect the agreement. Of course, we had no idea where he had gone until receiving a letter eighteen months ago that he was here, giving the exact location. I engaged passage on the Dolphin, which brought me directly to where he was residing. To my great sorrow, the Marquis perished in a storm some weeks before, leaving his daughter alone to seek her own survival.

"As our childhood agreement was already sanctioned by Rome, we at last were able to consummate the union by the grace of God. I found this island to be a wonderful place and have spent the past months fashioning a home for us, but it is now time to develop it further to provide as one should for a lady equal of the court."

Not all this explanation was fabrication. The Evreux family had status. Not a first-born son, Jean-Paul was educated with little hope for inheritance. A bit on the wild side, he pursued privateering as opposed to merely sailing one of the family's ships. To pass the long days aboard ship Jean-Paul taught François how to read, write, speak and act as a gentleman among other things, the latter not an easy task overcoming the influence of common sailors. François had a natural ability to learn quickly and mastered everything his mentor knew of courtly behavior.

Another ability François possessed was thinking on his feet. It also helped to have known that there was a degree of truth about the Marquis du Languedoc. He did have a falling out with his brother and left to seek his fortune. Unfortunately, the man died crossing swords with Captain Jean-Paul off Gibraltar. No one else knew about his end. The captain's remorseful letter to the family went down with the Fleurette.

"Yes, of course," the governor replied, completely taken by the lie. "Did I understand that your father is Captain Jean-Paul Evreux of the French merchant and shipping family?

"He was."

"Was?"

François had quickly sized up the governor before a full sentence had passed over the man's lips. He was not as stupid as he led people to believe, putting forth questions to verify what he already knew.

"My father died during an engagement with an English man-of-war. He bore a commission by the King Louis of France to attack English and Dutch merchant shipping, but only a few people were vaguely aware it was a covert adventure sanctioned by King Philip."

"I am sorry to hear of the death of your father. My sincerest condolences."

François merely tilted his head in reply.

"And the title you gave my Captain?"

François smiled impishly.

"Ah, yes, that. I am afraid I sometimes have a strange sense of humor and impatience with boorish people. Do you speak French?"

"Very little."

"My frolicsome response was to identify myself as Maître de Beaucoup Trucs."

The governor was silent as his face screwed into various contortions as he struggled to translate. It must have been painful and François nearly laughed when the pompous fool coughed, beginning a sporadic chuckle that crescendo into a rolling laugh which caused his belly to bounce up and down.

Finally able to control himself, he interpreted, "Master of many things? That, Don François is absolutely brazen in the face of whom you were addressing."

"Such are the whims of fancy my father hoped I would outgrow."

The governor took a gulp of wine, emptying the glass then said, "I have been seeking a Minister of Ports. You strike me as just the man."

François knew the offer was extended because of his supposed family connections and money. Politely declining, he said, "I am greatly flattered, Excellency, but for now I need to spend considerable time developing my newly purchased lands and see to the needs of my wife and family. When all is in order I would be more than agreeable to help in whatever small way I can."

Chapter 12

† A Bad Dream Returned †

The appearance of Ojos Oídos was often when least expected and not especially welcomed. Personable and disarming on the surface made being around him comfortable, exactly the relationship he desired. As the Governor-general's spy, what better way to get people to open up and impart information? When dealing with the man one always had to be on their guard, François and Mariah more so. When he suddenly appeared riding across the stream on his black Spanish horse just before the noon meal they naturally had to invite him to stay. Eating was difficult as François was tense, the food feeling as if barely managing to drop into the stomach to sit there.

Seated on the porch, Oídos sighed as he looked out at what the young man had accomplished. "I envy you, Don François," he said. "At such a young age you have more than older men could hope for. I don't just mean land and wealth, but a beautiful wife and a growing family. It is something I could have had if not for choosing a profession that precludes such things."

"You have been a spy all your life?" Mariah said bluntly drawing a surprised look then chuckle from the man.

"No, Señora Evreux. I entered the Army at the age of fifteen just ahead of my father's whip."

"Whip?"

"Unfortunately, my father was a sick man and overzealous with punishment. My two older brothers were already in the service of our king and encouraged me to join. At the same time my mother and younger sister took to living with her family."

"What is your rank?" François asked.

"Coronel."

"You command the detachment?"

"Hidalgo's replacement will command the garrison, while I . . . do other things."

"Many of the soldiers have family," Mariah said.

"Yes, but a military life is not conducive to anything considered as a normal life. Married life works well enough when one has an assignment such as here or one of the other islands, but far too many places would cause an undue hardship for the wife and mother, or being left alone in Spain not knowing the fate of one's husband. It really is not fair to the woman or to the children. But, we all make choices and must live with the consequences. However, I did not come to burden you with my depression." He handed François two folded pieces of paper, obviously dispatches of which the seals had been broken.

"The Governor-general sent communiqués to Spain and France to verify your story."

"At your suggestion," François said, taking the letters.

"Of course. I wrote them myself."

François opened the first. It was from Jean-Paul's father, lamenting the loss of his son and a surprise.

> "I regret not having the privilege to meet my heir, but Jean-Paul wrote often, praising him as a proud father should. I feared he had been taken as well when my son's ship was lost at sea. Your letter affirming the boy is alive and well has indeed been welcomed news. It would be my desire to hear from my grandson, and pray he may be able to come before my failing eyes are no longer capable to lay upon him. Please give him my love."

A tear formed in François' eye, not only at the senior Evreux's words, but at remembering the man who had publically declared him to be his son. He found it interesting that Jean-Paul had not mentioned his intentions of adopting him until remembering a day out of Casablanca he said something in passing about having a surprise for him when they next put into port. François passed off the remark, being too involved in something he could not even remember.

"The second letter is from the Duke de Languach, or rather from his secretary."

> "The Duke de Languach wishes me to express his regret at the news of his

brother's demise and to let the young woman who is his daughter know that her father's connection to the family and any of its inheritances were summarily terminated when he departed.

I have been associated with the de Languach family for many years and tried to assist Raoul through troubled times, but alas, there were some indiscretions, which could not be ameliorated. Nevertheless, I maintained correspondence with the lad in hopes of someday helping him to return into good graces with his brother. I was not aware that he had any children, although that should not be a surprise. That he appears to have been more of a father to this young woman, I can only find solace that he, for once, took responsibility upon his shoulders.

Please extend my sincerest regrets to M. de Clare at the loss of her father, and my best wishes upon her marriage to M. Evreux. I know the family and if he is anything like his father, he will be a credit to their proud name."

"May I show this letter to Mariah?" François asked, referring to the last one.

"I thought you might want to keep them."

Two months following Señor Ojos Oídos' visit and twelve months after little Jean-Paul's arrival, Mariah went into labor. Once more François was at her side, allowing her to squeeze his hand and pat her perspiring brow. Cirano's mother did not object and thought the idea had merit, although not certain many husbands would have the stomach for it.

As with little Jean-Paul's arrival, the specter of Mariah's mother dying during childbirth haunted him. The birthing went as the first.

When the child slid into the woman's experienced hands, Mariah looked up at François and smiled.

"It is a girl," he said.

It began crying, a wonderful sound to the parents. He looked at Rhea who smiled and nodded yes. As she prepared to sever the umbilical cord Mariah strained and cried out.

"What's wrong, child?"

"I . . . don't . . ." Mariah struggled to say. François felt panic.

"Dios mío! Señor, take the child. Hurry, there is another coming out."

Grabbing clean linen, he quickly wrapped the wailing baby and held her close to his chest and watched as another daughter entered the world. It was silent. Held by the feet, Rhea slapped the tiny bottom. It remained silent. She slapped again, the tiny child jerked, sputtered, and began to cry. It was angry.

As Mariah held one child and François the other, the mid-wife continued her duties to Mariah. François said, "Do you have any more surprises?"

An exhausted wife looked at him and began to laugh. "I think that is all for this time."

With the unexpected arrival of twin daughters, the garden was again expanded to accommodate the increase in mouths as Cirano and his family came to work at the hacienda, which underwent further expansion to add more rooms and the veranda where Mariah could sit with the children, sheltered from both sun and rain. The plantation was rapidly becoming one of the leading suppliers of meat, cheese, milk, rosin, timber, and wine, and the hacienda a small village.

Since that initial journey to Valverde to present

himself and purchase property, twenty-five months passed. Trips to the port became more frequent as imports and exports from the plantation increased, and each time François stopped at the Land's End hostel for food and refreshment.

Once considered a place for those of less means, his visits greatly improved its reputation and clientele. That resulted in enough income to undertake a physical reformation. The excellent food and service, however, did not change. Seated at a favorite table toward the back, he'd just taken a sip of wine when a burley hand rested heavily on his right shoulder.

"Well, lad. Fancy meetin' ye 'ere. Might ye be of a mind sharin' a pint with an ol' mate?"

A shiver crawled down François' back. That gravelly voice was too recognizable. A man believed dead had reappeared. It wasn't necessary to look into the fierce, brown eyes glaring down at him.

"Not at all Capt. Shaver. Please, sit down," François replied, motioning to an empty chair, trying to sound composed and waved to Onika.

The hostel owner's son was still noodle thin but had grown much taller over the year. Attired in a fine, white shirt, black trousers, and sandals reflective of many changes within the establishment, he brought a tankard of ale. His brow furrowed over a serious glare as he set it down.

"Thank you, Onika. It will be all right. The gentleman is an acquaintance."

Onika issued a quiet snort and left. Shaver watched him leave, a scowl on his face, and then said, "Done well fer yerself by the looks o' things, lad."

"Thanks to your gift."

"Ah, yes, that."

"I would have expected to see you better off," François said, referring to the captain's haggard appearance.

When they last met, Capt. Shaver had more weight on his five foot six frame. His face now appeared gaunt, his long, bushy hair and beard a bit grayer around the edges as were the heavy eyebrows. The long brocaded coat was a bit worse for wear, but his eyes still held a fire of perpetual anger.

"Aye. And so would I. So would I."

"Did you not find the treas . . ." François stopped, looked around, and then lowered his voice, "The item you were looking for?" He had no doubts Ojos Oíos was near. He thought to see something move in a particularly dark corner near the rear door.

"No, I did not. It appears the map be wrong," the Captain replied, keeping his voice low, which was not easy. His mood was sarcastic and bitter.

"I thought as much."

"Ye knew?"

"We found another map."

"Another!" he boomed, looked around, and then lowered his voice. "Another map?"

"Yes. It was on the bottom of the chest you gave me, beneath the coins," he lied, not wanting to reveal that there had been a second chest.

"And?"

"And what?"

"Don't toy with me boy," Shaver threatened with a low growl. "What'd ye do with it?"

"Kept it."

"So ye could fetch it fer yerself?"

"Captain Shaver, you are a very intimidating man, but don't unfurl your sail that way, not with me. If I had wanted the treasure, I could have well afforded to hire a ship . . . several ships, and well-armed . . . and gone after it. We made a bargain. You took the promise of treasure and I took the surety of gold coin in hand.

Whatever treasure may lie upon that island is yours. I kept the map safe expecting your return. It belongs to you by right of bargain."

No one talked to Aloysius Shaver in such a manner without the pirate lashing out. For a moment, he seemed dumbstruck. Glaring, he took a hefty swallow from his tankard to calm himself. Upon regaining his tongue, it was more civil.

"Sorry, lad. I've dealt too much with unscrupulous villains as meself. I should 'ave expected nothin' less from the son o' Jean-Paul. My apologies."

François startled. "You knew?"

"Aye, he mentioned 'is intentions some time back, when we shared a spot of rum in Casablanca."

"I wasn't aware you were there."

"Neither did anyone else. Despite me reputation and appearances, I can move 'bouts."

"I expected you long before this, then there was a rumor you had been killed."

"Someone's always circulatin' wishful rumors o' me demise. As it were, when I figured the map be false I decide ta shop the trades. That be when we met up with that Scot's ship, the *Agnes*. Only she weren't alone. Had a corsair runnin' alongside, both sittin' low in the water. Carryin' somethin' heavy. Since we didn't fare so well findin' the treasure, I thought ta appease the crew. You be right 'bout that ship. Didn't even get in range when she like ta blew us ta Davy Jones' Locker. Barely got outa thar with little more 'an a couple planks ta stay afloat 'an a rudder ta steer with.

"We was takin' on water bad like so made ta Tortuga fer repairs. While indulgin' a spot o' rum, I meets a brother who escaped El Sebastian some time before. That's the Spanish fort where some o' the brethren be sittin' in prison. All set for hangin' they was when the *Agnes* sails inta port bold as a lion seekin' the return o' a ship confiscated a few months before. Had this Spanish nobleman aboard ta negotiate the return and get the release o' a particular pirate the Spaniards be holdin'. Somethin' went wrong. When the smoke cleared, the bloomin' fort were a pile o' rocks and half the town afire.

"Anyways, me Quartermaster, a scoundrel named Shelly, ya remember 'im? Well, he be pretty unhappy with the whole affair. We made repairs, but the night before we was leavin' he got me drunk. It's a weakness I got, lad, I admits it, but I got me reasons. When I got me wits tagether, me ship and crew was gone. Well, thar I be, no ship, and no crew, and without so much as a shillin', but I been thar before. Finally acquired transportation so ta speak. Somethin' I could handle meself. Figured ta git me boat back, but Shelly were a bad captain. Got captured by the English. Serves 'im right. Earned a long drop on a short rope. Well, not much I could do so I start makin' me way here. Took some doin'"

"You have a ship of your own now?"

"Aye. Found me a sloop . . . as it were. However, I be in the market fer something perhaps a bit bigger."

"Why? It may not carry many guns, but it's fast and more maneuverable than anything you will board."

"Aye. Ye know yer ships, lad. We'll see what presents itself."

"Well, you'll want the map. I'll return home straight away and retrieve it. If you sail to the cove where we last met you can have it. No guarantees it's any better."

"Ye be honest, lad. Best ye got throwed up on this rock. Ye'd not make a pirate."

François smiled weakly. He had always thought himself a pretty good pirate, however while riding his stallion back to the plantation came the realization François Evreux de St. Nazaire was indeed missing one major ingredient to being a true pirate—larceny. He might be the biggest liar in the Spanish realm, but he was an honest one.

Chapter 13

† Kidnapped †

When the old pirate suddenly appeared and boldly strode up the streets of Valverde, his movements were watched closely although never directly. When he sat down for a friendly chat with Don François, gossip began to bubble up like an artesian well. However, that didn't much bother François one way or the other. He never attempted to hide a connection to privateering, which would have routinely crossed paths with likes of Shaver and the darker kind. All he really wanted was for Shaver to take the map and go far, far away so that his quiet, peacefully prosperous world could resume.

As François left Hogshead to finish his ale, he stopped at the table in the shadows where the governor's eyes and ears sat, and said so that his voice would not carry, "I am getting rid of him as quickly as possible. I will explain later. I hope the governor does not attempt anything heroic."

"No problem. The governor is a politician, not a soldier. Capt. Santana is under orders to do nothing as long as the pirate behaves peacefully. It's a matter of position. The garrison outnumbers the pirates, but the pirates have the superiority of cannon. The citizens would not react well to having their homes bombarded."

François knew there would be many questions after Hogshead departed. As expected, Mariah wasn't at all pleased to hear the pirate had returned either. They had a warm discussion, but the only way to be rid of the scoundrel was to give him the map. She just had a bad feeling about Shaver's trustworthiness.

As he emerged from the gap above the cove, Shaver's sloop, *Angelina*, came into view, rounding the north arm of basalt rock. At the same time the governor's eyes and ears gained a vantage point overlooking the cove where he could use a spyglass to see what was going on. Soon after the *Angelina* dropped anchor in the cove a longboat pushed off on its way to shore, arriving as François reached the beach. A jubilant Shaver slipped over the gunnel into the surf and swaggered ashore. François new the pirate had a limp to his left leg. Knowing the story, he hadn't given it much thought. This time limp was more noticeable as he crossed the surf-packed sand.

Grasping the map, he left the other three pirates to stand idle. "This be the only other one ye found?"

"Yes, but I can't say if it is any better."

"Hm-m-m. Shows the treasure ta be on the other side o' that cursed island. That makes more sense than where we was taken . . . swamps and all sorts o' nasties. Well, let's be gone."

"Have a good trip," François said, and under his

breathe thought, "and don't come back."

"Ye'll be comin' along too, lad."

"I don't think so."

"Ye don't 'ave a choice, boy. No one turns down an invite from Cap'n Aloysius Shaver."

"Times change."

Shaver whipped out his cutlass and pointed it at François chest. "Ye got spunk, lad, but not much common sense."

François had watched one of the sailors work around behind him. With the speed of a Tasmanian Devil, he bumped the man, taking his sword as the man was sent sprawling upon the beach. Drawing his own, François presented two swords against the grizzly, old pirate.

"The Captain needs to learn rejection."

Shaver laughed, "So ye wants ta cross swords, do ye? Well, let's see what Jean-Paul taught ye."

The pirate made the first lunge, which François easily parried, then deflected a barrage of blows before launching his own attack throwing Shaver backward in surprise. If his game leg had worsened, Shaver didn't favor it as back and forth across the sandy beach, into and out of the surf the two battled much to the older man's disadvantage.

"You're out of shape, Captain."

"Aye, but no less determined."

Suddenly everything went black.

"Damn ye Carson, ye better not 'ave kilt him," Shaver panted as he bent over his adversary. "Ah, good. Fer yer sake he be alright. Bind 'is hands an' feet an' put 'im in the boat. Amstedt, git ur things."

"Cap'n . . ."

"Now Benji, no arguin'. We discussed this all I intend ta. I be owin' a debt and this be the only way to repay it, but I'll not be leavin' 'is wench and brats without someone ta be carin' o' 'em."

"I ain't no nurse maid, Cap'n."

Shaver put his arm around the older man and spoke softly, "Benji, we been tagether a long time. E'er since ye took that ball meant fer me, yer health been gitten worse. It be time ta retire as it were and ye knows it, no arguin' the point. When we gits the treasure, we be comin' back ta drop the lad off with yer share. I trust no other man with 'is woman and brats. They be in yer hands. Anything happen to 'em whiles we be gone, and I'll feed ye ta the sharks alive—one piece at a time."

"Aye, Cap'n," Amstedt replied quietly, noting the twinkle in his eyes.

The Dutchman stood on the beach watching the sloop take sail knowing it would head north to Güímar on the island of Tenerife. By replenishing supplies at that obscure port, Shaver could avoid prying eyes and questions that would surely arise in Santa Cruz. They avoided a larger military force, as well. From Güímar the pirate would set sail to the new world . . . without him. Amstedt spat on the sand before sitting on the old log to watch his ship until it was gone.

With a resolute sigh, the old mariner took up his duffel, fastened it to the saddle on François' horse, and climbed the trail taking him up. Most men wouldn't have figured heading inland through the gorge, it looked impossibly blocked, but they had seen the lad appear here. Picking up the horse's tracks, he gave the animal its head. After some distance, he came to a pool and well-used trail beyond. The creature knew its way home.

Eventually reaching the meadow, Amstedt was surprised. It had been his impression the Frenchman and his woman were rustics and was completely unprepared for the large plantation house and number of people working about. As he approached, a young woman sitting on the veranda, stood to face him.

Dismounting, he removed his cloth hat exposing a thick head of snow white hair and said nervously with a Dutch accent. "Cap'n Shaver's compliments, ma'am. I am called Benjamin Amstedt. The Cap'n sent me here to vatch over the Frenchman's family."

"What do you mean? Where's my husband?"

"He sails with Cap'n Shaver, ma'am."

"He wouldn't do that!"

"Vell, the lad did not have much choice."

Mariah had feared such could happen, but held it inside as her husband left. There wasn't anything she could do but accept their fate.

Glaring down at the old man she said, "So be it, Mr. Amstedt. But don't believe yourself replacing my husband. Hassan, Mr. Amstedt, will be staying with us until my husband returns. Show him where he can bathe and where to sling his hammock. It would be a good time for you to bathe as well."

"Yes, Mariah," the slender, dark-skinned, Arab boy replied while casting a glowering, sideways glance at the new arrival.

"Vhat yer place here, boy?" Amstedt asked as the two made their way to the bathing pool built adjacent to the stream.

"I was sent to live with them three years ago. I am considered family."

"Vhat part of der Barb'ry Coast ya hail from?"

"My former master would not say."

"Hm-m-m. Interestin' pendant ya have," he said, referring to green encrusted half-moon pendant hanging about the young man's neck on a leather cord. "Yer master give that to ya?"

"No. I have always had it."

Like Lucy, Hassan came to Casa de St. Nazaire an orphan. He had been an orphan as long as he remembered. His master, a retired ship's carpenter, treated him kindly, but after completing a carriage for Mariah, he sent him to live with Don Evreux. He was fourteen. Small and thin, he looked much younger, if anyone noticed him at all.

Don François brought him to the plantation and treated him not only as an equal, but family. That took considerable adjustment, which wasn't totally complete. Better nourished, thanks to Mariah, now seventeen he stood as tall as most men at five foot six. A boy who's every bone could be counted, had filled out—broad shoulders, deep chest, narrow waist, muscled arms and legs. He was strong, agile, and good-looking. At least more than a few girls on the island held that thought.

Slipping through a stand of young trees shielding the bathing area from house and fields, Amstedt quickly changed the topic. "Seem like nice folk," he said, peeling off his clothes. It had been a long time since his last freshwater bath. "Is that vhat I think it is?" he asked as Hassan handed him a small, grayish bar. "Soap! Real soap! We run out months ago. Crossed a ship with barrels of the stuff bound for West Indies, but damn our luck, she sank taking da cargo with her. This will be a real pleasure," he sighed, and then looking at Hassan said, "Were you not to take a bath, too?"

"I'll do it some other time."

"Strikes me when the lady gives an order, you should do it, and by the look and smell now would be a goot time."

Hassan, who had spent most the afternoon caring for the horses, cast an eye over the man who was a bit shorter, more slender, and much older, and decided he wouldn't take orders from the likes of him. He had barely expressed that opinion when he found himself flying through the air and into the pool.

"Next time it vould be best to remove yer clothes before entering the water, ja?" the Dutchman scolded as he waded in and began singing noisily as he scrubbed.

Señor Ojos Oíos' report to the governor was not good. "I regret to inform your Excellency that Don François has been kidnapped. I saw him duel with the pirate Hogshead until one of those in his company struck Don François from behind. He was bound and taken aboard their ship. An old sailor was left behind, a Dutchman by the name of Amstedt. The pirates sank his ship off the coast of Africa several months ago and rescued him. He had no interest joining their crew, and not being in good health, they left him behind. Señora Evreux has given him shelter and work."

~ ~ ~ ~

Alone in bed that night following the news her husband was kidnapped, Mariah cried for the first time since the death of her father. Once again, she felt like that child years before, so hopelessly alone. What was she to do? What could she do? How could she manage the business her husband had built? Kneeling by her bed, she prayed into the night for God to protect her François and bring him home safely . . . and quickly. Then she prayed for help managing the burgeoning empire.

When her father died, she had three choices, move to either Valverde to the north, or Sabinosa to the west, or remain in the cabin her father had built. She prayed for guidance until exhaustion won out and she fell asleep on the ground. Awaking that next morning, she found Diablo lying just outside as if on guard duty. They had seen the great lizard hovering about the perimeter as they took up residency above the cove, but it never came close. From that time, he became a companion appearing frequently, even coming into the cabin.

Exhausted after praying for her husband and the plantation, Mariah felt she should stay, although her mind continued in turmoil as she argued with herself about the decision. Coming down stairs early the next morning, she stepped onto the front veranda. To her amazement, a nearly black lizard lay just out from the bottom step. She once again gazed at the creature with the inscrutable smile, feeling reassured, and comforted. It was Diablo.

"Thank you, God," she said, re-establishing their relationship.

In turn, Diablo flicked his tongue, rose up, and waddled into the brush, but never far, returning often to lounge in the sun a few meters from the veranda, a continual reassurance.

Chapter 14

† Dueña de la Casa †

Mariah stood on the veranda for a long time, first staring at the brush area where Diablo retreated, and then out at the plantation with its corrals, gardens, grass, and forest beyond. No one had begun work so the only things about were a couple of young lizards greedily eyeing the garden and two colts frolicking about in the largest corral as their mothers looked on. Every so often a puff of cool air touched her cheeks as if a kiss from her husband. Giving a deep sigh, she was about to head for the kitchen to prepare some coffee, when the aroma of that brew rose up to wrap around her like a fragrant blanket. Entering the kitchen, she found Mr. Amstedt seated at the table, a steaming mug of the black liquid in hand.

"Goedemorgen, Lady Evreux," he said, rising quickly, bowing slightly as two gnarled fingers touched his forehead in a salute.

"Good morning, Mr. Amstedt."

"I hope m'Lady do not mind. A habit I have since developing a taste voor de foul brew."

"Not at all, Mr. Amstedt, but it really isn't all that foul. It smells wonderful."

"May I fetch m'Lady a cup?"

"Thank you." She took a seat across the table from where he sat.

"Jou still have de look of vorry."

"Not for my husband. God will watch over him and bring him home, but he managed the plantation. I'm at a loss what to do about that."

"He have no overseers?"

"Oh, yes. He set people over different areas. One looks after the livestock, another the vineyards, another the crops, and one is over timber and rosin. Cirano takes care of things here. There is a man in Valverde who handles imports and exports, but I have no real notion how my husband did things. He has a way for organizing and getting things done."

"The answer be as jou say. He has men who know their job en he let them do it. It is vay a goede ship is run."

"How long have you been a sailor?"

"Most of thirty year."

"And before that?"

"I grew up on farm. I try dat, but too much bad weather. I took to sea ahead of debtor prison."

"Then you know about farming?"

"Ja."

"And how to manage men?"

"Ja. I waren bosun most of my time at sea."

"And you know how to handle strong-headed boys?"

"Like boy, Hassan? Ja. Ze be like young horse. Much energy, but do not know which direction to run so go in circles, causing lots of confusion."

Mariah had not thought she could laugh at this time in her life, but did. "I saw how you persuaded him to take a bath yesterday."

"Ja. It waren necessary voor understanding. When captain gives order, a goede sailor obeys. M'Lady say voor boy to take bath, but he waren feeling a bit mutinous. I waren juist showing him da error of dat course. I heft not mean to offend m'Lady?"

She smiled. "I was not offended. Will you be staying long?"

"Well, m'Lady, I am under orders to watch over deze family."

"By my husband?"

"No, m'Lady. Cap'n Shaver. He said to watch dat nothing bad happen to de young Evreux's family or I be fish bait."

"That pirate was concerned about us, yet he took my husband?"

"Well, ja. The cap'n believes he is repaying a debt."

Mariah stared at the elderly man waiting for an explanation that he seemed hesitant to discuss. Taking a deep breath, Amstedt let it out.

"Some years ago Cap'n Shaver waren at a meetin' of pirates at Salé on the Barb'ry Coast. It waren English trap set by Lord Chudleigh to destroy de pirate trade. Cap'n Evreux waren there, too. De two cap'ns weren on goede terms.

"De Evreux family always been a high en mighty family in Normandy, still are, but Cap'n Jean-Paul's side of family took to mercantile. He went to sea as cabin boy to learn de shipping part of trade, but he waren a little wild en went sailin' en met Cap'n MacArthur, de Scottish pirate. Well, de Evreux papa weren not too happy en got a letter of marque from de French king to pray on English ships en got his boy de Fleurette so get away from Mac Arthur. Dat were goede voor de family business, too. It please de king. He got to harassed his enemy en gain some fortune from it.

"Cap'n Shaver is a Monfort on moeder's side. Ze come from de same area of France as de Evreux's. De two families joined by marriage when they still in France long time back. De Monforts were met Villiam when he conquer England in de year 1066. Cap'n Shaver en Cap'n Evreux are cousins, but feelin's go a lot deeper.

"As I said, they waren this meeting at Salé when de English attack. There waren a fierce battle. I cannot say what happened voor sure. What I remember is this English officer pointing pistol at my cap'n's back while he waren fighting three soldiers. All I could do waren jump between the ball en my cap'n. Next I know, I waren aboard ship. What other sailors say, just after I took de ball Cap'n Evreux en men come. De English waren beaten off enough voor us to escape. Cap'n Shaver's ship waren sunk in de harbor, so Cap'n Evreux took us board de *Fleurette*.

"I waren in bad way met a ball in my chest, but by de grace of God, I manage to live a bit longer, tho it be met only one goede lung. Cap'n Shaver's leg waren nearly sliced off. Cap'n Evreux nursed us back to health en found us a new boat. It is a great debt Cap'n Shaver owe his cousin. I only guessing, but he figures to be repayin' part of the debt."

"By kidnapping my husband?"

Amstedt shrugged his shoulders. "I do not

know, m'Lady. Cap'n Shaver does not always appear to act like normal people. He has a reason, I'm sure. He is just a bit weak sharing his thinking. As voor yer problem, jou should be just fine managing this place."

"I don't know, Mr. Amstedt. My husband would speak to me about what he was doing, but I didn't pay attention to the details. Running this plantation is a man's work. Mine is to take care of the children and run the house."

"A ship's cap'n always keeps a log so dat it be known about de sailing. Yuw husband waren taught by a goede cap'n. He would have a log."

"François *did* write in a journal. There must be information there to help me. Wait here."

As Amstedt prepared more coffee, Mariah went to her husband's office and retrieved a large book. They were going through it together when Lucy appeared carrying one of the twin girls, with little Jean-Paul clutching her skirt.

"Oh my, is it that late? Where is Tabitha?" Mariah said.

"Isleta is cleaning her. She will be down soon."

"Pardon me, Mr. Amstedt, I must prepare something for them to eat, or we will have a very noisy house. This is Lucy. She lives with us. That is our oldest daughter, Talitha. Her twin sister, Tabitha, will be down shortly with the nurse. The young man is our oldest, Jean-Paul."

"Were you with the pirates that killed my father?" Lucy examined the pirate cautiously.

"I waren aboard ship met Cap'n Shaver looking voor yuw vader. The men who heeft dat waren not met us. I am sorry for what happen. We gaf him a Christian burial. I am sorry for yuw loss, Miss Lucy. May I hold da baby so jou can help Lady Mariah?"

Mariah glanced at the old sailor from time to

time as she put together breakfast. Her daughter was giggling and cooing while bouncing on the old man's knee. Jean-Paul stood by him, smiling. A bit of happiness seeped back into the house until Hassan appeared, black fury glistening in his eyes as he glared at Amstedt.

"You might find this difficult to understand, Mr. Amstedt, but I spent a great deal of time speaking with God last night. Once assured my François would be safe, I asked about running the plantation. I felt strongly that there was someone who could do that."

"I am not much of a religious man, m'Lady, not de way some make it, but I know er is a God. A person cannot sail upon de seas en not see it every day."

"Mr. Amstedt, I believe you are the one God said could help manage my husband's business. Do you feel up to it?"

"Dat a big responsibility, m'Lady, but I do my best."

Hassan's eyes grew huge. This interloper and mortal enemy had suddenly become his overseer.

Mariah was quickly reassured Amstedt was her godsend. François' journal detailed how he ran the plantation coupled with his expectations, goals, and timetable. Coupled with this knowledge, Amstedt continued the work faithfully. He also had a way of tempering Hassan's burgeoning attitude. The boy was sure Mariah had no idea of the hell he was cast into. He tried to defy the Dutchman one other time only to find himself seated on the ground trying to get his dazed head to reorganize the surrounding world back into its original coherence. In the ensuing months he bathed regularly, toiled in the garden and kitchen, and whatever else Amstedt deemed important. His saving grace was to be in charge of the horses which meant, according to Mr. Amstedt, "Ze must be exercised every day. Jou saddle en werk them into a goede sweat, den wipe them down goede. Give them special attention."

Mr. Amsted indeed knew what spirited animals needed. And Lucy? Yes, she needed attention, too.

Chapter 15

† Partners †

Concentration was a dismal failure courtesy of a splitting headache, due to the large and tender knot on the back of his head. Attempting to sit became a major challenge as the world spun wildly. Closing his eyes tightly, François fought down a wave of nausea. Breathing deeply, he waited for that to subside before attempting to gain his feet. Although disoriented, the smells, and familiar roll, and creak of timbers were strong indications as to where François was. Finally able to steady himself, he walked about the cabin to regain composure, surprised how quickly his 'sea legs' returned after being beached for so many years.

As his head cleared and eyes began to focus, François realized he was in the captain's quarters, more cramped compared to the *Fleurette*, but functional. Stopping at the table, he looked over the charts. One had an island in the Caribbean circled and he supposed this was their destination so memorized the co-ordinates. After snooping around a bit more, he stepped out onto the deck and instantly held up a hand to shade his eyes from the glare of daylight.

"Well, it be time ye were about," Shaver's gravelly voice called out. It sounded too cheerful.

François merely turned toward aft and glared at the man standing next to the big wheel. Looking seaward confirmed his fears. The only thing in sight was an open expanse of rolling, dark-blue ocean.

"Should have known you couldn't fight me without help."

The old pirate laughed, his gut bouncing up and down in rhythm. "The object be ta win, lad, but someday we'll continue that discussion without someone buttin' in. But, put yerself ta rest. I left a man behind ta see after yer woman and spawn."

François' anxiety peeked.

"Mr. Amstedt was a might beyond sailin' on such an adventure as this, but he be able ta handle yer farm whilst ye be gone. Benji'll take good care of 'em as if yourself were there or answer to me."

"The safety of my family is not the concern. You had better worry about Benji if he runs afoul of my wife," François shot back. "Even with two lungs he would be hard pressed."

"Well, so be it. Find something ta do and make yerself useful."

François walked over and stood next to the Captain, clasped his hands behind his back and stared at the ocean over the bow.

"I said find something ta do."

"I am. Keeping an eye on you with no one at my

back," he shot back.

Normally the pirate would backhanded such insolence, but he looked at the boy before slowly breaking out into a crooked smirk.

"Well, what'd ye know 'bout navigatin' a ship?"

"Tell me where we are heading and I'll put you there within a half point."

"Güímar on Tenerife Island. Due north from 'ere. Need ta restock our stores before headin' west. I be takin' a nap."

Turning loose of the wheel, Shaver let François grab it as he stomped from the deck. The limp was more noticeable. François was as fatalistic as Mariah. With no choice in the matter, rebelling would serve no cause. He was going on the venture. As for Mariah, he had no concerns. He knew Mr. Amstedt. Besides, Mariah really could handle him, even if he was whole.

In a way, he felt sorry for him. Becoming land-bound after life at sea was hard. Many a sailor had said retirement was only the prelude to the hell they were destined to inhabit. As for François, the last time he felt the pangs of loneliness he was bobbing in the middle of these waters. Added to that was a new sensation—a strong yearning to be home with his family.

As for Capt. Shaver, that was the last anyone saw of him although his presence aboard ship was obvious by the loud, raucous noises emanating from his cabin, something akin to a baritone cat in rut. The caterwaul ceased shortly after the midwatch stumbled on deck.

An hourglass sat atop a small pedestal just ahead of the compass. Marty, a small, ragtag boy of fourteen who looked closer to ten lay curled next to the ship's bell attached to the rail overlooking the main deck. Like two other boys about his age and condition who served as powder monkeys, one of their many menial duties was to watch the hourglass, turn it when the half hours' worth of sand finished running through, and ring the bell. That was one of several curious quirks François noticed as to how things ran aboard the ship. Somewhat like a merchant, even what he heard about warships.

"It's Mr. Gibbs' doings," Marty explained.

Gibbs was Quartermaster, the one who actually ran day to day operations. Shaver planned and conducted attacks otherwise generally did whatever pleased him which consisted of holing up in his cabin and consuming rum.

"He used to sail on real ships."

"Real ships?" François said.

"War ships," Marty said, snapping his head in a failed attempt to remove errant locks of straight, brown hair from his eyes, and sounding awed.

François had seen Gibbs on the main deck from time to time, but the man hadn't come to the bridge.

Another quirk was that after Shaver retired to his cabin Marty muffled the bell with one hand so that the loud, clear ring that normally carried to the bow was barely heard on the aft portion of the main deck.

Marty talked constantly, explaining all about the ship, what Mr. Gibbs expected of the crew under different conditions, and during a boarding. He was a complete log of each man aboard and François plied him with questions to elicit more details. However, just before the midwatch came on deck Marty fell sound asleep.

Slipping ropes over two spokes on the big wheel to secure it, he stepped to the rail, turned the glass, and grabbed the bell rope.

Clang–clang. Clang–thunk. Thunk–thunk. Thunk–thunk.

With the first sound, Marty easily put two puce between the deck and the seat of his britches. The second clang brought him to the realization of what was happening. Both hands wrapped around the bell as the second set of rings issued forth. The look on his face was of absolute terror as he knelt next to the bell, holding it tightly. When nothing happened, he released the death-grip and fell back against the rail.

"We don't ring the bell without a muffler after the cap'n's gone to bed," Marty said, his girlish voice quivering.

"I know," François said with a sly smirk, returning to take the wheel.

"Mr. Evreux, please. If'n the cap'n gets woke for no reason he'll throw me overboard." Marty was terrified.

"Oh, really? That would seem a waste. There isn't enough meat on your bones to whet the appetite of a baby shark. But don't worry, I'll throw you a line."

"What in Neptune's name is goin' on with ye, Marty?" a potbellied man whispered as loudly as he dared without disturbing the dead.

"Good evening, Mr. Gibbs," François said. "I am the guilty party."

"Oh. Well I better explain . . ."

"I know all about the muffling Mr. Gibbs."

"And ye rang it anyway?"

"That's the way it is done on a real ship, I believe."

Gibbs' lower jaw moved up and down, but nothing came out of his mouth. Nothing intelligible, anyway.

"If you aren't too busy, how about staying a bit and enlightening me about how things work aboard this ship."

Gibbs stayed and talked, occasionally leaving to check on the crew until 4 a.m. when he left to wake the mourning watch and retire, leaving Mr. Parker the sailing master in charge. As the glass was ready to turn, François lashed the wheel, walked over to the bell, and nudged Marty who rang out the muffled eight bells and curled up to resume the fetal position and resume purring, his youthful attempt at a snore. Alone, François savored his favorite time of day, watching the sun break the endless horizon.

Shaver remained in his cabin until mid-morning, leaving François at the wheel without relief, "A way to teach the insolent pup a lesson and to test his skills," he muttered to his Quartermaster before disappearing into his cabin. Staggering onto the deck, he stared at the island looming along their port side.

"Where we be?"

"Some sort of island," François replied.

"I can see that," the old pirate growled. His hangover was aggravated by the bright sun and a sour stomach. "Tenerife?"

"If your compass is not accurate than only God knows."

Shaver stomped up to wheel to confront the brat. "I'll tolerate no insolence from the likes of ye," he roared. "Twenty lashes should curb yer tongue."

"And how many crew can you ill-afford to lose? I'll tolerate none of your threats or we square off right here and finish what was interrupted on the beach."

Shaver feared neither man nor devil, but something in François' eyes startled him back to remembrance of his oath. To Harvey Gibbs standing nearby, Hogshead uncharacteristically faltered as two stood toe to toe.

Gibbs had been with Aloysius Shaver for most of seven years, signing on after being drummed out of the English navy. Like Shaver, he liked his rum a bit too well. There were only two times he hadn't sailed with the old pirate. The first time he'd been smitten by a Moroccan wench, ending up in a drunken stupor for three months when she left for another man. That's when the attack at Salé occurred. Two from Shaver's crew pulled him bodily from bed and sobered him up, not an easy task considering the amount of rum he had on-board. Brought on ship, he was standing on the main deck feeling confused and fuzzy-minded as Hogshead limped toward him on crutch-es, his face creased with pain.

"Ya sober, Harvey?"

"Aye, cap'n. More than usual."

"Walk with me," Shaver said, leading him to a pri-vate place near the rail. Ye be wonderin' 'bout me leg. Ne'r mind. Benji be below. He still be bad off." Shaver turned to face Gibbs. He'd never heard the pirate plead before. "I need ye back, Harvey, but I need ye sober."

"Aye, cap'n. Whatever ye need. Mind tellin' me what happened?"

"The brethren were havin' a meetin' at Salé. Turns out ta be an ambush set by Chudleigh. Benji took a ball intended fer me back. I'd be discussin' this with Davy Jones while holdin' a few body parts in me hands if'n it hadn't been fer him. I'd jist takin' a cut ta the hip when Jean-Paul and his boys shows up. He beat the scoundrels off and carrys me and Benji off to his ship and nursed us back ta health. I ne'r owed a man before, Harvey, ye know that, but I owe Benji, and I owe Jean-Paul."

One thing Gibbs knew about Aloysius Shaver, alt-hough an admitted scoundrel, he repaid a debt when the opportunity arose. The second time Gibbs hadn't sailed with Shaver was when he got wind of where Jeremiah Markel's treasure map was located. That time he had been laid low by Malaria, too sick to make the voyage. Gibbs figured it was because he'd been sober. Had he been aboard, Shaver might not have lost his boat.

"Güímar, a league off port," Gibbs called out, hop-ing to break the faceoff between Shaver and Evreux.

Shaver coughed once as if to clear his throat then said, "Well, enough of this." Then to Gibbs, "Put in so's we can replenish ar' stores. Did ye 'ear? I said put in!" he bel-lowed so that the co-captain jumped like a child at the bark of a big dog.

"Mr. Gibbs," François called softly after the departing man.

"Aye, Mr. Evreux?"

"It would not do for the crew to believe Capt. Shaver and I had a misunderstanding."

"Aye, aye, Mr. Evreux."

The last thing François wanted was for the crew to think less of their captain. The strength of his reputation might well be the one thing needed to complete this venture successfully. The Quartermaster was savvy enough to recognize that, too, notching up his estimation of the young man, and began looking upon him as an equal.

"You paying or stealing?" François asked after a lengthy silence.

"What be the difference?"

"Better to pay and not draw unwanted attention."

"Well, ye got any coin?"

François left the wheel, which Shaver grabbed to keep the craft steady.

"As a matter of fact, I do. Partners?"

His anger somewhat quelled, Shaver was still annoyed, which didn't help the head-splitting hangover. "And how much share ye be expectin'?"

"I took my share when you gave me the chest of coins."

Shaver smiled.

"But since you commandeered me . . . half."

"Half! Ye theivin' pirate!"

François smiled triumphantly and turned to walk away, throwing over his shoulder, "Half a regular share for someone who would not make a pirate. Consider it compensation for my being invited on this cruise." He then disappeared below to find something to eat.

A faint smile creased Shaver's craggy face and shaking his bushy head, muttered softly, "Too damn honest, boy. Be the death of ye, if'n ye ain't careful."

The *Angelina* was two days in Güímar taking on

stores as the crew spent time in civilization. It would be three to four weeks across the Atlantic barring any storms taking them off course, failed wind, or any of dozens of other problems. Then there would be however long it took to find and load the treasure, re-provision, and return home. François became resigned to the fact it might be at least three months before seeing his family again—if they were lucky.

During this time at Güímar, François met a boat captain bound for El Hierro who agreed to deliver a note to Captain Santana, who had become a good friend. In turn, he would deliver it to Mariah.

My dearest beloved,

As you are by now aware, I am in the company of Captain Shaver. Certainly not by my choice. I am well, sending you this note from Güímar where we are taking on provisions preparatory to sailing west. I do not understand why Captain Shaver wants me on this voyage as he has all the information to complete the quest. Having been a gentleman once himself, perhaps he simply desired civilized companionship, a weak excuse. I miss you and the children greatly and will continually have you in my thoughts and prayers, hoping to return in three months' time. As for Mr. Amstedt, he is an honorable man, left behind because of age and infirmity. Please do not be too hard on him as his current situation will be stressful enough. I will return as soon as possible.

My love for all time and eternity,

François

François wanted in particular to reassure her that he would be back. She knew promises were something he kept and that would hopefully quell any anxiety.

Chapter 16

† Competition †

𝒯he following weeks at sea were relatively uneventful. Shaver gladly yielded sailing master chores to the young man since François was much better at navigation. Reduced to spelling at the helm allowed him more drinking time. A couple of storms threw them slightly off course followed by three days of no wind adding several days to the journey each time. The temperature turned oppressively hot. Sleep was nearly impossible as below decks became like an oven. Tempers flared over trivial things. Quarrels erupted easily around the ship requiring watch officers to intervene. As the sun hovered directly overhead, eight bells signaled the end of the forenoon watch. The single bell a half hour later marked the 12:30 hour and a major fight exploded on the main deck. Too large for the officers to break up, Hogshead waded into the middle and discharged his gun. Three men felt the cat-o'-nine applied by the bosun, a large, muscled man.

Half way into the watch, François was near the stern checking their position with an astrolabe, noting that in the face of no wind, the current had carried them further west in the last twenty-four hours than expected. That was good news. The bad news was as Shaver discussed the condition of their food stores with Mr. Gibbs the bell beat out the time, clang- clang—clang-clang; another fight broke out. Wheeling around, no game leg slowed him as he grabbed the bicep of a sailor throttling another, smaller man.

"What be it this time?" he roared with a voice that could be heard over a firing cannon.

"I can't take no more of 'is muttering to 'isself," the man replied.

Shaver glared at the smaller sailor.

"I were jist hummin' a tune quiet like," the man said as he lift himself from the deck.

"Hummin', ye say? Well, I be partial to hummin'. Means a man likes 'is work." Without warning Hogshead, still holding the man's arm so tight to choke off the blood supply, grabbed the rope holding up his trousers, and picked him off the deck. Hauled to the gunnel, he was tossed overboard. "Any more fightin' and I'll cool ye temper in similar fashion. I'll tolerate no more," he leveled at the crew.

Hogshead then went to his cabin as François helped the man back aboard, thankful for the trailing rope.

"Two things I would suggest, Mr. Grayson. First, hide out below until tomorrow. The captain's temper should be sufficiently calm by then. Second, start another fight and you need not worry about coming back aboard. I will personally put a ball between your eyes, so you won't suffer the loneliness one feels before drowning in the middle of the ocean."

As the first dogwatch began at 4 p.m., François noticed scattered clouds beginning to come together. He smiled. Soon he felt a puff of wind on his cheek as the sails fluttered. By the second dogwatch at 6 p.m., the canvas was stretched tight and the *Angelina* sliceing through the water.

They skirted the heaviest showers, but did manage to get wet a couple times. A cooler breeze and forward movement calmed tempers as well. So did the gathering of thick, black clouds a day later as a hurricane moved to the north of their position. A glancing blow, they still battled wind and high seas.

Unless it was storming, François never let a day go by that he didn't use the time to hone his sword skills. The only one aboard who could give him a good workout was the captain, but he wasn't inclined to a re-match, usually remaining in his cabin. Cochran, a mid-twenties Irish lad showed the most improvement and as long as François didn't press him too closely, the young man offered a good report. Rifle and pistol practice helped to single out sharpshooters who would be good in the rigging to shoot down on the opposition.

He kept in physical shape by climbing the shrouds and lines. When the *Angelina* moved ahead, slowed by a light wind, he swam alongside, intending to grab the trailing rope and pulled himself aboard if she picked up speed, but that was never necessary. A pod of dolphins was always near and to the crew's amazement, watched them tow François to the Jacob's ladder.

As a partner in the expedition, François gladly assumed the duties of Sailing Master. Having competent helmsmen, he lent a hand wherever Gibbs needed help, but generally was found working alongside the ship's carpenter when not exercising.

On the morning of the thirty-seventh day, François came on deck early as usual. Checking their bearings and speed, he charted the *Angelina*'s position. By his calculations, they had traveled over 2,600 miles.

"Mr. Gibbs, I need a man with good eyes and a strong stomach."

"Mr. Cochran, present yerself," Gibbs called out.

Alan Cochran might have hailed from Ireland, but there was a Viking in the closet suggested by long, strawberry-blond hair, sky-blue eyes, and a total inability to grow a beard, making him the butt of many jokes. And, unlike most of the crew, his skin remained fair, the color of browned cream with a dash of red. The lad's endearing quality was a splash of freckles over the nose and the happy attitude worn like a pair of comfortable slippers.

François was quietly pleased with Gibbs' choice. Blue-eyed sailors had the best vision, and Cochran enhanced that understanding by sporting an earring in both ears. Although Mariah would have thought his ribs showed a bit more than they should and plied him with extra servings at dinner, he was a hard worker, and one of the few men aboard who could swim, sometimes joining the ship's Sailing Master and dolphins.

Handing him a spyglass François said, "Go aloft, and keep a watch for land."

With a quick, "Aye, aye, sir," he scampered up the rigging to the crow's-nest.

While this job seemed simple enough, for those seated high above the deck, every pitch and roll of the ship became amplified. Working up there kept a person's mind off the motion, but just sitting, contemplating one's discomfort necessitated a strong stomach. Continuing his own daily routine, François joined the bosun and embarked on a tour of the boat, something he'd just finished when the old pirate staggered onto the deck.

"How be it?" Shaver asked with slightly slurred speech, still in the grips of last night's drinking bout.

"All right. Expect a storm this afternoon."

Shaver scanned the relatively clear sky and horizon, sniffed the air, and grunted. "I coulda told ye that yes'erday. How much farther?" he asked with growing impatience.

"Sometime this morning. I have a man aloft."

Shaver glanced into the rigging then looked at him strangely, obviously wondering why he'd done that.

"I have a queer feeling," François replied to the unasked question, which was good enough. Shaver operated as much on intuition as anything.

Later that morning Cochran shouted down in his high voice, "Land, ho. Off the starboard bow."

"Mr. Gibbs, give Mr. Cochran relief. Have Mr. Martin take his place. We need to keep a close watch about the island," François said.

Shaver gave François another questioning look as Gibbs asked, "Anything in particular, Mr. Evreux?"

"As Capt. Shaver has said an island perpetually clouded in fog bears keeping an eye on."

Shortly before noon Marty, another blue-eyed, red headed, north Irishman shouted out excitedly, "Ahoy, on deck, two ships lay to anchor mid-island. Look to be sloops."

"How be this?" Shaver snarled, charging out of his cabin like a bull elephant in rut.

François grabbed the windward shrouds and hauled himself nimble as a monkey up the mast to join the lookout and see for himself. A sloop meant 14 guns and up to 75 men, something they could handle. Two sloops meant trouble. Neither flew flag nor pennant.

The *Angelina* plowed steadily ahead, her bow pointed directly at the center of the long, slightly concave spit of land barely rising above the ocean. It appeared there was an elongated cove sheltered by an outlaying reef and this was where the ships lay at anchor.

"Ye 'ave to stand off aways on the other side of this pile of sand 'cause of coral. There be a break in the ship-eater this side t'ward the nor' end of the cove. Deep water inside and ye can get close ta land," Shaver said.

A mile out Mr. Gibbs identified the intruders. "One be the *Dubliner*, Cap'n Penny's boat. The other I don't know, but they be workin' together."

François, standing next to Shaver, called out to the master gunner, "Señor Corvas, ready the guns. Load half of each side with canisters and the others with balls, but don't roll them out. Keep the gunners low." Then to Gibbs, "Everyone else acts normal."

"Still followin' yer instincts?" Shaver asked.

"Yes. Mr. Parker, take in sail and slow us down," François said to the Bosun, then to Shaver, "They're setting position to fight. Maybe looking casual will calm them a bit."

"I be fer blowin' em outta me waters."

"I suggest parlay first and see why they're here."

"Ye knows why they be here," Shaver rumbled.

"Searching with a foul map like you had. If they want trouble we're ready for your option."

Shaver cast an off-hand glance and arched an eyebrow at François. A cooler head might be the trick in this instance. As the *Angelina* slipped into the cove, they reduced sail and prepared to drop anchor, continuing to appear as non-threatening as possible.

"Mr. Corvas, be ready ta run out the guns. Mr. Parker, keep men aloft case we need sail. And keep yer bloody heads down!" Shaver instructed his crew. "Jist in case, boy."

"My feelings exactly. Taking them on would be like dealing with two hungry sharks. It's hard to get treasure home without a boat."

Shaver snorted displeasure at missing a good fight and wiped a sleeve over his nose.

Both sloops had run up enough sail to maneuver as Captain Penny called out, "State yer business, Hogshead?"

"I be sailin' this pleasure cruise about the islands, and this one looked interestin'," was his sarcastic reply.

"Well, there be nothing here 'ceptin' sand and trees."

"Actually, we need to take on some water," François interjected, trying to head off a confrontation.

"Ain't no drinkable water here."

"Damn liar!" Shaver growled under his breath. "Good spring mid-island."

François quietly laid a hand on Shaver's forearm.

Harvey Gibbs continued to be amazed. He'd never seen Shaver acquiesce so easily although he had no complaints. François seemed to know what to do and handled any duty with experienced ease. However, upon approaching the treasure island, he thought for sure Shaver would take over as a fight seemed inevitable, yet, the *Angelina*'s captain continued allowing the boy to give the commands. He certainly didn't disagree with a peaceable approach.

Continuing to reduce sail and appear a non-threat clearly put Penny at ease, especially coming from someone like Shaver who had the reputation of leaping into a fight. Not that the *Angelina* wasn't ready. Despite reduced sail, the ship was still maneuverable and more sail could be dropped quickly. A little addition acquired just before starting the Atlantic voyage enhanced their firepower.

As they neared La Palma, the western most of the Canary group, they spotted a merchant low in the water. Shaver just couldn't restrain himself as he nearly salivated while studying the ship through the spyglass. He just had to take a peek.

Looking as innocent as possible and flying English

colors, they worked their way close to the merchant. At the appropriate time, Shaver had his own ensign run up, a hog's head beneath two, crossed swords in silver on a field of black. As an exclamation point, a round was put over her bow. Taken by total surprise, the merchant's captain hauled in canvas and hove to so fast the *Angelina* nearly sailed pass.

Once aboard Shaver looked over the ship's manifest. His face clouded with disappointment. There was nothing more than trade goods bound for the New World. Any other time it might be worth the effort, but not now.

However, as François nosed around the deck something caught his eye. The ship only carried eight cannon, a way to reduce weight and increase cargo capacity, but beneath canvas were pieces capable of hurling a nine-pound ball. The *Angelina*'s compliment of cannon fired four-pound balls.

"Sorry ta 'ave interrupted yer voyage," Shaver growled as he thrust the manifest back at the merchant's captain.

"Excuse me," François said to the merchant's captain. "I see you are carrying extra cannon barrels."

"They are replacements for one of His Majesty's ships in the Caribbean."

"So?" Shaver said.

"Perhaps the good captain here would be interested in a trade."

"Huh?"

As the ocean was reasonably calm, they spent the next three hours exchanging four of the *Angelina*'s four-pound cannon for four of the merchant's nines, along with all her shot and most of the powder. Shaver generously left the merchant with twenty-five balls for the smaller cannon. Lightened of her load, the merchant rode higher while the *Angelina* sat a bit lower in the water.

Once underway, Gibbs took charge to have the

heavier guns positioned mid-ship, distributing the weight evenly. François worked with the ship's carpenter to refit the carriages to accommodate the new barrels, and reinforce the deck where needed to handle the added weight. The bigger guns discharged a heavier ball with considerably more force at a longer range to the detriment of whomever was on the receiving end.

Facing off against Capt. Penny and company, all five of the four-pound deck guns on each side were primed with canisters, which would shred the opponent's sails and deck before the two heavy cannons per side put them to Davy's locker. The crew had been drilled so that they could reload in just under two minutes, almost as good as any man-o-war. Yes, Mr. Gibbs was impressed. The lad clearly had a tactical head on his shoulders and showed a natural ability to command. The curiosity was that Shaver was letting him do so.

"Well, ye be damn unfriendly 'bout it all," Captain Shaver called back to Penny then to the amazement of the crew, he turned and shouted, "set them sails. We be findin' water elsewhere." Then to the sloop's skipper, "May crabs eat yer eyeballs, Penny."

As the *Angelina* turned and sailed back into open water he snarled, "They be searchin' fer the treasure all right. How many maps be there?"

"That is bothersome," François replied.

"So what be ar course now?"

"Tortuga. From what you told me, they are looking in the wrong place, too. We'll re-supply and come back when they've given up and gone, locate the treasure, and sail directly home."

As the *Angelina* made for deep water in a southerly direction, Mr. Gibbs stepped up. "Beggin' your pardon, Cap'n, but thought I better let ye know. As we were clearin' the reef, Cochran thought to glimpse a sail off to the north in that cloudbank. Not real positive. Might jist been seein' things, but it were Cochran who saw it."

"What kind of sail, Mr. Gibbs?" François asked.

"Believes it were a three-master, Mr. Evreux. Jist a glimpse mind ye. That be all."

"Thank you," François replied as he and Shaver looked at each other questioningly.

Chapter 17

† A Foul Wind †

Tortuga, hotbed of seething defiance, a thorn in the side of Spanish, French, and English alike, lay off the northeast coast of Hispaniola. Each power had tried to conquer its people only to have them rise from the ashes stronger, more determined, and more ruthless than before. The whole of the legendary island was lawless as François quickly learned while walking down one of the narrow streets, stepping over bodies—drunk, beaten, or dead. He found it exhilarating as if engaged in a boarding.

"I smells me a boy," the misogynist slurred, a bottle of rum in one hand, a pistol in the other. "I likes me boys young and firm."

François just nodded, smiled, and tried to step around him.

"Hows about a drink fer openers?"

"No thanks," he responded, trying to be non-confrontational.

"I wants me some company, and ye will do nicely," the man growled, leveling the pistol at François' nose.

François took a deep breath and relied on the survival skills learned years before on the streets of St. Nazaire and aboard ship. "Well, why didn't ye just come out and say so, mate? Where shall we go?"

The man grinned, revealing missing and rotted teeth, and lowered the pistol.

"There be . . ."

He didn't finish as François' left fist struck him between the eyes. Staggering backward, the pirate's eyes rolled up. A right fisted blow just below the sternum emptied his lungs, spraying a disgusting stench of stale rum-soaked air. A third blow with a left hook into a slackened jaw spun the man around to face away where he dropped slowly to his knees then flat on his face into a pool of muck.

"Well, seems ol' Petit got 'is self rejected," a voice remarked from the shadows.

François wheeled around, ready for whatever was to come next.

"Mr. Gibbs?" François said, greatly relieved as the potbellied quartermaster stepped from the shadows.

"That be some fancy fisting."

"Something one learns to survive."

"Well, better yer knuckles than mine. Would Mr. Evreux mind joinin' a common sailor fer a drink?"

"Aye," François replied, relieved to be in the company of a friend.

Stepping over his victim, the two proceeded to a tavern down the dirt street, a noisy, smelly den of humanity somewhat confined within rickety, wood slat walls with more holes than Swiss cheese. As they sat at a table toward the back, Gibbs stared at the boy for a moment before starting the conversation.

"Lucky Cap'n Shaver listened to ye or we might 'ave had to flex our muscles with those pirates then fight off an Englishman."

"Englishman?"

"Aye. That sail Cochran saw, the three-masted ship."

"He wasn't sure."

"Ye know Cochran has the best set o' eyes in these waters. Anyways, word's about a English ship o' the line set sail a couple weeks ago from over Port Royal way in search of pirate vessels. Now that just be rumor, but there be a couple boats unaccounted fer of late."

"They could be anywhere."

"Aye, but word is they be moored in Davy's locker," Gibbs said, taking a swig from the tankard of rum just served him. "You don't drink rum."

"No. You know us French. Wine."

"Aye. Had some once. Liked to knock me pegs out. Had a poundin' in me head for days."

Just then, a sailor staggered into the tavern shouting profanity about the English. Gibbs and François turned an ear to his story.

"Peavy got 'imself kilt an' the *Scavenger* sunk," the man reported. "Same fer Penny an' the *Dubliner*. Jumped by that English warship while they lay anchored at Loro Placida. Came right out o' the fog an' blew 'em all to hell. There be red coats on the island, too. Now we know what 'appened to Pike an' Blue Tooth."

Gibbs and François looked at each other.

"How ye be knowin' this?" the barman, a big, barrel-chested Scot called out.

"Ol' One-Eye Robyns were fishin' off the south reef o' Loro Placida an' saw it all. There were another ship there. Couldn't make out who they be, but it left a couple hours before the attack an' 'eaded south. Lucky fer them."

Gibbs took a big swig of rum.

"That island and all that treasure be cursed," another put in.

"Only thing buried there be our brethren," another added.

"Any survivors?" the barman asked.

"Aye. Picked up a couple o' the lucky ones who got away an' high-tailed it fer here."

"Could be a problem if that warship's hangin' around there," Gibbs said quietly.

François grunted soft agreement.

"What ya thinkin' lad?"

"I had a kid try selling me a treasure map not long after we made port. It was of Loro Placida and looked a lot like the one Captain Shaver had . . . the first one."

"Seems to be all sorts of them around."

"Believe I'll look that kid up. Have a question or two for him."

Gibbs gulped his drink, wiped his mouth with the back of a clean shirtsleeve, and followed François out of the tavern back down the street to where they met. The lecherous pirate had just staggered to his feet, leaning against the wall of a building trying to regain control of rubbery legs. As they passed, Gibbs smiled, doubled up his fist, and sent the man on a spinning face-plant into the stone wall with a resonating thud. He fell straight back into the same pool of muck, unconscious.

"Ne'r held with 'is politics," Gibbs remarked as they continued on. "Findin' that kid might be a bit challengin' in all this."

"Yes, but he was hanging out . . . there he is. Hey, kid," François called out.

The boy was still trying to peddle his map, but upon being called out, he started to run. He might have been fleet of foot, but not quick enough to outdistance François' long legs, who collared him in less than a dozen strides.

"Le' me go. I ain't done nothin'."

"Never said you did. Just had second thoughts about your map—my friend and I. How much do you want?"

"Five shillings?"

"How do I know it's any good?"

The boy, a short ten-year-old, skinny as a twig, and grimy as a pigsty, merely shrugged his shoulders.

"Here," François said shoving five copper coins into his filthy hand. "Let's see the map."

The boy pulled a sweat-stained parchment from inside a tattered shirt that hung to the knees and handed it over. Gibbs kept the youth close with a big paw latched onto his shoulder, but wasn't too sure about holding the boney lad, all the time studying the wild tangle of hair for any sign of lice while François studied the map. He didn't see any telltale spots, but that didn't ease his apprehension.

"What's your name?" François asked trying to sound pleasant.

"'Enry."

"Where'd you get this, Henry?"

"I found it."

François surprised Gibbs when he grabbed the boy by the shirt, picked him off his bare feet, and pinned him against a darkened stone wall with a knife at his throat.

"I asked where you got this."

"A man gave it to me. Said I could make good, hard coin for sellin' it," the boy squeaked in a high falsetto sounding like a distressed rat as his bare feet flailed the air.

"Where's this man, now?"

"I don't know, honest Mister. But he be back again. I be sure of it."

François set Henry back on his feet, but neither let go of his shirt nor sheathed the knife. Gibbs wasn't too anxious to hold him anymore.

"This man, has he done this before?"

"Aye. It ain't no good. He says so, but it be worth a coin or two, says he. I sells it and when he comes back I shows 'im the money I got paid. Then he gives me another coin."

"How many of these 'ere phony maps 'ave ye sold?" Gibbs growled.

"This be the fifth."

"Who's bought them?"

"Sailors."

"Sailors for who?" Gibbs continued to interrogate.

"One be from the *Devil's Disciple*."

"That was Cap'n Pikes' ship," Gibbs reported.

"Another be from the *Toreador*."

"That was Ol' Blue Tooth Grimmes' boat. Who else?"

"The *Scavenger*."

"Let me guess. The *Scavenger* and *Dubliner* ran together. That's why the two were at the island," François confirmed.

"And now they be on the bottom," Gibbs replied. "A decoy. No better way to hunt down pirates than have 'em come to you."

"A trap for the greedy. Would seem this Chudleigh likes setting traps."

François reached into his pocket then said to the boy, "Here. Three coins for the map. This is for your tongue," but held the coin back until he got another answer, "Where do you meet this man with the maps?"

The boy's light brown eyes flared with fear, and balked momentarily before admitting, "At me uncle's."

"And where do we find your uncle?"

Down the street and right. 'E makes shoes."

"I know the one," Gibbs confirmed.

François handed the coin to the boy, but still didn't let go.

"Understand this be for your tongue. Say anything about this conversation to anyone—your uncle, relative, friend, acquaintance, or stranger—I'll let it be known who's been responsible for many a good brethren meeting their end. I do not recall hearing a boy your age having been drawn and quartered, or even hanged, but that might be preferable to what will happen. Understand?"

"Aye, sir," the boy squeaked, shaking so hard he could barely grip the coins before bolting as fast as twig legs could carry him in the opposite direction they were to head.

"Thinks we ought to tell Cap'n Shaver?"

"Let's pay a visit to the shoemaker first," François suggested.

The shop was nestled among others toward the end of a dirt street. It was dark inside with shoes of all shapes hanging from the rafters, the smell of tanning leather so strong to smother the lungs. Hunched upon a short bench, a scraggy whiff of a man with a bald dome and long, greasy hairs hanging off the sides tapped nails into the sole of a shoe.

"What be ye wantin'?" was an almost unsavory

greeting as the man continued tapping nails.

"Something you're selling," François replied.

"Got money?"

He held up another gold coin. Gibbs wondered just how many coins François had.

The man's avaricious grin revealed badly dis-colored teeth, those that remained, obviously a victim of scurvy. As long, bony fingers closed in on the coin, it was also obvious his body was a victim of poor hy-giene. He smelled worse than the urine-laced muck Petit kept falling in. François pulled the coin out of his reach.

"What kind of shoes would sirs like?"

"No shoes. Information."

The man's countenance turned black as quickly as it shined welcome to the coin moments earlier.

"We have a certain map," François began.

"A treasure map as it were," Gibbs fleshed out.

"I ain't got nothin' doin' with no treasure maps," the shoemaker snarled and turned away.

"Now, that's not how we heard it told," Gibbs countered.

"The boy's a liar!"

"Dead men tell no lies," François replied.

The man's dark, wrinkled skin paled even more.

"You didn't . . ."

"This map or ones like it, are the cause of a number of brethren meeting their end," François con-tinued. "And they all came from this shop."

At that moment, François' ears picked up a muf-fled rustling noise behind a narrow passage covered by strings of beads. Glancing in that direction, he spotted the barrel of a pistol shove through the curtain fol-lowed by a husky man and another much smaller one also holding a pistol, both too well attired for sailors. Certainly not pirates.

"English!" Gibbs correctly whispered.

"So, our little secret seems to have surfaced," the smaller one said.

François wasn't one to wait long for events to unfurl, rather being a man of action and taking the offensive. Having backed against the narrow workbench his hand curled around a box of tacks behind him and in that instant showered the two men with them. Their reaction was predictable as they tried to shield their faces from the sharp barbs. François and Gibbs immediately drew their swords and knocked the pistols from the Englishmen's hands. They countered by drawing their own swords and the battle was engaged.

François' opponent may have been prodigious, but light on his feet; however, both were somewhat disadvantaged by their height as the hanging shoes kept banging them about their heads. The suspended merchandise also posed a problem in that a sword lifted into that realm could become entangled and useless. Gibbs fared better against the shorter man who was closer to his height, but François thought it unfair that he had to contend with someone closer to Gibbs' breadth while Gibbs' opponent was a better swordsman.

About the room the four dueled as the shoemaker hopped about shrieking, "Me shoes. Don't hurt me shoes!"

Not liking the confines one bit, François gave the workbench a quick kick, throwing it over in front of both opponents and with Gibbs in tow, ducked out the front door. The two attackers followed, expecting a chase through the streets, but were surprised to find the two pirates standing mid-street casually awaiting their arrival. This time it was Gibbs who got the bigger man and François the better swordsman.

Heads popped from windows and doors to

watch as the evening filled with the ring of steel, while those on the street hurriedly stepped aside or fled for cover. François' opponent knew he had an accomplished swordsman and spinning around shoved a shoulder into an onlooker, taking his sword to have two, but that wasn't much deterrence as François parried both weapons until hearing a familiar, rumbling voice to one side call out, "'ere, lad."

With a 360-degree spin, he caught the hilt of a sword and returned to face his opponent. He really didn't need it, but took the advantage to back the man toward a wall. He could have killed him at any time, but that wasn't going to answer his questions.

Covering another portion of street, Mr. Gibbs continued with his opponent, grateful for the sword practice with François during the crossing over. That's when Gibbs noticed Shaver standing partially in the street, undaunted as the two came particularly close.

"Nice footwork, Mr. Gibbs," Shaver said as casually as if at a tea party despite the two passing quite near. Shaver was a proficient swordsman, but spurned any practice himself as his partner gave the crew instruction and practice on the finer points.

"Thank you, Cap'n," Gibbs replied.

More accustomed to quicker results, Shaver began tiring of the entertainment, so as Gibbs and his opponent passed a second time, the old pirate stuck a boot out.

As François savored his duel, he suddenly heard a cry of pain. Out of the corner of his eye, he spotted Gibbs' opponent slump to the ground. Realizing he was outmatched and now alone, François' adversary attempted to flee. Flinging Shaver's sword, he caught him in the back of the head with the hilt, sending him sprawling face first onto the dirt street.

Like a lion, the boy pounced atop him placing

the edge of his own sword at the man's throat. "The shoemaker didn't seem able to answer my questions. Would you be answering instead?"

"Aye," was the winded response.

Jerking the man up roughly François shoved him against a wall, holding the tip of his sword at his throat.

"Where'd the maps come from?"

"Commodore Chudleigh."

"Commodore, be it now?" that deep, gravelly voice said. "What be this 'bout maps and Commodore Chudleigh?" Shaver asked, emphasizing the title with a sneer, a title that must have been relatively new.

"Our friends here have been distributing maps," François explained, "treasure maps. Copies of the one you had that was no good. Instead of treasure they are bait to lure the brethren to that island and this Commodore's warship."

"Well, well, well. That be the sails seen in the fog?"

"Yes. We got away, but the others didn't fare so well."

"Next time ye have a bad feelin' 'bout somethin' be sure ta let me know," the Captain said.

"Sorry, lad, mine's dead," Gibbs reported as he joined up.

"So be this one," Shaver said giving François' elbow a shove that drove the sword into the man's throat.

As he dropped to the ground, François turned on the captain.

"I wasn't finished questioning him!"

"What's more ta know?"

"How long that warship stays out, when it's due to leave and return, and where it hides."

"Oh . . . Well, sorry 'bout that lad. Might 'ave

been useful information, too," Shaver replied, sheathing his sword and walking off.

Frustrated, François stared at the shoemaker cowering in his doorway. Realizing the boy was looking at him, the weasel disappeared inside.

"Sorry, Mr. Evreux," Gibbs consoled, "the Cap'n means well, but he reacts more often than thinkin' bout things."

"I know," François spit out. "I know. Maybe not all is lost," he continued, stepping toward the shoe shop. "I'll be back directly."

Gibbs waited patiently; idly watching as a rickety, two-wheel cart pulled by two diminutive lads arrived and began loading the corpses. As he watched them handily toss the shorter, wiry one into the wagon Gibbs thought they looked a bit out of place. He would have expected them to be soiled waifs like the lad, Henry. While their shirts and trousers were soiled and tattered, they actually looked washed, even their bare feet, and each one's long hair was trimmed and combed. The taller, older-looking one was dark-complexioned with dark brown hair and facial features like lads from the eastern Mediterranean. The smaller was a miniature, blond, green-eyed Viking. In addition, unlike Henry and the other urchins prowling the streets, these two looked well nourished. To an observant man, they didn't seem to fit.

When it came to the big man, they struggled mightily, so Gibbs gave them a hand. They were about to leave when the shop owner's high-pitched voice screamed profanities followed by a hammer flying through the window. Seconds later a gunshot rang out. Gibbs took a step toward the shop as François walked out.

Spotting the corpse wagon, François walked over. Something about them struck him as odd, too, but dismissing it, pointed a thumb in the shop's direction. "There's one more inside."

"Did ye learn anything, Mr. Evreux?"

"Yes, but Tortuga will need a new shoemaker."

"And that boy be needin' a new uncle."

"Yes. That, too. I'll see you aboard the *Angelina*, Mr. Gibbs."

Chapter 18

† The Trap †

Late that next afternoon François rowed out to the *Angelina*, knowing Shaver would be aboard overseeing the loading of supplies. That was one quirk the pirate had, personally checking provisions alongside the bosun as they came aboard. He'd not allow spoiled food aboard. "Goes bad soon enough," he'd say. Whereas, Jean-Paul put a man he trusted to carry out his expectations and held him accountable.

"Welcome back, Mr. Evreux," he piped merrily while casting a wary eye on the diminutive boy cowering behind his Sailing Master.

It was a very different boy peeking around François' leg. Scrubbed, hair combed, he sported a new shirt and trousers, but remained barefooted.

"Sorry to interrupt, Cap'n. May we step to the rail a moment?"

"Who's the whelp?"

"The nephew of the shoemaker I shot last night. It was his only living relative."

"So, let me guess, ye want ta bring 'im aboard?"

"For the time being."

"So you couldn't find someone wet-nurse ta take 'im in?"

"Other than the three who are now dead, he knows the most about this affair with Commodore Chudleigh, but he's not saying much."

"Well, that be easy 'nough. A chicken squawks loudest when ye wring its neck. Then throw 'em overboard."

François stared at the captain.

"Oh, all right! But 'e's yer responsibility. Jist keep 'im outa my way."

At evening tide two days later, the *Angelina* sailed from Tortuga harbor, but not on the expected course.

"Pardon me for askin', Mr. Evreux, but I thought we was goin' back ta that cursed island."

"We are Captain, but I have a feeling we are being watched. I set a course to take us the opposite direction. Once out of sight we'll swing out to sea and circle back."

"That'll take us an extra day."

"Yes, time for the crew to sufficiently sober up."

"Hm-m-m. Perhaps ye be right. If we tangle with that Man-o'-War, ev'ry man jack'll need 'is wits about 'im. Oh, by the way, that whelp be a good hand. Shined me boots real good," the captain remarked, tossing the comment over his shoulder while strutting toward the bow, hands clasped behind his back, and whistling a merry tune, much preferential to his singing.

The next three days passed uneventfully, allowing the men to sober up and hone their fighting skills. Cochran and Henry spent much of their off time together sitting on the lee side of a longboat toward the bow.

"I see St. Elmo's fire last night," Henry said, having had the mid-watch.

"Aye, I heard. Jist one. That be a warnin'."

"Marcel says it means a storm's a brewin', but all the clouds I sees is on the horizon."

"There be a storm comin' sure 'nuf. The louder Hogshead sings the more rum he be drinkin' which means 'is leg be hurtin'. Does that when the weather changes."

"It must be hurtin' bad," Henry said of the louder than usual noises coming from the stern.

"But I thinks the warnin' be more than that. I hear that island 'as a Largarou tree. That be where unfriendly creatures gather, but I be prepared," Cochran said, tapping the hilt of the knife on his waist. "Which reminds me, I be wantin' ta give ye something."

The Irishman handed a piece of sailcloth to Henry. It was heavy. Opening it the boy discovered a sheathed knife. Made of iron, it had a black handle with a guard across the heel so that the instrument formed a cross. Henry was speechless.

"Keep it close. Ne'r know which part ye need, blade or hilt. Somethin' else." Cochran slipped a chain over Henry's head so that a silver coin lay on his breast.

All the men aboard, even Mr. Evreux, wore a charm for protection against the army of evil spirits inhabiting land and sea. Being Catholic, Cochran wore a St. Elmo's medallion close to his heart. That was the patron saint of the sea.

Later that day as Henry came to the poop for a lesson in navigating, Gibbs raised an eyebrow. "Ah, see ye finally got some protection."

"I suppose. How do ye know it'll work?"

"You don't," François said as he joined them, "until something happens. There are many things lurking in the sea to catch a sailor and take his soul. Once a man sets foot aboard a ship he constantly lives in death's shadow. Of course, there may be nothing to all the stories Gibbs tells, but on the other hand it costs nothing to take precautions."

"It be a daring man who courts trouble with no protection," Gibbs added.

The sun blotted out by a sheet of clouds, the boy spent his lesson learning to calculate the ship's speed by dropping a piece of wood at the bow, counting the time it takes to pass the stern, and working the mathematics. By the time they approached the island, a dark line of clouds had gathered on the northern horizon while a heavy fog obscured much of the island. By this time, Henry and Cochran were on watch in the crow's nest.

"Not bad navigating," Cochran whispered to Henry, seemingly reluctant at being heard as the *Raven* moved silently through the outer edges of the fog bank. "Mr. Evreux be one fine navigator. Dare say ye could drop a coin o' the realm and sail all the way round the world, and he'd bring ye back to that very same spot."

"Reduce sail," Gibbs called out to Parker, as they approached the cove, keeping his voice low as if it would carry all the way ashore as the fog seemed to amplify sound.

"As I understand it, Chudleigh has someone ashore watching for any ship that comes snooping about. They signal him so he can slip up from behind, trapping them in the cove, but this fog could work to our advantage," François said. "Anyone on shore won't be able to see us, and the Commodore won't be able to see any signals. By knowing where the treasure is really buried you might be able to slip in and out before he's the wiser."

"Aye," Shaver agreed, then calling out just loud enough ta be heard, "Mr. Gibbs, prepare a party ta go ashore."

The fog created another problem. They couldn't see the channel through the reef leading into the deep water cove; therefore, Gibbs had the skiff go ahead to locate the channel while two longboats towed the *Angelina* in. A tricky maneuver, but as soon as the way was located they slipped in quietly and maneuvered using a triangular staysa'l between the two masts, and a forean'-aft off the stern. Once at anchor, Shaver took twenty-five men and rowed ashore while François remained aboard to pace the deck.

He figured it would take the captain three or four hours to located the treasure and haul it back to the cove. Five hours passed and nothing. During the sixth hour, the fog began to lift just enough to see a fifty Toise, which gave him a fuzzy view of the shore and the channel out. As more time elapsed, François began getting a very unsettled feeling in his gut. Danger was about.

Based solely on that feeling, he had Gibbs set crewmen ready to deploy sail on a moment's notice, and others stationed along both rails and aloft to watch for any sign of either the landing party or an approaching ship. Gun crews unplugged the cannon and ran them out as quietly as possible. His worst fear was being caught in the cove with only one exit. It left him feeling like the lone chicken in a pen watching the hatchet-wielding farmer approach. He was regretting having remained in the cove. Then the feeling in his stomach began to churn.

"Mr. Parker, haul up the anchor and give me some fore-and-aft," he said to the Bosun.

"We leavin' Mr. Evreux?"

"Not exactly. Do it quietly, but fast."

"Aye, aye," he said, sensing the urgency, gathering crew as he hurried forward as the aft sails were run up.

"What have we got loaded in the guns, Mr. Gibbs?"

"Langrage in the fours, ball in the nines," Gibbs answered.

Using the fore and aft tri-sails, François had the *Angelina* piloted slowly toward the south end of the cove. That was just enough to make him feel a bit easier. The ship had just turned about when a series of red flashes lit up the fog bank from seaward followed by the dull thud of cannon. The water where their ship previously lay to anchor suddenly became a boiling froth of white spray.

"Mother of Mary, if'n we'd still been there . . . !" Gibbs said.

"More sail," François called out in a tone that sounded almost conversational as he piloted the ship hard about, careful to mark where the fog had lit up, "and torch the dingy."

Gibbs had silently questioned the need to deploy the small boat filled with oil-soaked rags, but then came a flicker of understanding. When François nodded, he called out to Gibbs, "Cut the dingy loose. Starboard guns shoot!"

When the starboard cannon discharged their loads, the smoke clouded all visibility. There was no doubt when the nines fired by the deeper roar and the way the boat vibrated as the carriages rolled back. Meanwhile the *Angelina* picked up speed, running back toward where she previous lay at the other end of the cove.

"At this speed we won't be able to turn without runnin' aground," Gibbs said.

"Aye," François answered sounding unconcerned as he strained to see through the increasing fog.

At that moment, the bank lit up again with red flashes followed by the distant thud of cannon. The water where the *Angelina* had been in the south end, now marked by the burning boat, sprang to life as a rain of balls and shot poured in.

"They've moved a bit south," Gibbs noted.

Passing the general area of the entrance to the cove François had the sails hauled in and the anchor lowered to stop further forward motion, then quickly raised. Another small boat immediately set out with two men and a lantern shielded so only those on the *Angelina*'s deck could see it. Their job was to locate the channel and lead them out.

When they gave the signal he said, "Hoist the anchor and deploy fore-and-aft. When we clear the reef, pick up the men and tack north, give me full sail, and get as many eyes as you can to watch for that ship."

Another volley from the unseen ship obliterated the fired dinghy.

"Aye, aye, Cap'n," Gibbs responded.

That was the first time anyone had used that title aboard ship regarding him, and for the moment pumped François' ego, but not for long as the weight of responsibility bore down hard.

"Sail off starboard!" Conner's youthful voice shouted from the gun deck.

Others glimpsed the ship, too, a three-masted frigate. It was there for only a second between rolling banks of fog, but that was enough to mark a bearing.

François was relieved. Had it been a first line man-o-war he'd be dealing with up to 140 guns. Chudleigh's ship would have sixteen guns per side on two decks with four in the stern and four in the bow.

"Full sail and shoot," François said calmly. Gibbs relayed the respective orders with less calm.

The *Angelina*'s starboard cannons answered with another volley. They couldn't see their target or assess the effectiveness of the fusillade, but Gibbs' experience told him their guns were on target and the grape shot alone would cause serious damage. The crew reacted quickly and efficiently as practiced. Sails dropped into place and snapped to the wind, lurching the sloop forward.

"I know she's been hit," Gibbs said, his chest swelling with satisfaction.

"I agree. Her captain will turn seaward so not to run up on the reef and back to give chase," François replied, then to the helmsman, "Bear ninety degrees starboard."

"That'll take on a collision course, Cap'n," Gibbs complained.

"Precisely what he'll not expect. Keep a weather eye."

The frigate appeared as a shadowy hulk slipping through the fog a mere hundred Toise slightly off the port side.

François had the *Angelina*'s bow turned hard to port directly in front of the oncoming ship.

"She'll ram us!" Gibbs protested.

"Starboard guns shoot as they bear," François told Gibbs still in a conversational tone.

Again, visibility was lost as smoke, flame, grape-shot, and ball belched from the *Angelina*'s guns. They were near point-blank range.

As the last gun fired François turned the *Ange-*

lina hard to the right and instructed, "Port guns ready."

Frigates were bigger and usually more nimble compared to sloops, but Chudleigh's ship wasn't responding as François would have expected. As they closed on it, he could see why. There was a fire rising in her fores'l and in the forecastle. To avoid a collision, it had turned left toward the reef. François' maneuver brought the *Angelina* parallel to its right side less than fifty Toise away.

"Shoot!" Gibbs shouted.

The volley struck the ship. The bigger balls bore savagely through its hull followed by a series of secondary explosions. Their return, despite the number of guns, was pitifully meager, but a half dozen or so balls found their mark. Reloaded well under two minutes, the *Angelina* turned a few degrees right to line up on the frigate's rear quarter and fired another salvo. With a turn to port the sails caught more wind and lurched ahead to disappear into the cloudbank. The frigate fired two shots, but François judged it was from the aft followers and they were off the mark.

"What about Captain Shaver?"

"We'll stand out to sea until tomorrow. If Chudleigh's ship isn't about we'll send in a launch to fetch him back. I will not be caught in that cove again."

"Aye. They didn't expect us to run quite so fast in there," Mr. Parker said.

"We were lucky, gentlemen. Very lucky."

By mid-morning the next day the fog lifted as all hands nervously searched for the frigate, but it was nowhere in sight. François then had the *Angelina* hold just outside the cove as a small skiff was prepared. Cochran was first to volunteer.

"Go ashore to the right of that big tree, and try to locate the captain and tell him where we are," François said.

The lingering wait was difficult as the tiny boat moved over the reef and across the cove. Its bow no sooner touched the beach than gunfire erupted from inside the tree line. Watching intently through the spyglass François finally made out the captain's party attempting to make their way back to the beach and the longboats; however, more than a small observation party was obviously put ashore and had them pinned down. The three men in the skiff hadn't been so fortunate. He thought they were all killed until spotting a head bobbing next to the boat, using it as a shield.

"Mr. Gibbs, have Señor Corvas set those nines on the tree line by that big tree with canister and open fire."

Each gun crew leader took careful aim before discharging the load, sending hundreds of fifty caliber-sized balls to rip the beach. François could only pray his captain had sufficient cover. At this range, it was like firing a blunderbuss. Everything downrange was fair game. It seemed to be effective as Shaver and half his men began running toward the boats struggling with two large chests. The other half continued protective rifle fire in rotation just as François had taught them during the voyage over, so that they laid down an almost continuous fire. All cannons on the port side laid a round of balls into the trees where they saw smoke from enemy rifles. The vegetation disintegrated. The enemy fire ceased.

As quickly, the treasure-laden boats headed across the reef breaching the surf toward the *Angelina*. Those on shore took a defensive position in the event of another attack while the gun crews prepared to answer if needed. The lone survivor from the skiff didn't seem able to take to his boat until two from the cover squad raced across the beach, lifted him in and oared back. An hour later, the last man climbed aboard, the wounded being tended on the main deck.

Sails were set as Shaver watched the last chest lowered into the hold before strutting to the helm.

"Well, that were an adventure. You sink Chudleigh's ship?"

"I don't believe so, but his ship is damaged."

"Make for Tortuga."

"We are well supplied. Why not just head home?"

"I got me some business there, that's why," Shaver replied curtly.

François gave the helmsman the bearing to take them back to Tortuga before going to check on the wounded. Cochran lay stretched out on the main deck, his left shoulder a mass of dried blood where he'd taken a ball, hair matted over the right ear by blood from a nasty cut above the ear.

"Looks like the luck of the Irish was with you," François said as Henry knelt next to him.

"Martin were Irish, too, but none for him. Too big a target. Stopped more than one ball that might have had me name on it," he said, valiantly trying to sound cheerful despite the excruciating pain.

Like most every ship on the seas, there wasn't a trained doctor, although Grover, the ship's cook, had more experience in such matters than anyone. Inspecting the wound he said, "Looks like the ball smashed the bone. It'll have to come off."

Cochran's face turned ashen as his eyes widened with fear.

"Let me have a look," François said. "One of my field workers ran afoul of a cow with a new born calf. Broke his arm in about the same place. The Guanches natives opened it up enough to fix the bone. Healed fine."

"Well, if you want to try, I got others needin' my

attention. There's another medical kit below. Marty, here, can fetch it back."

A few minutes later the cook's mate returned with a flat, black leather pouch containing several small knives and other tools then went to join the doctor.

"This is your choice, Mr. Cochran."

"If your way don't work, I'll lose the arm anyway."

"Well, boy, ye'll be needin' this," Shaver said from behind, passing a bottle of rum forward.

"I've never touched the stuff, Cap'n."

"Good. It'll knock ye out fer sure."

True to Shaver's observation, one healthy swallow and Cochran was blurry-eyed. By the third, he was unconscious, making the operation easier, although a couple stout crew pin his arms and legs securely.

"Mr. Evreux," Henry said, "these knives be duller than a marlin spike. If'n ye be cuttin' on 'im, use this."

François took Henry's knife. The boy was right. Grover's instruments were in serious need of a whetstone and Henry's blade was sharp enough to peel the fuzz off a cockroach. He then did something no one had ever seen. He had Henry pour some rum over his hands and bathed the instrument before using it, first to lay the arm open parallel to the bone enough to expose the break. Removing a couple pieces of bone fragment and ball, he worked the broken ends together and put the tissue back together with catgut, again using liberal doses of rum to wash the wound while sewing it closed.

"Keep him drunk, Henry, at least until this time tomorrow. I'll have someone take your watch."

Later that day, after Shaver retired to his cabin, Gibbs came alongside François, who was standing near the helm looking longingly at the ocean and said softly, "The crew who went ashore say the Commodore's ship weren't the only one involved in this 'ere treachery. The Cap'n be goin' after Jack Crane and the *Raven*."

Chapter 19

† Black Maggie †

ꝥew people took notice as the *Angelina* sailed into Tortuga's harbor. Under oath and threat of losing their share, the crew said not a word about the confrontation with the British warship. Most of their ship's damage was repaired. That still being tended went ignored, as it was common for ships to arrive in port in such condition, usually worse.

The people voiced more concern about the loss of the island's only shoemaker at the hands of one of Shaver's crew. Most felt no loss of the man who had been a liar, a cheat, and worse, a traitor, but feared shoes might come into short supply if someone didn't take his place. That's when one of Shaver's crew spoke up.

"Beggin' the Cap'n's pardon, but I know leather craft and I think this be a good time to set roots."

Shaver wasn't inclined to lose another man, besides it would be necessary to take an accounting of the treasure and dole out his. Of course, the rest of the crew would want their share, and that spelled trouble. The men would take what was rightfully theirs and disappear long before the time he wanted to sail. Worst, no longer accountable, they'd eventually talk up what Shaver wanted kept secret for a time. Besides, François had trained them well, and they functioned as any ship of the line, something else Shaver didn't want to lose.

When he finished expressing his concerns François spoke up. "Mr. Gibbs, Mr. Byrnes, and Mr. Grover make an accounting and just before we set sail give Mr. Westmare his share."

Shaver continued to balk, but the other officers agreed. In addition, Cochran was going to need more time to mend. It took François to persuade him to remain and help around the leather shop until fit to rejoin the crew. His share would be portioned and released as well.

With that decided, François spent the next two days helping put the looted shop back in order. On the afternoon of the third day a sleek, black oak Brigantine lay to anchor in the harbor, the most beautiful ship he'd ever seen. It was instant love. This ship bore news that warmed the heart of every person on Tortuga.

"Come out of a fog bank all of a sudden like, she did. Thought we be goners, but she was bad off. Mizzen gone, sails sliced to ribbons and burned. They be busy repairin' holes on her sides at the water line. Looked to have been in quite the battle. Cap'n Jack turned hard to outrun her, but they were in no condition to give chase. It was hard to make out the name, but she was flying the Union Jack and it were flyin' Commodore Chudleigh's pennant from the mast. Must've had a run in with a Spaniard or

Frenchie man-o-war."

A great din of cheering and increased drinking accompanied the officer's yarn. In a secluded corner were secret, knowing smiles. Later that evening François took a pipe while strolling among the small fishing boats overturned for the night along the beach. Finally, he spotted a half-Nubian-Portuguese and half English girl of perhaps twenty-five seated on the sand mending a section of net.

"Hello," he called out.

Her black eyes barely glanced up as she continued working.

"Any luck today?" he continued.

"Would 'ave if not so many holes in this bloody net. On the morrow it all fixed thanks to help from young 'enry, here."

"This arrangement seem to work?"

"Works for me," the girl beamed, her white teeth shining brightly from a dark mahogany face.

Upon putting ashore, François searched out the girl, and over liberal protests from the shoemaker's nephew, she took him in.

"Yeah," the boy added coldly. His hair had been trimmed more neatly so that it hung just above the eyebrows and over the ears to the base of his head.

"Well, I'm sorry your uncle got himself killed," François said.

"'E tried shootin' ye in the back."

"'Enry be upset cause 'e wants back to sea, in a real boat. Wants to be a pirate."

"You saw what it is like, lad. You need a couple more years to flesh out for that," François explained.

"How old were you when you went to sea?"

"Eight."

"I'm twelve. Marty an' the others ain't much older. Why do I 'ave to wait?"

François laughed. "I had no choice in the matter. I

was an orphan roaming the streets and getting into trouble with the soldiers. I would have never seen another birthday if a good man had not recued me and taken me under his wing. I spent nearly six years as apprentice seaman before returned to the land. The sea is as beautiful and enchanting as any woman, but can be unforgiving and ruthless. For me this voyage is almost over. I will put my back to the sea once again, and return to my family, and the land. If your desire is the watery mistress then apprentice here with Maggie. "

"To a woman! Fishing!"

"She wasn't always a fisherman," François replied softly with a wink.

"Maybe the boy needs a demonstration," she suggested, getting up and reaching under her overturned boat to produce a cutlass.

"Now, Maggie, be careful. You remember what happened the last time."

"Aye," she said, a generous smile spreading across her face and going on the attack.

The sound of steel rang loudly, François obviously had his hands full of the nimble woman until she suddenly stopped and held the sword upright in front of her face.

"Thank you," he said, bringing the sword up to his face then sweeping it down and outward.

The boy pretended to be only mildly impressed.

"Get as good as Maggie and you will find a birth."

Appearing unimpressed, the boy continued mending the net as the two spoke for bit in a foreign tongue. Then the girl drew her long, slender finger down the slight cleft in François' chin, raised up on her toes, and kissed his cheek.

"That be one fine body of a man," she sighed as he walked away.

"Why don't ye take 'im to bed?" the boy asked bluntly.

Maggie looked at Henry with some degree of surprise before replying softly, "That man different from any ye'll 'er meet. He don't give 'is word easily, but when 'e makes a vow 'e holds by it no matter how hard the wind she blows. 'E made a vow of loyalty to 'is wife and nothin' will change that course, not even me. Oh, to find such a man." Then twisting the corner of her thin lips into a mischievous smile said, "Ye be fair lookin'. Ain't made such a vow, 'ave ye?"

Henry's eyes shot wide with surprise and shock as he squeaked, "Me?"

The girl tossed her long, dark hair back and laughed, tousling Henry's fine, brown locks before resuming repair of the nets with a faint, teasing chuckle until the boy eventually calmed from the unhinging joke.

Eventually he stopped, looked up and asked, "If ye be a pirate 'ows come ye be sittin' 'ere with this fer a boat?"

"'Cause men don't like sailin' with no woman, especially a woman cap'n. Say it be unlucky."

Henry mended another knot before asking, "Why?"

"Don't take long after leavin' port for men to lust after woman. Havin' one aboard can cause anger. Next thing ye got fightin'."

"But he said ye were cap'n once."

"So it be necessary to care fer em all."

"All!" his voice squeaked again in surprise.

"And not get a bloody piratin' thing done. That be 'ard for both cap'n and crew, so the only course is 'oldin' a tight rope and let no man 'ave 'is way. None."

"Oh."

"That were French ye spoke weren't it?"

"Oui. That means yes."

"Ye meet 'im in France?"

"I 'ad a sloop once. A nice one, too. Was sailing off Madagascar, but pickin's weren't so good so I decides

205

headin' back to the Carib. Jamaica be my home. We put in at Meridian Island in the Canaries. They call it El Hierro now. Decent enough port to re-supply when me mutinous crew decided otherwise. Stole me ship and left me stranded. That be where I met that man. Took me in with 'is family 'til 'e found a ship 'eaded this way and paid me passage. Wasn't much in Jamaica anymore so I came 'ere lookin' to get another boat. That one's got a nice family. Never seen a man more devoted."

"Did he know ye were a pirate?"

"Oh, yes."

"If'n 'e's so devoted to is family what's 'e doin' 'ere?"

"Sailin' with Cap'n Shaver? Don't know why, 'enry. Somethin' strange goin' on there."

"Shaver's said to be the best pirate around."

"Aye, he be good, but if that man ever gets 'is own boat . . . well, the oceans won't be the same."

Standing on the wharf François looked out at the black ship silhouetted in the fading light, his eyes caressing her fine, clean lines, although the rigging of her two masts could use a bit of tidying up. Low charged, the forecastle was lower and set back compared to older designs, but still capable of deflecting waves from washing the deck while providing quarters for the crew. The poop rose up aft but not too high giving the officers and captain adequate space, and the helmsman a good view from the top.

"Pretty boat," a familiar, gravelly voice croaked.

"Yes, she is. Judge her to be 108 pied."

"Ye a good eye fer measurin', lad. Missed it by only a foot. She's a hundred-nine feet bow to stern, twenty-two at the beam. Draws eight feet. Strong as the shoulders of Hercules. Story be she were built up in Inverness.

"Seems this Scot gent were walkin' 'long the shore and 'ears cryin' and sees a mermaid sittin' on a rock. The tide's gone out and the poor lass be stranded in the hot sun. Well, he strikes up a conversation and she asks 'im to put her back in the water. Bein' a gentleman, he acquiesces. In return, she grants him one wish. Well, he says he wants to build boats that won't sink. Mind ye, he wants to build boats when he coulda had all the gold he could handle. Anyways, he gets 'is wish. N'er a boat he nor 'is brood 'er built 'ave gone down and that's made thenm a galleon load of gold in the process. She's a devil ship, though. That ain't black paint. That be her natural color. Black walnut."

"Unlucky?"

"She be like a wild woman, treacherous and dangerous if'n she don't take a likin' to ye, but she'll calm right down with a man that treats right."

"You know her pretty well."

"Aye, I know her." Shaver sighed. "Be cap'ned by Jack Crane now. He be the one in league with the Commodore."

"Oh?"

"Aye. Truth be, Jack Crane were on the other side of the island when ye took on the Commodore. Saw 'is ship at anchor when the fog cleared some, his self on the beach parlayin' with the red coats. You damn near sunk the Commodore's boat, did ye know?"

"I heard we hurt him."

"Word be ye killed or wounded a third of 'is crew including the ship's Cap'n and first mate, and put three holes below the water line. Jist missed the powder magazine, ye did. They still don't know it be the *Angelina*. Thinkin' it were a Frenchie man-o-war. The way the crew stood and fought all regular soldier like ta give me cover put the seal on that thinkin'. Crane be the traitor that's caused the death of many a good brethren."

"How'd you come by that?" François asked.

"One of 'is former officers be particularly informative."

François was quiet.

"I'm thinkin' 'e should be challenged," Shaver suggested.

"Folks should know what he's been up to."

"I'm thinkin' ye should challenge 'im."

"Me! Why me?"

"'Cause if'n I do it no one would believe it. Always been bad blood 'tween us. Ye be different. Neutral as it were."

"I sail with you. They would just say you put me up to it."

"Ye be a smart lad. Ye'll think of something."

Chapter 20

† The Raven †

François became so absorbed in thought on the problem Shaver put forth that he walked into the tavern unaware Captain Crane and another sat at a table near the back. At such times François wasn't good company so sat alone at a side table sipping a glass of wine when a group of three seamen strode through the front door.

"Cap'n Jack!" the leader called out searching for him in the crowd.

"What be the problem now?" Crane grumbled, obviously annoyed, then his face turned ashen. "Ah-h-h, a committee I suppose." his voice dripped with sarcasm.

"Aye. The crew don't hold with what ye been done. They took a vote Jack Crane. It went again' ye."

"The hell, you say!" the man bellowed, overturning the table as he stood up, pulling out a pistol and pointing it at the seaman's face. "Well, I take a vote and it goes against you and your traitorous mutineers."

Suddenly a cutlass appeared knocking the pistol into the air as Crane pulled the trigger discharging a ball harmlessly into the roof timbers.

"Traitorous is being cozy with Commodore Chudleigh and his plan to lure pirates to that bewitched island trap."

Crane swung to face toward his new accuser.

"And who are you, boy?" he bellowed.

"François Evreux."

"And jist what ye be accusin' me of?"

"Three days ago my ship was at an island following a treasure map picked up here. It was foggy, but when our men made high ground it cleared enough to see your ship at anchor on the west side of the island and you standing on the beach talking to English red coats while unloading provisions."

"I'll rip your lyin' tongue out."

"You won't fare any better than the Commodore did with the *Angelina*."

"Liar! The *Angelina* could never take on an English war ship or stand against regular soldiers."

"How much did they pay you to betray the brethren?"

Crane threw the pistol aside and drew his cutlass, slashing viciously with a ferocious down cut. François nimbly sidestepped and parried the attack. Crane's associate moved to joined in until a pistol lay on his shoulder just below the left ear.

"It's jist between the two of 'em, mate," Mr. Gibbs said softly.

A wild, undisciplined swordsman, Crain attempted to overcome an opponent with brute strength. The room was packed, but as the fight commenced customers scattered, overturning tables, and chairs in flight. Some of this Crane used by throwing into François' path or lunging forward, forcing him to take a step backward and hopefully trip over some debris.

Countering Cranes' attacks and keeping track of where his feet were in regards to the furniture became a challenge, and in one instant François didn't see the broken chair that sent him sprawling backward. It was déjà vu. Capitalizing on the misstep, Crane raised his sword high overhead to cleave his victim, but François kept his wits and shot a boot into his attacker's groin. The pirate froze in pain just long enough for François to roll backwards over the shoulders and spring onto his feet there to deftly knock the cutlass from the man's hand. With wide-eyed disbelief, Captain Jack staggered backward a couple steps into the arms of two other pirates, who held him as if clapped in irons. François then stepped to where Harvey had Crane's companion pinned against the wall.

"How many ships did your plan send to the bottom?" François asked, his voice cold, eyes boiling like an approaching squall.

The man hesitated knowing he was condemning himself, but when François' sword nicked his throat he blurted out, "Five."

"And how did you do it?"

"Cap'n Crane had this treasure map. He knows it be worthless 'cause we followed it. We got caught in a storm and put in a cove along Hispaniola for repairs when the Commodore slipped up on us. He was set to hang us all, but Jack struck a bargain, our freedom in exchange for luring pirate ships to Loro Placida.

"The Commodore put soldiers on land then lay to on the lee side. When a pirate ship come into the cove, the soldiers gave him a signal and he'd circle in. There be no escape. With those big guns he'd stand out to sea and send them to the bottom. Any crew lucky enough to make shore were captured by the soldiers, then they'd have a trial and hang them."

"And how much did you get paid?"

His eyes were wide with fear as he glanced around the attentive gathering. François nicked his throat again. "A thousand pieces of gold for every ship and five for every pirate."

"And what about your crew here?"

"We didn't tell them. The oafs thought Jack bargained a pardon until he put in at the island like you said. We was just deliverin' supplies, that's all."

Those in the pub listened intently. With this confession they lurched forward with cries of outrage, grabbed the two men, dragging them outside, and down the cobbled street to the livery where they were found hanging the next morning. Their fate was no concern to François once he proved his accusation. Instead, he returned to the beach where the small fishing boats were stowed for the night. As hoped, no one, especially Maggie and the boy, was around. He wanted to be alone.

Sometime later, while seated on the keel of a small fishing boat, he heard a soft foot fall in the sand. Turning, he spied a short, stocky man with a short, dense, white beard and a sailor at each shoulder approach, the same men who had brought word of the crew's vote to Jack Crane. As they didn't have weapons drawn, he figured it to be a friendly visit.

"I am called Mendoza, Sailing Master on the *Raven*, formerly under Jack Crane. This is Masseur Girard, our carpenter, and Mr. Yates, Master Gunner."

"You were the committee."

"Si. The crew were angry because of Jack's relationship with the English. Had no idea what he was actually up to until we anchored next to Englishman's ship. Your words against Jack brought justice."

"It was right to be done by his own kind."

"I am most grateful standing for me. A ball between the eyes would not have been to my liking," the sailor said, his cheeks puffing up as his lips curled into a warm smile.

François instinctively liked the man and acknowledged the words of gratitude with a simple nod.

"No longer having a capitán, we were sent ashore by the crew to find one. Capitán Shaver speaks highly of you. He say to us you are the one who capitáned the *Angelina* and nearly sank the Commodore's ship. He say you might be young, but are more than capable. We think anyone who can do that is the kind of man we want for capitán."

François was taken back. A long pause followed as his mind tried to comprehend the sudden offer, finally asking, "That is the vote of the crew?"

"Qui, *chaque homme*, yes, every man," Monsieur Girard said with a French accent thick as the fog when the *Angelina* encountered Chudleigh.

"And you say Capt. Shaver endorses this?"

"Si, he does."

"Then I accept."

"We will need more crew before sailing, fifteen men, and provisions," Mendoza said.

"Put out the word and see what shows up. Have them assemble on the dock a nine in the morning."

"May we escort Capitán Evreux to his ship?"

"Yes, Señor Mendoza, that would be fine."

With long, proud strides, François accompanied the committee back to the wharf and rowed out to the ship he had admired. Climbing up the rope ladder, he stopped short as one leg crossed the gunnel.

"Anything wrong, Capitán?" Mendoza asked, standing below him on the Jacob's ladder.

Harvey Gibbs was standing on the deck, silver whistle in hand.

The escort joined their new captain on deck, not quite sure what was happening. They'd never heard of a pirate captain piped over the side as they did on a ship of the line. Having been a bosun during his younger years before the ale caught up to him, Mr. Gibbs blew the shrill notes. For him, that brought back a flood of memories.

François stood erect until Gibbs finished. Almost immediately, the thud of feet upon the teak deck echoed like the soft beat of a drum through the rigging as those who had once served aboard a regular ship responded instinctively and lined up. The others followed with a great deal of confused hesitation. François saluted before walking across the smooth deck to mount the ladder leading to the bridge atop the quarterdeck. Stopping at the large wheel, he gently caressed one of the spokes. Perhaps it was just his imagination, but he thought to detect the ship to groan. He hoped it was a satisfied sound.

Turning to face the crew he said, "I am François Evreux. You voted me to be your captain. I accept that responsibility and pledge to serve you and this ship to the best of my abilities. We will of course, become a companion to Captain Shaver's ship, the *Angelina* . . ., at least for a time. Also, there will be some changes as to how this ship will run. All I ask is that you go along with these changes even though they may not seem right for a pirate ship. Understand, it was these things that enabled the *Angelina* to take on an English ship of the line and all but sink her. For now, get some rest and be ready to set sail on the morrow eve's tide. Mr. Gibbs, I assume you are staying? Good. Gather those officers that remain and come to my cabin in one hour."

"I brought your things over," Gibbs said with a

broad smile. "Figured ye be stayin'."

"Thank you. Señor Mendoza, have some men make my quarters suitable while we inspect the ship."

"Aye, aye, Capitán, and welcome aboard de *Raven*. Three cheers for our new capitán! Hip, hip, hooray!"

The cheers drifted across the quiet bay to settle over the village like a warm blanket. Somewhere among the ramshackle buildings beneath the guns of Fort de Rocher, curled next to pleasurable companionship, Aloysius Shaver smiled. He'd kept the vow made to his cousin.

Chapter 21

† Making of a Reputation †

Following a tour of the *Raven*, François met with the officers. What with Crane and his Quartermaster hanging at the livery, and absence of the bosun who confessed to Shaver, the only officers remaining were the committee and Mr. Lowery, a Bosun's Mate.

After a lengthy discussion about the ship and crew, François said, "Sr. Mendoza, I would propose to the crew that Mr. Gibbs be Quartermaster, you, and Mr. Yates continue with your duties, and Mr. Lowery be bosun. I shall recommend others for positions as I see how they perform."

After the crew approved of the officers, he spoke to them about his expectations. Only Gibbs was not surprised, and after some discussion, they decided giving the new order a try.

Late the following morning, Lowery personally checked the quality of provisions being loaded aboard, being very selective as instructed. One of Capt. Jean-Paul's lessons to a young François was:

> "A good captain learns to delegate. He cannot do all things himself. Be specific about your expectations and let the men do their job. If it is not exactly what you envision be sure your orders were clear, then help them to succeed. This makes for a good ship."

François only wished the *Fleurette*'s helmsman had listened better.

Leaving the crew to their work, François accompanied Gibbs to sign on additional crew. He was surprised to see the number of sailors lining the wharf, many having come early upon hearing the call for men to serve the black ship. Word had gotten out that the new captain of the *Raven* was the one responsible for defeating the pirate's scourge, Commodore Chudleigh, and many were anxious to join his crew.

It was a motley, hard-looking lot, and the first thing François did was look into each man's eyes. He'd have no one who showed up drunk. That was not a problem with the first in line.

"Hello, Marty. Capt. Shaver know you want to jump ship?"

"Aye, sir. Told him I wanted somethin' better than bein' a powder monkey."

"And what be 'is reaction?" Gibbs asked.

"He throws me overboard. So I swims ta shore and stands in line. Well, actually there weren't no line at the time."

"See Mr. Lowery to sign the articles."

"Thank ye, cap'n," he said, giving a quick salute.

"Well, if the lad has anything goin' for him it be enthusiasm," Gibbs chuckled as the boy practically skipped to the small table where Lowery sat with the ship's log.

"Assign him to Mr. Lowery as a mate."

With Gibbs at his shoulder, whispering suggestions, the two proceeded down the line interviewing each man. François considered his quartermaster's comments inviting this or that man to sign the articles. He had actually gotten the fifteen needed, but there were less than a half dozen left. Feeling inclined, they continued the process until coming to the last one.

"Yes?" François asked warily.

"I be 'ere to sign aboard, Cap'n."

"You are still be too young, Henry."

"He be ready," a familiar voice replied from some barrels stacked nearby. Flashing a broad, white smile, Maggie DuBri stepped forward.

"So soon?"

"The cap'n of such a grand ship has need of a cabin boy, and I don't see a better one here 'bouts," she replied, looking around. "He couldn't learn from anyone better, either."

François remained silent for a moment as the hot sun beat down on them. "There is always someone better, Maggie. All right. Mr. Gibbs, sign them both on."

Henry's mouth broke into a wide grin showing adult-sized teeth except for the canines which were just sticking through.

Gibbs choked. "Beggin' the Cap'n's pardon, but it be bad luck to 'ave a woman aboard," he protested softly, but earnestly.

"Your concerns are duly noted, Mr. Gibbs, but I think I will risk it to have this one aboard the *Raven*."

"But what'll she do?"

"Anything you can," Maggie snapped defiantly, which caused him to wrinkle his face as if he had just bitten into a green lemon.

"Larkins expressed great displeasure working the galley, and if breakfast was a sample of his skill, it might be best for all, in particular him, if he had other duties. Maggie can take the galley. That should meet everyone's approval. Henry can be cabin boy and work in the galley as well."

Gibbs' mouth opened and closed like a fish out of water, finally mumbling, "Aye, aye, Cap'n." With a wave of his hand, he motioned the two new additions to sign the articles and go aboard. "It still be bad luck."

That evening the *Raven* moved out of the harbor leaving the *Angelina* behind. Shaver had persuaded him to join up for a raid on the Spanish treasure fleet, perhaps as a way to keep François around longer as they really didn't need more treasure. The old pirate was well versed in the art of manipulation. In return, Shaver agreed to allow François two weeks to get the *Raven*'s crew in order. At that time, they would join up and set out together doing what pirates do best with treasure-laden galleons, only better. What Shaver didn't know was that François had something in mind in the way of improving the *Raven*'s performance, more than just training the crew.

While not the most successful privateer, Capt. Jean-Paul was a capable officer and motivator of men. François learned those lessons well before tossed ashore on El Hierro, as demonstrated by the development of his plantation. The *Raven* no sooner cleared the harbor than he gathered the officers in his cabin to lay out the specifics of how the ship would run. Expecting some initial resistance, he was very precise explaining their duties, and explaining the reason behind each peculiar expectation. Of course, they questioned having a woman aboard, but when the meeting ended, she served a satisfying meal and an extra pint of rum, which further buoyed their spirits and lessened objections about the galley assignment. They were at least interested in trying the new order of things.

Mr. Gibbs suspected there was more to this voyage than just a training cruise. Being an observant and thoughtful man, he had seen François spend some time with two expatriate Spaniards, conversing intently in their language. Intuition told him the young captain was up to something. When he alluded to this, François merely smiled.

"I am considering seeking Spanish help in a minor refitting the Raven," he said, but no more.

On the third day out the crew was working more efficiently and in good spirits, their minds filled with expectations of fortune. Keeping the coast of Hispaniola off the port side, they sailed west through the Windward Passage, across Gonáve Bay, and along the southern shores of the Island until reaching Santo Domingo.

Despite flying the Spanish ensign, François kept the *Raven* well south of that port before rounding the eastern end of the island and heading back along the northern coastline. They made an exceptional speed of six knots during the circumnavigation of the island due in part to a favorable wind and some minor changes in the rigging. Several hours before dusk on the fifth day, François had the bow turned directly toward land.

The officers and crew, even Gibbs, thought their captain had inhaled too much water during the latest swim as they boldly approached Puerto Plata and the deadly long guns of El Morrow de San Felipe. As they came within three leagues, François reappeared on deck attired in a Spanish naval officer's uniform.

"We have a cache of Spanish uniforms below in barrels marked with a yellow spot on top. Have half the men change into them. The rest are to conceal themselves below for the time being. And Mr. Gibbs, no one is to say a solitary word except me. Not so much as a cough."

Gibbs had come to appreciate the twinkle in his captain's eye when he was up to no good, but really wondered what he had in mind as the *Raven* dropped anchor off the Amber Coast under the guns of the formidable fortress. Night was in full swing. Those on deck of the *Raven* could barely see the launch on its way to gr0000eet them, its lantern bobbing to the rhythm of the waves. When it knocked against the *Raven*'s hull Gibbs was ready to welcome them aboard also dressed in a fine uniform.

"Good evening, gentlemen," François greeted as the three climbed aboard, a lieutenant, a sergeant, and a corporal.

"Good evening," the officer replied with a smart salute. "I am Lt. Pedro Mendez de Cordillo, representative of the Master of Ports for his Majesty's Puerto Plata."

"Captain Francisco Meridiano de Ortega Guzman, at your service," he replied smoothly with a courtly Spanish that dumbfounded Gibbs who knew enough of the language to know what was being said. He kept his mouth shut as ordered. Harvey's pronunciation was atrocious.

"Guzman?" the officer replied as his eyebrows shot into his hair line, obviously surprised.

"Yes," François replied coolly, referring to the

richest and most powerful family in Europe. "Duke de Medina-Sidonia, Alonso Pérez de Guzman, Captain General of the Ocean Sea by appointment of Philip the III is my great uncle," he continued with an aloof manner, referring to the family's patriarch.

"It is an honor," the lieutenant blubbered. "Your arrival has taken us by surprise," he said, now looking over the obviously British-built ship.

Turning sideways, hands clasp behind his back, François looked into the rigging and said, "Like my acquisition? Its previous master was most reluctant to turn it over to my command, but could not resist the offer . . . to hang around and contemplate his misfortune."

Despite the earlier admonition, Gibbs nearly choked at François' explanation, concealing a cough behind his hand.

"It looks to be a fine ship."

"Frankly, I like it much better than the Cordova del Sol," referring to a Spanish man-of-war rumored to be in the waters off Florida. "It is fast and not nearly so crowded. That is why I have selected this as my flagship."

"The Cordova del Sol? Is she coming here as well?"

"Yes, as soon as she rids the Floridas of the pesky French trying to settle there. That won't take long, then we shall regroup. I came ahead to prepare to clean up the pirate mess in these waters."

"We have received word that the pirate Hogshead has reappeared," the Lieutenant said with a hint of awe in his voice. "Shipping was reasonably safe during his unexplained absence. We had hoped the rumors of his death were true, but now that he is back . . ."

"Yes. That is precisely why I am here, because

he has returned from the dead. However, the situation is graver than you know. He has joined with another pirate known as the Dolphin."

"The Dolphin? I do not know that one."

"He terrorized the Mediterranean and African coasts. If the pirate Hogshead is in league with the devil, this Dolphin is worst. He is the devil incarnate."

The Lieutenant visibly shuttered before changing the subject. "Will you be coming ashore?"

"Not tonight. It is late and I am sure the Governor would like some time to prepare for my arrival."

"Most assuredly, yes."

"I will come ashore in the morning. I am not an early riser, though. Perhaps, say, eleven?"

"The morning fog will have lifted by then. The governor will be most excited to meet you. Until then, is there anything I can do for you?"

"Ah," François paused as if about to ask for something, then finished, "no. I shall personally take care of our needs later."

The lieutenant saluted crisply and left so anxious that he was easily heard commanding the oarsmen to stoke faster to get back with the news that a very important person had just arrived.

"Cap'n?" Gibbs said softly, clearing his throat. "Jist how far ye be takin' this charade?"

"About as far as that Brigantine," François replied, nodding toward a huge ship at anchor one-hundred Toise to the left of their bow, its lantern light slowly being enveloped by fog.

"And jist what could be of importance about that ship?" he continued to query; referring to the fact the ship was riding high.

"We shall see when we get there. Prepare a boarding party."

"Aye, aye, Cap'n," Gibbs responded, still baffled,

and then paused before leaving. "Dolphin? That be a good name for ye." He wondered about the young man being the devil incarnate, though. That might be stretching things a bit far.

As soon as the lieutenant was away, Francois left the Raven to Gibbs and lead three longboats through the now dense fog toward the Brigantine. At the Jacob's Ladder, he climbed ahead of the men up to the amidships rail. Following instructions, all stayed out of sight as he, Mendoza, and Henry stepped onto the deck. Instantly a guard challenged their arrival.

"Who is in charge?" François snapped in Spanish.

"Sargent Vega," the young soldier replied holding his rifle on them as two more soldiers hurried to his side.

"Please advise Sargent Vega that Capitán Francisco Meridiano de Ortega Guzman of his Majesty Philip's warship Raven has come aboard."

"Si, capitán," the boy croaked, sprinting off to return shortly with an overweight man whose tunic was partially unbuttoned and grease from something still being chewed shining around his thick lips. He stopped, went ridged, and saluted as soon as he came into the dim light.

"I am sorry, Capitán. There is no one aboard to receive you. Capitán Ruiz and all officers are in town."

"Is this all that is aboard then?"

"Si, Capitán."

"Good. Then you will kindly lay your weapons upon the deck," François said politely drawing a double-barreled pistol from his waistband and laying it on the tip of the sergeant's nose. At that instant, his men swarmed aboard.

"Take the sergeant and his men below. Courteously. Be mindful of their needs."

"Cap'n, the harbor patrol is coming," Henry whispered.

"Do not answer. Let them come aboard."

When the patrol sergeant's head peeked over the gunwale, he became angry. The ship's guard were standing toward the back of the main deck, laughing. They made him remove from a comfortable seat and climb the ladder to find them too busy telling jokes.

"Who is in command?" he shouted while stomping toward them.

François turned slowly so that his uniform was plainly visible. The sergeant went ridged, offering a frozen salute.

"I believe that I am, Sergeant. How many more ships do you have to inspect?"

"Two, Capitan."

"I am afraid the Lieutenant that greeted us earlier forgot to give the password so they will not know it."

"The hale is, the King is in good spirits. The return is, He is with the Queen."

"That is rather crude."

"A-a-a, yes, but I do not made these."

"No matter. Mr. Mendoza, pleases relieve these gentlemen of their uniforms and allow them to join the others below. Pablo, Reyes, and Corvalis will put them on. Corvalis once served in the Spanish navy, they shall finish their rounds and return so nothing will seem out of order. Henry, signal the *Raven* to extinguish her lights and come alongside."

"Aye, aye, Cap'n," they responded, and then Mendoza asked, "What exactly do we need from this ship, Capitan?"

"You will notice, Sr. Mendoza, this is a new ship. So are those guns. Have the men make ready eight barrels. Barrels only. When the Raven comes alongside, swing them over . . . carefully and quietly. After taking sail, we will put two at the bow forward either side of the bowsprit, and two on the poop. They shall serve as our chasers and followers. Place two each side amidships. We will also need appropriate shot and more powder. And Sr. Mendoza . . ."

"Aye, Cap'n?"

"Quietly, please."

"Aye, aye, Cap'n," his sailing master beamed as he spurred the men to silent action. "I would like to see their faces when they wake in the morning and find what happened."

"We all would. However, that is only a few hours away and that interesting response must occur some distance behind us. No lights so they can't see the direction we leave."

"Aye, and what direction shall that be?"

"North until out of sight of land then south-west."

As Mendoza went about supervising the transfer, he saw François speak to Henry who in turn went below with Marty and two of the crew. He was aware they transferred something other than shot and powder, but was too busy to tell exactly what.

A sliver of light was just cracking the blackness along the eastern horizon as the *Raven* sailed from Puerto Plata.

Even at that early hour, François wasted no time. Under full sail the *Raven* drove into a brightening, clear, blue sky while the boarding and transfer crew slept. Those who had not been involved spent the day placing the guns. Morale was high. Their captain had taken them into the jaws of the enemy, stolen some of their teeth right from under their nose, and left unmolested. The Spanish prisoners, bound hand and foot, sat in a longboat idly bobbing next to the top ten feet of mast of the once new ship now sailing the bottom of the harbor.

At four bells of the forenoon watch François ordered a change in direction to west by southwest returning to the coast of Hispaniola. As the second dog-watch crew came on deck, land was sighted.

Slipping into the well-protected and uninhabited Chouchou Bay, they anchored off the arcing strip of sandy beach on Hispaniola's northwest coast. The next morning he selected a target on the beach, a particularly large tree standing above all the rest. It was a delightful sound when the first cannon unleashed its deep-throated roar, as pleasing as any siren's song. Maggie laid the shot within fifteen feet of the target. Before allowing another round, François checked with Masseur Girard, the carpenter.

"No problem, Cap'n. She's a strong ship."

The Raven was slightly smaller than Chudleigh's frigate, but earlier modifications had provided an unusual complement of thirty-two, six-pound cannons on two decks weighing twelve-hundred pounds each. The new acquisitions were capable of propelling a three-inch, nine-pound ball with sufficient force to penetrate two feet of oak at 1500 Toise. The usual weight for a gun this size was twenty-four hundred pounds, but not in this case. New metallurgy had trimmed each gun's weight to not much heavier than that of a six.

The first shot impressed Harvey and the crew, but when Maggie's gun crew laid a second shot even closer to the target, they were astounded. When she lay a third ball in the same area, they were in disbelief. Such accuracy at such an extreme range was unheard of.

"The Spaniards apparently learned of a Scot forced to flee his homeland who was experimenting with a different approach to making cannons. There is a groove inside the barrel," François explained. "Using a more accurately formed ball, he was able to achieve a snugger fit. That causes the ball to rotate, which is supposed to improve accuracy. Obviously, it works.

"The English learned of his work and sent an army detachment to take him to London. Not having sworn allegiance to England, they labeled him an outlaw with plans to steal his technique. The Spanish spy told him of their approach. Persuading him to leave was not difficult.

"The spy said a ship would take him to Sweden, but instead went to Cuba where he built enough of these for three Brigantines. The three ships are undergoing sea trials and training before they are unleashed upon the French and English . . . and the brethren.

"However, there is more. A German made some modifications to the powder and shot which came into French hands. They sent a shipment to the Caribbean, but the Spaniards captured it. Okay, Mr. Yates, show them the other surprise."

Opening a box next to the new cannon, he removed a cylinder and shoved it down the barrel; the gun crew set the cannon into position and fired. All eyes were on the target. On impact, the shell exploded, but as Gibbs turned to express his delight, the cannon fired a second time followed by a second explosion ashore. Before they could gather themselves together again a third round fired.

"What the . . .?" Harvey's expression of shock spoke for everyone.

Yates stepped up holding one of the cylinders.

"As you see, the German mated the ball to a powder charge. All one needs do is swab the barrel and ram a new round down the barrel, cutting reload time nearly in half."

"But, how'd she light the fuse on the ball?"

"There is no need to light a fuse separately. The ignition of the main powder charge does that. The ball being hollow and filled with powder breaks upon impact and explodes, or it lies dormant until the fuse reaches the powder."

"What of the Scot? He will just build replacements," Gibbs said.

"That will be a bit difficult. The good man unfortunately died when an explosion destroyed the foundry. The Spaniards are attempting to duplicate his work, but all the drawings went up in smoke with him. I understand a son in Scotland knows the technique, but he is in Sweden, sent ahead by his father before betrayal by the Spaniards."

Under Yates' and Maggie's tutelage, the gun crews peppered the island to improve their fire and reload efficiency. Using competition, Yates spurred them to cut the time between discharges on the old cannons to one minute and thirty seconds. That was as good as the best English man-of-war. Those using the new cannons reloaded in under a minute. Other crewmen worked with François to improve their rifle marksmanship, sharpshooters singled out as a unit. Maggie worked with others on their swordsmanship.

The following day François took his riflemen ashore to begin instruction in rank firing like the professional armies. As dark closed out the fourth day, everything had been stowed allowing a tired, but happy crew to dine and make merry with an extra ration of rum. As Gibbs patted his lips with a napkin, he had to admit having a woman like Maggie aboard to cook made pirating a sight better. The following morning the *Raven* was under sail heading west as if bound for Tortuga.

An hour under sail Henry cried out from the crow's nest. "Sail ho off the port bow. A Spanish sloop turnin' this way."

As the two ships bore down on one another it was obvious the Spaniard meant trouble.

"Alright, Henry. Come on down. I've need of ye," Yates called up to the boy.

"Maggie, you and Henry take the chasers. Henry below deck, Maggie topside," Yates said. They were gun captains for those cannons.

"Mr. Gibbs, take charge of the ship," François said. "I will lead any boarding party. Señor Mendoza, take charge of the riflemen."

At 1500 Toise, François gave the order. The two topside chasers fired. He patiently waited for the smoke to clear so to assess the effect. Both balls struck home. Then Henry's cannons fired. One appeared to hit. The other sent up a tall column of water short of its target. A second round from each caused the sloop to break off.

"Three points starboard," François said calmly to the helmsman.

The Raven's bow turned to the right aligning the port guns. As soon as they had a target both decks released a rolling discharge. The combination of ball and canister devastated the small vessel. Its mainsail snapped in half as the whole of the ship seemed to shudder. By order, the new guns held fire until the older ones were ready. A minute and a half latter a second round of shot struck the ship, but that was unnecessary as it was already listing badly preparatory to sinking.

"Survivors?" Gibbs asked.

"Set out two longboats, Mr. Lowrey," François replied. "They already have two in the water. Find out what they were doing, and then we'll tow them close to shore, and drop them off. After that, resume our course through Tortue Straits."

"We putting in at Tortuga?" Gibbs asked.

"No," François answered, going to his cabin.

With survivors in tow, the *Raven* headed for land six leagues distant. As the crew busied securing the ship, Gibbs came into the captain's quarters.

"The Spaniard was bound for Puerto Plata carrying a secret message from Havana. Unfortunately, the captain and first officer got killed. If it were written, it's being read by Davy Jones. No one else was told of it."

Rounding the western end of Hispaniola once again, the *Raven* retraced the route when it first began the cruise until coming within sight of Isle de la Gonáve in the gaping mouth of Hispaniola's western gulf. When another ship was sighted early the next morning the crew was eager to try out their skills once again.

"Set a course to intercept," François directed Mr. Mendoza as the other ship turned toward them as well.

Chaptder 22

† The Baracoa Raid †

"It's the *Angelina*," Marty shouted from atop the forecastle as he lowered his spyglass.

"How'd he know . . .?" Gibbs said.

"We planned to meet here," François replied.

Several hours later as the two ships ran side-by-side Shaver called out, "Grab a line and swing o'r. Well, what were ye about, boy?" Shaver rumbled as François landed nimbly onto the *Angelina*'s worn deck. "The bloody Spaniards be more upset than a pack of penguins watchin' a shark cruisin' off shore. Seems someone slipped into one of their ports, rode alongside a new war ship, and removed some cannon, then disappeared."

"And those new ships sink really well, too," François answered.

"That were you! That be one of the most fool-hardy stunts I 'er 'eard," Shaver began as if to chastise, then grinned. "Come across a sloop makin' fer Florida outa San Felipe. They be in a uproar fer sure. Sayin' it jist weren't natural. That black ship's Cap'n must be in league with the devil. The governor were sendin' fer that big, fancy warship of their'n to come make things right."

"What did you do with the sloop?"

"I don't need no stinkin' Spanish sloop. Weren't worth the price o' powder nor ball to blow her up. The only thing keepin' her tagether were its maggots holdin' hands. Should've been scrapped long ago."

"And the crew?"

"Now, I ain't bloodthirsty, boy. I let 'em start swimin' ta shore before scuttlin' it, but ye keep doin' things like that'll be givin' piratin' a new name in these waters."

François just smiled and tipped a two finger salute coupled with a slight bow. "For someone who wouldn't make a pirate?"

"Ye jist ain't gonna let me forget that, are ye? No matter. Come ta me cabin. We got affairs ta discuss."

Inside, Shaver's steward offered each a tankard, one containing rum, and the other wine.

"How be that ship of yern? All right? No . . . strange noises and alike?"

"The Raven is a fine ship. Tight as a new casket, well balanced and responsive. No problems, and no unusual noises."

"Humph. Well, now about that treasure shipment we discussed a while back. Seems the Spaniards be makin' a change in the route accordin' ta the sloop's captain. Right chatty fella before I . . . anyways, after the fleet leaves Panama they normally pass along the southern side of Cuba and meet up with the Tierra Firma Squadron at Havana," Shaver explained while tracing the route on a chart with a gnarled finger. "Word is they be stoppin' at Santo Domingo fer some reason or other, then west along the south coast of Hispaniola. But this where the Spaniards be gettin' tricky. Instead of followin' along the south coast of Cuba as usual, they figure ta slip through the Windward Passage ta Baracoa, then along the north side ta Havana. I figure ta intercept them 'ere," he said, stabbing the crooked digit between Hispaniola's grand peninsula and Navassa Island .

"How many ships?"

"Two plus escort."

"How soon?"

"When the big storms be done. A month."

"Good, that gives me some time."

"Fer what?"

"These new nines are much lighter. I'd like to acquire a couple more. The ship we raided was part of three new ones sent to these waters to control pirates. They're not doing a very good job. I hear tell another is at Baracoa."

"You wouldn't! Not twice!"

"They'd never expect it twice."

"Yer a devil alright. Ye say nine pounders?" Shaver asked, stroking his beard.

"Aye. And more accurate than what anyone else has," François replied and then explained.

"I could use a couple of those."

"I'll meet you in two weeks. Let's say in this bay off the end of the north peninsula."

"Columbus' Bay," Shaver identified the place. "That be where he arrived in ninty-two and lost the Santa Maria."

The land jutted out into the ocean and curved

slightly inward like a crab's pincers creating a nice harbor three-quarters of a mile wide and a half mile long.

"Good harbor. There be a native Taínos village near the ruins of Columbus' La Navidad. Also a small garrison of French there, though the Spaniards don't know of it."

"What have you done to the French?"

"Nothin', really. Their ships don't usually 'ave much exceptin' trade goods. I be on good terms with 'em, generally, and those native girls are bit o' fun."

"Sounds like a good place to have friends."

"Ye be suggestin' I don't go upsettin' things."

"Always good to have a safe harbor. Well, I'll be off to stir a hornets nest."

"That it be. That it be."

Shaver shook his head while watching his young protégé nimbly swing back to the *Raven* where he charted a course for Baracoa on the southern tip of the Cuban across the Windward Passage from where they were. However, he wasn't about to enter the small, confined bay without more information.

Pushed by a strong westerly, the *Raven* sped across the Passage at a crisp seven knots so that by first light of morning her helmsman eased the ship into the sweeping, sandy bay near the little fishing village of Cayo Güin well north of their target. As Gibbs waited impatiently in the long, gently curved cove, François, Maggie, and Henry went ashore.

The native village lay on a flat plain a half mile inland between swamp and dense rain forest. Making friends with the villagers was not difficult as they shared a mutual dislike for Spanish politics. Not only did they get directions to Baracoa, but the services of a guide about Henry's age. To create less suspicion, François purchased peasant clothes to facilitate blending in with the populace consisting of a cotton shirt and trousers for him and Henry, and a cotton dress for Maggie. He fell in love with the sandals, a reminder of home. Considering the heat, they would be more practical to travel in as well.

Leaving the relatively open area around the village, their guide took them into the forest. A few steps in felt as if swallowed by some giant creature. Almost as quickly, the heat and humidity had their clothes drenched with perspiration. The trail, not much thicker than a halyard, was well defined as it drove through the thick growth of palm, mahogany and a hundred other varieties. Two miles from the village, they picked up a small stream and followed it down a steep gorge where it joined the Toa River.

Despite being a narrow section of river, it still looked dauntingly wide. Using a rope spanned across, François pulled a small canoe to the opposite bank. Once across, they took time to refresh themselves in the cool but muddy water before re-entering the forest and a hike of just under one league around the base of el Yunque, a flat top sentinel rising over Baracoa's north side.

By noon, they reached the second river, Rio Duaba. There hadn't been rain for several weeks so crossing was mostly navigating through the rounded boulders about the size of large melons. François' companions were glad to hear it was only a half league to the last river crossing, Rio Joa, and their destination. At least a suspension bridge was available according to their guide.

Unaccustomed to long hikes, Maggie and Henry considered the three leagues an eternity, while it seemed as nothing to François who hiked El Hierro regularly. It was humidity that sapped his strength.

While Baracoa straddled the river, what interested François most lay on the other side of the deep, muddy water coarse. True to their guide's knowledge, a suspended footbridge crossed the river; unfortunately, it was damaged during the monsoon season and still under repair. A fisherman living by the river eagerly volunteered to boat them across—for a fee. This obviously had become the man's source of hard cash and not the myriad of chickens clucking about. Truth be known, he wasn't anxious to encourage repairs, either.

This bay was the first landfall Columbus made on the island and fell in love with the region's beauty. Cut off from the rest of the country by the rugged mountains of Cuba's interior, Baracoa was isolated, but that actually lent to its prosperity. Illicit trade with both the French and English flourished so François wasn't surprised to see vessels from all three countries as well as the ever-present Dutch. However, his interest was in a specific Spanish vessel at anchor close to El Castillo, the intimidating fort spread upon a hill overlooking the bay and the town hugging the near-circular harbor.

Once across the river the travelers passed women doing laundry along the banks and entered a jungle of huts. Strolling into town the trio easily blended into the populace. As they passed a food vendor Henry's stomach issued a loud protest.

"I think we better buy the boy food or they think a bear wondered into town," Maggie suggested.

"I was thinking the same thing. My gut's been scratching my backbone for the last couple hours as well," François answered.

Henry always seemed to be hungry and ate twice what they did, drawing a wry remark from Maggie. "That boy never shows much for all he eats."

Wandering past more food vendors and shops, François kept an eye on the Spanish Brigantine at anchor toward the middle of the bay. At appropriate times, he made passing remarks to locals about the ship, people who would know about it. As night began to descend, he decided not to negotiate the trail back to the *Raven* in the dark. To maintain appearances, he secured lodging for the night in a stable loft, returning to the *Raven* the following afternoon.

Once back aboard, he gathered the officers and lay out a plan, then waited for dusk before moving out. As el Yunque cast a long, dark finger over the ocean, the land slipped into darkness, the town marked by dots of yellowish lights. Displaying a bright blue flag with the white Cross of Burgundy, popular among Spain's merchants, the *Raven* approached the mouth of the harbor as a fog began spreading its blanket over the area. Again, their timing was perfect. Those on El Castillo's ramparts watching incoming ships understood a prudent captain would wait until morning before entering the harbor.

"Have Mr. Lowery take in the sails and drop anchor. We'll lay to here for a time."

Gibbs chewed on his lower lip. "This be the most insane thing I've 'er done in thirty years at sea, other than almost gettin' married."

An hour later three longboats with muffled oars left the *Raven,* passing through the narrow neck of water into the harbor. There seemed to be no world as they glided over the glassy surface, the eerie silence seeming to amplify the gentle slap of waves on the bow. Hulking merchant ships loomed ominously then disappeared. Mendoza wondered how his capitán knew to find their quarry, when he could barely see the other boats, until coming alongside the new ship. Hoisting themselves onto the main deck, François lead the assault crew aft. From his casual inquiries, he had learned that only a skeleton guard was aboard which was quietly and efficiently neutralized, and bound. As one group worked among the decks to be certain all on board were accounted for, the others set about their assigned tasks.

Half of the forty crew brought aboard scurried into the rigging to release sails when needed while others unplugged and primed some of the main deck cannon. François took upon himself the task of slicing through the heavy anchor rope while Henry made tow ropes ready. Once free, he gave the signal for the six rowers in each of the longboats to begin turning the bow seaward. Crandal, a gunners mate, stopped François who was making his way aft to pilot the ship.

"Cap'n," he whispered excitedly, "These guns have a better mechanism to change elevation."

"If you can raise them quietly, target the fortress, but that small garrison off the port side will be a bigger problem."

"Aye. We're ready for them."

François watched the compass by the big ship's wheel until it pointed easterly toward the entrance. With a wave, crewmen stationed along the length of the ship passed the silent command. The men in the longboats dipped the blades of their oars into the water to begin a silent run for open water. François would have liked to spread a bit of canvas to assist, but the wind was too variable, which would cause them to flap and create noise.

Now every man's heart beat strong as the ship inched through the harbor. Aside from detection by sentries on land, they had to thread their way passed other ships. To avoid a collision, he set a skiff ahead of the longboats to plot a clear course, using a small lantern as a guide. Maggie, who was in charge of the rear guns, nervously rechecked each piece, hoping to avoid the worst. It happened.

As the ship neared the entrance and open water, a muffled thud echoed across the bay followed by a flare casting an instant, eerie, red light over the harbor.

The small garrison on the south shore must have heard something to arouse suspicion. Now the whole island knew what was happening. The fog had lifted some. As the first flare died a second filled the night with its reddish, moon-like light and the garrison's cannon began targeting the tow boats.

François shouted since there was no longer any need of secrecy. "Silence those cannon, Mr. Crandal!"

The men sprang to action as cannon on the main deck opened fire. From the spacing François could tell the crews were firing only as a target came to bear. He was impressed as the first seven shots obliterated the garrison. They were obviously using canister to spray the area like a blunderbuss. That caused secondary explosions from their powder. Contending with the fortress' big guns was another issue. The pirates were severely hampered by the lack of gun crews for all the weapons, answering best they could, until from the blackness outside the harbor the *Raven*'s guns began to assault the fortress.

"Give me sail!" François directed, "and pickup the tow crews up on our port side."

With the fort to their rear, the main guns were unable to target it, so that they could only answer the fortress guns with their four followers. Fortunately, the big, land-based guns were old which meant they just lobbed shells in their general direction, hoping for a hit while avoiding innocent ships moored in the bay. Had the Spaniards known it was their own, prized warship, they probably would have stopped shooting altogether. Few shots came close although one of the abandoned longboats disintegrated from a direct hit. Some shrapnel ripped through the rigging killing one crewmen and injuring three others, but the sails continued to unfurl so that the big ship gained speed as it put the harbor behind.

"Cap'n, there be a Corsair makin' sail," Mendoza warned.

François turned to see the ship illuminated by yellow fires from the destroyed shore battery and more red flares from the fort. It looked like a ghost moving between the other ships. At near full sail the purloined Brigantine plowed through the remainder of the harbor as if a sluggish arrow thrown from a bow.

Maggie's four aft guns targeted the corsair. As it entered the harbor's narrow throat the *Raven* turned its cannon on it, as well. They were less than 250 Toise apart. The first volley crumpled the Spaniard's masts as fires broke out followed by a horrible explosion that seem to lift it out of the water.

"Got their powder," Mendoza shouted. "That'll block the channel."

"We're still not clear," François warned as another ship charged the entrance intent on pushing its way through.

"Mr. Crandal, stop that ship!" François called from the wheel as he turned to present the port side guns.

The deck guns began pummeling the attacker. The *Raven*'s guns poured out chain, canister, and ball, catching the brig in a brutal crossfire, but it looked like it would make open water until the guns below decks belched red flame and smoke one by one. Whoever was below had deployed some of those guns for a try. The brig's captain tried valiantly to push pass the burning wreckage blocking his exit, but the firepower of the two ships cut its sails and masts to ribbons. It stalled and caught fire as the two rogue ships disappeared into a fog bank.

"Signal Mr. Gibbs to follow," François called out. "Mendoza, take the wheel and bear 170 degrees. Mr. Lowery, give me all the sail you can." He then turned to

Maggie who was helping direct the gunnery crews to secure the cannon and clean up.

"Fine job, men," François complimented the crew. "Mr. Crandal, thank those men below . . ." He didn't finish as Henry and ten crewmen appeared up the hatch. "Don't tell me he was . . ."

"Aye, that be him," Maggie said.

François shook his head slowly then smiled.

"Henry," he called out in a booming voice that commanded attention even on the forecastle.

"Aye, Cap'n?"

"Fine job. Fine job indeed. You have learned your gunnery lessons well."

"Thank ye, Cap'n," the boy called back beaming broadly. "That mean I don't 'ave to be cabin boy no more?"

François just shook his head from side to side slowly as he smiled. "No, but you can add gunner's mate to your duties. Mr. Crandal, young Henry will be apprenticed to Mr. Yates and you."

"Aye, Cap'n," he replied tousling the boy's long, unruly hair as the two immediately went to work caring for the powder, shot, and guns. During a fight Henry's good eye would be useful sighting their target, but François wasn't ready to turn all of the boy's education over to someone else.

Chapter 23

† The Treasure Fleet †

(D)uring the early afternoon a week following the raid on Baracoa, the *Angelina* lay off the white beach of La Navidad bobbing gently within the quiet bay. Shaver had just stumbled out of his cabin into the glaring sunlight restarting the pounding in his head, the result of too much rum the night before. After a week of indulging in all the pleasures offered by the Taínos and mestizos, he was feeling the need to have a salt wind in his face.

The likelihood that English or Spanish would venture into the sheltered bay was as remote as finding a mermaid sitting on the bowsprit. That's why he decided to take the opportunity to have the boat's bottom scraped and resealed.

Sailing up the narrow side bay, he had the cannon off-loaded with sufficient powder and shot and the *Angelina* run up on the beach at high tide. As the water retreated, she lay gently over onto one side. Not being a trusting soul, half the men stood sentry with the off-loaded cannon while the other half made short-order of the job so that the exposed hull was almost like new. Then to be fair, the crews exchanged places and the other side was careened.

Job completed, he returned to anchor off the village, the cause of last night's celebration. Stepping onto the deck the bright light blinded him. Covering his eyes with one weathered hand, he did an abrupt about face and retreat to the darkness of his cabin for another swallow or two of rum. That's when the hatchet-pounding headache was further irritated by the peace-shattering cry from above as if the main mast had just cracked.

"Two ships comin' in. One's the *Raven*, the other looks to be a Spanish warship."

The old pirate's heart skipped a beat. Either the kid actually pulled off the fool-hearty stunt or he was about to take on two heavily armed ships and no maneuvering room to make a clean run for it. With the efficiency taught by his protégé, the *Angelina*'s crew quickly prepared for action, but as the *Raven* approached, its sails lowered to slow down. The Spaniard followed suite. When Shaver saw her smiling captain on the forecastle waiving, he was beside himself. The boy had not just purloined cannon off a Spanish warship, "The brat's stole the whole bloody ship!" With the prize safely anchored in the bay and the *Raven* and *Angelina* lashed together, François swung over.

"I thought ye jist be gettin' guns. So ye had to bring the whole bloomin ship?" Shaver chastised lightly as he watched the first of the nines made ready for hoisting aboard his ship. "Any trouble?"

"A little," François said, tantalizingly vague.

"And . . .?"

"Those guns are really quite nice. Had a Corsair give chase so we blocked the channel."

"And what did ye use to block the channel?"

"The Corsair," François responded casually, "and a Brigantine. Look at these gun carriages. They have a new mechanism to more easily change elevation."

Once the transfer was complete, they hauled the *Raven* closed to shore at high tide. When she lay over, they began careening. There were no bad timbers to replace so the work went quickly. With that accomplished, the hull was covered with an ointment of sulfur, tar, and tallow. Not a pleasant chore, but necessary. It was speed which often kept a pirate ahead of warships and overtake the merchants.

Once completed, François had Mr. Yates replaced the remaining small cannon with the new nines giving the *Raven* an unprecedented thirty-eight guns on two decks, more than doubling the usual number. Meanwhile, Henry and Marty took charge of installing the smaller, swivel guns by adding brackets fore and aft on either side rail.

"Not plann' ta carry much booty," Shaver commented as his crew replaced cannon as well.

"Not being much of a pirate, I am not planning to shop for common merchandise."

"A dog with a bone," Shaver grumbled as he stomped away and shaking his mane. "A dog with a bone."

While this went on, Lowery set to replacing the original sails and modify the rigging by adding trysails, triangular-shaped canvas, between the *Raven*'s two masts of square sails.

"I seen this in England just before signing on with the captain," Lowery said. "They were trying them out and I could see they helped in light, quartering winds and allowed the ship to move about much better."

"Where'd you get the new canvas?" François asked.

"Well, while you were busy acquiring those guns an' all at Puerto Plata, young Henry and me found these new sails in their stores and brought them aboard."

"Black?"

"We been dyin' them for weeks. Thought it'd add a special touch to the *Raven*. Never seen a *Raven* with white feathers," Lowery said.

"Neither have I," François agreed. "They do lend our ship a sinister appearance."

"All pirates 'ave somethin' identifin' 'em," Henry said. "Black sails will be yer mark."

"Us," François corrected. "It will be our mark. The Raven and its crew are one."

As the crew continued stripping the prize of its finery down to the dinnerware, the two captains considered adding the ship to their fleet. However, that would require more men than they could spare or desired to recruit and train. Although a new ship, Shaver didn't like it, opting to keeping the *Angelina*.

"Grown kinda fond of the 'ol whore," he said during more lucid moments between bouts with rum to sooth the pain in his leg.

Overall, the raid on Baracoa had been a profitable venture in that the two pirate ships became the heaviest armed of their kind. A menacing tandem on any ocean, they were rivaled only by war ships and maybe those merchantmen escorted under Lord Douglass' pennant.

Just to tidy things up, the purloined Spaniard, now equipped with the old guns from the two pirate ships, was sailed around the peninsula to Tortuga for ransoming back to the Spanish for a "fair" price. That transaction they left in the hands of one of Shaver's old cronies who slid about the New World as broker for anyone with goods to sell, and buyers looking for the perfect gift.

After completing the arrangement, the two captains tacked into the Windward Passage and across the mouth of Gonave Gulf. Turning east around the southern peninsula, they followed the coastline, passing Port-Salut some distance out to sea so as not to attract attention. Swinging back toward land, they were approaching Ile a Vache near dusk when the cry, 'Sail, ho!' rang out. François glanced up at the lookout who was pointing due west.

Unable to see anything from the deck he shimmied aloft, curling an arm around a line to peer through a fancy, brass spyglass purloined from the stolen ship. Silhouetted against the last golden arc of sun, the Spanish treasure fleet was five leagues further west than either captain had guessed, and ahead of schedule. Apparently blown further from land than intended, their bows were now pointed toward the passage.

From the information Shaver gathered, their intention was to hug the Hispaniola coast, and then sail through the Passage, around the east end of Cuba, and on to Havana. That was to avoid Trinidad, another uncontrolled pirate's haven, and certain ambush.

"Take us hard to starboard bearing west by northwest Njiru," François shouted down to the African helmsman who joined them at Tortuga.

It wasn't necessary to alert now Admiral Shaver—with two ships under his command he rightfully promoted himself—as the *Angelina* was already turning. The problem was that the wind helping to speed the treasure fleet toward the passage was not friendly to them. François feared they might not be able to intercept the ships as the same wind was like a big hand holding them back. The *Angelina* didn't fare well against such winds. On the other hand, the trysails helped the *Raven* move ahead.

Sliding down a rope back to the deck he called out, "Mr. Lowery, all the speed you can."

The chase was on and so was nightfall. The two Spanish galleons, despite wallowing low in the water, made good speed as darkness descended. With all lights extinguished except what the sailing master on the *Angelina* could see, François took their bearings before retreating into his cabin to hover over the charts and make some quick calculations.

Another gift from the Spanish warship was a set of new Portuguese charts and several new, brass compasses. Giving course directions to the night watch with instructions to listen close that they may be drifting close to shore, there wasn't anything left to do but retire to his cabin.

Sleep was impossible as the excitement of the morrow crept over him, so François found himself repeatedly venturing on deck. By midnight, he began to see the Spaniards' lights without climbing the mast and was thankful for having skinned the speed-reducing barnacles from the *Angelina*'s hull so to keep up. Using a single, directional lamp they kept sight of one another to avoid colliding, but with the dawn their presence became known.

The galleon had developed from modifications to Carracks, built for carrying cargo on the open ocean, but heavily laden as these were, speed and maneuverability was compromised. That necessitated an escort of five sloops. Two were the larger, reddish Jamaican type and three slightly smaller common variety, none of which carried more than fourteen cannon. However, they were dangerous and effective escorts. Their job was to dissuade attacks by quick response.

"Prepare for action, Mr. Gibbs," François said as casually as if speaking to a cabbie going to a court ball.

"Cap'n Dolphin," Henry said as he approached François who was standing near the helm. "Should we show our colors?"

Studying the Spanish fleet through the spyglass as he said, "That would be appropriate, Henry. A piece of black cloth, or whatever might be aboard will do."

One of the first acts the Raven's crew did when François came aboard in Tortuga was throw the former captain's pennant overboard. After studying the ships, he put the spyglass down to speak to Gibbs, surprised to see many of the crew looking aloft. Turning, he looked up.

"Now where did that come from?

"Maggie and the sail maker did it. Said ye needed somethin' so folk know who they be dealin' with," Henry answered, a prideful tone in his high voice.

From the top of the main mast, a large, black ensign stretched before the wind. Clearly evident was a dolphin leaping over a skull, the flag of the pirate Dolphin.

Now having advantage of the same wind, the *Raven* sliced through the swells as if a demon through a crowded street. The Admiral was having a tougher time. The *Angelina* was a good ship, but its helmsman did not have had the delicate touch or the extra sails to coax every breathe of wind to their use so the *Raven* was first to overtake the trailing galleon—a lumbering behemoth. The *Maria del Crispin* also had more guns than a porcupine had quills, however the *Raven* had to first attend with two sloops charging ahead of the pack to intercept.

Aboard the treasure ship the captain and crew must have gloated at the impending demise of the pirate ship, until it opened fire at more than 1000 Toise. The first sloop's sails and mast were hit leaving it crippled and helpless. The second defender literally disintegrated in a shower of pieces when its powder exploded. To the Spaniards' horror, two defenders had been swept aside as easily as flicking a cockroach off dinner. A third sloop, some distance away, fared no better as the *Raven*'s long reach peppered it unmercifully with a rolling fusillade. As Shaver caught up, he unleashed a broadside on the fourth ship. The Jamaican list badly, capsized, and sank in minutes. Having no death wish, the fifth sloop turned tail to flee with the other galleon.

As the *Raven* closed to within 750 Toise of the *Maria del Crispin* the Spanish captain apparently expected the pirate to be stupid enough to run up for a broadside, but at the proper moment Francois nodded to Henry who was standing next to the chasers. Now began the artillery ballet.

Henry waited a second for the *Raven*'s bow to lift into the right position before touching the hole that fired the charge. With a hissing squeal, the big gun spat a whitish-gray cloud and thundered backward from the recoil, but Henry had already jumped to the second gun and fired. The two canons below took their cue to join the overture.

As the crews began their reload, Henry stood with hands on the rail to watch. His first shot struck toward the forward waterline of the massive hull sending up a towering column of white water. The second smashed into the towering rear castle. The other balls burrowed through the ship's timbers, each exploding after a delay. With this information Henry turned to the first gun's powder monkey and said something in his ear to which the boy ran below as Henry took aim. Francois was well pleased. The crews had reloaded in one minute.

A second volley was a repeat of the first except Henry kept the balls above the waterline. The gun crew swung into their practiced dance. No sooner had the gun carriage been stopped in its retreat than a wet swab was run down to dampen any sparks. Next, the powder cartridge and shot were shoved down the bore. As this happened the prime was set and the gun run forward. Henry stepped up, checked the aim, and touched the hole. With the third discharge, the Dolphin could hear a minute difference in sound from the guns below. They had changed from ball to canister.

Though grievous to the Spaniard, the deadly, sail-ripping concoction was more like the stings of a wasp upon an elephant, something it would not long tolerate, and it was for that moment François watched. When the lumbering giant began a right turn to present its guns, he was ready."

"Mr. Njiru, to port if you will."

It was during this prelude François realized to whom he paid allegiance. First was Mariah; however she and he had mistakenly thought the second to be the sea. It wasn't. When the smell of sulfur from the first shot wrapped about his body in a loving caress, he realized the siren that called and kept him from his family was the smell of gunpowder and attending thrill of battle.

The *Raven*'s sixteen starboard guns began their assault at 1500 Toise. They discharged a second volley before the Spaniard finally swung into position to answer. Her shot fell pitifully short as the sea erupted in foaming, white columns of water.

Now began the pirouette, a maneuver that

would become the Dolphin's signature of attack. As the starboard crews reloaded a second time François had the ship's bow brought around. The chasers once again fired, then the port guns had an opportunity to display their expertise. Two rounds and the *Raven* swung back allowing the guns to cool.

They barely came within effective range of the beast's guns when he sailed behind the Spaniard's stern rendering its main guns useless while continuing to pummel the cripple ship. Smoke began billowing from below decks, shredded sails flopped useless in the wind, and then Henry sent a round of chain that sheared the foremast like a scythe in a corn field.

François glanced at the *Angelina* which was now making strides to join the battle, before training his glass back on the galleon. More of the *Raven*'s guns used canister as well. It wasn't their intent to sink the ship, only cripple it into submission. Henry's chasers fired on the towering stern resulting in considerable damage, and then it became obvious the *del Crispin* lost steering. Shortly thereafter, they struck their flag signifying surrender resulting in a roaring cheer to spring from the *Raven*'s decks. They hadn't been touched during the entire encounter.

"Adm. Shaver can handle this one. Go for the other one," Francois said indicating a galleon making for the Cuban coast with the remaining guard ship. It had nearly a league on the Raven.

"Signal the Admiral to take the *del Crispin*," he said Gibbs.

Their new target was equally over-burdened and unwieldy in the rolling surf. The wind that had favored them at first now became an enemy, driving the hulking brute closer to the coastline. Even as the *Raven* raced after it the ship still had a sufficient lead to make François wonder if it were possible to catch it at all. He didn't desire its treasure as much as he wanted to prevent it and the remaining escort from rounding the point of land that would bring it to Baracoa and alert the garrison that would dispatch warships.

Lagging behind, the surviving escort knew it was out-matched, yet summoned the backbone to attempt interference, hopefully enough for the galleon to escape. Henry's chasers pummeled them unmercifully until it began listing badly, a prelude to capsizing. As for catching the treasure ship, it was going to be close as the Raven sprinted to within firing distance and encountered the same problem—a wind pushing them toward rock-strewn shoals along the coast. Suddenly the treasure ship lurched to port so severely Francois thought it would capsize, then righted, but not all the way.

"Mr. Lowery, take in sail."

The crew worked furiously hauling in the big, square sails, leaving the trysails for control. As the Raven slowed he called out, "Hard to starboard!"

Both men watched the galleon closely, and when she lurched they instinctively understood the danger. By reducing sail to just the s and tacking right, the *Raven* better handled the wind without being thrown over as they put away from land. The galleon, however, plowed into another submerged rock as its crew began to abandon ship. The first collision must have taken a sizable chunk from her bottom. Certainly, the second did as the ship rolled over and went down incredibly fast.

"Take us back to the first ship," François said sadly.

"What about the Spaniard's crew?' Henry asked, having come back to where François stood as he was ordered.

"They're not far from shore. Those who can

swim should make it ashore right enough. Fetch my navigation instruments."

Taking a reading, he noted a particular geographic landmark on the island, recording it and the coordinates in a small book. Handing the instrument to Henry he had him take a reading as well.

"Very good. That is very near what I obtained. Now, plot us a course back to that galleon and let us become wealthy," he said, tucking the notebook inside his coat and walking down to the main deck to congratulate the men and prepare them to board the Spaniard.

After plotting the course, Henry worked with Njiru, learning to steer as they returned towards the galleon floundering in the undulating swells. However, Henry took a moment to record the location of the treasure sunken ship, drawing a fine picture of the coastline at that spot.

"Looks to be the Admiral's gone aboard, Cap'n," Mr. Gibbs called from the bridge as François reappeared from below decks.

"Bring us alongside. I will join him. Mr. Gibbs, you have the *Raven*."

Swinging aboard the *del Crispin* François met up with Shaver who was having a meeting with the ship's captain and looking over the manifest.

"See ya lost yours. Too bad," Shaver said.

François just stared at him, refusing to take the bait.

"Oh, ye be no fun a'tall Cap'n Dolphin," he said and handed the manifest to him. "Cap'n Romero 'ere's got lots of fine merchandise aboard. The kind that glitters."

"Capitán Romero. Instruct your men to throw tow lines to both our vessels."

"And where we be takin' this fine ship ?"

"I prefer a more leisurely stroll through the cargo holds than having to hurry because of that storm building on the horizon and the Hag starts her laundry. We can let Capitan Romero and his men ashore on the south peninsula then proceed to a nice, quiet place to sort things out."

Shaver cast a glance at the western horizon and the cumulus clouds stacking up. "Sounds reasonable enough. Send over forty men ta join me and my crew. I'll stay aboard and see things stay peaceable like."

"And you will show Admiral Shaver where spare sails can be located," François said to Capt. Romero in fluent Spanish.

"Si." The captain was not happy, but compliant.

Shredded sails replaced, the storm passed to the north and aberrant winds abated enough to allow them to bringing the prize within a safe distance off the Hispaniola peninsula. At Shaver's command, the Spanish crew took to launches or swam for shore as they crossed over to the protection of La Navidad as more squalls passed to the north. There they were free to fill their holds to capacity, and the French garrison and natives to replenish both supplies and purse as well.

"I be of a mind ta put in at Trinidad. The old girl needs a bit of mendin'," Shaver proposed.

"I have something needing my attention."

"Like goin' home?"

"Not just yet. I'll meet you at Loro Placida in two weeks at which time we will discuss that issue."

"Mind tellin' what ye have in mind?"

"A little more pirating business to visit upon the Spaniards."

Shaver was not happy, but an accord was reached to meet at their secret base of operations.

"And what do ye suggest we do with that galleon?"

"What pirates do with excess treasure, Captain, bury it."

As the scuttled *Maria del Crispin* disappeared beneath the surface, a number of the crew approached Gibbs. In turn, he approached the captain.

"A moment of the Cap'n's time," meaning he had something important to discuss. "Some of the crew 'ave it in mind to return home. They be gone a long time, and now that they be rich, well . . ."

"I understand completely, Harvey. I am entertaining similar thoughts, however, we need to take a slight detour." Walking to the table François looked over several charts before pointing to the string of islands south of Hispaniola.

"Take us south by east."

"Where we be goin' Cap'n, if I may ask?"

"Barbuda. I have it on good account there would be something suitable there for the men to return home in."

"Again?"

"We've not shopped that far south so they would not expect our visit. That third ship possess a serious threat to the brethren. I want it removed. Besides, I made a promise to a young Scot in Tortuga."

"Aye, Cap'n. I'll tell the men."

Chapter 24

† Room of Toys †

Each of the four oars silently dug deep into the black water propelling the longboat ghost-like through the fog. François' heart pound within his breast, excitement growing as each stroke brought the pirates closer to the impending attack. Priding himself on being independent, fiercely so, a slave to neither man nor the elements, in these ultra-quiet moments as the bow sliced toward the objective, he knew this was not true. He was enslaved.

The sea was neither his master nor mistress many sailors used as an excuse. The true inducement was exactly this—the excitement and attending fear filling every pore with a prickling sensation. That addictive force stealthily seduced and chained him to the present course, keeping him away from Mariah, the children, and home. That, and a promise made to a young man whose father the Spaniards forced to build cannon for three ships.

Somewhere ahead they heard a patrol checking each ship laid up in the harbor. If the challenge went unanswered or the incorrect password given they went aboard to have a word with the watch. By the way the fog distorted sound, locating the patrol's location was difficult until realizing it was hailing a hulking, Portuguese galleon just ahead. Slipping beneath its stern they hid until satisfied the patrol had moved on, and then following like a distant shadow.

When the patrol approached their target, the officer called out, "*Ahoy, lo que es para el desayuno?*"

"*El diente de un tiburón,*" a voice responded from atop the stern castle.

Listening closely, they heard the patrol challenge another vessel some distance away. Several strokes brought them to their target's side. Oars raised, rolled canvas put over the gunnel, they allowed the boat to glide in until coming against the ship's hull without a sound. There, they secured to the bottom of the Jacob's ladder. Most of the ships in the bay, had lanterns ablaze and men talking—sharing crude jokes and derisive laughter. The pirates' target was dark and quiet. With the same excitement and fear beating in their own breasts, each man followed their captain up the rope ladder to the main deck.

Nearing the top, François cautiously peeked over the gunwale, quickly scanning where the guards stood—two near the stern, two forward. Those were the only places lit meaning they could secretly work across the main deck to neutralize those guards before working their way below to secure the vessel.

Mr. Lowery took three men forward while François led four aft. Henry followed close to his side. They had just reached the bottom of the steps leading up to the quarterdeck where the guards stood talking when he heard a peculiar noise followed by the rushing thud of boots. Turning, he found a dozen rifles pointed at them. Resistance would be plain stupid.

"Well, it seems we have captured ourselves some pirates," he heard a youthful voice announce in Spanish as a man, not much more than a boy, strutted from behind the soldiers into the dim light, hands held contemptuously behind his back. "And who would you be?" the officer said arrogantly.

Francois did not reply thinking it best they not know he understood Spanish. One could learn a great deal that way. On the other hand, it would not be wise to use English since the two countries were at odds, despite recent diplomatic ventures. As his reputation spread, thanks to a prideful crew, the story circulated was that the Dolphin was French, therefore to use French might betray his identity, and that was certainly a path to a quick rope over the yardarm. His men would follow his lead.

Because he had obviously been giving directions, questions were directed at him. He answered with puzzled expressions. The officer repeated the question, "What are you doing on the king's ship?" François continued acting as if not understanding.

"What is he, dumb as well as stupid?" the young officer said, becoming frustrated. "Who among you speaks Spanish?" Most knew enough to get along, but no one spoke up. He then repeated the question in bad French, then English, which was atrocious causing Henry to giggle

"You think this is humorous?" the officer said, slapping his face. Henry kicked him in the shin.

Before he could retaliate, François stepped between the two and said in Arabic, "Leave the boy alone."

François had first learned the language from

shipmates aboard the *Fleurette* and improved with Mariah's tutoring, and a tutor from Valverde to help Hassan. It would not fool a true son of Esau, but good enough to befuddle the young officer who paused and looked at his soldiers hoping someone understood. The crew remained true to their oath of silence despite interrogation.

Frustrated, the officer said curtly, "Sergeant, put this slime in chains. We will take them ashore. They must have some knowledge of where the Dolphin's ship is to be found. It cannot be far. Someone at the fort will understand this contemptible black'ard's gibberish."

Henry's move was so sudden to catch everyone off guard. With a twisting spin, he slipped between two soldiers and made for the rail. The soldiers were so close together that turning to aim their cumbersome rifles was awkward, but just as Henry reached the rail the officer drew a pistol and fired. There was a cry of pain followed moments later by a splash. Two soldiers rushed to the side to peer over, pointing their rifles toward the water, but did not fire. After what seemed an eternity, they returned to report.

"Your ball must have found its mark, Lieutenant," one of the soldiers said. "He went straight to the bottom."

"One less to worry about. Take these ashore."

Shackled, all nine were taken ashore, and roughly thrown into a large, dank cell deep inside the fortress. Isolated from the rest, François knew he would have to come up with a way to escape, and soon. However, that did not seem possible at the moment with the large guard standing watch just outside the cell door, so he settled against the cold, mildewed rock wall.

He tried to be careful as they approached the island, but someone obviously saw them. Where was the Dolphin's ship, the Spanish officer asked. "Just outside the harbor, you fool," François thought, "and a sitting gull for the fort's guns at first light when the fog lifts." Then his thoughts turned to Henry. Had they killed him? Wounded or not, it was a long way back to the *Raven*, too long even for him. The boy wasn't that good of a swimmer, yet. François deeply regretted bringing him on the raid. He should have said no, but Maggie insisted. Maybe Mariah was right. Women could intimidate him.

A crack high up the slimy, stone wall of his cell allowed the first rays of sunlight so he could at least tell time. If the Spaniards had guessed the *Raven* was not far outside the harbor they might have dispatched boarding parties to capture her. That he heard neither cannon nor gunfire might mean Mr. Gibbs sailed away. Did the Spaniards give chase? François hated not knowing the fate of his ship and crew. The scrape of metal signaled opening of the cell door. Immediately four armed soldiers entered, rifles leveled. Behind these followed the same junior officer who captured them.

"You, come with me," he said, attempting a poor imitation of sounding tough, while waiving a pistol carelessly. "Our comandante wishes to speak to you."

François gazed at him stupidly as if not understanding. Frustrated, the officer waived for him to come out of the cell. When he didn't respond quickly enough one of the guards grabbed an arm and roughly jostled him down a narrow, stone corridor to a room filled with the instruments of inquisition.

"So, Lieutenant, this is their leader?"

"Sí, Coronel. He was clearly giving the others directions."

As two burly soldiers pinned his arms, the officer stepped close to François' face and asked, "What is your name, pirate?"

François responded by tilting his head questioningly. The flat of the man's hand lashed out. The slap stung, and by the taste of blood, had loosened a tooth.

"Your cowardly ship fled into the fogbank leaving

you alone. If you value your life, you will answer me. What is your name?"

François continued mute for a moment, relieved Mr. Gibbs had held close to orders and effected safe escape. He then blurted an obscenity in Arabic. That stymied the officer for a moment.

"Bring that slave in here, the heathen called Sa'id." The comandante's anger and frustration piqued.

That someone was available who could instantly recognize his masquerade sent a surge of adrenaline coursing through François's body until he prickled from the toes on both feet to the top of his head. Fighting to not let recognition of what was said be transmitted, François randomly looked about the darkened chamber of horrors as the Colonel slowly moved among the fiendish contraptions designed to bend and break the strongest will. Occasionally he stopped to glide long, bony fingers over part of a device fashioned by the hands of some sadistic, mentally disturbed mind.

Screwing up his face into a faint, malevolent grin, the Colonel looked at the captive with a sideways stare. The only sound was the faint dripping of water somewhere in the black reaches of the torture room and the crunch of Colonel's boots on the stone floor.

François guessed the man to be in his forties. A small scar on his pockmarked, left cheek suggested he was familiar with battle. Indeed, his face was angular giving a hard appearance accentuated by a thin line beard seemingly drawn by a quill from each ear to an austere moustache and goatee.

After a painfully long wait, the shuffle of footsteps announced the arrival of the Arab, a young man being shoved roughly into the room. His black eyes were wide and glazed with terror as he first looked at the machines then at the Spanish officer.

"It appears this pirate only speaks your foul, bar-

barous tongue. I want to know where the pirate Dolphin has run off to," the Colonel commanded.

"He wants to know where the pirate Dolphin has gone," the nervous translator stuttered in Arabic.

"I know exactly what that filthy bag of human excrement asked. If you want to die a slave to this creature you can tell him I'm not an Arab. If you want to escape your position I can help despite my current predicament. Tell him my name is Hassan from Morocco and I do not know where the Dolphin's would have taken her ship, which happens to be the truth."

The slave instantly realized the prisoner knew enough of the language, but wasn't Arabic. Having heard greatly exaggerated stories of the Dolphin's reputation the boy also realized his life now hung in a precarious balance between these two men.

Listening to the Spaniards talk, they said that the Dolphin was in league with the Devil. For that Sa'id could not vouch, but the Spaniard at his elbow certainly was. He had, over the course of several weeks, resolved to escape the tyrannical brutality of this captivity even if it meant death. He had in fact, considered committing the greatest sin, to kill himself, as others had, but suddenly, here might be an opportunity to escape the living hell now consuming his young life, or at least die with honor in the attempt.

"He is called Hassan, from Morocco. He does not know where she has gone."

"She!" The Colonel shrieked. "Is that vile creature saying the Dolphin is a woman!"

Sa'id put the question to François who nodded eagerly and said, "Yes," in Arabic.

"Where will that ship go?"

"He does not know, Comandante."

"How convenient. He doesn't look Arab. He looks French," the Colonel said more calmly, studying his prisoner closely."

"He says you don't look Arabic."

"Tell the horse's backside my mother was Arab, my father was a French soldier who left after the occupation."

The boy translated a wisely edited reply.

"Let's see if there is something we can do to change his story. Strip him and lash him to the rack."

Struggling was impossible against the two brutes with muscles like the great, black, African apes as they ripped off his clothes and secured his arms and feet with ropes extending from each end of a long table. François had heard of this torture devise as the sailors aboard ship spoke of it—a favorite of the French and Spanish church—something definitely to contend with.

The Colonel gazed down on his victim, again studying him as a scientist would a new insect. As a child in St. Nazaire, François' skin had been a pearly, almost sickly white, but after years at sea it was now a deep brown. The Colonel had doubted François' explanation of his Arab background.

When ripping off his trousers, the Colonel became mildly surprised, showing a faint expression of beginning to believe the fabrication. Sun and wind burned European sailors a dark brown, but upon shedding trousers to bathe, their skin from the waist down almost glowed white as a cloud making them look ridiculous. This prisoner's legs were the same dark brown as the torso. Hooking a finger beneath François' loincloth the Colonel pulled it down to expose the hip. It was the same dark color.

Having a great love of diving from the dragon's back, keeping anything about is loins was impossible upon impact. As it was only he and Mariah, François didn't bother with clothes when swimming at home or aboard ship. The result was a uniform, rich, dark brown coloring not unlike some of the Moroccans. With a slight shrug, the commandant began to accept the story.

Poised near the foot of the table, the Colonel caressed the spoke of a large, wooden wheel taken from a ship while a heinous grin split his lips again, spreading the edges of the beard encircling his mouth. With a slight push on the wheel, a slow series of loud clicks echoed among the stone walls as the ankle ropes tightened, removing the slack, and pulling him along the table.

"Now, I wonder just how much you really do understand what I say," the Colonel said while pushing the wheel another click.

The ropes about the ankles pulled. In response, François went into his best act showing as much fear as possible and jabbering in Arabic.

"What did he say?" the officer snapped at the slave.

Sa'id did not dare repeat most of what François said so replied as way of interpretation, "Please do not do this in the name of Allah. I have told you the truth."

"Has he?" the officer replied, turning the large wheel one more click.

François felt the muscles in his shoulders, hips, and knees stretch. Once again, he rattled in Arabic, the distress becoming real in his voice.

"Well?" the officer snapped.

"He pleads mercy. He is only a poor boy taken by the pirates and made to sail with them," the translator replied now making up a response as François reverted to less dignified language.

The officer turned the wheel another click. The cry from François' lips was not acting as his sinews and tendons burned, on the verge of tearing. In response, he cried out again.

"He has told you all he knows."

"He is more than a simple sailor. He was leading the attack."

The Arab boy translated the Colonel's words to which François struggled to reply, "Tell him it is my place to find what we needed. I am the cook. All we wanted was food."

The Colonel's eyes lit up upon hearing the response, declaring, "Food! The Dolphin needs food that badly? How interesting. How interesting, indeed. Conditions must not be good aboard ship."

After a quick exchange, the Arab returned the answer, "Most of their powder and stores were ruined by a storm several days ago," referring to a squall line of thunderstorms that passed through the area earlier. Of course, the *Raven* steered so to skirt the storm's edge.

"Perhaps he is telling the truth, Coronel," the young Lieutenant said. "That might account for the child being with them."

"Hum-m-m. Perhaps."

Then François cast a bargaining chip.

"What did he say?"

"He pleads for mercy, your Excellency. He swears allegiance to you, to your god, whatever you want. He will be your slave."

"Hm-m-m," the officer responded, stepping to François' side and staring at him intently, before sliding an icy-cold hand over his stomach and chest. "Perhaps. He is young and strong. He might actually be useful. He does not appear to know more than he tells. Yet . . . Where will your ship go?" he said, leaning very close to François' face, his black eyes glistening as if on fire.

François wanted so badly to spit in those eyes, but waited for the slave to translate before answering, "He is not sure. He overheard something about Barbuda."

"Barbuda! Barbuda! Again, Barbuda!" the Colonel snarled like a wounded demon while standing erect and turning his back. "A haven for the devil's own, and on our soil! Someday I will destroy that place!" He slammed an open hand against the wheel. François was grateful it didn't move.

Anger vented, the commandant traced a finger slowly along the edge of one spoke, looked back at his prisoner, lowered his voice, and said with an oily tone, "Tell this one that he will indeed become my slave, but do not betray me or he shall feel this devise pull his pretty body apart inch by slow inch."

With that translated, he pushed the wheel one more click, chuckled at the cry wretched from the prisoner, and walked off, tossing over his shoulder, "When he is whole, see that he is bathed, then bring him to my quarters."

As soon as the Colonel and soldiers disappeared, the Arab boy released the wheel and ropes, and helped François struggle into a seated position on the edge of the demonic table. Sa'id's gentle message of the shoulder joints relieved the burning pain there.

"Thank you," François said quietly.

"You are the Dolphin?"

"I am called that."

The boy moaned. "I have sold my soul to the devil. You said you could help me escape from here."

"Yes."

"But your ship has run away."

"Not far. It will return, then that dog will receive payment for this," he said, rubbing his thighs and knees. "You shall not only receive your freedom, but a sizable reward."

"Please, I do not do this for money. Follow me if you are able to walk."

The first steps hurt, but slowly François regained the use of his legs as he followed the youth up several flights of stairs then along a narrow corridor passing through an open arch and into the kitchen. With only a cotton garment about his loins he became the instant center of attraction among the scullery maids flitting about like fire flies. To shorten the embarrassment he quickened the pace, pushing Sa'id as they passed through the kitchen and into an alcove toward the rear.

"I am sorry. There is no other way here," the boy apologized.

They had come to a bathing room for servants, an open area with a large, oval, iron tub behind the brick ovens, conveniently placed so that water could be easily heated and added. After checking that no maid was skulking about he slipped out of his garment and settled into the tub. It reminded him so much of home, and for an instant felt pangs of homesickness wash over tender joints. Those thoughts were quickly pushed aside so to concentrate on a plan of escape.

"This bath is unusual," François continued in Arabic. "They seldom wash in Europe."

"Yes. So I have been told, but Colonel Macaria prefers his servants not to stink. He, himself, washes often with his women. I have attended him in such matters."

"What do you think this Spaniard has in mind?"

"He will give you to his wife. She will enjoy you for a season. When she grows weary you will be sent to the mines to die."

"What?"

"They have a very unusual relationship. One of the girls who attends her says that the Colonel and his wife were married when very young, perhaps seven or eight years of age. When their families decided it time, they were instructed to—how is it—fornicate? No. I do not remember the word. They were to lie together in bed for the first time."

"Consummate," François said.

"Yes. They had no love for each other. He likes other women. She likes other men. It was an important alliance for their families. Very important. When they were to spend the first night together he went out of the bed chamber through a secret passage to the arms of another while sending his wife's lover to her."

"They never sealed the marriage? That is incredible!"

"He continues to sleep with any woman he likes, and she with other men, most who he finds for her, like you."

François shook his head in disbelief. He had heard of prearranged marriages forced upon children of nobility for the gain of the parents, but this went far beyond anything he imagined. Yet, this was something that might just work to his advantage.

"How many others here speak Arabic?"

"Only myself. You have a bad accent,"

"What of my crew?"

"They will be sent to the mines."

Relieved of one worry, but burdened with another, he lifted a leg to scrub as a maid stepped in with fresh clothes and giggled. She slowly placed them on a small table nearby, but François was too absorbed in thought to take notice. He had just put on pantaloons when Sa'id sprinkled scented water over his shoulders. Again reminded of home and Mariah, he slipped the knee-length, loose shirt over his head just as the girl returned. She had him sit on a chair so to comb the tangles out of his curly hair. Another memory.

Cleaned and dressed, Sa'id escorted him back through the kitchen to the corridor, drawing more stares and smiles from the women. Up two flights of stone steps and down another hall the two eventually reached a heavy, wooden plank door. Sa'id knocked, heard a muffled response, and entered.

Ushered into an opulent chamber, François came face-to-face with Col. Macaria once again. He was now wearing an impressive-looking uniform trimmed with gold. Staring at the man seated at a large desk by the window overlooking the harbor he hoped the anger surging within his chest was not noticeable. A woman stood next to the colonel, her pudgy, round face barely visible above the fluted collar of an immense, billowing dress. François immediately felt violated as her lecherous eyes played over his body. There was the feeling as if being smeared with toilet.

"Baroness Güttruda, this is my new slave. He only speaks Arabic, but he should prove entertaining." Then turning to Sa'id, he instructed, "Tell this heathen if he does not do exactly what the Baroness wants I shall remove every inch of his skin with a whipped." The Colonel paused a moment as a smirk crossed his lips before continuing, "Or better, returned to the rack where I will remove his skin with a blade while pulling him apart."

"I heard the swine," François replied after Sa'id translated,

"He understands. Your word is his command, master."

The woman fanned a small pink hand before her face and giggled.

"Very good. I may have use of him later myself. The Baroness will call when she desires company. Make sure he is presentable at all times." The colonel spoke brusquely, waived a hand for them to leave, and resumed some work on the desk. Baroness Güttruda's beady, blue eyes followed them out like a snake watching it prey.

There was a foul taste in François' mouth as his guide quickly gave the Arabian bow. He mimicked it while retreating back into the corridor and returned to the kitchen. Without shackles and a guard, he was free to move about, limited, but free.

"When will your ship return?"

"Upon my signal."

"They are not in Barbuda?"

"No," François replied with a faint smile.

That afternoon he managed to work out onto an upper gunnery level and look over the harbor. There were nearly two dozen ships moored in the bay including the Brigantine that had been the instrument of their capture. Besides a Portuguese-built galleon, there were also two other, small war ships, and several merchants, some low in the water. There were also a number of fishing sloops, but one in particular caught his eye with its bright yellow pennant. Returning inside, he discovered a route to the main powder magazine.

Expecting the Colonel's wife would summon him that night, he nervously fretted through the day, but such did not happen, a definite relief. The troubling news was that Lowery and the others had already been moved to the mine. Life was becoming very complicated. Escape was a simple matter for himself, give the pre-arranged signal, and meet up with the *Raven*, which would brazenly return. However, his men were several miles inland, and if at all possible he would not leave them behind. The Dolphin's thoughts became occupied with finding a way to rescue them while effecting his and Sa'id's escape, and staying as far from the Baroness' groping hands as possible.

Chapter 25

† The Ruse †

Over the next two days, François and Sa'id received menial tasks affording François ample opportunity to familiarize himself with fort's maze-like interior. At the same time, the call to entertain the Baroness hovered over his head like an executioner's axe. Providence intervened early the morning of the third day when the young Lieutenant, who had been instrumental in his capture, stormed into the kitchen where they were seated.

Stopping just inside the arched door his gaze fell on Sa'id. Calling out angrily he shouted, "You. Heathen. Come with me and bring that one with you," indicating François.

The officer, barely sprouting little more than fuzz

on his face unworthy of shaving, spun around and headed down the corridor without further word. Sa'id sprang up quickly, nearly upsetting the table at which they sat, and ran to catch up. At the end of the narrow passage, they exited into a small courtyard and from there onto the large, grassy field north of the fortress used to train and drill the soldiers. Near the middle of the field, an older man and two associates stood waiting. François instantly knew there was going to be a duel.

"Good morning Lt. Ramiro." The man's greeting was smug. "As is my right I have chosen swords."

"That suits me well, Señor Amadeo," the young man replied.

"My sons will act as my seconds."

François judged Amadeo to be in his fifties, stout but not fat, and light on his feet. His sons were in their early thirties, placing Ramiro and his seconds practically in the sandbox league.

The choice of weapons would be rapiers, delicate in appearance, but in practiced hands as deadly as a stout cutlass. After the Lieutenant chose his weapon, Amadeo took the remaining sword and whipped it back and forth. The young Lieutenant certainly was no stranger to the blade as he slashed the air and made a couple practice lunges; a warm-up prelude to someone's death.

"This will do," Ramiro said, handing the sword point down to Sa'id. Removing his military jacket, it was handed to François who wondered if the young man had even attempted shaving yet.

The two men squared off and at the signal began combat. The Lieutenant was proficient, but the older man was definitely better. It was during the exchange that a plan began to come together in François' mind, however timing would have to be near perfect.

The duel continued for a time, the older man smiling while defending, making half-hearted attacks, obviously playing with the Lieutenant. Finally, the young officer deployed an offensive move he'd used several times before, something the older man expected, and tiring of the game, neatly executed a pirouette of the blade, ripping Ramiro's sword free and sending it sailing off to the side. Thus beaten the Lieutenant stood erect, awaiting his fate.

Señor Amadeo was almost salivating as he savored the moment, pressing the tip of the sword against the boy's exposed chest just below the sternum, drawing a trickle of blood.

"You are very fortunate that it is I who defends the honor of my daughter and family, not one of her brothers. You shall die quickly. They would have chopped you into little pieces while you lived," Amadeo's discourse rang with an oily expectation of pleasure.

Just as the victor was about to thrust his rapier into the boy's heart François stepped up, grabbed the man's wrist and with a painful twist loosened the weapon from his grasp. Immediately the seconds raced forward, but François pushed Amadeo aside and met their charge with a fist to one and a powerful backhand to the other sending both sprawling on the grass. Picking up the sword, the Dolphin issued an icy stare at the older man before breaking it across his knee.

"This has not ended, Ramiro. I shall have my rightful satisfaction."

François turned to Sa'id and said, "Tell this man if he attempts to harm my master again I will come by night and slit his throat and everyone in his house."

Sa'id relayed the message, which seemed to have a sobering effect on Amadeo who looked into François' eyes. Turning away, he snatched his coat from the ground and left the field, his two sons in close pursuit holding bloodied noses. It was then Macaria appeared from the courtyard where he had been watching.

"Well, Lt. Ramiro, it seems you have narrowly

avoided yet another visitation from the angel of death, thanks to this slave. He would seem to be a good man to have about."

"Si, Coronel Macaria," the Lieutenant replied stiffly while hastily buttoning his jacket.

"Return to the fortress and clean up then attend to your duties. As for you my big slave . . ., you two of you follow me."

Instead of returning to the fort, Macaria strode along its northern wall to the stable where an open carriage was waiting. Climbing inside, he directed François and Sa'id to step onto the back to hold on, which they barely managed as the driver snapped the whip, spurring the two horses into a canter.

The wind blasting his face and whipping his hair reminded François of being on board ship and found it enjoyable. On the other hand, Sa'id gripped the bar so tightly his knuckles turned white, terrified of falling off which would certainly prove fatal at this speed. François wrapped an arm around his skinny waist and held them both fast to the carriage.

They had traveled nearly a half hour along a twisting road before suddenly exiting the jungle and coming upon a stockade in the middle of a clearing. Just beyond François could see the opening to a mine and wondered if his interference had condemned the two to this place.

"Good morning, Coronel Macaria," an officer saluted as the commander stepped down.

"I want to see the books," the Colonel said as he brushed by the officer and stepped inside.

As the carriage ground to a stop before the waiting officer, François' heart nearly stopped as well. The man opening the carriage door was Capt. Hidalgo, former commander of the governor's garrison at El Hierro and François' bitter enemy. If he were to recognize François . . . Fortunately, he was too intent on attending to the Colonel to pay attention to two loathsome slaves behind the carriage.

Having received no instructions, the two remained by the carriage as the sun beat down on them unrelentingly. Yet, their predicament was far easier than those laboring under the lash in the mine a stone's throw away. After a time François went over to the building to sit in the little shade it provided and listen.

"You have done well, Capitan. I am pleased," Macaria said. "We sail on the morrow's tide rich men."

"What will you tell the king?"

"That brainless, inbred will believe anything. As for the queen, she will take her share and remain quiet, as she has done before. Begin loading the shipment at once. I will leave the two I brought. They are ignorant heathens, but loyal. Use them to transport the shipment to the port. Dispose of all evidence here before joining me."

"What of the prisoners?"

"They are evidence. So are the guards. Mining accidents happen all the time."

"Si, Coronel. What of those slaves and Lt. Ramiriz?"

"Ramiriz is a young fool. He knows nothing, but will die a hero. The pirate Dolphin is in the area. His attack on the fortress will result in an explosion in the main magazine." The two laughed.

Knowing the conversation was coming to an end François got up and moved Sa'id to the back of the carriage before they came out.

When Macaria appeared he called to Sa'id, "You two remain here. You are to drive a wagon directly to the dock. I will meet you there. If anyone attempts to interfere it would be better you forfeit your life than hand the wagon's contents over willingly. Do you understand?"

Sa'id bowed and replied, "Yes, master."

François looked at Sa'id, imitating a puzzled expression and bowed, as the Comandante regained his carriage and left. François could not believe the sudden turn of events nor planned it better, except Hidalgo was a worry.

Looking in François' direction for the first time, the furrows about the captain's eyes deepened as he obviously thought there was something vaguely familiar about the slave, but could not place where. That François was taller, broader, darker, and sported a thick, but a short, black Van Dyke befuddled his memory. Fortunately, it was a passing question as Hidalgo had too much work ahead to prepare the shipment and close down the operation.

Returning to the shade near the building, the two men waited and watched as prisoners began loading gold bars into several wagons. Near dusk, soldiers herded the prisoners together. Obviously, Hidalgo wanted to maintain some semblance of routine so to not cause a panic. François was grateful his crew had remained close to one another. When he and Sa'id appeared during the evening feeding, their faces lit up with hope, but François quickly indicated for them to ignore him. As shadows lengthened and the last wagon was filled with reformed gold, Hidalgo gave the order to his sergeant.

"We are finished here, Garcia. Are the charges set?"

"Si, Capitan."

"Herd the prisoners to the back of the mine and shoot them. When you hear the shooting, seal the entrance and we will be finished with this place."

"Along with the soldiers?"

"Unless you desire to share with them."

The sergeant saluted, a malevolent smile parting his cheeks, turned, and headed to where the prisoners huddled near the mine entrance..

As Hidalgo approached François, he again furrowed his brow trying to place where he had met the slave before.

"You seem familiar," he said.

"You still have the face of a horse's rear," François said in Arabic.

"We have met, that I know. It will come to me," then pointing to the last wagon said, "Get on your wagon,"

François replied in kind, "As you wish, Mon Capitan."

The officer's eyes went wide with the sudden realization who was standing in front of him, but there was no time to react. François' fist sent him flying backward, striking his head against the log wall of the building. Grabbing the stunned captain's pistol, he fired a shot into the air. That was Lowery's signal.

Unbeknownst to anyone, Francois purloined a key to the prisoner's shackles and slipped it to Lowery during the meal. Hearing the pistol shot, they sprang upon the soldiers. Armed only with stones and sticks, they outnumbered the Spaniards three to one, easily overwhelming them. Lowery and his crew broke free and ran for the wagons. Meanwhile, the Captain and François faced off once again.

"I cannot believe my luck that we should meet again," Hidalgo said as their swords rang out a greeting.

"I'm afraid I haven't much time for conversation, Captain." Then to Lowery he said, "When the prisoners have finished their revenge, remove the soldiers' uniforms and put them on. You are going to become soldiers of the King—at least for a while. I'll just tidy up a bit and be with you in a moment."

Once again, Hidalgo became enraged by his opponent's arrogance, which exceeded his own, and knowing this must be a duel to the death. However, François had no time and pressed the Captain until his back was against the log office wall. Hidalgo slashed recklessly, forcing François back.

"Capt. Dolphin, we must be going or that colonel will send troops to investigate," Lowery said as they watched the duel from the wagons.

"Dolphin? You are the Dolphin?" Hidalgo said.

"Unfortunately for you, yes," François said.

Energized, Hidalgo realized that by killing his bitter enemy, he would also become a hero. His attack was vicious, but every maneuver, every trick he had learned went for naught as François deflected everything almost effortlessly.

"Well, it has been entertaining as usual, but I must go," François said, and to Hidalgo's consternation once again found himself back against the log building, exhausted and desperate.

Employing a feint to the left Hidalgo spun completely around sweeping his sword with both hands waist high only to find his opponent wasn't there. With cat-like reflexes, François had seen the maneuver coming and jumped back out of range of the blade. As it passed, he sprang forward, driving his sword through the captain's right shoulder with enough force to throw the man backward and embed the tip in the joint between two logs.

"I hate to leave you hanging Capt. Hidalgo, but we must go."

"This is not done. It will never be done until you are dead," the captain said, grimacing with pain.

"Such seems to be our relationship. As for yourself, I suspect the prisoners really want to have that discussion with you, as well. If you are a lucky man we will meet again."

Leaving the wounded Spaniard to contend with the rampaging prisoners, François and his men began the trip back to the fortress. It was during the return Lowery conveyed some very interesting information. Everyone knew there wasn't gold on Antigua, but Macaria had fabricated the story and mine as a cover. The gold actually came from the galleon moored in the harbor. What he had built was a smelter to reform it into coin and ingots earmarked for his private use.

François wasn't sure what to expect when they arrived at the wharf, but at least a detachment of soldiers. To his surprise, only the Colonel and the Lieutenant awaited them on the dock amid a number of torches. The near total darkness aided the pirate's deception.

"Use these soldiers and the slaves to load the gold onto the corsair, but do so quickly. You must be finished by first light so that any pirate spies will not see what is going on," the Colonel instructed his officer.

"What of the Dolphin's ship? Might this be why he is in these waters," Ramirez said.

"Perhaps, but the shipment leaves on the tide before anyone can signal our departure, and with the escort, she will not dare to attack. I and Capitan Hidalgo will accompany the shipment personally. You will be in charge of the garrison until the new comandante arrives."

"Me?" The boy's voice cracked as if still in puberty, which wasn't that far behind him.

"Yes. My replacement was supposed to have arrived weeks ago, but by my orders, I cannot delay any longer. The necessary papers transferring command to you are on my desk. When you finish loading the kings gold, send me word, but stay aboard until I come. This is one shipment the pirates will not get." Then turning to Sa'id he said, "Tell this fellow to follow me. The Baroness desires his company tonight. If he pleases her, he will come with us to Spain. She can entertain herself teaching him to speak properly."

Sa'id maintained the rouse and quickly translated into Arabic as before. François bowed acknowledgment and replied to Sa'id, "Do as we planned, my friend, and await my signal," then turned to follow the Colonel.

So far, everything was working well, but transferring four wagonloads of gold would take at least until dawn. Now, he had to devise a way to stay out of the clutches of the Colonel's apocryphal wife and send the signal, which would return the *Raven*. As they headed up the cobblestone street leading to the cavernous fortress, Macaria suddenly stopped and cursed.

"Damn my impatience." Turning around he addressed François by using sign language to convey his desire. "I want you to bathe then come to my chambers."

The gyrations were so comical François had all to do to keep from laughing. Cocking his head sideways and lifting hands with a shrug to indicate ignorance forced the Colonel to go through it again until becoming totally exasperated. François thought the man would explode, until a familiar voice from the door of a mercantile interrupted that interesting prospect.

"Can I help?"

"Who are you?" he snarled.

"Maggie DuBri! I just brought in a load of fish for the garrison."

"Unless you can speak Arabic, be on your way."

"I can."

"Thank God! Tell this heathen to bathe then come to my chambers."

Maggie turned to François and said in Arabic, "What is this donkey's problem?"

"Never mind that. What are you doing here?"

"Waiting for your signal."

"Move just before first light."

"He understands and will do as you say," she said to the colonel.

"Humph!" Macaria snorted and stomped off with François close behind as Maggie stared in amused wonder.

François now had to stall for time. The first way

was to take a long bath, but that was cut short when a servant and two soldiers interrupted and prodded him to hurry. The Baroness was obviously impatient. He still wasn't sure how to resist her perversions and keep from violating his oath to Mariah.

Originally, François was supposed to report to the Colonel's apartment, but instead the servant and guards took him directly to the Baroness' chamber door. With grunts and gestures, he tried to convey the original orders to them as another way to delay. That bought another five minutes. At this point, every minute counted.

"Oh, that," the servant said. "The coronel has changed all that. He is entertaining a young woman. You are to go directly to the Baroness. Oh, you don't understand," the servant snorted. Then jabbing a finger at the door simply said, "In there and be quick about it. No, not quick about that. Go in quickly and take your time, oh . . . , whatever!" The man rolled his eyes and threw up his hands. "Just go in.

Pushed through the door, it was quickly closed behind him with a ominous thud. Taking a deep breath, he quietly entered and stood in the shadows, understanding how early Christians must have felt prodded into the arena with a waiting lion. In this case, it was a waiting hippopotamus seated beneath the covers of a very large bed as a maid braided her long, yellowish hair. François guessed the Baroness had a Viking ancestor or two in the family closet, an adventuresome people who knew their way through countries, or around in them?

Spotting him, the Baroness waived her attendant away and motioned for François to stand by her. As his bare feet padded across the cool, stone floor his stomach churned even more with anger, frustration, and disgust. Then he noticed the arched doors covered by red draperies. Beyond was a balcony overlooking the harbor.

"You goot lookin' for Arabic," she said, swinging

cannon-sized legs over the edge of the bed and standing, letting the nightgown drape over her voluminous body.

As hinted by her face, the Baroness was fat and the lack of height accentuated that obesity. She not only had the face of a plow horse, she had the body of one that appeared old and broken down. More than ever, he had to find a way to avoid this situation. As she drew close, François moved to the balcony and pointed toward the harbor.

"Do you speak Arabic?" he stuttered.

"I not speak your tongue," she cooed. "I know language we all speak," and stroked his arm with two pudgy fingers.

"You have the face of a pig's rump," he said trying to control shivers running rampant up and down his body.

"You pretty," she responded with a heavy Teutonic accent that even carried through inane giggles while sliding her hand around to unbutton his loose, muslin shirt.

When her puffy fingers began to play on his chest he almost choked. Instead, François deftly slipped out of her clutches to head straight for a table of leftover food—poultry, fruits and raw vegetables. Having not eaten since morning, and that had been interrupted. He was seriously famished. Grabbing a leg bone, he eagerly tore off a sizable chunk of meat with his teeth.

"Foot? You vant foot? Poor dear, you no eat today? Youst like that man no feed servants. Verk, verk, verk. Alltime verk. You like have voman feed? Güttruda feed pretty one," she volunteered, taking a plump grape and jamming into his mouth.

"Well, that may not be a bad idea," he thought to himself as she popped another in. "This could consume a lot of time."

Apparently, the woman had been among the Arabs at some point in time. Waddling to the bed, she retrieved a blanket and numerous pillows to make an Oriental dining place on the floor where François could recline while she sat next to him stuffing him with food. He actually thought this a very nice custom, and for the most part enjoyed the attention except for her incessant giggling which was beginning to drive him to distraction. However, after an hour, he began to feel like a fatted hog and very drowsy which was leading to his downfall as she finally managed to completely unbutton his shirt and slip it off his shoulders.

"Goot boy like go bed now?"

Surprisingly strong, she easily pulled him to his feet and with a death-grip on one arm, stomped toward the bed. It really looked inviting after all that food and a long day, but not for what she had in mind.

"I really do not think this will work," he said in Spanish.

She stopped short, thick lips parting in surprise.

"I think you no speak da Spanish?" she gushed.

"The Dolphin can speak many languages, Baroness Güttruda."

Judging by the size of her lungs, he expected her to raise an alarm that would reverberate across the harbor like a canon shot. Instead, she drove a right hook into François' gut knocking the air from his lungs, quickly followed by a shot to the jaw that sent him sideways, bringing on lots of twinkling lights swirling about his head. He barely blocked a third punch that would have finished the deed, but still made a glancing blow to the side of his head. She was about to issue forth a resounding cry when he got his wits together.

"I'm very sorry, but sleep well."

With that, his fist connected to her robust jaw sending the woman tottering backward to fall unconscious onto the bed. With a great many grunts and groans he lifted the rest of her onto the bed, and retrieved several pillows from the floor to make her comfortable. Next, he made sure the Baroness would not sound an alarm. Ripping down drapery cording she was bound hand and foot, and by necessity, he gagged her ample mouth, finally pulling up the covers to make her comfortable.

Now came the difficult wait. For this to work the gold had to be loaded aboard which would take most of the night. If he appeared in public too soon someone might become suspicious. He dared not attempt to sail out of the harbor until the hour just before changing of the guard, when they would be most sleepy and few would be in the corridors.

When eight bells sounded faintly across the harbor, he shook alertness back into a groggy mind before rising from where he sat on the floor next to the bed. It was 4 a.m. and the morning watch was coming on. The Baroness had aroused earlier and thrashed about until exhausted, then remained quiet until he stirred at which time she issued a series of muffled grunts.

"I am truly sorry, dear lady, but I must consider the welfare of my men and ship thus you shall remain in this most undignified manner until servants arrive later this morning. Our visit was entertaining, and I thank you for the delicious food, and unexpected exercise. Perhaps we will meet again under better circumstances. Until then, adieu," François said softly while gently patting beads of perspiration from her forehead.

She thrashed more vigorously until either realizing escape was futile or from exhaustion and quieted as he reached the door. Cautiously opening it he peeked through the crack. There was a lone guard standing to the side partially bent over the barrel of his musket, but straightened upon hearing the creaking hinges. Quickly stepping into the corridor, he shut the heavy door as quietly as possible, smiling weakly at the guard, and drew his forearm across his brow. The guard gave a disgusted glare before turning a blank face the opposing wall.

Moving along the dimly lit corridor, he heard the rhythmic cadence of soldiers. Slipping into a small, darkened alcove, he watched as a troop moved past, the changing of the inside guard had begun. There was little time remaining. Reaching the courtyard entrance, he slipped out into the cool, damp ocean air, a much-preferred smell in contrast to the musky odor of the interior. There was just one guard, but he was young, obviously new, and dutiful.

"Halt. State your purpose."

"On orders of comandante," François replied officiously in Spanish.

"And just what were those orders?" an all too familiar voice sounded from the shadows followed by the appearance of Macaria with a scullery maid at his side. "My wife must be a good teacher. Your Spanish is greatly improved."

Allowing the young soldier no time to react, François drove an elbow into his side hearing bone crack and the wind driven out of his lungs with a loud, "Humph." This François followed with an elbow into the boys jaw that turned him completely around to fall unconscious, face first without bending a knee.

In one smooth motion, the Dolphin pulled the soldier's sword free as he dropped to the ground. The Colonel pushed the girl gently aside, smiled, and withdrew his own sword with great deliberateness.

"This will be a great pleasure, Captain Dolphin, I presume."

François brought the blade of the purloined blade vertically in front of his face, point up in the traditional salute, and then swept it gracefully down and outward in a courteous salute. The Colonel reciprocated.

"I do not believe we have been formally introduced. Under such circumstances you should know the name of the one who will kill you. I am Baron Desiderio Bernadino Fernández de Velasco Sanchez-Macaria of Zaragoza, Baron of Aragon, Duke of Konesburg and soon, by the grace of proper birth, and wealth, Lord of Almenara."

François tapped his mouth with an open hand and yawned, "Oh, excuse me, are you through?"

Colonel Macaria seized upon the base insult to lunge forward, but François responded almost casually, deflecting the attack. From that moment, the ring of steel filled the courtyard as the two swordsmen matched skill and wits in a deadly duel.

"You are not a bad swordsman, for a pirate," the Colonel complimented as they parried back and forth. "I think, however, you have not met anyone of my expertise."

"You are good, Colonel, but unfortunately appear to be out of shape. Perhaps too many young women and not enough exercise. You would do well to engage your wife. She certainly could provide you with all necessities to improve your condition. She is a very robust woman."

The Colonel was tiring enough to forfeit a reply. Perhaps the boy was right. He had neglected his usual workouts in recent months and realized this encounter could not go much longer. With a grunt, he launched a vicious attack, but François deflected each blow.

"Really, Colonel, is that the best an officer in the King's army can do?" François taunted, and then with a flick of his sword laid the Colonels left shirtsleeve open, drawing a trickle of blood.

Staring briefly at the sudden wound Macaria redoubled the attack, but François merely opened the other sleeve. For the first time, true fear shown in the man's eyes. He had to do something, anything, to reverse the present course of events. Seeing an opportunity, the colonel lurched forward. François yield ground, failing to see the unconscious soldier's legs and toppling backward.

Macaria's sword arched straight for his unprotected chest, but suddenly there was a thud, a sound akin to a melon dropped on the ground. The Colonel's eyes rolled upward as he slowly dropped to his knees and pitched forward to sprawl face down into a bed of flowers next to François.

"A woman called Black Maggie sent me," Sa'id said as he stepped from the shadows, a wood ax handle in hand. "Gold is loaded and the crew is waiting. Sorry to interrupt, but the woman says you should stop playing with your enemies. We must go. First light comes. Will I accompany you from this wretched place?"

"Maggie's quite right. We were about finished anyway. Yes, you shall accompany us. I gave my word. Now listen carefully and do exactly as I say," François said, then explained his plan before each hurried off in separate directions, Sa'id into the fortress, François to the pier.

Stopping short of the dock where the ore wagons stood empty, he could see a squad of a dozen soldiers standing at attention. The change of the dock guard was in progress.

Taking a deep breath François launched into a run toward them, screaming. "Help! Help! Pirates!"

"What are you babbling?" the officer in charge replied with incredulity.

"Pirates have taken the galleon. We will all be killed!" he explained with great earnest.

"Captured the galleon?" he laughed. "I heard no noise of battle."

"Coronel Macaria just learned the ones who loaded the gold from these wagons were escaped prisoners from the mines. They've used their knives on the poor, sleeping sailors, but one made it to shore," he moaned. "The Coronel's orders. To the battlements immediately! Sound the alarm!"

"Soldiers to the fort!" the officer shouted, leading a charge up the hill back to the citadel.

"That was pretty good," Henry chuckled as his head popped up from where he was hiding just beneath the pier.

"I told you he be the best liar in these waters," a woman's voice called out from a small boat moored beneath the dock.

"Hello, Maggie!" François called out happily loosening the mooring rope and jumping aboard her fishing boat. "Make for the far side of the galleon." Then tousling Henry's head said, "Glad to see you alive. They were certain you had been shot."

"Missed me by that much," the boy replied, holding his thumb and forefinger a puce apart. "When I hit the water I went deep and swam to the stern."

"How did you warn the *Raven*? Did you swim all the way?"

"No. I swam ashore and ran out to the 'ead-land. That's where I met Miss Maggie coming ashore. Mr. Gibbs be waitin' south of 'ere for the signal to return."

François was impressed by the boy's swimming ability and endurance, and grateful he was alive. As they passed near the stern of the huge galleon François said to Henry, "Shoot a ball into the air to get their attention."

The boy eagerly pulled out a heavy pistol and holding it in both hands took aim at its main mast. A flash of fire accompanied the shot from the barrel and sent a loud report echoing across the silent harbor so that it sounded much like a small cannon.

"What's going on?" A voice called down from the galleon.

"Pirates have attacked the fort. The Colonel is fighting them. He says to make ready. They plan to fire on the harbor," François shouted back, then added, "man your guns."

Whistles and yells instituted a flurry of activity as men rushed into the rigging followed by the rumble of cannon run out on the other side. Meanwhile, the Colonel had lifted himself to all fours, shaking his head back and forth slowly trying to clear away the pounding. He had just reeled to a standing position when a contingent of soldiers came running up from the dock.

"Coronel. Pirates have taken the *Maria de la Cordova!*"

Staring blankly first at the man then at the dark outline of the ship seemingly lying peacefully in the harbor he struggled to make his mind comprehend.

"Coronel Macaria? Are you alright?"

"Yes!" he snapped returning to his old self. "Who captured the *Cordova*?"

"Pirates, sir. Escaped from the prison."

At that moment, a shot echoed over the port.

"Sound the alarm!"

The officer had barely entered the fortress when he heard the bell atop the edifice. Someone else must have seen the pirates, too.

Once they passed the *Cordova,* Maggie's fishing boat eased up to a corsair anchored just beyond the galleon. François grabbed a rope hanging off the side from its yardarm and swung up, calling back, "Make for open water. It is about to become very unfriendly in these parts."

As she cleared and approached one of the merchants on the way out someone from the ship called out, "What's all the noise?"

"Pirates 'ave taken the fort," Henry yelled back. "Get away before they use the fort's cannon to sink you."

As the signal rang out from ship to ship, the boy flashed a huge, mischievous, toothy grin.

"You learn quick," Maggie said, her white teeth shining in the sporadic light.

"Mr. Lowery, set the foresa'l and standby the mains," François called out as his feet touched the deck and headed for the quarterdeck ladder.

Men were already in place to unfurl the ship's rigging and roll out the seven cannon on the port side. It only took Lowery's call for an immediate response. He then strolled back to the stern to stand next his captain.

"Welcome aboard Cap'n."

"Is everyone aboard?"

"Aye. The gold is secure below and the prisoners from the mine arrived an hour ago, at least those that could make it. The natives headed for the interior. Have near a full compliment."

"What size guns do we have, fours?"

"No. Nines."

"Nines!"

"Aye. They bare the mark of his Lordship Douglass. Accordin' to a former occupant she was called the *Edna Dumfries* before the Colonel had the name changed."

"Now how'd he come by an English ship?"

"Confiscated for smuggling."

"Lord Douglass smuggling? That is interesting. Where are the former occupants now?"

"Locked below."

"I doubt they would be interested in joining us, however, propose the offer of adventure, gold, and freedom. Those who do not wish to accept such a generous offer put over the side before we make open water."

Lowery had only taken a couple steps when a brilliant flash of light issued from high up on the fort momentarily bathing the edifice in an eerie yellowish light followed by a resounding boom. Moments later they could hear a ball cutting the air. Landing close to the *Maria de la Cordova*'s bow, a huge column of water erupted into the air. As Lowery reached the hold to release the prisoners, a second cannon at the fort fired, from a lower level seaward. This time the ball struck the hulking galleon a glancing blow near mid-ship. François lashed the wheel, gathered up a coil of rope, and tossed it over the stern, securing his end to the rail. Resuming the wheel, he piloted the ship on a reckless, careening course through the crowded harbor toward open water as the galleon's guns returned on the fortress.

Within minutes more cannon came alive from shore while the *Maria de la Cordova* laid down a massive assault from her three decks of guns reinforced by other ships in the harbor. From the upper observation level Baron Desiderio Bernadino Fernández de Velasco Sanchez-Macaria of Zaragoza, Baron of Aragon, Duke of Konesburg, and maybe not so soon by the grace of bad luck, Lord of Almenara, watched in horror. The entire harbor sprang to life firing on the fortress as its giant guns returned fire. Suddenly, he realized this was all a horrible mistake. Each had been lead to believe the other to be pirates! He shouted for a cease-fire, but no one could hear him over the roar of cannon and explosions of incoming balls. He started down the rampart to personally silence his guns when a ball destroyed the only stairs leading from his high position. Trapped, all he could do was watch in dismay at the destruction of his fleet, the fortress, and ultimately his career and titles as the silhouette of the corsair with his gold made for open water, steering close to the north point of the harbor entrance.

"All ashore that be goin' ashore," Lowery bellowed, spurring an exit of soldiers. Then returning to his captain said, "Twenty-two stayin' with us. What about this one?"

"Good morning, Lt. Ramiro."

"You speak Spanish!"

"Yes. May I introduce myself . . ."

"You're the Dolphin!" the young man sputtered.

"Yes," he said, looking beyond toward the closing point of shoreline.

"I was not a part of Coronel Macaria's plan. I was told the transfer was to fool pirates. It being vitally important to the King, the Coronel was taking it to Spain personally. I only became aware that this may not be true when I observed the markings on the gold bars and coins."

"So I heard Col. Macaria tell Capt. Hidalgo."

"What be ye lookin' fer, Cap'n?" Lowery asked as François seemed distracted.

"A friend."

"Sa'id!" Lt. Ramiro exclaimed.

Wheeling around François saw the very wet face of his Arabian friend peering over the aft rail, a huge, white-toothed grin splitting the dark face. François quickly grabbed his arm and hauled him on deck.

"Welcome aboard, my friend," François said in Arabic, then in Spanish, "and freedom." Then to the Lieutenant as he cut the man's bonds, "It has been a pleasure to make your acquaintance, Lt. Ramirez, but unless you have decided to become a pirate you may want to leave before we clear this point of land."

"Captain Dolphin, you are incredible. Sailing with you would certainly be an adventure, but my career is with the King's army, which may prove to have been greatly enhanced by the Coronel's blunder. As he personally named me comandante of the garrison, I shall have the privilege of placing him in a dungeon . . . if there will be one left to use."

"You might be interested to know Capt. Hidalgo is also deeply involved in the plot," the Dolphin said as the Lieutenant sprang lightly to the rail, "If he has been lucky enough to escape retribution from those he guarded."

Ramiro paused briefly, holding a rope in one hand while giving a smart salute with the other. "Do take note of the reefs beyond the point. Bear left during low tide," he said, before saluting and jumping feet first overboard.

When the *Edna Dumfries'* bow met the first open swells, she dipped as if to curtsy in prelude to a long awaited dance. The Dolphin looked back. Ships and the fortress were ablaze, the flashes and resounding of cannon filling the air. Ahead was open water, the first light of a bright, clear day, and to starboard, the *Raven*.

Chapter 26

† Homeward †

Anchored in the lee side cove of Loro Placida Island, François saw the *Edna Dumfries* name restored and properly fitted for the voyage home to avoid any bad luck caused by the name change. As most of the men were Irish or Scot they would put in on the Norman coast to disembark those from the continent before sailing to Donegal to let off the Irish and Dutch, and then sail around Malin Head into the Irish Sea with a skeleton crew to their final destination of Ayr on the Scottish coast. From these less conspicuous ports, the men could quietly return home leaving the ship at Ayr for Sir Douglass to reclaim. François saw that the ship's log detailed the events of her recovery and a message to Sir

Archibald from the Dolphin.

Preparations completed, it was with great sadness François saw almost half his crew set sail under the command of Mr. Lowery, each far richer than they had ever dreamed. The downside was doing the Scot a favor by returning his ship; however, being in the Scot's good graces might work to the Dolphin's advantage when the time came as it surely would. The *Agnes,* however, was still a cursed ship.

Taking advantage of a dense, morning fog Gibbs, Maggie, and Henry helped their captain haul a sizeable barrel ashore and into the interior. Over protests, Gibbs and Maggie helped bury his portion of treasure beneath a large tree that towered over all the rest.

While François noted the location in a small book, a second journal apart from the one concerning his exploits, his friends put some distance between them and the tree.

"What be the problem with that tree?" Henry asked.

Gibbs spoke very quietly. "That be a Lagarou tree, lad. If'n I'd knowed what the cap'n were up to, ye wouldn't find me 'ere."

Maggie watched the tree closely for any movement with eyes open so wide Henry was afraid they'd fall out. She alternated between mumbling protective spells and nodding agreement with everything Gibbs said, one of the few times they agreed on anything.

"It be the devil's tree, lad. Evil spirits come to learn their trade here. If ye were fool enough to come at night, ye would see them, little lights going from branch to branch."

"Ye be here at night, they see ye, they suck out yer blood before ye could scream," Maggie whispered nervously.

"If there'd been any clouds 'ere, ye n'er git me

close to that thing. See those other trees next to it. Burned they are. God tries to destroy that thing with 'is lightenin' but it can't be killed."

Heading back to the coast, François had to slow Henry down several times until they had put some distance between them and the Lagarou.

"Of course, the fact that tree is the tallest thing around wouldn't have anything to do with drawing lightening, would it Mr. Gibbs? Or that fire flies like its leaves. Still, it has a useful reputation. Safest place to bury treasure I know . . . especially after Maggie put a curse on it," François said and winked.

Several days later, the *Angelina* limped into the little harbor suffering from the effects of a storm off the southern tip of Puerto Rico.

His crew was more than happy to reach the island despite its reputation. Shaver had been in an increasingly sour mood until reunited with his prodigy at which time he relaxed, content to lounge about the soft, white beach with a keg of rum. On the other hand, François didn't feel like frivolously wasting time. Remaining aboard the *Raven,* he was satisfied making a log entry concerning the worthiness of the ship and overseeing repairs to the *Angelina.*

"You wanted to see us, Cap'n?" Gibbs asked, poking his head through the door.

"Yes," François replied, getting up from the table where he had been working. When Gibbs and Maggie sat down, he poured each a tankard of rum and wine for himself. "I want to discuss our future.

"I don't see much left in the Carib. We have all the gold and jewels we could possibly want. With the word out about the Admiral's fleet and firepower not even Commodore Chudleigh dares stick that big nose out of his stronghold, he's so out-gunned, and the Spaniards are holding all shipments until it's fleet of warships arrives.

All that seems to remain is to drift from island to island for no reason and get into trouble. However, any decision is up to the crew. I would like to return to my family, but will continue to captain the *Raven* if it is their desire . . ., for a while longer."

"We be of a similar mind, Cap'n," Gibbs replied. "The crew would like ye to stay on, but knows your feelin's towards family. It be their mind to sail to Madagascar and shop around the trades as it were, and bein' as El Hierro is on the way, well, we could drop you off."

"Thank you, Mr. Gibbs. What about a new captain?"

"Well, they be undecided about that."

"May I suggest Maggie?"

"A woman!"

Her glare could have cut Harvey's tongue out.

"She is not without experience, and I think she has proved herself, and then some."

"Aye, she has. I'll bring it to the crew," he acquiesced soberly.

"Don't I 'ave a say in this?" she interjected.

"Of course. You can say aye or nay." François grinned, knowing she dreamed of being captain of her own ship again and would do a fine job. "The *Raven* will ultimately have the last word, but my feeling is that she will approve."

Gibbs' left eyebrow raised. "Well, there is that to consider, too, I suppose." Something in his voice expressed hope the *Raven* would object.

Three days later Hogshead and the Dolphin set sail north, the *Raven* preparing to catch the winds and currents home. As the Spanish, French, and English gathered their individual forces to root out the greatest pirate threat in the Caribbean, it was about to split up and vanish as mysteriously as it appeared.

As the two pirate ships casually sailed north their

mere presence struck terror in the hearts of cities and governors. The news spread rapidly throughout the Caribbean of what happened at Antigua. The stories bore little resemblance to truth as tellers plied with rum embellished it to bring attention upon themselves, increase their importance as being someone in the know, and garner the surety of another free tankard. While the Dolphin engineered the fort's self-destruction, storytellers ascribed it to his fleet of ships, which grew larger with each re-telling.

Their fear of attack by the devil's fleet was unfounded, although the islands would continue to contend with Hogshead from time to time who was setting sights on semi-retirement in the Carolinas. Finally, the two ships reached the Florida Keys and the point for the *Raven* to catch the easterly winds and currents that would speed him home.

It was a time François deeply regretted for in this profession chances were good he would not see the irascible Captain Shaver again, nor those with whom he had been close these past two years. As the solid world of land melted into the ocean, a melancholy feeling began to infiltrate the Dolphin's normally cheery disposition. Nor was his depression assuaged as it took forty-three days to traverse the Atlantic, two weeks longer than it should as a seemingly endless string of squalls and becalmings besieged the *Raven* as if nature herself attempted to prevent his retirement. Following a feeling, he rationed food and water early on, but the crew grew increasingly uneasy until the coast of France hove into view.

François' melancholy only deepened when the *Raven* put into St. Nazaire for provisions, the telltale black sails changed out for lighter tan ones. The name was covered over by securing a plank across the stern. For the time the Brigantine became the *Jean-Paul*.

There was little he recognized as he walked the

streets of his youth, now only a very hazy memory. The people only remembered the old Jew and his wife as "those Jesus killers driven out of the country."

Shifting allegiances now pitted France against Spain. Spain was forcefully resisting incursions by French settlers into her coveted areas of the New World, and complaining bitterly of attacks by French privateers on her treasure fleets. François found it amusing that Admiral Shaver's fleet somehow became a part of France's Caribbean navy.

Spain's Queen Mariana did not take the sinking of the *Mary de la Cordova*, gracefully. It was not only one of her favorites, but she had personal designs on the contents in her hold, as she acquired other of Spain's treasures. Adding insult to injury, with the Spanish fortress in ruins and the garrison unable to defend, the English moved to occupy the island of Antigua and then Barbuda. The French denied most of the allegations vehemently, but secretly smiled with satisfaction.

When François sailed from the place of his birth, most likely for the last time, he tried to focus his thoughts on Mariah and the children. The growing excitement at having them cradled in his arms again greatly mollified an almost debilitating funk. However, as they passed the entrance to the Mediterranean his thoughts slipped back to that last time when he was a happy, carefree youth aboard the *Fleurette* with Capt. Jean-Paul, and their travels along this same path skirting the African coast.

Several days later, he stood quietly in his cabin running an idle finger over the charts finding it interesting how he remembered the co-ordinates. They were the last taken as a crewman, part of his training. Going on deck he stood at the rail, the wind whipping his long ponytail as a pain burned in his heart. Somewhere below laid the *Fleurette* and his shipmates.

Finishing a silent prayer for their souls he was

about to retire to his cabin when Gibbs approached carrying a small cask in his arms.

"It'd be proper to leave somethin' fer yer shipmates," he said.

With pained smile, François took the cask of rum and gave it a toss. After a moment, it sank out of sight, which was surprising. Being lighter than water, it should have floated.

Leaning over the gunnel to be sure he'd seen correctly, Gibbs said, "I do believe they've taken it aboard, Cap'n."

"Thank you, Mr. Gibbs. May they share it with the sea so that we might be granted safe passage."

His friends dispensed with the ritual evening meal that night, understanding and respecting their captain's grief by seeing he wasn't disturbed. François appreciated the time alone to remember his captain and friends over a bottle of wine. Feeling tired, he was about to lie down when a slight movement in the shadows near the door caught his eye.

"Mr. Gibbs?" he said, trying to focus on the area. Someone was there.

"It's not Mr. Gibbs," a familiar voice replied. François staggered back against the chart table as the figure stepped forward. "You've grown some, lad."

"Capt. Jean-Paul!"

"Aye. The crew sends their regards and thank you for the gift."

"But . . . I thought you were . . . in Davy Jones' locker."

"Well, I would have expected that, too, but it seems we were not all that bad, some of us anyway. We have been blessed to birth at the other place, what my Irish Bosun calls Fiddler's Green."

François' mind told him this was a dream and to shake his head back to reality, but dream or not, he didn't want to lose the moment and took a step forward. He so wanted to wrap his arms around the man who had become like a father, but hesitated. Was that possible? Jean-Paul stretched out his arms.

Locked together François wept on his captain's shoulder. He'd been there before, but something was different this time. His visitor smelled of lilac water, as he did before going ashore.

After a time Jean-Paul stepped back, holding the young man by both arms and said, "A captain, a fine ship, you have done well for yourself, well indeed."

"I have been fortunate."

"You made your fortune using what you have been blessed with—a good mind. So, tell me all that has happened since we parted."

Seated at the table, sharing a bottle of wine, François explained all that had happened. "I was concerned you might not have approved using your name and assuming a relationship, but then a letter was received from your father explaining you had declared me to be your son."

"I was going to tell you on your next birthday. A surprise . . ., however all has turned well, and my cousin has fulfilled his oath."

"Oath?"

"If you remember, Aloysius was in a bad way when I brought him aboard the Fleurette that time the brethren were ambushed by Chudleigh at Salé. The cut on his thigh barely missed the artery, which would have been certain death. Just before we parted, he agreed to swear an oath that if anything happened to me he would see that your education continued so that you would become captain of your own vessel.

"Well, I cannot stay beyond my time," Jean-Paul said as he stood. "Do not worry about me or the crew. We are well off, considering."

"Will I see you again?"

"Perhaps, if you happen this way again, and God is willing. There is one thing, though, I need to warn you. Over the years I tried to temper your anger, something you must continue to guard. Just remember, do not let anger rule your actions."

The two hugged once more, Jean-Paul drained his glass, and stepped back into the shadows.

As the sun rose above the horizon at the stroke of five bells, François stepped from his cabin, took in a deep breathe of the salty spray, and let it out. He'd not slept so well or felt so rested since leaving Casa St. Nazaire. Joining Gibbs on the poop, he took his stance next to the wheel, the wind blowing his long, unbraided hair.

"The cap'n appears well this fine mornin'," Gibbs said.

"Yes, Mr. Gibbs. Amazing how well one can rest when the soul's burden is lifted."

"It be good to talk things 'or with another."

"You heard?"

"Young 'enry was on watch and heard voices from yer cabin. Knows ye be troubled and thought ye be talkin' in yer sleep 'till hearin' two voices, yours and another. Didn't listen, mind ye, but came straight away to me. I told 'im it be alright."

"I had a visitor."

"Thought as much might happen. Jist after ye took to yer cabin a flock of petrels and a couple albatross began circlin' the ship. Ne'r seen so many all at once. Counted sixty-one all told. Well, that would mean only one thing. Yer shipmates didn't have a decent burial so they will haunt this place. They obviously be cordial to ye so there be nothing to fear, so I had the canvas taken in and we sorta lay-to 'till it got light. It all be well?"

"Yes, Mr. Gibbs, it all be well."

As the wind blew more favorably the next days,

François' spirits continued to lift, especially when looking down from the bowsprit to see a pod of dolphins leaping alongside. It would have been in this area they first met and became the source of his rescue and companionship, and that meant Mariah and the children were not far.

The *Raven* quietly approached Tenerife, standing off to by-pass Santa Cruz during the night. Slipping ghost-like along the eastern coast, it rounded the southern-most tip of the island before making for El Hierro, Ptolemy's western end of the world—the tiny, volcanic rock poking through the azure waters of the south Atlantic, and home.

At three bells of the First Dog Watch a day later, Crandal entered the Dolphin's cabin to announce, "Cap'n, El Hierro off starboard."

"Very good. Stand off five leagues. Are we flying the Spanish flag?"

"Aye. A merchantman."

"Good. If anyone notices, we will appear to be nothing more than one of the king's ships on a southerly course. No reason to draw attention."

Once past Valverde and the north end of the island Sa'id set the *Raven*'s bow on a westerly course directly toward two projections of land reaching into the ocean as if arms of embrace welcoming home a loved one. Just before dawn, the anchor splashed into the placid waters within Dolphin Cove. After lowering three longboats, a large sea chest was lowered into each before François stepped into the one oared by Henry.

As the boy leaned into the sweeps, François said, "Henry, would you like to stay ashore and live with my family?"

The boy stopped rowing and stared at his captain. The bow scraping the beach seemed to galvanize his thoughts. "I'd like that, Cap'n, but I'd like to spend a bit more time at sea. We be comin' back this way. Maybe then?"

François understood and smiled faintly, winked, while nodding agreement.

Once the chests were set on the beach the boats returned to the *Raven*, which immediately set sail around the southern tip of El Hierro to the village of Pozo de Sabinosa nestled above the shore of El Golfo. Here they planned to take on the supplies needed for the trip around the Horn of Africa and on to the rich trades of the East Indies.

Chapter 27

† The Señora †

Two weeks following her husband's abduction Mariah sat upon a woven settee in the shade of the veranda, the picture of strength and serenity as she hemmed a nightshirt for one-year-old, Jean-Paul. It was exactly the appearance she wanted—the appearance she needed to portray, both for herself and for those working the plantation. Looking up, she saw Alessandro Santana appear out of the forest astride his reddish-brown stallion, followed by two soldiers.

Replacing Capt. Hidalgo, Alessandro and François become good friends and he frequent visited, especially on the way to and from El Gulfo. However, she could tell this was not a social call as he dismounted. Flashing a broad smile, his dark eyes could not hide that something was troubling him.

"Good day, Señora Mariah," he said with a bow, and taking her hand, kissed it.

Amstedt was off toward the outside kitchen area in conversation with Cirano. Stopping, he glared at the new arrival.

"It is too late in the day to be on an inspection tour and your eyes tell me there is something troubling you." She was one to go right to the root of any problem.

Capt. Santana learned very early in their acquaintance that Mariah was very observant and outspoken. "Well . . . yes . . . I . . ."

"Have your men water the horses while we sit in the shade and you can tell me what is so disturbing. Isleta, please fetch the captain and his soldiers a cool drink. Now, you must have something about my husband."

"Women frighten me, Señora Mariah, but you more than any. You seem to have the ability to read a person's mind."

"Not at all, Alessandro. I've lost my husband to pirates and there is great worry in your eyes. My father taught me to be observant."

The captain reached inside his jacket to extract a piece of paper. "A ship's captain arrived this morning from Güímar. He met Don François there who asked tht this be delivered to me. I'm afraid that I read it. My sincerest apologies. It was meant for you."

Taking the folded message, she saw that it bore Capt. Santana's name on the outside in her husband's writing. She read it, fighting desperately to not cry.

"Actually, I think he wanted you to see this. Well, there is nothing either of us can do except wait for his return."

"Will you be alright here?"

"Oh, yes. Mr. Amstedt is staying on to help. He is a very capable man."

Santana looked toward the old sailor who was still standing in the yard glaring at him.

"Are you sure he is just an old sailor and not an old pirate?"

Mariah chuckled. "You are being suspicious."

"That is part of my duties, Señora Mariah."

"And what does the eyes and ears of the governor say?"

"That he was with the pirate Hogshead and left behind when they took your husband."

"And what role did Mr. Amstedt play in the kidnapping of my husband?"

"None. He stood back and watched. He did not attempt to help your husband."

"And how much help would a man with one lung be? Not to worry, Alessandro. He is a good man and his arrival very much appreciated." She patted his hand.

During François' absence, the captain stopped at least every two weeks, sometimes more often. Mariah enjoyed his visits, although at first was suspicious of the soldier's intentions. At twenty-seven, he cut a dashing figure in a military uniform with curly, dark brown hair and dark eyes, a strong jaw and chin, a regal bearing with an effervescent smile. After all, she was a wealthy woman whose husband was kidnapped by pirates with no word concerning his whereabouts, or if he still lived.

Then there was Lucy, equally wealthy, developing into a beautiful, young woman. The two often sat on the veranda talking, mostly about Spain and grand ladies of the court. Isleta was present during such visits if Mariah had to be elsewhere, however even her presence would not have been necessary. If Mr. Amstedt wasn't hovering nearby keeping an eye on the visitor, Hassan practically sat between them; however Santana's intentions were entirely virtuous. As he bashfully admitted, Mariah reminded him very much of his sister. He was a lonely boy far from home. He made no such distancing comparisons with Lucy.

Chapter 28

† Reunion †

Barely mid-morning and the oppressive heat continued to rise as it had for the past week. Like the others, Hassan rose in the dim light of pre-dawn to work his portion of the vegetable field. Even then, it was warm. An hour after the sun appeared he looked over the remaining area to be cultivated, estimating at least another hour and a half of labor remaining.

Beads of sweat began gathering to become cascading rivulets down his brown body, the blue bandanna about his head barely managing to keep the stinging, salty liquid out of his eyes. Likewise, the burnoose draped over his shoulders was drenched and clung like a second skin intensifying the discomfort.

Not finishing the chore would put him further behind. He only stopped long enough to gulp ladles of cool water as a little girl continually circulated about the fields with a bucket. He had decided to push on and finish one more row when Lucy came along carrying a large basket over one arm.

"Hello," she called out in that sweet, lyric voice that caused his heart to skip.

He smiled weakly while wiping a forearm across his brow.

Turning to Mr. Amstedt who circled the work area like a hungry shark, she interrupted his conversation with Cirano and several workers, "I'm tired of this heat, Mr. Amstedt. I have decided to go to the cove."

True to his word, Don François had cared for Lucy following her father's death. Not just to Hassan's notion, she was frightfully spoiled, but secretly liked her anyway. It was difficult even for the normally stern Mr. Amstedt not to smile when she was about. Bubbling joyfully, she always had a smile and a kind word for the old man.

From the time Hassan came to Casa de St. Nazaire she was aloof and distant toward him, sometimes downright rude. Cirano, whose friendship to Hassan was like a brother, suggested that she might be jealous of his coming to the plantation. However, over the past few months, she began speaking more kindly to him, and then unexpectedly become irritated over some triviality. For the boy, she had become a frustrating pain in the buttocks.

Hassan tended to being quiet and withdrawn. He readily worked a portion of the field, quick to respond to anything Mariah needed done, and tended the horses. That job he enjoyed the most, spending hours exercising each one, brushing their coats, and keeping the barn and corrals immaculate. Once finished training Lucy's filly, she began riding almost daily and brushing the coat until the hairs reflected the sunlight as if they were tiny mirrors.

Amstedt kept an eye on Lucy, especially when she was in the barn area. Not that he mistrusted Hassan, but remembered himself at that age. When she came to ride, Hassan always stopped whatever he was doing, and quickly saddle the filly. The two then rode out, generally with Jean-Paul as company, and always staying in the open areas.

Returning, she brushed down the animal and stayed to talk to Hassan as he swept out the stall before putting the horse in. Hassan was always proper and kept a respectful distance, best he could with a girl constantly at his shoulder.

Amstedt also noticed their interactions at the dining table as they sat across from one another, she with the twins on either side, and he with Jean-Paul who adored his big brother. Hassan said nothing unless asked a question. Lucy chattered constantly. What Amstedt noticed was how her eyes would move to look at Hassan then away. Face buried in a plate of food, the young man lift his head up every so often just enough to look at Lucy, and then return to the plate. Once in a while the two looked at one another at the same time at which point each instantly divert their eyes elsewhere. Mariah also saw the same peek-a-boo game as they all sat on the veranda in the evenings.

"Go with Miss Lucy," Amstedt said to Hassan.

Hassan groaned inwardly. The assignment would put him seriously behind in his other chores as well. Before Amstedt arrived he would have protested, but learned early on one did not argue with the overseer, so dropped everything. Of course, it would be nice to cool off in the ocean.

As she continued along the path leading to the

hot pool and down to the beach, Hassan looked at the old man, spreading his arms as to silently say, "What about this work?" Amstedt returned Hassan's stare and simply cocked his head in her direction. Leaning the hoe against the split rail fence, he vaulted over and quickly jogged up to follow behind the girl.

"Oh, are you going to escort me?" she teased.

"Yes, Miss Lucy."

"Without your clothes?"

Wheeling around, Hassan sprinted back to the big rock where he had cached his burnoose and a pair of tattered sandals, and slipped them on, aware of Amstedt's scowl. The normally dour expression was there, but the man's eyes flashed something different.

Thinking Amstedt was acting strangely, Hassan dashed to catch up and fall in behind the girl just as she was about to enter into the forest and shade. He thought it would be cooler, but instead found the air even more humid, hot, and stifling. It didn't get any better as they passed the hot pool and followed the cataract of steamy water adding to the heat.

Upon breaking out of the forest onto the barren mountainside, the sun's rays bounced off the volcanic rock intensifying the discomfort. Normally he didn't bother with sandals, but was glad for the small protection they afforded from the frying-hot rock.

There wasn't a hint of breeze here either, as the ocean lay near motionless like a huge sheet of lightly rippled glass. Angling downward across the exposed rock face toward the beach felt like being in a huge oven; the heat radiating through the thin soles of his sandals as the unrelenting sun baked him inside his own garment. The only relief was the thought of diving into the turquoise water.

"I've never seen it so calm," she said, setting the basket on the large log laying partially buried in the sand just beyond the high tide line. Then pulling off her thin dress, she tossed it over the log next to the basket and sprinted across the searing, black sand and into the water.

Hassan stood motionless and swallowed hard as he stared at her lithe figure barely concealed beneath the thin, linen garment. Dumb-like, he watched as she swam into deeper water and disappear beneath the surface for a moment. Reappearing, the long, strawberry-blond hair lay flat against her head, beads of water glistening like small diamonds on a browned face.

"Well, are you just going to stand there and bake or come in?" she shouted.

Taking up the basket carelessly left in the sun, he set it in the shade of the log, and removed his sandals. After some hesitation, he slipped the burnoose over his head, draping it over the log next to Lucy's dress. Still hesitating, he stood as the water lapped up around his feet, suddenly feeling self-conscious. Finally, he ran out to dive in and swim to where she waited. The instant cooling effect shot a surge of energy through his body.

Lucy swam further out, then with an arching kick slipped below the surface. Hassan followed, coming alongside the girl as they angled downward.

The bottom was smooth sand with only a few scattered boulders that ran out perhaps thirty Toise from shore before angling steeply down. Near the end of the dragon's head the water was deeper and the abundance of sea life greater, especially with lobsters and other shellfish. The area had always proved to be good fishing.

After several dives, they surfaced next to the base of the rocky projection and faced each other. She laughed. They had been playing a game of tag and she just barely touched his foot before he reached the 'safe' zone beneath the arched hole through the southern promontory.

"You are a good swimmer," he said.

"Thank you kind sir," she replied sweetly with an infectious smile that was so alluring. "I'm hungry."

He swallowed hard while looking into her dark, green eyes. "Me, too." It was late and he hadn't stopped for breakfast that morning.

"If you fetch the basket we can eat up in the shade of the eye. It will be cooler."

As she climbed up into the natural hole, he retrieved the basket, returning by using a side crawl while balancing it above the water. Pulling onto the flat rock where Lucy sat, he watched her open the basket, remove a chicken drumstick, and hand it over. There wasn't much discussion as they gnawed on the pieces of baked chicken and raw vegetables—enough for two. Although hungry, Hassan found it difficult to eat as he kept glancing at her while trying not to be noticed. The girl's thin garment, now wet, didn't hide much.

When he came to live at Casa de St. Nazaire she was a skinny, little girl already on her way to becoming annoying. During the intervening three years she became a beautiful woman—long, light, cream-colored hair with a reddish tint, deep green eyes swimming in pools of white, and a petite, well-sculptured body tanned a deep, rich, amber from head to toe. The effervescent twinkle in her eyes and infectious smile always set his heart beating a little faster, but in recent months it had sent his blood into a boil.

Lucy was secretly staring at him, too, and then tossed a cleaned leg bone into the water. "You have never said how you came to be with the old carpenter that built Mama's coach?"

"The man who owned me sold me to the old sailor when I was about five or six. I don't know why, but there was some kind of trouble and he said I had to leave. The old man was a ship's carpenter and took me as an apprentice. As we neared this island, he took ill so they put him off. I went overboard as the ship began to make sail and came ashore."

"But I thought you couldn't swim? François had to teach you."

"I had an empty powder keg to cling to. I was very frightened, but I wouldn't have stayed on that ship. It was not a good place without the old man. One of the officers wanted me for a woman."

"He wanted you for what?"

Hassan shrugged his shoulders and continued, "Capt. Shaver didn't approve, either."

"That is the same pirate who took François away."

"Yes. The Captain and the man argued about it, and then the Captain tossed me an empty keg after throwing me overboard. It was not all that far to shore. What about you? How did you come to be on this island?"

"My father was a seafaring man. Mother died seven months before he came home. I was living with my mother's older sister by then. Papa was already very upset about something that happened on his voyage. He never explained except to say there were men trying to take something away that he had. We left and moved many times before coming to this island. He didn't think they would find him, but they did." A tear formed in her left eye and trickled down her cheek.

"There was a terrible fight. He managed to kill most of them. One ran off, but papa said he would be back. Papa was hurt and could not run. We heard someone coming and hid. It was François. The one who had run away returned and they fought. Papa knew he was dying and shot the man and then asked François to take care of me." Her thin lips quivered as she choked back a sob, tossing her head to whip strands of the shoulder blade-length hair from her face, trying to cast off the moment.

"Papa gave François a small chest of gold coins, so we were not without money. The pirates returned and we had to run away. François returned the next day to give papa a Christian burial, but the pirates already did that. He then began to gather any usable items. That's when he found another chest of coins with a treasure map. When Captain Shaver appeared, he gave him that map. No one was aware of the second map in my chest until I found it later. Have you ever wanted to go back home?" She said, changing the subject.

"My ship put in there once. There was some kind of trouble and we had to leave very fast. Life aboard ship was hard, but we seldom went hungry. I was not a very good sailor and think that was another reason to maroon me here."

"Is that the way you think of being here—marooned?"

During the discussion, Hassan's eyes had been pinned on his feet dangling over the edge of the rock, kicking at an occasional wave that sloshed through the arch. With this question, he raised his chin so that their eyes met for a brief moment before resuming his feet and answered softly, "No." Following a long pause he said, "At first I missed being at sea, but less as time passed. I came to like being on El Hierro and especially at Casa de St. Nazaire. Don François and Lady Mariah have treated me well." He chuckled. "In a way I kind of like crotchety Mr. Amstedt, but don't you tell him."

Unsaid, the fact remained that he increasingly

felt drawn to this girl despite their being from two very different worlds and stations in life. It was easy to toss off any serious thoughts as mere fantasies, but not the feelings inside.

While the two sat silently side by side listening to the waves gently slosh against the rocks he could hear his heart pounding in his breast. He had tried to not look at the girl because her eyes, her hair, her smooth, dark skin, her breasts, were causing a stirring deep inside.

"Do you like me?" she blurted out.

His chin snapped up as he looked at her directly before lowering it.

"Yes, Miss Lucy," he said weakly.

"Why do you always call me Miss Lucy?"

"Because that is the proper way for a person of my station to address a young woman. Mr. Amstedt has so instructed me."

Curling the index finger of her right hand, she tucked it under his chin, lifting it to turn his gaze back to her. His eyes were like liquid pools of coal, penetrating, mysterious, bottomless. She wondered if he could feel the quiver radiating through her body.

"I've never thought of you as that way."

"But that is my life."

"Not here, Hassan. Not in this place. You have never been considered or treated as a servant at Casa St. Nazaire. I know I have often treated you rudely. I don't know why, but I never thought you as someone beneath me." Leaning forward she kissed him on the cheek.

Hassan didn't turn away this time, but looked deeply into her eyes for a long time before leaning forward until their lips met, lingering, as the desire smoldering deep in their breasts struck a tiny flame. Encircling arms about each other the passion grew as they kissed.

"Bring the basket and come with me," she said and slipped into the water to swim back to the beach.

Hassan lifted the much lighter basket into the air and swam behind her although he felt as if it might be possible to stand on the surface and skip back. Reaching the beach, she gathered up their clothes, took him by the hand, and ran toward the cabin.

Stepping onto the porch of the beach house, she tossed the clothes over a railing and ducked inside. Wheeling around in the middle of the single room, she faced him. Hassan was growing apprehensive as he entered the cool darkness.

"Did you know this is where Mariah and François first lived? Well, not the same cabin, but on this same spot."

"Yes," he replied, sounding vague, surprised to find his teeth chattering as if he were cold.

"Mariah's father built the first cabin. She was living in it alone when François came to the island."

"On the backs of dolphins," Hassan filled in, still a bit skeptical of the legend.

"Mariah told me they exchanged a pledge to become husband and wife on the beach, then came here," she explained pointing to the hammock bed.

Hassan shivered again despite the warmth.

"Do you like me?" she asked.

The boy immediately saw the direction the girl was taking, feeling as if struck in the gut while something akin to a lightning bolt shot through his body.

"I've always liked you."

"Will you be my husband?"

"Is not that to be the man's question?" he said, stalling, fear now digging its talons deep into his body.

"Mariah said sometimes it is for the woman to ask, when the man is too shy."

"It would not be right. You are a lady. I am a lowly . . ."

"Will you stop that nonsense? You are not."

Hassan continued to avoid the situation. "It would be proper to wait for the return of Don François and ask his permission."

"He's been gone three years. Some say he may even be dead, although neither Mariah nor I believe that. Do you love me?"

Hassan desperately wanted to change the subject, to turn, and run out of the cabin.

"Yes," he replied weakly then thought to himself, "Why did I say that? I will be a dead man when Don François returns."

"You do not sound very sure."

Hassan stuttered, stammered, and stared at his feet. They remained planted to the hard-packed floor. True. To wed this girl was something he had fantasied. What he feared was not so much what François would say, but do upon his eventual return.

"Do we not need a religious man . . . like a priest?"

"Why? Our family has never had need of them. Papa was a Calvinist. François said many times that he distrusts them."

"But the Don," he continued trying to beg off, seeing in his mind's eye the tip of François' sword plunging into his chest.

"I am almost twenty. Are you not also the same age?" she said.

"Yes."

"Then are we not old enough to make up our own minds about such things? Mariah has seen how we are when in each other's company. She sees things more clearly than either of us. We spoke until very late last night about that. Do you love me as your eyes speak."

"Yes," Hassan stuttered, coming to understand his true feelings and voicing them.

With great curiosity, he watched as the girl slowly placed one very warm hand on his breastbone, looked into his eyes and said, "I pledge my loyalty and love to you for all the days of my life, no matter what sorrow or pain may befall us, to be your wife in all things, and mother of your children."

Hassan was mesmerized and only vaguely aware when she gently placed his hand flat over her heart. Neither was he entirely aware of the words that tumbled from his lips, but something that mimicked her vow. What he kept seeing was Don François' evil grin as he twisted the sword buried in his chest just before pushing him backward over a cliff.

"I am a dead man," he groaned within himself.

It was late the following morning as husband and wife lay nestled in one another's arms when his bladder called. Slipping slowly away, he quietly made for the door so as not to disturb the girl. Having relieved himself in the bushes around back, he returned to stand on the porch and stare out at the blue expanse of ocean. Ever since moving into puberty an increasing ache racked his body to bond with a woman, but the opportunity never presented itself to fulfill that destiny. If it had, he was certain to have been too afraid.

Thinking back, their first union was so frantic, but each successive episode became more deliberate and satisfying as they sought to please each other rather than just their own lust. Now he must return to the hacienda and face whatever would come. Then a nagging thought slipped into the back of his mind like an itch one couldn't reach. What if Lucy did not have Señora Mariah's permission? When she discovered what happened would she understand? Mr. Amstedt, on the other hand, would take a different view. A strict, foreboding man, he closely guarded Lucy's welfare. Entrusted to protect this girl, Hassan could only hope Mariah would mediate. Then there was Don François. A quiver ran through his body. How would he react? Could anyone quell his certain anger?

Two arms encircled his chest as Lucy's soft body pressed against his back, her breath warm against his right ear as she whispered, "Is something wrong?"

"No," he lied.

"François always said that next to an oath the most sacred thing was to be truthful."

Hassan didn't respond.

"You are worried about what François will say when he returns."

"More what he will do than say, if Mr. Amstedt does not kill me first."

She laughed softly. "He will not kill you."

"I know him differently. Anyway, we must go back. My portion of garden needs tending."

"That has been taken care of."

"How?"

"Look on the beach, next to the old log."

Hassan hadn't looked closely at the beach, but next to the salt-water-hardened tree were several boxes.

"Where did those come from?"

"Mariah said she would have provisions brought if we did not return last night. She said it was important that we have time together, alone."

"She conspired?"

"Well, you are so shy. Everyone could tell you had feelings toward me; everyone except you. I would cry every night after you left. I am sorry if you feel tricked."

"You are right. I would have never dared approach you," he said, turning to kiss his bride.

Slipping the ankle-length shirt over his curly, black hair, Hassan made his way down to where the boxes were neatly stacked and stared at them.

"When did these come?"

"Mr. Amstedt arrived several hours ago. You were sound asleep."

"Mr. Amstedt?"

"Aye," a deep, baritone voice said from a jumble of large boulders behind them.

"Mr. Amstedt!" Hassan's body went rigid causing his voice to squeak.

"Congratulations," he responded with a big smile while pumping Hassan's hand in a vice-like shake before giving Lucy a fatherly kiss on the cheek. "Congratulations ARE in order?"

"Yes," Lucy said.

"I waren to leave these here, but ze are heavy. Jou are strong, jongen, but thought jou would like a hand moving zem to de cabin." Then unexpectedly, the old Dutchman curled a big, rough hand behind Hassan's neck in a gesture of affection. "Besides, I want to be de first to congratulate de newlyweds."

"How did you get all this here?" Hassan asked as they began toting the wood crates over the loose sand and up the steep incline to the cabin.

"Longboat from de village. I send zem away after unload. Easier to go back up de trail."

Hassan still harbored uneasiness around the Dutchman. He'd been a hard taskmaster over the past months leaving little time during the day to become bored. After making his expectations clear, he accepted no excuses for poor work, nor did he tolerate talking back. Yet, Hassan found the old man patient when one tried their best, and readily responded to questions if something seemed unclear.

Although robust for his condition, the work was strenuous for a man with only one lung, necessitating frequent stops. Hiking back to the hacienda would not be an easy task for him, either. There obviously was something more to his visit.

Just before taking the last box up to the rock steps Amstedt paused, but not because of being winded. "I not aware jou two had such strong feelings voor each other. Well, dat not exactly correct. I could see how jou two looked at de other, or perhaps meer correctly, try not look at de other. I see how jou both act, nervous, like mouse en cat. I never have children, en it too many years since I courted de wife, God rest her soul, so I forget, but I am happy voor jou both. Jou are a likable jongen, en would have been proud if jou warren my son. Dat said, a little vader advise. Do Miss Lucy wrong en your manhood be in danger, jou catch my drift."

"Aye, Mr. Amstedt. I gave my word and am bound to it."

"Dat is a goede thing. Don François is one of de few men I hear dat never gave his word to anything but he kept it, come the duivel his self. Well, jou two love birds take all time needed and nit worry about werk at hacienda. It will be done proper if I have to do it myself."

"Thank you, Mr. Amstedt," Hassan replied, much relieved.

"No telling what Don François will say about deze, though," he said, putting an arm around the boys shoulder, "but I stand voor jou. Make this island jou home. Do not leave. Dat be best," he said with a wink, touching the half-moon pendant at Hassan's throat before returning to hoist the last box up the rocks. That was the second time someone made that admonition.

Once the box was stacked with the others, he turned to leave, but not without a final word to Lucy. "Jou glow like de sun, Miss Lucy. Jou papa would be pleased, real pleased." Then in a whisper and jerking a thumb in Hassan's direction, "He is goede jongen, a little slow in some things, but has goede heart."

Without further words Amstedt took off up the steep trail alongside the stream leading directly to the hacienda, the same trail Hassan would use returning to work several days later.

During the next three months, Husband and wife settled into a daily routine not unlike that of François and Mariah when they lived on the coast. It was an idyllic life of work mixed with the pleasures of each other's company on a secluded beach, and life at the hacienda, until Lucy became ill in the morning, sapping her strength.

They were excited knowing they were to become parents, but concerned about the lingering sickness. Seeking advice, Mariah smiled and told him not to worry about his duties at the plantation, but stay and comfort his wife. Returning with Guanches medicine to ease the morning sickness of pregnancy, he remained close.

Several weeks later, they felt a sporadic rumbling and heard what sounded like distant thunder. The fear was that there might be a renewal of volcanic activity somewhere on the island. Neither slept well. As the sun cleared the watery horizon Hassan stepped out onto the porch. Gazing out upon their protected cove, it didn't open upon an unobstructed expanse of ocean. A black, foreboding ship lay at anchor.

"Lucy!" He whispered, shaking her. "Pirates! Their ship is in the cove."

Vaulting from the bed, she joined her husband to watch from the secrecy of their cabin as three long boats came ashore, each containing two men except for the lead boat, which had three. Upon reaching shore, the third man jumped ashore to begin issuing directions.

The intruder stood in sharp contrast to those who brought him ashore. They wore little more than knee britches and tight-fitting shirts. He was dressed as going to a ball in shiny black, knee boots, gray and white stripped pantaloons, and a flowing, maroon, silk shirt beneath a black long coat with silver stitching. An ostrich plume waived in the gentle breeze from a large-brimmed hat.

The sailors immediately set to unloading a sea chest from each boat, their struggles indicating each was very heavy. When the third and last chest was stacked on the dry sand, the sailors shook the man's hand, then saluted before returning to the longboats. One appeared to be a boy who hugged the man before joining the others to row back into the gentle waves leaving him to stand on the beach alone.

"Climb up along the stream and go to the hacienda. Tell Mr. Amstedt pirates have marooned a man here."

"What are you going to do?" she whispered.

"I will stay here and watch him. Now hurry, before he turns this way and sees you."

Pulling on her clothes as she fled, Lucy hastily began the ascent using boulders and vegetation to cover her escape. When she was safely out of sight, Hassan again turned his attention to the man on their beach who stood motionless with hands on hips watching.

When the sailors reached the ship, he turned to walk inland toward the cabin. He seemed to know exactly where to go as both the cabin and trail leading to it were well hidden from view, either from the sea or the beach. If Hassan tried to take cover in the surrounding trees now, he'd be seen. The only thing was to back into the cabin where he stood firm, feet apart, sword in hand next to the back wall.

Gaining the porch, the man turned to look seaward, glimpsing the ship as it vanished from view, heading south around the dragon's snout. He then drew a cutlass and pistol.

"Alright, come out," he ordered.

Hassan slowly emerged and the two faced each other.

"Don François?" the young man said, finally breaking the heavy silence. "You've returned!"

"Hassan . . .? Well, you have grown," he said, putting the weapons away and hugging him. "So, you are living here and not at the house?"

"Yes," Hassan said with some hesitation.

"Well, it is good you are here." Without another word François stripped down to his britches, laying the clothing over the porch railing. "Come on, I can use your back." Returning to the beach, he put on a burst of speed to sprint into the gentle surf throwing up a great wake of water.

With effortless ease, his long arms stretched out pulling him with amazing speed through the water. Despite having become a good swimmer, Hassan was hard put to keep up. Arriving at the eye of the dragon, François scampered through the opening to the other side, then along the rocky base of the promontory leading back to the mainland. Hopping from one rock to another, he nimbly made the waterfall, and ducked behind its curtain into a small cave. Hassan stayed close behind, confused, and curious.

Just inside the veiled opening sat a lantern and tender box on a high ledge. Striking flint and steel against the wick produced a bright, yellow light by which he proceeded deeper into the cave until coming upon an over-turned longboat on a shelf above the high tide mark. This they righted and oared back out and around the projection of basalt to where the chests rested.

Wrestling one of the chests into the boat took every bit of their strength. It was indeed heavy. Fortunately, there was hardly any waves otherwise the boat would have been swamped, it sat so low in the water.

Hassan rowed the boat back to the cave while François returned as they had initially gone. Once pass the curtain of water, François took a rope to pull it along, penetrating the cave some distance further beyond where the boat initially had rest. Coming to a large slab of rock laying across the stream, they pulled the bow onto a soft, sandy incline. Here, the two again struggled with the round-top chest until it was stowed in a small room well hidden from the stream. The last chest they stacked apart from the others.

Near exhaustion, they secured the launch where it had originally lain and returned to the entrance, but instead of going the way they had come, François ascended a nearly invisible, vertical, hand and toe trail up the face of the cliff to the top where the long trail home drove into the cleft. From there he strolled out to the end of the promontory and peered over the edge. Hassan gingerly crept close to the edge. It was a long drop and certainly looked higher from here than from below. In the crystalline waters, he spotted a large, black shape moving slowly about the cove close to shore.

"I love it up here," François said and then eyeing the young man peering apprehensively over the edge, said, "A long drop, aye?"

"Oh, yes," the boy gulped.

"And it is now has a pirate's friends."

Hassan was horrified to realize a shark had moved into the cove.

"You have become a good swimmer. Have you never jumped from here?"

"Yes, but never realized there were sharks," he stuttered as a second black shape joined the first.

François stepped back and drew a long dagger stashed in his belt and pointed it at Hassan's chest.

"A pirate's treasure should be safe, aye?"

Hassan's eyes opened so wide his black pupils appeared as tiny dots awash in a sea of white.

"I swear secrecy, Don François," he stammered, remembering the horrible vision when Lucy proposed marriage.

François replied by stepping forward. Hassan inched back to the edge.

"Please, sir," he pleaded, trying to avoid the sharp point, "I swear not to reveal the location of your treasure."

"I knew that would never be a problem, but you need to learn a lesson about overcoming fear," François replied as a mischievous smile etched across his burnt face just before lunging forward.

Instinctively jumping back, Hassan realized too late that it was a step into thin air. François leaned forward to watch as the body plunged toward the ocean and its black forms.

To Hassan the fall seemed to take an eternity. Managing to twist around to hit the water feet first, a great roar filled his ears. Kicking frantically, he stretched for the surface, hearing what sounded like a dull boom just before breaking the surface. Whirling around, he desperately searched for the tale-tell fins. When the first one broke the surface he knew it was approaching too fast for him to make the promontory. He was about to suffer the destiny of those whose mouth must never be allowed to reveal the secret of buried treasure. He only hoped the end would be swift. Suddenly François' head burst upon the surface next to him.

"I would say your lesson is complete my Arab friend."

"Sharks!" Hassan cried out pointing at the approaching fins.

"Do you know you squeal like a woman," François laughed as he slapped the water with outstretched hands. "How long have you been here? Have you ever seen sharks in this cove?"

The nearest fin disappeared beneath the surface a mere fifteen pied from the two, and then as suddenly the bottle nose of a silver-gray dolphin popped up in front of them chattering excitedly as François stroked the beast gently. When a second nose broke above the surface nearly nose-to-nose, Hassan squealed in surprise.

"Pet him," François said as a third came to the surface. Reaching out a hand, he grabbed a fin. "Oh, how I have missed you my friends. Take hold, Hassan."

With that, François gripped the large fin and stretched out on the water to be carried away. Hassan latched onto the nearest fin. Just as quickly he felt the wake from the mammal's powerful tail as they shot forward.

With other dolphins leaping alongside, the two were briefly towed about the cove with amazing speed, and then toward the beach. At the last moment, François let go as the creature turned sharply, propelling him onto sand where he sprang up and stepped ashore. Hassan, too, was beached, but not so gracefully. Rolling onto the sand, he staggered, breathing hard, and stumbled, falling near François' feet. In the small cove, the pod of dolphin heads bobbed in the water, watching, and chattering excitedly before one rose upon its tail to swim backward, capping the show with an impressive leap into the ocean's depths.

"Oh, it is so good to be home." Then as they dressed François said, "Well, we are rich men."

"Rich?" Hassan replied in surprise.

"One chest belongs to Mr. Amstedt. He is still alive?"

"Oh, yes."

"The other two are for the family Evreux. You are part of that family."

"Thank you, sir," was the stunned reply, then his eyes bulged and mouth dropped open as he comprehended the sudden turn of events in his poor life, but his excitement was dampened by the thought of what his benefactor would say upon learning of his marriage. He thought it better to explain when Mariah was around to temper any ill-feelings. "You will be going on to the plantation?"

"Yes. I am anxious to see Mariah and the children. But, we can't leave that girl hiding in the trees behind the cabin."

Hassan spun around and stared toward the back of the structure shrouded by dense growth of trees and undergrowth, but saw no one until a slight movement caught his eye. Lucy had not left. Her presence known, she boldly stepped out to stand next to Hassan, hugging his arm.

"Surely, this is not the little girl I left behind. Lucy?"

"My wife," Hassan replied boldly.

"Yes," she replied firmly.

"My word, but you have turned into a fine woman. And now married?"

"Yes," she replied. "With Mariah's blessing."

"And soon to be a mother."

Reaching out, François curled a left hand behind Hassan's right ear and a right behind Lucy's left to gently pulled them to forward, kissing each on the forehead.

Chapter 29

† Call to Arms †

 Typically, Capt. Santana rode up to the hacienda at a canter, his horse stepping proudly as its long, silky tail arched high to catch the wind and shimmer in the sun. However, on this day, everyone could tell this visit was not social. He arrived at a full gallop with four soldiers trailing behind, their horse's sleek shoulders and flanks white with lather.

"Good afternoon, Captain," Mariah said as he stepped onto the veranda. Her vivacious smile faded upon seeing his worried expression, making him appear older.

"Good afternoon, Señora Evreux." He bowed and kissed her hand. "I am afraid I cannot stay long. I come with bad news. Spain and France are at war. We have been warned to expect trouble."

"Here? What possibly would bring the French to our doorstep? We are so far from anything important."

"Apparently they intend to take the Canary Islands to control shipping to the New World. To do that would require a base from which to launch an invasion of each island. Regretfully, our defenses are the most vulnerable, suiting their plans. I have come from the Governor-general with a request to seek volunteers for an armed resistance."

"Begging uw pardon, Lady Mariah, but do I understand de Captain seeks to raise en army?" Mr. Amstedt said as he joined them on the porch.

"That is correct," Santana said.

"I have a little experience in such things. I assume jou intend meeting de French invaders as ze step ashore?"

"That is the plan, as impractical as that may be."

"The Captain understands. De only sensible defense is to allow them to land en confine them to Valverde. With Lady Mariah's permission, I can make these farmers into soldiers."

"Yes, of course, Mr. Amstedt."

Those on the plantation between fifteen and fifty responded eagerly and divided their time between their labors and the capable marshaling of Mr. Amstedt. Each day the feeling around the hacienda became one of a military camp. This Mariah dreaded because if the rumor came to fruition it would mean some, if not many, would die.

~ ~ ~ ~

When Lucy began to flee up the steep trail, it quickly became apparent pregnancy would make the journey nearly impossible. That's why she returned to the cabin. Besides, she wasn't about to leave her husband alone with a pirate, even if it were just one. They would fight him together.

Reunited with Francois was a joyous event, but the exertion had been too much and François was far too anxious to return home by traveling the long way. That's why Hassan and Lucy insisted he go ahead and they would come at a slower pace.

Just before stepping from the trees into the meadow, François looked over his home. It had changed a great deal during his absence. The hacienda had grown in size, obviously using the plans for the expansion detailed with diagrams in his journal.

Amstedt admitted at not being very good at working wood, but recognized good construction. A journey to Valverde to personally inspect various individuals' work helped to secure first-rate artisans. The home now stood two stories surrounding a central courtyard with a covered balcony stretching atop the veranda.

The once small field for vegetables was significantly larger, and the trees planted to shield Mariah and Lucy when they bathed in the stream stood tall and dense. When he left, four people were needed to work the fields, now he counted ten. A number of well-bred horses grazed on lush grass within large, pole-fenced areas. A larger barn peeked from behind the volcanic outcrop that served as the hacienda's back wall. However, more importantly was the woman seated in the shade of the veranda, just as he had envisioned for nearly thirty-six months.

~ ~ ~ ~

As mothers and wives watched their men train, apprehension and fear increased. These women were now more than ever her responsibility, for the fear and anxiety filling them was close to the surface. They needed to see her indomitable strength, especially when what must surely be the sounds of war—sporadic, muffled thuds carried on a fickle wind—reached their hearing. When the sounds came more loudly and the land quivered it generated great anxiety among the people for only the biggest war ships had such weapons and certainly not the small island's meager defenses. She worried greatly as they expected the call to arms at any moment. When the dull thunder stopped, she knew the battle must have ended. With the eventual arrival of the victorious French, her life as such would come to a close.

Despite this, Mariah continued to sit quietly on the porch, in clear sight of all, sewing, calmly waiting. As the shadows from the mountain behind the house lengthened and stretched toward the eastern forest and hills, it remained insufferably warm. For nearly three weeks the cooling, ocean breeze failed. Suddenly the pines moaned softly. Gazing at the towering tips, she saw them sway gently. When another puff of air came, it encircled and caressed her moist skin—cooling, refreshing, renewing. Closing her eyes, Mariah inhaled the freshening air. It felt good.

When an excited feeling stirred her bosom, she opened her eyes to see a tall man standing in the shadows a few Toise out from the porch. Blinking, she tried to focus. Hand over mouth her cry turned the heads of the children playing at the other end of the veranda.

Standing abruptly, the sewing flew from her lap and scattered over the floor as tears welled up and flowed down her smooth, brown cheeks. Then with the surprising speed of the big lizards, Mariah flew from the veranda, sobbing as she threw herself into François' arms. At the other end of the porch Jean-Paul rose up from play with the others and stared at his mother, wondering what was afoot as the reunion unfolded, until Isleta shooed him forward.

"It is your father, little one. Praise be to God, he is

home!"

~ ~ ~ ~

Later that evening Mariah and François cuddled close to one another on the veranda, continuing to share all that had happened over the past years. Jean-Paul curled on a seat next to his father, the twins reluctantly put to bed some time before. Cradled in his arms was the daughter he hadn't known about since Mariah's pregnancy didn't become apparent until a month after he'd been kidnapped.

That next morning, as the sun slipped over the eastern hills and into the second-story bedroom, François slowly opened his eyes, feeling cramped. Between he and Mariah lay baby Esmeralda purring softly. On the outside lay Jean-Paul with one arm draped over his father's chest as if to be certain he would not leave again. The twins curled at their feet. It drew a smile. With a gentle finger, he swept back a long lock of dark hair from his beloved wife's face. She opened her eyes and smiled, an alluring smile filled with content and love.

As consciousness slowly formed, she noticed the children and giggled, kindling giddiness in her husband. Jean-Paul awoke, rubbed his eyes, and with a squeal, dog-piled his father. Startled, Esmeralda began to cry. François wanted to assuage her fear, but became overwhelmed by the giggling assault of a son and two daughters.

Breakfast was a challenge as people stopped to see for themselves that the master of the plantation had indeed returned and express their joy. Jean-Paul doggedly followed his father on a brief inspection tour of the plantation. Later, as François and Amstedt sat on the veranda talking, he listened patiently, curled in his father's strong arms, understanding little of the conversation until the steady drum of horse hooves reached his alert ears.

Turning to look, he spotted Capt. Santana's flashy stallion burst from the trees at a gallop, through the stream, sending up a shower of water, and then back onto the dusty road, kicking up little puffs of dust as the hooves bit into the dry dirt. Approaching the house the rider brought the steed to a sliding stop, neatly stepping off, and trotting up the steps to face Mariah who was sitting as usual on the north end of the veranda.

"Señora Evreux, my sincerest apologies. Word has come a French warship has been seen off the coast of Tenerife heading this way. We expect it to arrive by tomorrow. The governor requests you send as many armed men as possible to Valverde."

Mariah smiled pleasantly and nodded toward the two men standing at the opposite end of the porch that the young officer had ignored. "Perhaps you should discuss this with my husband."

"Don Evreux!"

"Good day, Alessandro."

The young man stood rigid a moment then hurriedly stepped forward so the two men could embrace. Taking a step back Capt. Santana said, "I presume Señora Evreux and Mr. Amstedt have told you about the impending war."

"Yes."

Standing at rigid attention, he delivered the official message. "Miguel Rodriguez Martini Hernandez, Military Governor of El Hierro, calls upon all able-bodied men age of fifteen and above to assemble at Valverde to defend our Island from the French attack."

"So, Miguel is still governor. I shouldn't be surprised. El Hierro is sufficiently distant from Madrid to keep him from under foot. My wife has told me of your frequent visits." François seemed totally unconcerned about the call to arms.

"I hope you are not offended, Don Evreux," he said nervously, relaxing a bit. "I felt it my duty to keep an eye on your family during your prolonged absence."

"And for that I am deeply grateful. Mariah told me of the rumor concerning a French invasion. I was in France only a few weeks ago. There was much complaining, but heard nothing except unsubstantiated rumor of pending hostilities between the two countries."

"We are not sure what is happening, however, a sloop arrived this morning with a communiqué from Spain. It advised that the French dispatched a fleet of warships to capture one of the Canary Islands. El Hierro was specifically named, as it is the weakest. They are to establish a base from which to launch invasions of the other islands. On its way here, the captain of the ship came upon two French war ships north of Gran Canaria heading in this direction. One fired on him and gave chase, but he managed to outrun them."

"El Hierro would be a reasonable objective. As you say, its defenses have always been meager. I assume they have not changed much."

"Unfortunately you are correct. An invasion has never been a concern."

"Which means you will meet them at the beach and the war ships will use its cannon to destroy you."

"What do you suggest?"

"Who is your commandant?"

"Don Roul de Salazar."

"The governor's pompous bastard?"

Mariah winced. So did the captain, but not so noticeably.

"Yes."

"My suggestion is to set him with a squad of your poorest soldiers on the beach to meet the enemy."

"But he will surely be killed."

"That would at least give you and the rest of your soldiers a fighting chance."

Mariah coughed. The young captain blushed. Amstedt unabashedly laughed.

"In any case, do not meet the French invaders on their terms. In the New World, the native inhabitants there lay in wait under cover to attack at will. Quite an effective strategy; strike and run, strike and run. Do not give them an opportunity to use their cannon on you."

"That would mean abandoning Valverde."

"What is important? A few buildings or the lives of the people? It would cause the enemy so much trouble they would not be able to launch an effective attack the other islands. They would give up and leave."

"I see you are right," Alessandro agreed thoughtfully.

"Jean-Paul," he then said to his big-eyed son. "Run to the ridge overlooking El Golfo and see if there is a black ship there, then return and tell me. Take a spyglass with you."

"Yes, papa," he chirped, speeding off on the trail south, his little legs churning in a blur, returning an hour later so breathless as to be unable to speak.

"Is the ship still there?"

He nodded, yes, while gasping for breath.

"Very good," he said, tousling the boy's long hair, then to the captain, "That would be the ship that brought me home. They are re-supplying before sailing. If you ride there and explain the situation to the captain and say that I ask they return to the cove where I disembarked, I am sure they will help. When you return here, Mr. Amstedt will have men ready to move to Valverde. And my suggestion concerning Roul—I was serious."

"I thought as much. What do you plan to do?"

"I will rejoin the *Raven* and attempt to intercept the French ship before it makes the island."

"The *Raven*! Here? I have heard of this ship. It is captained by the pirate called the Dolphin."

"Yes. When you go there, seek out her master, a

woman called Black Maggie."

"The invincible pirate Dolphin is a woman!"

François shrugged, a deliberate response to create more fodder for rumormongers and story tellers.

"She would fight for us?"

"If I ask."

"Then good luck, my friend, and God be with you. I would not want to know you traveled all the way from the New World to only see your wife and family one day."

"Neither would I."

The two shook hands, then the chivalrous captain turned to Mariah, kissed her hand, and galloped west.

Chapter 30

† Battle for El Hierro †

"Are you going away again, Papa?" Jean-Paul voice was etched with a fearful quiver.

"For a short while only." Kneeling to answer, he tenderly stroked the boy's curly, dark brown, locks.

"I do not want you to go away, Papa," he said as tears began to stream down tanned, cherubim cheeks.

"I do not want to go away, but this I must do for you, and your mother, and the little ones."

"But you might be hurt."

"Has your mother told you about making promises?"

"They must be kept. Will you promise to come back?"

"No, I will ccan not make such a promise, for I have learned that life is something we have no control over."

The boy's countenance fell as he looked down, tears splashing upon his bare feet.

"I will make this promise to you. Whatever may come, I will always be in your heart."

The boy turned his face upward with a puzzled expression. Cupping the little, plump cheeks in each hand François leaned forward and kissed the boy on the forehead then pulled him tight against his body. The child could not comprehend that his father felt as if on Macaria's rack being torn apart. After a time François set the boy at arm's length. Before, he entered battle for the thrill, but this time it was for something more—this was for family and their way of life.

"Gather up what you can," he said to Mariah. "It will be safest for you at Dolphin Cove until this is over." Then to Mr. Amstedt, "Gather your men together and prepare to accompany Capt. Santana to Valverde when he returns. You heard my suggestion how to engage the French?"

"Aye. What of dat peacock pretending to be general?"

"It is better one man die than an entire people. Capt. Santana is a good man. Help him as you would Capt. Shaver or me."

Amstedt smiled and with a sailor's salute left to attend his duties.

Turning to Cirano he said, "Your wife and family will be with Mariah. I want you to stay at the hacienda."

"I am not to join the fight?"

"I need someone to oversee the hacienda. You will have only young boys, but they will work hard, however your main responsibility is to protect the wives and mothers who remain here. If the French approached you are to see them safely to their villages."

The heavy weight of responsibility replaced the youthful excitement of going to battle, as he seemed to age ten years before François' eyes.

All gathered, François led his family and friends into the forest. He had never known the trip to the beach to take so long. Mariah carried Esmeralda, he their belongings, as Jean-Paul helped the twins, going only as fast as their little legs could walk. Cirano's family and other followed in tandem.

Hassan and Lucy started the trip up the mountain the preceding day, but were forced to return to the cabin. The strain had been too much causing labor pains. Seeing Francois' leading a band of refugees clear the V-shaped gorge and begin the descent toward the beach, Hassan hurried to help.

François quickly filled in the details as the two men did their best to settle the women and children into the small cabin. A dozen boys came along to help, assembling shelters for the rest. With that accomplished, they would returned to the hacienda before sunrise the following day. Meanwhile, Francois and Hassan went to the beach, the inseparable Jean-Paul closely behind his father.

"I wish to speak in Arabic," François began, surprising Hassan with the improved command of the language with only the slightest accent. "I do not wish for my son to hear for he is too young to fully understand. The *Raven* is a good ship with a good crew and most capable of doing battle with any war ship, but battles are not always predictable. If it goes badly I will not return. I trust the safety of my family into your hands.

"There are ample resources in the cave behind the house. The cave on the other side of the Dragon continues beyond where the treasure is hidden. When come to a waterfall, the passage divides. To the right one part angles upward and comes out in the cave behind the house. That route is marked with three horizontal lines. The main passage continues along the stream. It is marked with a horizontal and vertical mark overlaying one another similar to a cross. That trail enters a large room.

"At the far end of that room is another passage that will take you through the island coming out not far from Los Toscas overlooking El Gulfo. See the man there called Enrique. He has a small boat. He will help you sail to Portugal. When you arrive there buy a caravel and make for Loro Placida Island. I have written the coordinates in this book. It is a good island on the western side, and as you will see by my notes, a very rich place."

"Yes, sir," Hassan replied somberly as he received the small book. "But, it would be much better if you return . . . for the boy." There was an obvious lump in his throat as the words came with great effort.

Celena stayed with Lucy in the cabin. The labor pains had calmed for the moment, but the arrival of their child was very near. Meanwhile, as she slept, François' family spent the evening on the beach around a crackling fire. Conversation was stifled because of fear and distress until François responded to a question from his son.

"Papa, what was the most frightening thing that ever happened to you?"

François paused for a moment to reflect, and then smiled. "I would have to say the most frightening thing to have happened was a very large . . .," he began holding his hands up to indicate a very large-breasted woman, but Mariah's glance suggested he fore-go that part so his hands continued sweeping out to indicated, "A very large-statured woman."

François then related the adventure with Baroness Güttruda in such a way to cause Jean-Paul to begin laughing so hard he rolled on the ground holding his belly. Soon everyone was laughing. Finishing the tale, François began to sing a Celtic seaman's chant, his melodious baritone a surprise even to his wife. When he began another mariner's song, Hassan harmonized. When at last, François sang a seaman's prayer, that achieved the effect of putting the children to sleep. Hassan and the others carried the sleepy little ones and shepherded a reluctant Jean-Paul up to the cabin and bed leaving husband and wife alone.

"I would like to go for a swim," he said as a large, orange moon rose above the horizon.

"I would like to have another son," Mariah replied.

François looked at her as the fire light played over her face. That honest, frank quality always startled him, but he did so appreciate it. The darkness made it difficult to see into her eyes, but knew what they were saying. Stroking her cheek with one finger, each leaned toward the other and kissed.

"A son? Is it possible to place specific orders?"

"I will pray to God."

"Just one?" he continued to tease.

"It is possible for more, I suppose. An even more wonderful gift."

"If God allows this to be a boy I would like to name him Emanuel Gusman."

"Emanuel Gusman?" she replied, wondering why until memory evoked a story of many years ago. "Is not that the man you met aboard the English ship that sunk the Fleurette?"

"Yes."

"Why name your son after an enemy?"

"I do not know who or what he was, but he became a friend who seemed to be there at the times in my life when I needed one most. I believe he would have found a way to prevent them from hanging me had I not taken matters into my own hands and jumped overboard. He was in many ways very mysterious, but a kind and honorable man. A person with that name would have much to live up to."

At mid-morning the next day the *Raven* arrived and dropped anchor. Mr. Gibbs brought the longboat ashore himself.

"Don't forget your promise, Papa," Jean-Paul said as his father kissed him on the forehead and smiled. He then kissed each of the other children in turn before facing his wife.

"Come back to us," she said very softly.

Her lips were warm and moist and he very nearly changed his mind, but turning away, François climbed into the boat and said, "Shove off, Mr. Gibbs. We have work to conclude before either of us can resume our former course."

~ ~ ~ ~

"**W**elcome aboard, Cap'n," Maggie greeted as Henry's piping died away.

"Let's get underway," he replied.

The black sails of the *Raven* unfurled to billow taunt in the wind. The sleek ship canted to port, and sped from the cove with the regal grace of a great Orca at the chase. Clearing the northern projection François looked back at his family standing on the shore determined to see him to the last unaware of the great dragon hovering protectively over them. From an overlook not far from the cabin Diablo watched and flicked his long tongue.

"Flag, Cap'n?"

Standing next to Sa'id who had the helm, hands folded behind his back, feet spread for balance, François looked up at the masthead. The white Burgundy saltire on a field of blue stretched out boldly—the ensign of a

Spanish merchant. "That will do . . . for now."

Passing Valverde, the *Raven*'s bow bore into the swells with a determined ferocity speeding them northward as if eager to battle once again. After a time a sailor perched high on the main mast called down, "Sail, ho, five leagues due north. It's flying a white flag "

"French," Mr. Gibbs spat. "How many?"

"One."

"Only one?" Francois said to Gibbs, and then called up, "Do you see another sail?"

The lookout scanned the horizon carefully before answering, "Nay. Jist the one, Cap'n."

"I thought there be two ships?" Gibbs said.

"To our advantage, call him down, Mr. Gibbs. Maggie, load all guns with langrage."

The next hour seemed interminable as the ships closed. The tension grew, yet the Dolphin had a sense of serenity as he stood resolute, the wind whipping both hat and coat.

"Well, they read us to be Spanish," Mr. Gibbs reported as he viewed the ship through a spyglass. "Mother of Mary she's big."

"Big and not easily managed in this wind," François replied looking up at the sails stretched taunt. "Let's make it a little more difficult for them." Turning to the helmsman, he spoke quietly in Arabic, "Sa'id, when turning, not too fast in this wind, I want to engage that Goliath with guns relatively level."

"Aye, aye, Captain."

François turned to his gunner's mate. "Henry, let this Frenchman know exactly with who he is about to dance."

"Aye, aye, Cap'n," the boy resounded, a great smile splitting his face as he disappeared into the captain's cabin returning with a large black cloth cradled in his arms as if a baby.

With help of the aft gun crew, the Spanish ensign was hauled in.

Aboard the French man-o-war, Captain DeMers turned to Admiral Dammartin and smiled. "A Spanish merchant. She appears to be striking her colors to surrender."

Dammartin gloated. "She knows who rules this sea."

"But what will we do? It will only slow us down and interfere with what we are doing. I suppose we could use its guns on the Spanish garrison."

"A merchant does not carry many guns and we have more than enough. As it comes parallel fire a broadside."

"You wish to sink it, Admiral?"

"Yes. And do not worry about survivors. We have an island to capture."

The order given, DeMers resumed observation of the approaching ship, but by this time something odd was happening. The *Raven*'s crew struck the square sails on both masts leaving a fore and aft configuration so that the sails were set along the line of the keel rather than perpendicular to it. The configuration provided an advantage in the wind. As he pondered this, a different flag unfurled causing the French captain to suck in a deep breath. In his spyglass, he saw a black flag mount the main mast bearing the unmistakable leaping dolphin over a skull trimmed with a broad, silver border.

"Mon dieu! Le Dauphin!" he exhaled.

At 500 Toise François smiled. "Señor Mendoza, show this French invader what we are capable of doing. Ask Henry to extend an invitation with our chasers," he said, having sent the boy forward to take his place with those guns.

The Bosun's marvelous voice needed no relay as it could be easily heard over the roar of sea or cannon.

The order was followed by Henry's shrill voice, "Chasers shoot!"

As prearranged, the boy commanded the first of four bow cannon to fire sending a billowing, grayish-white cloud of smoke rolling over the deck. François inhaled deeply and then watched the shot spray the approaching galleon with hundreds of rifle bullets. The chasers fired slowly, maintaining a near-steady rain of shot ripping through the Frenchman's sails and rigging so that when the last fired, the first was loaded and ready to discharge.

The first shot stunned the French captain. They were a long way from coming into range with their cannon and already incurring damage. The second volley so soon told him this was not a common, undisciplined pirate ship. The *Bridgett* was an older Carrack and her cannon old. Dammartin could not count on any kind of accuracy in the heavy swells over 100 Toise. Anything else would only be lucky shots, but his opponent was already pummeling him at three times that distance. After receiving eight rounds of canister, the black ship switched to ball. The Frenchman wasn't expecting exploding shells, either.

After the third round of shells his battery officer swore. "Damn him to hell. He's still too far off. We just can't sit here, Captain."

"Return fire," DeMers shouted back, and then mumbled to himself, "Pray we have luck."

The warship turned left to present her starboard side to the incoming Brigantine, disappearing behind a massive cloud of grey and white smoke. After a time the ocean erupted as their balls landed, well short of the *Raven*.

"Thank you," the Dolphin said with a chuckle. "Now I know your range." During this entire time, the *Raven* charged directly at the huge ship. Following the seventh volley from Henry's guns François gave the order. "Come to port, Sa'id. Let us give this one a full measure of our song. Señor Mendoza, ask Maggie if she would be so kind to sing a note or two?

"Aye, aye, Cap'n. Maggie, say hello," he roared across the main deck.

The *Raven*'s top starboard cannon fired, filling the air with the acrid smell of burnt sulfur and rolling thunder as the below deck guns rang out in harmony.

Naval warfare strategy was to get in close and deliver a devastating blow early on. Against a massive warship such as this Frenchman that would be suicide and neither the Dolphin nor his crew had a death-wish. The warship's hull would be thick to withstand bombardment, but by standing off, the *Raven*'s balls would lob in to crash through the thinner decking.

"Keep us just out of their range, Sa'id and bear around his stern," François said.

Henry's volleys punched enough holes in the Frenchman's sails caused them to rip so that blue sky easily shown through. Severed rigging lines flopped in the wind while topgallants and royal sails at the top were loosed and useless. The mass of square sails ill-equipped the warship for maneuvering in the stiff wind, and turning easterly sorely disadvantaged the French giant. Thus encumbered, the *Raven*'s cannon rained exploding balls upon it creating havoc as they bore deep into its interior. By switching sails, the Raven was able to use the wind no matter which direction it turned.

"Henry, one more round as we turn to share the fun," Mendoza called out.

The forward gunner's mate had one more surprise for the French giant. Hugging the deck DeMers and Dammartin watched in horror as something whistled through the rigging, setting fire to the mizzen sails, some falling to the deck—long, white-hot iron rods.

"Fire arrows!" DeMers said as he jumped up, waiving his fist. It was his last act of defiance as a shaft of iron passed through his chest becoming embedded in the deck and starting a small fire.

"Well, that put a few holes in 'im," Mr. Gibbs reported cheerfully as they maneuvered to bring the full complement of cannon on the starboard side to bear. Using a rolling discharge from bow to stern, the main deck guns discharged, followed by those below deck. The crews were reloading well under a minute and a half.

"The guns be gettin' too hot," Maggie called up after repeated rounds.

"Sa'id, bear to port."

The Raven swung away from the battered ship, it's aft guns now able to throw more canister at them, before the port guns resumed the broadside pummeling. The Frenchman continued totally ineffective fire as the *Raven* again came across the warships bow as it tried to charge. The maneuver was useless. The black ship remained out of range moving far more quickly.

Admiral Dammartin's arrogance evaporated, realizing the pirate's reputation well-earned as he picked himself off the deck where he had thrown himself to avoid flying debris. He had expected the two ships to pass and exchange salvos in the traditional manner, but the pirate unleashed a deadly rain of shrapnel before turning to pound his ship unmercifully.

Even with whole sails the warship was too unwieldy for quick maneuvers as the *Raven* circled his stern. Ordering a turn to the right to position his own starboard guns, his own bow had barely begun to swing around when the *Raven* did a neat pirouette to present its port guns, continuing to remain well outside the Frenchman's effective range. To add insult, the *Raven*'s two stern cannon caressed the Frenchman with more langrage and shot, this time heavily damaging the exposed helm.

A month earlier, then Capt. Dammartin dined with colleges aboard Admiral de Ponthieu's frigate in Nantes harbor to idly discuss their respective missions. He would proceed to the Canary Islands and establish a base on the remote island of El Hierro. The invasion fleet consisted of three vessels, but an epidemic broke out on one the first week out forcing them to return. A storm north of Tenerife damaged the second so that it had to put in at a friendly North African port for repairs. Not expecting much resistance, newly commissioned Admiral Dammartin forged on.

Another larger fleet went to the Caribbean to protect France's interest against attacks by the Spanish and to seek out the pirates Hogshead Shaver and the one known as the Dolphin. While the pirates had not bothered French colonies or shipping in the Caribbean, they expected it would only be a matter of time. At the conclusion of the meeting, Admiral de Ponthieu admonished his gallant and battle-savvy, Caribbean-bound officer to be very cautious, especially when dealing with the pirate known as the Dolphin.

"Whether man or woman, this devil is obviously a very experienced captain and treacherous. Expect the unexpected.

Those words rang loudly in Dammartin's ears and the question, "What more could he do that would be unexpected?" The answer came when after four volleys from the starboard guns, the *Raven* swung to head-straight on. Ordering a turn to port the Frenchman attempted to bring those guns to bear, the problem being the black ship turned right just before coming within range of his six pound cannon. The *Raven* unleashed all seventeen cannon, again shredding sails and timbers. When able to fire Dammartin could only watch the *Raven* move away, showing its stern, and the smallest possible target. Out of desperation all 50 guns unleashed with hopes of inflicting some kind of damage. The sea erupted around the *Raven* with small columns of water, but the shot seemed to fall horribly short. A sinking feeling seized Dammartin's gut. His opponent was not only quicker, but with bigger guns could to stand out of range to inflict considerable damage.

As the French war ship continued turning in an attempt to follow the *Raven,* Dammartin beat his fist on the rail in frustration. "Stand and fight you coward!" he shouted, knowing there was no way his ship could catch the Brigantine even with a full set of undamaged canvas. Then to his amazement the *Raven* lost wind in its sails. His hopes soared.

Looking carefully through a cracked spyglass, Dammartin tried to ascertain the problem, but was too far to tell except that the pirate ship seemed to be having trouble steering. Could it be? As the gap shrunk, it became more obvious that was exactly the problem. By the grace of providence, one of the frigate's balls must have damaged their rudder. At 1500 Toise he could see the *Raven*'s helmsman spinning the large, spoke wheel furiously as the wind first filled the sails then dumped, leaving them to flap uselessly. Two-hundred more Toise and he would put an end to this nonsense and the Dolphin's career.

While Dammartin was counting his victory medals, the Dolphin resumed his usual stance, legs apart, hands clasped behind his back. There was a smile on the pirate's face, which, had Dammartin been able to see through his glass, would have troubled him immensely.

"Mr. Gibbs," he called down to the main deck, "reconnect the steering cable."

"All done, Cap'n."

"Sa'id to port if you will."

To Capt. Dammartin's astonishment, the *Raven*'s

sails filled as she rolled to the left.

"Starboard! Turn starboard!" he shouted realizing he had been tricked. Instead of having use of his side guns, all that was available were six chasers. The *Bridgette* was a formidable ship, but out-classed by modern technology. All he could do was watch for the gray smoke to appear indicating the pirate had fired, then wait. When it came the destruction was staggering. With painful slowness, the Frenchman turned until its guns were in position.

"Return fire!" he shouted during another rain of balls that splintered deck and timbers.

"They are still too far," his master gunner shouted back.

"*Le feu*, damn you, Fire!"

The sea around the *Raven* erupted in water columns as ball after ball hurtled toward them. François winced as nearly a half dozen actually struck his beautiful ship. Dammartin was unable to assess the effectiveness of his gunners as he was forced to dive once again for cover as another volley rained upon his beleaguered ship. The pirate's reloading speed was startling.

Hugging the deck, Dammartin saw torn bodies litter the deck following another round of shrapnel slice the big ship to ribbons. He could feel the balls bore through the ship's heavy timbers and explode. Secondary explosions added to the damage He was frustrated, angry, and frightened. He'd been in sea battles before, but never receiving so much damage so quickly—not without reciprocating.

Blood streaming down his face from a scalp laceration, he picked himself off the deck, again. The damage was staggering; the top third of the foremast leaned back into the main sail. Smoke issued from below decks near the bow. The center of the ship looked like a refuse yard with broken and shredded timbers. Worst of all, most of the topside helm was shot away and no helmsmen left. Capt. DeMers lay dead as well as more crew than he could count. Cautiously peeking over the remnants that had been a railing, Dammartin looked through a cracked spyglass to watch the *Raven* continued to turn to cross his bow.

"Lt. Gravois, secure the weather helm before we are thrown over!" he shouted hoarsely.

"There is a fire in that area," the man called back.

"More enjoyable news!" Dammartin hissed under his breath. "Get it under control! I need steering!" he yelled while trying to help manage what remained of the topside helm. "Damn you pirate!"

Dammartin was positive some of his shots struck the black ship, but obviously not inflicting sufficient damage. On the other hand, his ship was battered and another salvo on its way. His best guess was that the Dolphin would continue the circle. In desperation he spun the broken wheel best he could to turn right and elevate his port guns. As he did a column of water shot up and drenched him. Other balls missed, but many found their mark; he could feel every one as they bore through ship's hull. Then came more secondary explosions and he prayed the main powder magazine was still safe. His gunners returned fire hoping against all odds some of their balls would find the enemy. Dammartin tried steering the bulky ship to the left then felt the wheel working without his efforts. Lt. DeMers had taken control with the weather wheel.

"Seven points to port," he shouted into a speaking tube.

The behemoth's bow slowly turned left.

"Hard to port!" he screamed, almost joyfully, as the pirate ship came within his outer, effective range, and by leaning to the left his right side guns were elevated.

"Le feu!"

"Shoot!"

The command was simultaneous by both captains. Both ships suffered, but the Frenchman was by far the receiver of the most damage as the whole forecastle disintegrated in a series of huge explosions sending flames into the foresail. Dammartin had no choice, but to break off before suffering the unthinkable.

François gazed down on the *Raven*'s main deck. Despite the number of hits taken the damage didn't appear too severe, but what of below? After a quick inspection, Gibbs returned to report.

"Nine crew dead, twenty-six wounded. Three cannon starboard an' two port side knocked out. Four be reset shortly. Some hull damage near the water line, but Mr. Carmichael and 'is boys have it under control, and the pumps be 'andlin' the water. All-in-all not bad considerin'."

Suddenly Gibbs stopped, his eyes gazing beyond François' shoulder. The young captain slowly turned around. Maggie was coming onto the bridge, tears staining her brown face, cradling a small, limp body in her arms. François stepped forward, to receive the body of his gunner's mate, and gently lay it on the deck, the stump of a wood splinter embedded in his chest.

"He was workin' the chasers below on that last exchange," she croaked through a strained voice.

François gently brushed hair from Henry's eyes, eyes that had danced and sparkled with the joy of being at sea, now fixed in death. With loving care, he closed them as a burning tear fell from his cheek and splashed upon his weathered hand.

"Break off, Mr. Gibbs," François said with a husky voice, taking the limp body into his arms.

Carrying Henry into his cabin, François kicked the door closed behind him. He was surprised how slight the boy felt as he laid him on the long table. Slumping into a chair, he covered his eyes with one hand and wept.

After a time he felt the Raven's movements change and knew Gibbs had lay to. Shortly thereafter he knocked and entered.

"Beggin' the Cap'n's pardon, what would ye like us to do?"

François mentally shook himself back to the present. "What is the Frenchman doing?"

"Tryin' to put out fires. She can't move much. Her sails are pretty much done in. Should we make fer El Hierro to bury the men?"

"They were men who lived on the sea, let them live in the sea. See they are prepared proper burial."

"And the lad?"

"Fetch me a bucket of water, if you will?"

When Gibbs returned a few minutes later, François had cut Henry's clothes off and was pulling the shard from his chest. The coin Cochran gave him had been driven in Henry's chest by the ragged point.

"Didn't do him much good," François said.

"It's supposed to be carried in the right pocket. Cochran shouldn't 'ave put a hole in it. I'll be seein' to the others."

As François finished bathing Henry's body, Maggie entered carrying clean clothes and helped put them on, and then combed his hair.

"Such nice hair," she said. "Ne'r tangle no matter what."

Finally, they placed the body in a canvas shroud, a nine pound shot at the feet. Just before sewing the last together François and Maggie each leaned to kiss the boy's forehead.

~ ~ ~ ~

The death of one's friend, often in their arms, was difficult and heart wrenching, but seeing their body enshroud in canvas and weighted with cannon ball disappear into the ocean depths had a mysteriously soothing effect.

"What the sea wants, the sea takes, so we commit these bodies unto the bosom of the ocean upon which they sailed to join with their brethren who have gone before. May they find birth on Fiddler's Green." François struggled to speak.

One by one Gibbs read the names from the ship's log as friends tilted the plank upon which that person lie, sending the remains sliding overboard.

"Fredrick Holcomb, Carlos Phillipe, William Pitkin, Pierre Languine, Edward Lynch, John Zeiler, Peter Ulbrech, Juan Santee, Austin Pratt."

As Pratt's body slipped overboard François stepped forward taking one side of a plank across from Maggie. Upon the board lie a small canvas with only one ball for weight.

"Henry . . .,"Gibbs began, and then stopped.

François turned to his Quartermaster to see why he hadn't finished reading the boy's full name. Gibbs, his cheeks tear-stained, stared at the log a moment then at his captain and shrugged.

"He ain't written a last name, Cap'n."

"It's 'cause of 'is uncle," Maggie explained. "He were ashamed to carry the name."

Turning back to look at the small shroud on the plank François said in a broken voice, "Captain Jean-Paul this one is Henry . . . Henry Evreux. Take care of him as you did me." Together François and Maggie tilted the plank, sending their little friend away.

The planks upon which their dead had laid were set aside as the bodies of their friends silently descended into the ocean's depths. François silently returned to the bridge overlooking the ship as the crew finished clearing away the damage. Gibbs looked up from the main deck.

As seen so many times, his captain stood as if one with the ship, feet apart, hands behind his back, the wind whipping his long hair and coat tails, while he stared out passed the bowsprit to the ocean beyond. However, it was the set of the jaw and narrowed eyes that sent a chill tapping at his soul. Gibbs shivered despite the warmth. He had never seen such darkness in a man's eyes. They almost seemed to glow, not unlike a nightmare he'd had where he saw one of the devil's red-skinned own coming for him.

"Set sail, Mr. Gibbs." Then François said so softly the helmsman barely heard, "Bring us about, Sa'id." As the ship turned, the wind filled her tattered sails and the *Raven* began to move forward with increasing speed until it sliced through the swells with a ferocious determination. "Straight at her mid-ship, Sa'id." His barely audible order had such a cold edge to cause the helmsman to wonder if an evil spirit had possessed his captain.

"Yes, Captain," he finally replied in Arabic.

"Mr. Gibbs, prepare the cannon. Exploding iron ball."

The enemy ship rocked at the whims of the swells, its mainsails shredded and flapping useless, it's bare and smoldering foremast leaning back into the main mast. Smoke billowed through gaping holes in the front third of the ship as it list to port. But that didn't mean it was without teeth. The crew redoubled their efforts; continuing to clear debris from the decks and preparing what cannon were still serviceable.

When they first engaged the war ship an electric feeling of excitement flowed over the *Raven*'s decks, but now a different feeling permeated the air spurring the men to action, the black feeling of revenge.

"Two-hundred Toise, Cap'n," Gibbs called out as

the *Raven* bore down on the smoldering warship. "50 Toise."

Aboard the French man-o'-war, Dammartin watched as the pirate ship approached, mentally preparing his surrender. Admiral de Ponthieu warned him, but arrogance led him to a humiliating defeat.

"What be yer intentions, Cap'n?" Gibbs asked.

"Bring us parallel, Sa'id."

Despite her wounds, the *Raven* seemed eager to obey, swinging with a smooth quickness that brought their starboard parallel to the listing ship.

Gibbs had been secretly praying to hear his captain call out for the Frenchman to surrender, but in his heart knew what the words would truly be. Even more deeply in his breast, they were words he wanted to hear.

"Señor Mendoza . . . shoot."

Dammartin realized what was about to play out when the pirate didn't reduce sail and turned broadside. He yelled out the order for his cannon to fire, but the response was pitifully small. There was considerable damage below decks and fires prohibited gun crews access to their cannon. Sporadic explosions only added to the problems. The ship was taking on water and listing enough to direct the muzzles downward. Only the main deck cannon had a chance at hitting the pirate.

The roar of cannon deadened hearing, smoke suffocated the lungs with the acrid stench of sulfur as balls from the *Raven* bored through the Frenchman's heavy, oak timbers and ornate workmanship like fingers searching for the its heart. Whether one penetrated that heart or a fire below, the cause was immaterial as the main magazine exploded with the thundering violence of a Vesuvius. As a dazed and bloodied Dammartin staggered to his knees. His ship was sliced in half, the remaining bow section a blazing inferno.

Aboard the *Raven* its captain and crew stared in

shock, unable to do little except watch as more explosions ripped through the warship's convulsing carcass. The bow of the 100-gun ship disappeared first followed by a catastrophic blast consuming the stern that felt as if someone opened furnace doors releasing a wind from hell to sear the on-looker's faces. The Raven lurched sideways, knocking many to the deck. The larger pieces slipped quickly beneath the swells with the loud hissing of an angered leviathan leaving behind a cloud of steam boiling up from the depths among splintered and burning remnants littering the sea. In an incredibly short time, a once powerful ship of the French navy and all aboard were gone.

It was then the gravity of what he had done bore down upon François as an anchor of shame hung about his neck. He forgotten Jean-Paul's last admonition and in a moment, allowed anger to become his master and he the needless cause of hundreds of deaths. The foul taste of shame and remorse filled his mouth as a clammy hand laid upon his soul. No amount of regret would . . . could undo what he had done. Standing in shamed silence, François made an oath never to succumb to such anger again, and to his dying day sought forgiveness, knowing in his heart more than earthly repentance would be required to overcome this crime of passion.

Chapter 31

† Home to Stay †

Early that following morning El Hierro's Governor-general and entourage hurriedly gathered on the rocky shore below Valverde. Yesterday, while standing on the balcony of his mansion high on the mountain, he watched the approaching French warship with great anxiety. Then the ominous, black ship appeared, racing toward it from the south, the wind at its back. From where it came, he had no idea, but was thrilled to see the Spanish ensign flying from its stern. When the black flag suddenly appeared, he became confused. Were the two ships allies or was the much smaller vessel incredibly attacking the much larger one? Those questions would have been answered if the governor's son had bothered to relay Capt. Santana's information about the return of Don Evreux, but he didn't.

When the two ships came together great clouds of smoke issued from each followed by the ominous, staccato boom of cannon. Finally, the Frenchman stalled, some flame and much smoke visibly spewing from its battered carcass amid exuberant cheers among the onlookers. Even the normally dour Minister of Finance joined in the revelry as he slapped the governor on the back.

When the black ship withdrew, it seem to sit on the water as a dog licking its wounds after a fight until turning back, and in a ferocious assault destroy the helpless war ship before disappearing into the darkening eastern horizon.

Small fishing boats went out, but there were few survivors. Information gathered from those lucky few, there had been over 800 crew and soldiers aboard. What remained barely filled the governor's meager prison.

With the new sun, the mysterious ship lie at anchor just off shore, its black flag bearing a leaping dolphin and skull clearly visible as the wind stretched out the cloth. The governor's entourage reached the docks as a broad-shouldered man stepped from a longboat into the surf and walked toward them.

The governor leaned over and whispered to a tall, skinny kid in a fancy uniform, "Mother of God, protect us. I think that is the pirate Dolphin!"

"Yes, father. Such a flag could belong to no other."

"Yet, we must be grateful to this pirate," the Minister of Finance admonished. "We can only hope he does not require more than we can afford to pay for saving our city."

'He's along. I could arrest him.'

The governor looked at his son as if to say, "Don't be stupid."

Knee-high, black boots sounded like a deep, bass drum on the wood planking leading up from the beach as the tall man in a long, maroon, broadcloth coat approached the crowd. A huge, plumed hat covered his face, but it was not something the governor wanted to gaze upon. He'd seen the evil-looking faces of pirates before when such boarded a ship he had been a passenger on years before. It would be craggy, scared, and frightening to look upon.

"Good day, your Excellency," the visitor greeted, removing the hat, and with great flourish, swept it across his body while bowing in the manner of a salute.

"Don Evreux?"

"At your service, Excellency."

"But . . . that ship . . . it is a pirate ship . . . that flag!" the obese governor blubbered. "Is not that the ship of the pirate Dolphin?"

"Yes," is all François would say, relishing the consternation convulsing the pompous oaf.

Turning, he waived to the men standing by the longboat. After acknowledging, they set their bow toward the ship.

"How is it you are aboard that pirate ship?" the young man closer to François' age and dressed like a peacock in a fancy, military uniform asked.

François merely looked at him with contempt. It had been a long time, but he well-remembered the governor's son, a contemptible, disgusting braggart with the mettle of a mouse.

"Ah, you remember my son, Don Roul. He is the commander of our garrison."

The boy straightened his shoulders throwing out his chest to bask in the glow of his importance. François cast a demeaning glance, but paid no more attention to him.

"I was kidnapped by the pirate Hogshead Shaver three years ago, as you may have heard, and forced to serve him on a voyage to the Caribbean. Thanks to some good fortune he became quite wealthy and retired from that line of work leaving me free to return home. That ship was my transportation."

"I have heard stories of that black ship and its dreaded Captain Dolphin," the governor's son interjected, eagerly trying to become a part of the conversation. François continued to take no notice of him or his comment.

"It is said this Captain Dolphin actually stole one our kings galleons from beneath the guns of a fortress," the Finance Minister said.

"Many stories surround the *Raven* and its Captain. Most are exaggerations. That one happens to be true. Twice, in fact."

The governor gasped.

At that moment, Captain Santana rode through the crowd upon his prancing stallion to join them.

"But how did the pirates know we needed such help?"

"I returned home the day before when Capt. Santana rode to the hacienda to gather soldiers and apprised me of the situation. I suggested he ride to where the *Raven* lay at anchor in Gulfo Bay taking on provisions and speak with the Dolphin," he replied as the young man approached.

"You are to be complimented, Captain. It took great courage to face the dreaded Capt. Dolphin."

"She was most amenable to assist Don Evreux and his people."

"She!" the governor nearly choked. "The Dolphin . . . is a woman!"

"Yes, the captain of that ship is a woman. I am

glad you are safe, Don François," Santana continued as the governor tried to come to grips with the revelation.

"It is good to finally be home," François replied, and then to the governor, "If you will excuse me, Excellency, I am anxious to rejoin my wife and family."

"Yes, yes, of course, but, please, when you have attended to your affairs come to the palace and bring your beautiful wife so that I may honor your return and our victory over the French invaders."

François bowed politely.

"Please, take my horse," Santana said.

"Thank you Alessandro."

"Will any more of them be coming ashore?" the governor asked, casting a nervous glance toward the ship.

"No. They are anxious to be on their way as well."

His sigh of relief was an audible wheeze.

As always, Ojos Oidos stood back from the throng of people, patiently holding the stallion's reins, taking in all he saw and heard. "I have never witnessed such masterful tactics, truly befitting the captain of that ship," he said, and displaying a rare smile, handed over the reins. "Welcome home, Don François."

"And where is that ship going?" the governor called out as Francois settled into the saddle.

"The *Raven* is returning from where it came, the Isle of San Borondon."

"No such place exists," Roul pronounced, but should have saved his breath and embarrassment.

"Quiet, you fool. Everyone has seen Aprositus, the Inaccessible," the governor admonished, saying the name with an air of reverence, then aggrandizing himself added, "I have seen it myself . . . many times."

"Let the Guanche drums resound

and the conch shells blow,
for the mysterious island is appearing
in the midst of the waves;
here comes San Borondon,
showing up in the mist like a queen
with the surf as her suitor;
Island of the Seven Cities."

Capt. Alessandro Santana, soldier-poet, recited the ancient verse with reverence as François nudged the horse's flanks and rode off amid grateful cheers from the people.

Chapter 32

† Epilogue †

Just before disappearing over the *Raven*'s side and down into the launch that would carry him to the waiting throngs on El Hierro's beach, François looked one last time upon his friends, Maggie, Harvey, Sa'id, Mendoza, and the others. In all likelihood, they would not see one another again, but then he had that thought four days earlier.

"May the East Indies be a profitable for you."

Harvey coughed. "Well, we've given some thought to that. Spotted this island off to the west when we was takin' on stores at that village other side of the island. San Borondon, they call it. Figure to put in there fer a spell. 'Ear it be a good place accordin' to the native folk. Outa the way and all."

"With beautiful women looking for rich husbands," Sa'id interjected, his brown face practically swallowed by a huge smile.

Riding Santana's stallion home, François crested a hill overlooking the broad expanse of ocean stretching out to the east from El Hierro. Below, the ship he so loved was making its way south once again. He waived, knowing they would not see him until the steady thud of seven cannon reverberated off the volcanic rocks—a farewell salute. Capt. Santana's horse reared, waiving its hooves.

At Dolphin Cove, fear was taking its toll on Mariah and the distant rumbling and shaking of the earth did nothing to assuage that fear. The little ones sensed her distress until Hassan climbed to the Hacienda to see if everything was all right. Finding all well, he went to the highest point. Using a spyglass, he could easily see Valverde. All seemed right there, too. He looked across the sea, but it was empty. Then something caught his eye. What Hassan strained to recognize warmed his heart as he verily flung himself back to the cove with the news.

"All is well. The black ship is sailing this way. No other ships. And the thunder we hear, is not the noise of war. A volcano erupts on the island to the north."

Mariah muffled a relieved laugh with her hand, and then gasped. Over Hassan's shoulder she saw Santana's spirited bay working down the steep trail, however, it was not the more slender, almost boyish officer she was familiar with who straddled the horse's strong back, but someone broader and taller. Reaching the bottom, the steed willingly kicked into a gallop, sliding to a stop twenty feet from the buried tree allowing a dark, flamboyant man to dismount. With outstretched arms she met and embraced her husband. François was home—safe.

~ ~ ~ ~

With his return, the adventures of Don François Evreux de Nazaire, known better in other circles as the pirate Dolphin, came to closure, at least for a time. Merchants and governors in the Caribbean eventually breathed a sigh of relief. The people of El Hierro wondered if François, too, had been as successful as the man who kidnapped him three years before, often asking in hushed voices, "Did he return with treasure?" They could only speculate as Don Evreux continued to pay business transactions as always—with coin of the realm garnered from a successful plantation.

A few months after François' return home Mr. Amstedt lie ill, struck down with a fever and burning in his chest, grasping for each breathe. As Mariah sat next to the old Dutchman, holding his hand, François at her shoulder, he struggled to speak, "Dat Jongen, Hassan, is goede boy. See ze gets my share. I have no use voor it. En keep hem on island. Uw understand, Cap'n. Is not goede voor hem to leave."

That night the Dutchman stopped struggling to breathe. His was a life of hardships and sorrow that found joy and contentment in the end. However, as he went to his eternal reward, François knew there would be no such rest for his soul when that time came. He'd brought a curse upon himself that the old shaman from the Guanches village declared could only be lifted by another.

Sean Patrick O'Mordha

(Aboard H.M.S Surprise)

Sean is the author of six novels and numerous short stories and artcles. The Urchin Pirate is book two in his historically accurate, **A Pirate's Legacy** series. Book one, **For Glory, Truth and Treasure** began the saga with the Dolphin's 21st Century descendant, launching the two generations separated by 400 years on a common quest.

www.oldguey.webs.com

Also By

Sean O'Mordha

A Pirate's Legacy

Book 1: For Glory, Truth and Treasure
Book 2: The Urchin Pirate
Book 3: CIC (The Canary Island Commandos)

Incident at Beaver Creek

For All Time and Eternity: Waters of the Deep

Death by TOP SECRET

† Print editions available wherever books are sold †

† eBook editions at **www.smashwords.com** †

.